"You're not invincible, you know. The stories of the Blacks are rife with the gruesome murders of Black Protectors. Why ole Meriodoc Black had his eyelids sliced off and boiling oil fried his living eyeballs right in their sockets. Only then did they tear his entrails out with such precision he lingered for days having to fend off rats and other vermin in their dungeon." Jones stopped and gave Harry a lingering look. "When Meriodoc fell, another Black rose to the cause. Another Black always follows."

Harry choked down the bile rising from his stomach. "She never explained it like that."

"No, she wouldn't. She didn't spare you, but describing what she knew of certain unfortunate members of your family would have been excessively cruel."

Praise

"S. P. Brown's spell-binding talent explodes in this new and terrifying sci-fi tale. But the author's real gift in this genre is easing the reader to a shocking conclusion: is the veil in the modern world between ancient evil and avarice that fragile?"

- Nancy A Hughes, Multi-published
Crime Fiction Author

Black Legacy

by

S.P. Brown

Black Legacy

Contact Information: info@thewildrosepress.com

Cover Art by *The Wild Rose Press, Inc.*

The Wild Rose Press, Inc.
PO Box 708
Adams Basin, NY 14410-0708
Visit us at www.thewildrosepress.com

Publishing History
First Edition, 2024
Trade Paperback ISBN 978-1-5092-5318-0
Digital ISBN 978-1-5092-5319-7

Previously Published: 2017 'Black Opal'
Published in the United States of America

Dedication

To Coraline Hansen, the sweetest granddaughter in the universe.

Chapter 1

Near Jackson, Mississippi

Day broke over Black Manor, a morass of despair assailing Harry Black's mind. Punishment, perhaps, from some ancient, vengeful deity, as if the countless, sleepless nights weren't enough.

The woman, the screaming woman.

Her pain still echoed in his ears as he clutched the bedroom drapes, his body slick with sweat. In the early morning light, Celtic statuary littering the expansive front lawn faded into view as if settling back into the waking world from their nightly excursions, their ugly, fierce stares warding off whatever evil lurked around the edges of the property.

No doubt something was out there, watching, waiting, prevented from entering. But that was his grandmother's paranoia, not his.

He turned from the eloquent window as the faint sound of feeble steps invaded his struggling ears. He kept trying to hold onto the woman's screams, searching for something that could identify her. The squeaking door drove the last vestiges of her terror from his mind, replaced now with Agnes Black's morning scowl.

She didn't often invade his private quarters, and never at this hour. He turned more fully to her. She hadn't even bothered with a robe, instead appearing in her nightdress, the ancient lace gracing frail, white ankles. Surprisingly, she still had some strength left, marshalling enough to drag the tank everywhere with her, shunning the more modern device delivering the necessary oxygen her weakening lungs needed.

Not since his boyhood years had she been in his room. But here she was now, stooped but not broken, hesitant but alert, taking in his appearance, understanding slowly dawning through her piercing blue eyes.

"Trouble sleeping?" she asked, her voice deep and raspy from too many years of cigarettes. She was stronger than she had been only days before as though her nurse had found a miracle cure. It was an oddity because the doctors hadn't given them any reason to hope.

Her question contained no hint of concern. Instead, there was an underlying accusation, a harsh judgment. He shook his head, but not in answer. It was only to acknowledge her determination, her dogged grasp at life, her sheer stubborn will.

"Ha…I know better. Gerta has told me otherwise."

"So, you're using her now to spy on me."

"What if I am? I'm paying her enough for two jobs, you know. Might as well use her to keep an eye on you." She looked around the room as if searching for something. "Oh, I've heard all about your troubles at night, my boy."

He grabbed a discarded tee shirt from the floor and put it on to cover his nakedness. It had been years since his grandmother had seen even this much of him. Her eyes searched him, searched the room again, and he knew all too well where this was leading.

“Get dressed. We need to talk.”

She swept from the room, channeling the old flair for dramatic exits. The graceful movement stunned Harry, as though years had melted from her, replaced by renewed youth and purpose.

Always a purpose with her.

Harry turned from the closing door and considered the window again, the grounds beyond. He knew where this was leading, but what the hell else could be going on?

Chapter 2

It had been an incredibly long night, allowing Harry's general, *I don't give a shit*, attitude toward his grandmother's schemes to chase away a growing weariness. Instead of following his grandmother dutifully down to the kitchen and a hearty breakfast, he waited more than a half hour to make an appearance.

Likely, Jones was with her anyway. The two together could be real ball busters. So, he waited just to stir them up a bit, and remembered the night and his dream.

He'd woken soon after turning in, always the same pattern. The wailing woman assaulting his brain. Afterward, he would fall into something bordering on insomnia and a fitful sleep. And in the morning, he would remember, like he was doing now.

The last few weeks had him doubting himself, his decisions. Maybe he should heed his grandmother's warnings rather than dismissing her bizarre rants as insanity, like he'd been doing for years.

Twenty-four long years of living with Agnes Black had him on the verge of breaking. Her ridiculous stories—should he embrace them, become like her, acquiesce to her lunacy, accept all she had been trying to teach him?

Maybe then there would be no need for these nocturnal cries, no more circling through claustrophobic woods, no demon eyes staring at him as he searched for the screaming woman who didn't exist.

If believing his grandmother would free him, could he do it? Was it really as simple as accepting her worldview? This legacy business. It would mean going against a lifetime of ignoring her rants about the dangers he would have to face. Would conceding to her really end this torment?

****

Like a flimsy negligee, a slip of cloud slid from the shoulder of the waxing moon cutting a silver swath across the manicured grounds of Black Manor, bathing his room in an eerie glow. The cool air sucked the heat from his naked torso, making him shiver. As his head cleared, the woman's cries grew more distant, less urgent. Staring bleary-eyed through the window, the screams died altogether.

Relief flooded him like cooling rain. He waited, listening. He closed his eyes and tensed as the vision returned—the woods, the disorienting darkness, the insistent heat and humidity of a summer night in Mississippi. The nightmare reached for him then, pulling him back, her screams reverberating through his mind like phantom wails, compelling him to run, to seek her out. That same light appeared, some sort of fire glowing in a clearing, people in hooded robes—chanting, circling, chanting.

Something gripped him, some sense, not of horror or despair, something crucial, some feeling he couldn't quite grasp, something vital trying to break through to his subconscious. He kept his eyes clamped, a feeble attempt to hold onto the vision as long as he could.

The woman twisted in her captor's grasp, her

tortured face almost revealed.

Almost.

Fire…chanting…

****

Remembering this scene, Harry had been clenching his jaw. Now, his aching muscles cried out for relief as he opened his eyes.

Was she real? She always seemed so real.

He needed to see her fully, but as usual the vision melted away at the wrong time, her image fading in the flickering firelight of the dwindling dream.

Still at the window, still fighting this nightly visitation, he noted that the morning sun shimmered through sheer drapes.

He ran nervous hands over the back of his neck. They trembled as he examined his body, remembering how red-eyed demons had leered at him from the gloom in his dream, slashing at him with hooked talons. So real—so damn painful, but not a mark on him.

In the night, shadows had danced across the far wall of his bedroom, a sudden new visitation forcing him to flinch. Remembering them, he staggered away from the window, turned toward the wall where he had seen them. Nothing was there now. No shadows. Nothing substantive like a real person. His grandmother had been the only real thing to enter his room, but that was much later, after daybreak. Yes…it had been after daybreak.

"Dammit," he muttered, shaking his head, trying to release the fog invading his mind.

He never wanted to tell his grandmother about the recurrent nightmare, but now she evidently knew through her nurse spying on him. And now that she knew, there was no doubt that Jones was down there with her, ready to assail him again with their cockeyed stories.

Agnes had conjured many fantasies over the years in the kooky dream world she inhabited. But were these fantasies only stories? Could they be Harry's actual family history, the one true legacy of Clan Black? He'd fought this idea, denied all her weird stories and other things she'd tried to teach him, but he seemed now to be losing the battle. Somehow, her crazy shit had invaded his mind, her fantasy world claiming him as it had done her.

She wanted this, of course. It was his turn to carry on like she had. Become the figurehead of a clan that no longer existed. The patriarch of a family estate that could easily pass for an insane asylum. Be just like her, a true Black.

He ran a nervous hand through his hair as he pondered the question, shaking his head like a teenager arguing with a parent, the force of her words haunting him.

You are the last inheritor, the last of Clan Black. If the family legacy does not come to you, it will be lost forever. And they will have won.

They…who the hell were they? If his grandmother knew, she had never made it clear.

****

He made his way to breakfast, ready to face the inevitable, and found Jones, irritable, picking through the remainder of his breakfast plate. Agnes sat at the end of the long table tapping a skinny finger on the rich mahogany, her plate untouched.

They both looked up as he entered the room but

neither spoke, so he walked straight through to the kitchen and fixed a serving of sausage, grits, scrambled eggs, toast, and some assorted fruit.

"Glad you could pull yourself from whatever the hell you were doing to join us," Strom Jones said, the words spoken with ice forming at each syllable.

"Don't mention it." Harry lifted a fork of grits to his mouth as he made his way to the table. "Wonderful."

"Sit before you eat, Joey. I taught you better than that. Manners matter, you know, especially with the company you'll be keeping."

It was the old refrain. He just ignored it and continued to eat as though he had run a marathon through those woods in his dream. He finally pushed the plate away and waited for it to begin. Strom took the cue and pulled some pages from the inside pocket of his signature seersucker suit coat.

Harry knew his grandmother wanted him to carry out her agenda after her death, but he wasn't going to do it. Given her frail condition and how easily she could be offended, he didn't want to aggravate her more than could be helped. Her temper would rise, and she would probably have a stroke, or worse. He couldn't live with the guilt something like that would bring.

She had painted him into a corner, no doubt ready to color in the rest of her trap, the rest of his life. He met Jones's eyes as the old man handed him what appeared to be legal paperwork. Something binding was about to be sprung on him, something not easily dismissible after her death. He gave Agnes a long, hard look, but got nothing in return. The parameters of the playing field would soon be revealed.

"What have you managed, Grandmother? Tell me in your own words, not something drawn up by Jonesy."

Agnes pressed her lips into a fine line, the second time in under an hour she'd managed to keep a lid on her temper. Instead of answering, she placed a shaky hand inside her robe and drew out two legal-sized pages and handed them to Harry.

This was it, their ploy. Harry fought the temptation to throw the pages down but instead he scanned them. "I'll have to let Jack read this over and get back to you." Trying but failing to put as much ice into each word as old Strom had done.

"Don't be ridiculous, boy."

"He's my lawyer. We have a plan for the estate after—" He stopped, embarrassed to speak the obvious truth.

"Oh, you're being polite. I might not live out the week, you know, and I'll be damned if I'll let that reckless friend of yours have a say on my activity with the estate."

"He won't. He'll be helping with *my* activity because *my* actions will be the only ones that matter then."

She stood slowly and leveled her stark blue eyes onto Harry, revealing something in them beyond the long, tiring years. Resolve, but mixed now with a kind of sadness she'd never shown. The old fighting spirit he knew so well had suddenly come back in the midst of her decline, but the sadness was what scared him.

"That's just the thing, son. You won't have control."

His head suddenly thumped, his eyes losing a little

of their focus. He stood slowly and placed a hand on the table to steady himself. Glancing around the room, he expected to see twin shadows flitting across the ceiling, but nothing was there. He finally said in a shaky voice, "The hell I won't. I'll be—"

"Jonesy!" Agnes said. "Tell him about the will."

Strom Jones cleared his throat and then that smirk appeared, the one he wore whenever his grandmother had something on Harry.

"Gladly, madam. When Agnes dies, control of the estate falls to me as executor. There are certain, shall we say, *extraordinary matters* that must be confirmed before you're able to acquire control."

"And you know what we're referring to," Agnes said.

Harry placed a hand to his forehead and walked off a step or two. "I already know most of this. You're attempting to keep control of the estate from the grave."

"Only until..." She let her words trail off.

"Until what?"

She shook her head and nodded to Jones.

"You are to meet with Senator Rankin. Here...at the party tonight. And mark my words, you *will* be here. Everything will be made clear then."

Rankin's coming out party. Agnes's pet project. Then he made the connection. "Why haven't I been shown the will? I want to see it."

"Soon. Not before the meeting."

Harry shook his head. "How about now?"

"No," Agnes said with finality. "I want assurances my support of Bill will be uninterrupted when you do assume control."

"And when will that be?" Harry asked.

Agnes managed a weak smile as if pleased with herself.

The trap had been sprung, and Harry had walked right into it. As the sole heir, he nevertheless wouldn't have control until—how had Jones put it—some *extraordinary matters* had been cleared up, or come to light, or some other such crap.

Everyone knew the Blacks were wealthy—some, no doubt, suspected how rich. But no one knew of their secrets. No one knew how or why Harry had been reared by his grandmother, nor of the crazy stories she told to a growing and impressionable boy. Jones had gotten a good taste of these stories too over the last several decades of his employment with the family, making him, effectively, a member of the clan. And no one knew how insane Agnes really was.

Harry didn't have the details of the will, but he had pieced together some things over the years. He returned Agnes's steady gaze. "I understand, but I still want Jack to have a look at this other document. I'm not signing anything until he does."

And with Agnes caught midway between seated and standing, he threw his napkin onto the table and stormed out of the room.

Chapter 3

Desperate to escape the place, he pulled his keyring from his pocket and headed for the Mustang. Halfway to the car, he stopped. Drawn by an uncontrollable urge, he turned back to the house, thinking of his grandmother.

If the doctors were right, she had mere weeks to live. When she passed, perhaps the greatest matron this place had ever known would no longer stalk the deep veranda. The memory of her there was so strong he could almost hear her clicking steps echoing off the white facade, her long dress slapping at slender ankles. This was her domain. She had remade the antebellum home and christened it Black Manor, the name that once belonged to the ancient family estate before they abandoned England well over a century earlier. The stately oaks and cypress, the carved landscape, was more her creation than any of the others who had ruled here.

But the physical structures of the estate were the least of the changes she had brought to this property. It had become the Black Manor of her tales, inhabiting the walls, the furniture, seeping through the framework of the place to challenge his sanity.

Harry looked down and found his cell phone in his hand. He thumbed the smiling icon, wondering when his friend would finally have enough of him and his need to talk his problems through.

Jack Hallowell answered in a whisper. “Yeah.”

“Paula with you?”

“Yeah.”

“Let her sleep. I need to talk.”

Jack sighed. “Didn’t you get wasted like I said?”

“Didn’t help. Got this pounding head for my trouble, and here I am talking to you again.”

“Bitch.” There was a low moan, a soft rebuke. “Not you, honey. I’m talking to Harry.”

“Told you to clear out.”

“Look, man, it’s Saturday. Can’t this wait?”

“No.”

“Okay, where?”

“The greasy spoon on the highway. Ten minutes.”

Harry entered his car, doubt eating at him, and turned the ignition. The engine roared to life. With his mind free of the phantom’s wails, he tore along the winding drive and pulled onto County Road 384, making for the I-55 interchange north of Jackson, the classic Mustang hurtling down the road.

Minutes later, the Cold Fish Diner loomed in the distance. He hadn’t visited the place in months, since about the time Paula Grisham had come into Jack’s life.

The Harley sat in easy view of the diner’s window, chrome handlebars and splashes of red gleaming next to two eighteen-wheelers. Jack Hallowell sat alone at the table, sipping coffee, and admiring his ride. Harry pulled alongside, and Jack raised his cup.

A pretty waitress Harry didn’t recognize ambled over as he slid into the booth opposite his friend. Harry ordered a black coffee and noticed the amused look Jack gave him when the waitress lingered longer than she really had to.

"You can do better than that," Jack said when she left.

"What?"

"The smile. Crank it up a bit."

Jack's own smile was contagious. His auburn hair and light, almost golden eyes had turned plenty of heads. Harry looked at her but turned away when he saw her staring back.

"Not my type."

"Hell, she's not!" Heads turned, so Jack lowered his voice. "I know you, bro."

Harry shook his head. "No more waitresses or bartenders. I'm into more sophisticated women now. You know, like Paula. She's a lawyer, you're a lawyer."

Jack nodded, his eyes dancing to some private memory. Jack had fallen hard. Harry assumed the feelings were mutual. He glanced at Jack's bike, hoping he would take the hint and change the subject, but hints and Jack had never really been all that close.

"Look," Jack said, "you might as well. You need something to do with all the time on your hands at night."

"I manage to get around."

"Sure, you do. When?"

Harry shrugged, instead of answering.

Jack raised his cup, hesitated, and put it back down. "When's the last time you slept more than a couple hours straight?"

"Two…three weeks…maybe."

Jack whistled. "How you holding up? You look pretty good, considering."

"Adapting. I was exhausted all the time at first, but now it's better. Tonight was too much, though." Harry looked past his friend, remembering. "The intensity is way up."

"Same damn dream?"

"Every time. Screaming woman. I'm looking for her, running hard, and finally find her surrounded by people dressed really weird. Some kind of pagan ritual, I think."

"Ritual," Jack said, his eyes locked onto Harry. "Got any idea what it means?"

Harry shook his head. He sure as hell didn't want to know the meaning, even if there was one. He could already hear his grandmother harping on the legacy crap. She'd attach every lunatic idea that popped up in her crazy mind.

The waitress came back with the coffee and placed it down, letting her fingers brush Harry's hand. She fussed about the table, trying hard to get his attention.

"Thanks," Harry said. "We're fine for now."

Jack turned red, trying to suppress a laugh as she walked away. "You *have* reformed."

Harry sighed. "There's too much crazy crap going on right now to chase women."

"It's never *that* bad."

"I haven't really slept in five nights, but I feel like I could run a marathon. I'm hearing women who don't exist screaming their pain and horror into my brain. I'm running around some fucking woods so real I can smell the decaying carcass of some dead animal, and you're the only one I can really talk to. So, knock it off about women."

Jack held up his hands in a sign of surrender.

"Easy, Hoss. You know I'm with you."

Harry had been leaning over the table without realizing it. He glanced around the place. Heads had turned, uneasy eyes staring at him.

He shrugged an apology and sat back down. "I didn't mean to jump your ass like that. It's just all this shit happening at the same time as Jones and Agnes refusing to show me the will."

Jack sighed, bent forward, and massaged his temples. "She's still insisting on using the will to enforce her legacy idea?"

"Claims it's ironclad. I won't get a dime until…"

Jack had heard most of this, except the strangest parts. The bits and pieces Agnes let slip to Harry during her crazier times, those things Harry had kept to himself, even when he and Jack were kids. There were some things you just didn't tell your friends.

The lawyer in Jack always kicked in at about this point. "The burden of proof if we go after Agnes's mental state is pretty stiff. From what I hear, Jones has the probate judge locked up."

"So, unless we have some solid evidence that my grandmother is bat shit crazy, I'm screwed."

Jack nodded. "It would be nice if I could actually see the damn will."

"It's out of my hands, Jack. I know some rudiments from the first page, but that's it. I haven't seen it either. It's a simple, two-page document as far as I know, but I wouldn't put it past Jones to lie about this to me."

"If we take Jones to court, he'll have to release it. Of course, you'd want to wait until after Agnes—"

Jack stopped and looked away. It was better left unsaid. Complicated was the best way to describe

Jack's relationship with Harry's grandmother. Jack's history with her was almost as complex as Harry's. And now she was dying.

They sat for a while, staring out the window. Harry finally broke the silence. "I'm not ready to knuckle under to Agnes, even if she is right about it ending the nightmares. I've got my own plan. I think a psychologist can help. I even know one."

Jack put his cup down. "What are you thinking?"

"I need help."

"You're not crazy, Harry."

"Yeah, well, I'm beginning to worry her fucking brainwashing seriously messed me up."

"But going on the couch?" Jack hesitated. "Is he any good?"

"*She's* legit. Young. Someone I know, sort of. Virginia Rankin."

"Rankin." Jack sipped the coffee, thinking. "That the family I'm thinking of, as in that old racist?"

Harry yawned and rubbed the back of his neck. "Maybe, but could be a separate Rankin family. Why?"

"My knee-jerk liberal parents hated people like that, what they stood for."

"Your parents didn't much like my grandmother, either."

"Agnes is many things, but racist isn't one of them."

Harry nodded. "But Agnes is plenty conservative. Same thing in their mind. Anyway, the racist stuff was decades ago. We aren't talking politics here, just my mental health."

Jack nodded. "Speaking of politics, when's the big party?"

"Tomorrow night."

"You looking forward to it?"

The honest thing would be to say no, but Harry had an ulterior motive for wanting to be there, and it wasn't to support Agnes's latest political venture. Changing the subject, he said, "I'm going to see Dr. Rankin as soon as I can. I need help."

The waitress returned with some apple pie to go with their coffee. She placed generous slices in front of them. They both smiled, and she started to walk away, but Harry reached out and touched her arm.

"Listen, thanks for the pie. I'll make sure Buddy knows what good service you provide."

She walked away, beaming.

"You've got an admirer," Jack said.

The waitress strolled to the counter, her short skirt a distraction, but not enough of one.

"Anyway," Harry said, turning back, "Agnes claimed to know this *gift*, or whatever it's supposed to be, was in me even though it had skipped two generations. She said it had to be since I was the only heir left." Harry glanced around the nearly empty diner and leaned in over the table closer to Jack. "But how would she know? She's never seen any of the weirdness firsthand. As far as she knows, somebody could have made it all up and put it in the Black family diaries, right? There's no proof the stories are true. It's all just a stupid fantasy."

"Or something worse," Jack said. "She could actually be insane. A family trait, maybe?"

Harry snorted. "Funny."

"But if the stories aren't true," Jack went on, "why the nightmares?"

Harry smiled. "What if they're the effects of her brainwashing? That's what her storytelling was really all about. Just a lonely old woman bent on believing fables about our glorious family. She's been frantic to get me believing it all, to somehow sustain her belief system. That's the way I see it. I guess some of it rubbed off on my subconscious."

Jack straightened. "You think the psychologist can sort you out?"

"That's damn sure what I'll ask. Or point me to someone who can. I think the dreams must be a jumbled mess of the images pulled from stuff Agnes forced on me as a kid, nothing a good therapist couldn't fix. And when I do get better and prove to Strom Jones this stuff is phony, that I'm normal and not going through some sort of metamorphosis, I'll be able to force his hand. And my crazy grandmother can just—"

Harry grimaced, ashamed with what he had been about to say. The woman didn't have long. He hated feeling so negative about her all the time. She was holding onto life, it seemed, to accomplish some final act. That big political bash coming up was undoubtedly central to her plans, and Harry suspected he had a significant role to play. He just didn't know what it could be.

Jack took a bite of his apple pie. "Crazy, eccentric, what's the difference? The tack I'll take with the judge will have him believing she's demented. Bring that story to court with a credible expert saying the nightmares are cured, and you'll win. You've lived up to your part and more, I'd say."

"Your opinion as a lawyer."

"Damn straight."

Harry smiled again, feeding off Jack's energy. It was the second page of the will that was the problem, the part that threatened his inheritance. But Harry didn't have any details from it, just an impression gathered from Agnes and her sidekick. Strom Jones, her personal assistant and lawyer, seemed to be making that part of the will decisive, strongly hinting that without acquiescing to the second page, his inheritance was null and void. He could avoid it by proving the legacy had come to him, but how was he supposed to do that? Rant and rave like a lunatic as she had done.

He could still hear the awe in Agnes's voice when she talked about it, using words like destiny, a faraway look coming over her. *Black Manor will never be yours unless you do as I say.*

He'd nearly forgotten those words, but in the grip of insomnia, they'd come back to him with regularity these last few nights. Agnes had made it clear the inheritance wasn't merely the mansion and the money. It was far more than that, encompassing the family legacy, some tradition he hadn't really grasped, some sort of duty that rested with him as the last living member of Clan Black. The house and the money came with that second page, not the reverse. Jones had been clear about it. Complying with the second page would make him rich, but he didn't have control over when the second-page provisions would activate. If Jones and Agnes were right and he couldn't break the will, he would be subservient to his grandmother even after she died.

Jack's eyes brightened, and Harry could almost hear his brain working the possibilities. "If the doc can help you get rid of these dreams, it'll prove to old

Strom the stipulations are all invalid. Whatever it is he has in the will."

Harry nodded.

"You know," Jack said, "he'll probably relent without us having to take him to court."

Harry smiled at Jack and his newfound enthusiasm. Then he caught some movement outside—a pudgy man of about forty walking past the Mustang, head bent, dragging his left hand across the hood, the other stuck inside his blazer. He lifted his head and stared into the diner, locking eyes with Harry.

Harry saw darkness there, a sense of malevolence, the shadow of a sneer. Harry's head thumped, strange words blossoming in his mind.

A priore sensum.

In the dull light of the parking lot, against the creeping light of the sun rising in the east, formless shadows flickered over the Mustang and engulfed the man. They were the same as had appeared in his room. The man stopped walking. Something about him wasn't right. Head held high, he seemed to lose substance as if phasing out of this dimension and entering an alien one.

Harry gripped the table, his throat suddenly dry. He tried to cry out, tried to make some sound, any sound. In the next moment, the man blinked out altogether. A moment later, he shimmered back to solid form. With a tortured look, the man grabbed his throat and collapsed.

Harry still couldn't speak, but his brain was screaming, trying to break the spell or whatever it was that had taken him over. He clutched the edge of the table, staring at the stricken man lying on the outside walk.

Jack looked up, his mouth wrapped around a now

empty fork. "This is better than what the last cook used to whip up."

Harry rose, head thumping, still silent, still staring at the stricken man.

Jack finally noticed something wasn't right and followed Harry's gaze. "What the—"

"Shadows," Harry finally gasped. "They just—"

The waitress cut him off with a screech that could be heard in Yazoo City, forty miles away. All heads turned. People scrambled to their feet. The commotion jolted Harry into action. Stumbling from the booth, he pushed through the door, the waitress tight on his heels.

Blood oozed from the man's nose and mouth. Harry placed two shaking fingers to the man's throat and glanced up at Jack. "No pulse."

The waitress latched onto Jack's arm. "He's d-dead?"

Jack tried to pull away. "Why don't you call an ambulance?"

"Buddy's doin' it."

Harry looked closer and noticed the dead man's ears and eyes had also begun to seep blood, lots of it pooling around his face. He could smell it. Harry's head thumped again, making him stagger back a step or two as he stood.

Moonlight and blood don't mix.

The phrase floated through Harry's mind as sweat beaded on his forehead. Something seemed to take control of him, lifting his head to the enormous moon now vanishing into the western sky, its pale light being chased away by the quickening sun.

The phrase seemed to carry some sort of warning.

Harry tried to swallow but his throat felt like a

parched desert floor. Those things, whatever they were, had murdered that man.

The pretty waitress left Jack and came to Harry, nestling close. It had the effect of pulling him back to the moment. She trembled as they stood over the dead man.

“Ambulance is coming,” someone called from the crowd.

Harry nodded to no one in particular, and walked the waitress back into the diner, trying not to look at the Mustang and what he feared lurked inside.

Chapter 4

Harry made it back to Black Manor, its front gardens basking in the morning light. But the beauty of the place couldn't chase away the visions of the dead man. No one at the scene had mentioned anything odd regarding the death. Harry knew better. He'd watched the shadows glide over to the man, seen him lose substance, then come back into full view. The bleeding started then.

He'd been murdered. Somehow those shadows had murdered him.

Harry slammed his car door and raced into the mansion as if drawn again by some irresistible urge. He tried to be quiet so as not to disturb Agnes or her nurse caretaker, but he couldn't be still. He went straight to his room but stopped in the doorway and watched as twin shadows flickered through the window and onto the ceiling. As if reacting to his presence, they froze over his bed, motionless except for a peculiar quivering.

His stomach tightened, and he would have bolted, but those words came to him again—*a priore sensum*—the same words that had sprung up in his mind right before the man fell. Instead of producing fear, the shadows seemed to be beckoning him.

His breathing slowed. His pounding heart calmed. It didn't make sense. His grandmother, her nurse, they should be warned, but a sense of quiet spread over him.

He walked to the bed, examining the shadows with each step. They were real, impossibly real, continually shifting—eyeless, headless, nothing that could indicate intelligence. Harry had a strong sense that they were here to observe him. Could they be sentient? Had something, some*one* passed unimpeded through the walls of his home?

A thousand ideas cascaded through his brain. Run, leave Black Manor, forget the money, the will, the legacy, his grandmother's insanity, and be done with the whole damn mess. Start a new life somewhere else. Forget his past.

He groaned. This was his property. He wouldn't see it, and the money would go to some charity Strom Jones would pick on a whim.

Keeping his eyes on the shadows, he rounded the foot of his bed. *Intelligence*—suddenly, the idea didn't seem so farfetched.

They drifted back to the wall, hesitating at the closed drapes. Harry took a step toward them. In response, their flickering doubled in intensity, almost as if they wished him to follow. Then they dissolved through the curtains and left the house.

He dashed to the window. In the intensifying morning light, they were hard to see, but they were there, flitting across the lawn before blinking out of existence.

****

Harry paced the mansion through the morning, each hour a torture. He'd resolved not to let this thing paralyze him, but the memory of those shadows passing over that man, the agony on his face, the smell of the blood.

Those things were real; they had murdered. And more than that, they seemed somehow connected to him and the mansion. But how? Why?

He fielded these questions, always replaying the last few weeks in his head—the dream ramping up in intensity, and now last evening with these sudden significant changes. He hadn't told Jack how the man died. He hadn't dared. And now the murdering shadows were here, in his home, his bedroom, part of his nightmare, part of him, killing, murdering.

Harry didn't want to go in to work, but he wouldn't give his grandmother one more reason to hound him, so he dropped the Mustang off at the shop and took a cab to the offices of Schuster and Howard Financial Advisement.

Throughout the day, he went through the motions, trying to act interested, trying to stay out of sight. Peggy, his assistant, was loyal enough to help, but it didn't work. Big Hank Howard pestered him constantly to lobby his grandmother's political contacts since Agnes Black hadn't seen fit to invite her grandson's employer to the big bash everyone knew about. He and Harry had been arguing for weeks about it, but Harry steadfastly refused.

He nearly quit twice and used some choice words to tell Howard just what he thought of his brilliant ideas. The end of the day hadn't come fast enough. Retrieving the Mustang, he drove for an hour, needing time to think. Finally, after much debate, he decided that Jack had been right.

He had to stay away from the mansion for a few nights. Maybe that would clear his head and interrupt the nightmares. He hadn't seen those shadows all day.

No foreign words or strange phrases had popped into his mind. He needed to think, but a little companionship at the same time could help. He veered off the expressway before exiting the metro area. Maybe his off-again, on-again, almost-girlfriend would give him a sympathetic ear.

She appeared at the apartment door, still wearing her airline flight attendant uniform. The surprise on her face turned quickly to a wry smile.

"You're lucky," Jenn said, kissing him on the cheek. "I just got back a half-hour ago."

Harry returned the kiss and threw a small duffle bag onto her couch.

She stared at the bag, hands on her hips. "This had better mean that you're back."

Harry didn't know what it meant. All he knew was that he needed a break in his regular routine. This was something he hadn't yet tried, and it was worth a shot.

"I know this is sudden," Harry said. "I could crash somewhere else if it's awkward."

"What, did Agnes finally kick you out?"

"No, nothing like that. I just need to talk."

She went to him and placed a hand on his chest. "What's wrong, Harry? Why would you bring your bag just to talk?"

"I'd hoped you wouldn't mind a sleepover, just platonic. I should have called first, but it's just…everything. I'm…I really do need to talk. I don't expect us to…you know…" He let the words go, hoping she would understand.

"I ought to be furious with you, and I have been." She gently touched her lips to his, putting her hands on his hips. "Do we have to talk? That's never been our favorite activity."

Instead of kissing her back, he pulled her into a hug, but she pulled away after a moment.

"You're trembling." She held him at arm's length. "Something's wrong."

Harry took a deep breath. "Listen, I know I've been an ass to you, Jenn. Maybe we could have dinner later tonight. I just have to make an appearance at that party to mollify Agnes, and then—"

"Oh, I'd forgotten about the party."

"I would have invited you, but things might not go well. In fact, I'm pretty sure they won't."

"You forgot to say Agnes wouldn't approve of me."

Harry took her hand. "I approve. That's enough."

Jenn pulled it back. "Apparently, not enough to bring me." She looked again at the bag, frowning. "I haven't seen you in, what, a month, and you think you can just come here without calling, bringing your things?"

Her cheeks were flushed now. Harry stepped closer, needing to head this off before it got worse, but she pushed him away.

Jenn looked up at the ceiling as if the words she wanted to say were written there. "And the thing is…I really wish it weren't this way, but I'm okay with it. You know how I feel, Harry. Just say the word, and I'm all yours. But not like this. I want it to be for good."

Harry hadn't anticipated this. Jenn was carefree, a female version of how Jack had once been before Paula corralled him. Apparently, his thick skull hadn't let in the signs she had undoubtedly given off. Major misstep. He tried again to say something, but she wouldn't hear it.

"I haven't 'dated' "—She put quotation marks around the word with her fingers, meaning something else entirely—"in two months. I've waited for you to come back, wanted you to come back to me, and when you do, it's this half-ass thing about talking and you not being able to stand up to your damn grandmother."

The words washed over Harry, and he knew she was right. He put a hand on her shoulder, but she jerked away. She let out an exasperated growl, spun on her heels, grabbed the duffle bag, and pushed it into his arms. She threw open the door for him to leave.

Harry stood outside her door for a moment, listening to her cry, her words ringing in his ears. He would have pounded his head against the wall, but that would draw her attention. He'd have to make this right, somehow, but in the next breath, he knew he shouldn't give her any more mixed signals. It was time to move on with his crappy, screwed-up life.

****

The bar was some dimly lit dive he'd never seen before. Stale cigarette smoke stung his eyes as he sat there alone. A few customers were drinking in the shadows at the far end. He wanted to get drunk, but he needed company, so he called Jack and got lucky. Paula was shopping, so a few beers were just what he needed.

With three beers down at Phil's Tavern, the conversation turned to their rides.

"The hell you could," Harry said.

Jack snorted and took the last sip of his whiskey. "Look, you know I love you, man, and I think your Mustang is…cute. But the Harley could whip your ass three ways to Sunday without trying very hard."

They bought two more bottles apiece and ended up taking them to Miller's Road just east of Black Manor, the light fading fast on a hot June day. A lonely stretch of ragged asphalt in a place that would make the middle of nowhere appear cosmopolitan, Miller's Road enjoyed a bad rap as a place where idiots and hotheads went to settle arguments behind the wheel.

It was a quick race, the Harley barreling along to the right of the car, inching ahead at the last possible moment. Passing the agreed-upon finish line, the two supercharged machines skidded and skirted to a stop, barely a foot apart.

Harry sat there, head pounding, forehead pressed against the steering wheel, as Jack nudged his bike to the driver's side window.

"You okay?" Jack asked.

"Empty stomach, too much beer, and a kick-ass ride. Dangerous cocktail."

"Don't know about the kick-ass part. Did you hear it?"

"Yeah, skipped a beat right at the end."

The rebuilt engine purred most of the time, but top-ending the classic Shelby muscle-car revealed the problem. The mechanic responsible for tuning had turned in a crappy job.

"I'll have to take it back tomorrow."

"Still has plenty of flat-out speed," Jack said. "You sure you aren't obsessing just a tad?"

Probably, but Harry didn't want to admit it. "I want it right."

"Then find another shop."

Harry nodded and glanced at his watch. "Shit."

A crooked smile crossed Jack's face. "Agnes sure

as hell won't like the way you're dressed. She prefers New York chic, to Mississippi swank."

Harry looked down at the blue blazer covering his starched white shirt. The jeans were new, but Jack was right. Agnes wouldn't like it, but appeasement wasn't on the menu after what Jenn had said.

"Grandmother has more to worry about tonight than what I'm wearing."

"If you say so," Jack said, "but that's not my experience."

It was the old game Jack loved to play. Pit Harry against Agnes, something he'd perfected in their teen years. Lots of fights resulted from that. Harry would have punched him now, but he couldn't reach Jack through the car window. Instead, he held out his fist, and his friend bumped it with his own, that goofy smile still playing on his lips.

"Why don't you get Paula and come over tonight?"

Jack shook his head. "I don't match too well with Agnes's taste in guests."

"True," Harry said, "but I know how your boss gets when lobbyists and politicians come together. Same as mine. And there will be lots of legal-eagle work if you have the right connections."

"Doesn't matter."

"So, making partner before thirty is no longer part of the plan? You tell Paula that?"

Harry had him there. Paula Grisham had wrapped up Jack faster and tighter than any woman ever had, and the funny part was that he'd let it happen, hadn't resisted at all. In the last two months, Harry had seen his best friend maybe three times besides today.

And that meant this thing with Paula was damn

serious.

"I'm on track, but Paula's cool with whatever."

Harry looked off down the road, nodding.

"So, who you with tonight? Jennifer?"

"Jenn's history," Harry said, frowning. "I'm on my own."

"Didn't you just leave her place?" Jack leaned over his Harley, looked through the back window, and pointed to the duffle bag. "That's cold, man. Breaking up after an overnight."

"It was never going to be an overnight, not like she wanted anyway." Harry grimaced, thinking of the scene he'd left earlier. "I needed to blow off some steam, maybe talk to someone who wasn't on the inside."

"So that's why we're out here acting like a couple of stupid seventeen-year-olds." Jack pulled one of his beers from the compartment behind him, popped the top, and took several swallows. He gave the car a good once over. "Ten years ago, when you got it, the 'Stang would have eaten this bike up."

"We're both getting older, I guess." Jack lifted his watch for the second time in as many minutes. "Ah…Paula calls," Harry mocked.

Jack's smile was back, a bit sheepish this time. "Better find a tie to go with the blazer, or your grandmother will have your ass. Probably been looking for you."

Harry shrugged. "I can handle her."

"Sure, you can." Jack lowered his eyes, and he turned serious. "Tell the old girl goodbye for me and that I appreciate everything. I never got the chance to thank her properly. I mean…" He let the thought trail off. "I know she's a loon, but I wouldn't be where I am now without her."

Harry looked up into his friend's face and could see sincerity there and not a little concern. "She wouldn't have let you. It was enough that your parents knew how you financed your education."

Jack sighed, and a pained look crossed his face.

"She knows you appreciate what she did. Don't beat yourself up over it."

Jack nodded. "You're right. It's just that I probably won't see her again before—"

"I know," Harry said, cutting him off before he could say the words. It hurt too much to hear it.

Jack turned away, the long stretch of black road before him. It didn't matter that they wouldn't speak more words over his grandmother's condition or what she'd done for Jack. Brothers wouldn't have to mouth such sentiments or talk about the bond they shared.

Jack revved the bike and gave the Mustang two slaps on the roof. He took a couple more swallows from the beer and threw the bottle into the weeds. "Later, bro."

In a roar, the Harley sped off in the opposite direction, its rear tire swerving and throwing loose gravel, making Harry duck his head.

Through his rearview mirror, Harry watched his friend recede into the quickening night. He gripped the wheel harder, a twinge of jealousy welling up from somewhere in his gut. Time would tell how permanent Jack's new flame might be, but something did seem different about this one.

Harry couldn't help the coldness that crept over him like icy tentacles, closing around his chest. When Jack's parents had rejected their son, Agnes had practically taken the boy in. Now Jack had found someone. The jealousy Harry felt didn't really have anything to do with Jack or what he had now with Paula. It was more a complicated *something* Harry couldn't quite put his finger on, a mixture of the imminent loss of the only family he had left and Jack's preoccupation these last few months. It was a feeling of despair that had nothing to do with the nightmare and the sleeplessness that had been stalking him for weeks, culminating in that man's death this morning. And now he had to throw in the loss of Jenn. She wanted something Harry wasn't willing to give her, but she was still a friend. He hated that he had run roughshod over her feelings, even if it was inadvertent.

Harry gripped the wheel harder. He had to pull himself together, or his foul mood would overtake this night too and make it a total wreck just like all those years ago at Agnes's other big political bash. It couldn't happen again. He had too much to prove this time.

As Jack disappeared into the east, a slither of cloud crossed the path of the early rising moon reflected in the driver's door mirror. It caused Harry's heart to skip a beat. He tensed, but the shadows didn't reappear. He shook his head, trying hard to escape the irrational fear gripping him.

He put the car in gear and took a deep breath, letting the frustrations of the day leach out of him. He stared straight ahead. His path lay due west, to home, and a destiny he needed to embrace.

Chapter 5

Near Muscat, Oman

Arie Peeters materialized at the surf's edge, the air shimmering where he stood as though the bowels of the earth had suddenly unleashed a blast of heat. The effect would last only a moment, undetected by those watching. He checked the GPS in his watch to confirm his location. A stiff wind blowing in from the Gulf of Oman peppered his white shirt with spray. He didn't care. He wouldn't be stuck in this shithole very long.

The cry of gulls filled the air as Peeters got his bearings. He turned east and let his senses drift out. In a moment, his own magical working wafted to him as a combination of smell and touch. He threw his cigarette to the sand and lifted his head higher, arms spread, and extended from his body. He couldn't see them, but his contacts were there in the dark, waiting about a hundred meters off. The cigarette's dying embers vanished as a flood of lights from several motor vehicles backlit the silhouettes of three men. More Jihadist bastards were near, just over the dunes to his right, but he didn't need his unique ability to know this. He expected nothing less of his three contacts. They would make sure he'd come alone. He chuckled, imagining the confusion of the watchers as they puzzled over how he had gotten ashore.

Peeters dropped the bag containing the cash just out of reach of the surf. His three contacts gave each other sideways glances and started toward him at once. The million dollars was a powerful draw, an inducement to get them here, and more importantly, it would provide them with something to inspect. The promise of ten million more would keep him safe from any treachery these three might hatch.

It had taken too long to piece this part of the operation together, almost a year of bribing and plying them with sex on the yacht, waiting for him far enough offshore to remain unseen. He'd convinced these three principals they would be needed, not their underlings. It had also taken a fair amount of aeromancy to pull it off, but he had managed it with his own power.

During his dealings with the three Jihadists, their appearance had never changed—heavy stubble, keffiyeh headdress, standard thawb—all unremarkable except for the ammunition belts and automatic weapons now slung over their shoulders. Peeters carried nothing but the large knife hidden inside his boot.

"So much to protect against one man?" Peeters asked as they neared, his native Dutch producing an unwelcome accent as he spoke to them in Arabic. He chuckled through the comment as though talking to old buddies.

"And more across that ridge, my friend," the tallest one said, leveling his weapon on Peeters with a contemptuous smile.

Peeters nodded, a conciliatory gesture as if to say, "Do with me what you will." It didn't matter. They would soon realize who was in control. Arms spread wide in a welcoming gesture, he said, "You needn't have doubted me." He moved alongside the bag, watching the three men eye it greedily. "The down payment is all there. Please, look for yourself."

The tallest one took the lead and unzipped the heavy bag, stepping aside to let the others see the bundles of cash. Their distrust of each other very nearly equaled their hatred of the West. The three had insisted on American money, had laughed at the irony of American currency bringing calamity to the great Satan.

This had been part of his master's grand plan. The American administration would be confused to think these three had worked together to achieve such a feat. Peeters smiled, thinking of the American president focusing on this part of the world, ignorant of his real enemy.

Unable to resist fondling the cash, as foreseen, the fat one reached in with both hands. Peeters's heart thumped. He took a step forward, anticipating the working that had been planted for just this moment. But before the trap could spring, the tall one fired a short burst from his AK47 into the sand a half meter from the bag, making the Palestinian cry out and fall to his fat ass.

Peeters tensed as the tall one spoke to his shocked companion in deep guttural tones.

"I can see that it is all there, Gabrill," Khaled Mashaal said before turning his eyes to Peeters. "There has been a change of plans. We know you are off our shore." He looked out over the gulf. "And we know you must have the rest with you. One million will not be enough, my friend, to turn American eyes onto us. The other ten will be required. Now, not later when you will, no doubt, forget what we have done for you."

Peeters looked at the three men, their smirks confirming that his aeromancy had not been as complete as he had thought. He grimaced. The master wouldn't be pleased. These issues were supposed to have been resolved with Peeters's last bit of mind sorcery dulling the will of these men. Apparently not.

He glanced to his right. The watchers had come out into the open, about thirty of them, all as heavily armed as the three bastards before him.

"My mas—" He caught himself. "My people will not like this, Khaled. We had a deal."

"Yes, but this is only a slight change, and we do not know your people, nor have we seen them. They are mere ghosts. We do not trust ghosts."

His comrades laughed at Khaled's joke.

Peeters ached to cut the man, make him bleed in great arching spurts, but he kept his composure. He needed to return their attention to the bag, or his master's plans would be ruined.

"You will have your money. Just give me something to communicate with the boat. I've left my cell phone."

Mashaal reached into his garment and pulled out his phone. It seems they had planned well. But not well enough.

Peeters drew near and took the phone from the tall Arab, but in doing so, he grabbed his hand at the same time. The skin-to-skin contact was enough. Mashaal stiffened, and Peeters got a firm grip on his wrist, completing the connection.

"Now," Peeters said calmly. He glanced at the group of men about fifty meters away, but they were unaware. "You were about to inspect the money,

Gabrill. Please do so."

Under control now, Mashaal nodded, and the others, confused, did as they were told. It happened as planned this time. The magical working snapped with an audible buzzing sound when Gabrill stuck his hand into the bag. It clicked in their minds the preparatory aeromancy Peeters had worked into them over many drunken nights. The three men remained frozen as if their brains had ceased to function.

A mist rose from the bag, all but invisible, unseen by those spying through night-vision field glasses. Peeters waited as the translucent mist formed into the semblance of his master, taller than the tallest of the three, now-pliable men.

The psychogeist began to speak, the words coming to them as through a long tunnel. "You will go now. When it begins, the three of you will immediately claim responsibility, insist that your group and yours alone will bring the infidels down. Then wait for further instruction."

The apparition waved a vague hand as though parting a curtain. As it did so, three streams of a misty grayish-black substance broke free and floated to each man, penetrating their skulls. The three men rose to their full height and turned as one to Peeters, their faces placid, their eyes indicating that the leaders of Hamas, Hezbollah, and al-Qaeda now had a new master.

Peeters smiled, grabbed the bag, and vanished. Back on the boat, he ordered the crew to get underway while he placed a call on his secure satellite phone.

Chapter 6

Near Amsterdam, The Netherlands

The sorcerer searched the eyes of his confidants and knew they were ready. Over the last year, he could feel his old power returning. It had been many, many decades since the trickery of Clan Black had broken him, nearly destroying his own clan. His people had made it through, but the toll had been enormous, for it had taken him well over a century to reconstitute his strength, to nurture it, coax it into a semblance of what it had been. And, in all that time, they had planned well.

Their intelligence indicated that Clan Black had fled to America from England. A long search ensued, and finally, after two world wars, the rumor of them had come as if on the wind. They'd finally found the cursed Blacks in the American South, hiding like snakes in the most unlikely of surrounds. The once-proud opponents in the great struggle reduced nearly to peasantry.

That discovery had been nearly sixty-five years ago, a lifetime by the standards of normal men. Luckily, he had worked his magic before his clan's failure. His life force had been spared, but not his power. Its return had been slow.

Now the time was at hand. With the sorcerer's strength rapidly returning, Clan Black would also rediscover itself. It had always been so, that truth as evident as Newton's Third Law of Motion. Every action produces an equal and opposite reaction. Likewise, when Clan Mage rose again, there would be a balanced response from Clan Black. Unfortunate, but true. The Blacks had opposed them at every turn.

"Has there been no word yet from them? No whisper that a new Protector is rising?"

"No, Lord, not yet."

"Most unusual, don't you think?"

"Not the standard pattern, no. But we have eyes on the ground there. The boy lives a normal life, grows in maturity, does a man's work. But we are limited in what we know of him. We cannot follow his every movement because of the veil."

"Normal, would you say?"

"Nothing extraordinary, I assure you. The young man appears quite ordinary in every sense."

The group chuckled, and Desmin Von Ausberg nodded. He turned his back on them and stared into the giant stone fireplace. Regardless of the report, he had just been given, the old pattern would manifest. It always did. Why should this modern world be any different?

"Have we maintained control of the lackeys in the Middle East as Arie assured me?"

"They will make suitable and logical targets for the Americans. The distraction will be beneficial. The Americans won't suspect any other possibility."

"Good," Desmin said. "It is time. Arie should remain in position and inform us if he can make a breakthrough in Mississippi."

The skinny man nodded before saying, "Lord, if I

may?"

Desmin motioned for him to continue.

"Is it not possible that we, in fact, destroyed them unknowingly? With your power back, we should have seen something by now."

"It is the twenty-first century, Johannes. The usual may no longer exist, but it is my opinion that this boy will develop. Mark my word. Nothing else makes sense."

"Yes, Lord, forgive me."

"Proceed with the plans, then. Teach the ritual to those chosen to attend. We must be certain this time that they will be utterly destroyed."

"He is unmarried and childless. He is the last. When he is dealt with, there will be no others. We will have won."

Desmin remained calm, not choosing this time to show the anger he felt at such hubris. "You seem so confident."

Desmin said it such a way that left no doubt. The surety Johannes unwisely assumed was not an opinion shared by his lord. A low murmur broke out among those assembled, but their lack of foresight aggravated Lord Desmin. They were inflexible, incapable of seeing that times change. It was the usual weakness of youth, though, by the mere look of his people, they would all pass as much older than he. But looks, in this case, were most definitely deceiving.

Desmin must take no chances this time, for he feared there wouldn't be another. He had conquered death, man's terrible enemy, had regained his glorious youth, had held it, but if there was another mishap, and it backfired onto him alone like it had that last time, he wasn't so sure he would survive. He'd come too far to fail again. Those assembled would serve as a buffer for him, though they suspected it not.

"Clan Black has always shown itself to be most resourceful. Take no chances. If we cannot dispose of him through normal means, all our power must be brought to bear through sorcery. Clan Black must be cut off—for good."

Johannes bowed to him, and it was enough.

"When the protector shows himself, inform me at once."

Chapter 7

Black Manor, Near Jackson, Mississippi

By the time Harry made it to the massive twin gargoyles at the entry gate to the estate, limousines were already rolling past, blocking his entry. He veered to the left and pulled to a stop at the command of a sheriff's deputy directing traffic.

Harry cursed under his breath, knowing his grandmother would have gone all-out for the occupants of these cars, including inconveniencing anyone who might be innocently passing on this stretch of road.

Like sleek black snakes, the limos crawled along the winding drive where majestic oak and cypress cast a foreboding gloom as though the visitors approached some ancient European castle and not a gothic mansion in the heart of Mississippi. The first of them halted before the front entrance, depositing VIPs attired for the evening's gala festivities. Trailing behind, Harry found an inconspicuous parking spot and killed the engine. He caressed the steering wheel, trying to calm himself. He needed to be here; this time around things would be different.

He stayed in the shadows after exiting the car, watching Agnes stalk the expansive gallery as best she could, welcoming her guests. Dressed in starched white shirts, black coats, and bowties, her crew busied themselves, helping new arrivals navigate the front acreage.

As dusk gave way to the black night, the grounds lighting snapped to life. Harry smiled at the faint cries and nervous laughter of those trying to manage the winding paths alone. Agnes's tastes in outdoor decoration could be a bit macabre. Angry-looking Celtic statuary was placed at strategic spots for maximum effect. Tripping motion sensors caused a sudden illumination sequence, making it seem like demons were invading from some unknown realm. That was just the effect she wanted. He thought of the occupants of his dream, and his neck hairs stood on end. He looked out into the night, but things seemed in order—no demons, no roaming shadows.

Harry shook off the heebie-jeebies. This was a big night for his grandmother. The Governor of Mississippi would already be inside, flanked by his many aides. They were lucky Agnes hadn't blackballed them and a great many other Democrats. After all, the party was in honor of Dr. William Rankin, Republican extraordinaire. The minority leader of the U.S. Senate was one of Agnes's two obsessions. Rankin had been her project for as long as Harry could remember, and she played the role of mentor with a single-minded attention to detail. Her financial backing had put Rankin in Washington. Years of scheming and enough money to feed a third-world country would put him in the White House. Agnes damn well meant to make it happen, but that would be after her death, and there was nothing she could do about that.

Agnes paced the deep porch as best she could, the trailing oxygen tank her constant companion these days.

She appeared aggravated, searching for something, then a servant approached from behind and leaned into her ear. Agnes smiled at a small group nearing the gallery. Gathering her flowing, ankle-length chiffon, she strolled imperiously toward them, head held high despite the stiff back she'd been complaining about. The tall redhead walking beside the senator pointed Harry's way, bringing Agnes to an abrupt stop.

Agnes's eyes flashed at Harry as he and the Rankins converged on her. With one sweep of her head, she took in all of him and without comment turned to the senator.

Speaking with a hoarse voice caused by chain-smoking, Agnes said, "Bill, Lisa—so glad you've finally arrived. And the children." She patted the young girl and boy on the head and turned to the senator's sister. "And the second Dr. Rankin. So happy you could make it, Ginny."

Virginia Rankin smiled broadly and clasped Agnes's hand with both of hers. "Wouldn't miss an evening with you." They hugged. Ginny whispered to Agnes, "I see you've managed to corral him this time," loud enough for Harry to hear.

Head slanted to Harry, but speaking to Ginny, Agnes said in stiff undertones, "You remember that after ten years?"

"I remember a defiant young man who didn't like his home being flooded with politicians."

"He still doesn't," Agnes said. "See the way he chooses to dress? Really, son, boots and jeans for tonight? At least you've managed some sort of decorum from the waist up, but not much." Agnes shook a crooked finger, scolding him like a school kid. "I taught you better."

Ginny laughed but covered her mouth when Harry turned to the family, standing a few feet off, waiting. "You're neglecting your guests, Grandmother." He extended his hand, and Rankin took it. "Senator…Mrs. Rankin…I'm Harry Black. Welcome to our home."

Harry turned to Ginny with a smile and a slight bow. "It's been a long time."

Ginny Rankin locked onto him with green eyes so bright they could light the porch. "Our meeting then was pretty brief. I'm surprised you remember."

Agnes huffed. The episode ten years back had been one of the blackest of Harry's formative years. He gave his grandmother a quick wink and flashed an impertinent smile, the kind he knew she hated.

He could tell she wanted to dress him down but would never show her darker side in front of the senator.

Harry turned back to Ginny. "Brief, and I'm embarrassed to admit, not the way I would have wanted. I'm older now and hopefully a little more mature." He put his arm around Agnes. "And more tolerant of my grandmother's need to display me."

Agnes gave him a feeble shrug and pointed to his jeans and cowboy boots. "Well, that makes quite a miserable display, young man. Goodness, boy, do you know who's in this house tonight?" Leaning in closer, Agnes lowered her voice. "And do you know who it is standing next to us? He's not just any senator, you—" She stopped short, her aggravated look getting even worse. "Is that beer I smell on your breath?"

"Don't get worked up so much, or you'll need more than a nasal cannula to get enough oxygen."

Harry kissed her on the cheek. “You’re the only person I know who could bring this much power into one house.” She tried to give him a good poke in the ribs, but he intercepted her elbow and gave it a gentle squeeze. “Let’s go in and have a good time, shall we?”

Agnes relaxed a bit at his unexpected show of affection. There had never been much of that between them. She broke off from Ginny and Harry, hobbled over to the Rankin family, and led them inside.

As Ginny watched her family disappear through the massive set of doors, Harry studied her. Ten years earlier, she had been a twenty-year-old college coed working for her older brother’s first campaign for the senate seat from his position as Congressman. Harry was a graduating high school senior battling his grandmother’s every attempt to orchestrate his life, trying to turn a seventeen-year-old into a carbon copy of herself. The result was predictable. He stormed out of the party, telling her not to expect him back, ever. It was all bluff. He always returned.

He’d often thought of Ginny Rankin since that night. Weeks ago, when Agnes told him about this gathering, Harry wondered why she had kept it a secret so long, given the event would have taken her months to pull together. The answer was that something was up. Agnes obviously wanted to keep him off balance and without much time to wrangle her intentions from Strom Jones, which also explained Strom’s absence from the estate in the last few weeks. Agnes hadn’t trusted Harry to act like an adult this time. That in itself was a slight, but after so many years with her, he was used to it. Instead of being upset, he took the opportunity to check up on Ginny Rankin, quickly filling in the missing years.

If possible, she was more beautiful now. At thirty, she had lost her girlish look, but not the intelligent eyes. Her bright red hair flamed against pale shoulders left bare by a pearl-white gown accentuating slender hips.

His unwavering attention caused Ginny's face to flush. "Agnes will want you and Bill to talk at some point tonight," she said.

Harry nodded. "That's a given."

"You up for it?"

"I knew it was bound to happen at some point, but that's not why I'm here. I'll try to cooperate. Grandmother doesn't need the aggravation, considering her condition."

Ginny gave him a concerned look. "No, she's not doing so well."

"Not for a while now."

"I've given some end-of-life counseling to pulmonary patients and their families. I know the signs. How long does she have?"

"Maybe two months—best case." He glanced at the front door again. "She's marshalled some strength but could just as easily take a downturn again."

"How do you feel about that, Harry?"

"Trying to psychoanalyze me, Doctor?"

"So, you've checked up on me. Or has Agnes filled you in?"

He chuckled. "My grandmother doesn't talk to me about such things. I got all the details myself—finished Ole Miss three years before I did, studied for your psychology doctorate at UMMC, nearly five years in clinical practice. Doing great, I think."

"Very well done." She gave him a mock hand clap.

"So, you seem okay now with Agnes's involvement in Washington politics."

Harry's guard went up. He wasn't okay with it, and Agnes damn well knew it. He turned once more to the massive front entrance. An attendant had opened the door to admit someone. People were laughing, drinks in hand. "Let's just say my grandmother's goals are not my own. She wastes too much money on Washington, trying to change the unchangeable."

Ginny acknowledged him with a stiff nod. Harry knew the implications of what he had just revealed. Without the Black family money, her brother's political future and financial backing would become less clear. With the Black family matriarch out of the way, the sole heir to the family fortune would be free to find better uses for it. Harry studied Ginny's face in light of the sudden revelation. If it angered her, she didn't let on. He liked that. Emotions ruled his grandmother, but Harry preferred to be circumspect and had a deep need to be his own person. He had never fallen prey to his grandmother's schemes. She wasn't bad, just crazy, and he definitely didn't want to be like her. His plans for the inheritance certainly wouldn't meet with her approval.

Ginny had been toying with a diamond pendant she wore. She lowered her hand and looked up at Harry, breaking the long, uneasy pause. "My brother has been doing well in Washington. He's a unifier and part of the president's inner circle on financial matters, though he's in the opposition party." She hesitated, but Harry didn't respond. "He's a positive force for change if it makes any difference to you."

"I'm sure he is," Harry said, knowing his comment could be taken many different ways.

Everything she said was essential to Agnes, not him, but Harry didn't want to tell Ginny Rankin that. Not just yet. He wanted to get to know her better, show her he was different from the rude, angst-filled kid she'd met so long ago.

He wanted to change the direction the conversation had gone, so he said, "I would have expected some kind of entourage for the Senate Minority Leader, even here in Mississippi."

Ginny shook her head. "Not really, though Carl, his Chief-of-Staff, was supposed to come." She turned and looked about the porch as if searching for the person. "I would have heard if he had canceled."

Harry noticed Ginny eyeing a waiter carrying a tray of drinks. "With what I suspect my grandmother is serving me tonight, I could use one of those."

"Shall we go in?" Ginny asked.

Harry smiled and offered her his arm and was glad when she took it.

****

The party was in full swing when they entered. The huge Swarovski crystal chandelier in the entry hall sparkled as an easy-listening band played in one corner. The crowd was a mix of young and old, a change for the better in Harry's mind, probably a calculated move by Agnes. Bring in new blood, people he could identify with, most from well-connected families, perhaps all Republicans, though he could see the Democrat elite had also been invited.

"Hungry?"

"Starving," Ginny said and snagged a glass of white wine from a silver tray carried by a passing waiter.

Harry guided her to the large dining room. The central table had been removed to allow for more people. Five smaller tables were placed at equidistant spots along the walls. His mouth watered as they approached the table with the big gulf shrimp and sirloin strips.

Other tables had different themes and food choices, but he hadn't eaten since a quick breakfast and needed something substantial.

"There you are!"

Harry and Ginny turned to find an older man dressed in a white suit coming toward them.

"That's Mr. Jones, isn't it?" Ginny whispered. "I remember him."

Harry groaned and looked around the room. He spotted Senator Rankin holding Agnes by the arm, leading her into the library. No doubt, Strom Jones had been sent to drag Harry to the private meeting, which meant the brief gathering on the porch hadn't been enough for his grandmother. The big introduction was on, just like ten years ago, when Harry foiled her plans in a fit of teenage rage. The urge to storm out again was strong, but age had brought with it an appreciation for the inevitable. It would be his time soon enough if he could just secure his inheritance. He might as well start acting the part and think like the head of the estate, especially given Agnes's imminent decline. But she had so many irons in the fire for wielding influence it might take months, if not years, to pull them back. He didn't want to influence anything in the political arena. Under his control, the name Black would be synonymous with—*private, stay away*.

Strom Jones made it to Harry and Ginny through

the packed room. Jones's shock of neat white hair surprised Harry. He had never seen it combed down so well. As Agnes's only assistant, the old lawyer hadn't practiced properly in forty years, and his appearance sometimes showed it.

"Follow me," Jones growled as he swept by.

Harry grabbed his arm and pulled him to a stop. "This won't take long, will it?"

Jones returned Harry's stare with coal-black eyes. "It'll take as long as Agnes thinks necessary." He noticed Ginny standing there and seemed momentarily surprised when she edged closer to Harry. Recovering quickly, he put a fake smile on and said to Ginny, "You're welcome too, of course, Dr. Rankin."

Ginny lifted her glass. "I'll wait here." She put the heavy crystal to her crimson lips and took a small sip.

"Perhaps it's best," Jones said, before abruptly turning and marching off toward the library.

"Smart," Harry said to Ginny as Jones made his way through the crowd. He leaned in close to her. "Wish me luck."

She touched his hand, and with that small contact, darkness fell over the room, sucking all sound away as though they had fallen into the void of space. The cacophony of voices ceased. The band no longer played in the front entrance. Even Ginny's lilac scent disappeared. Harry staggered back into the emptiness, breaking the brief connection they shared. The room spun back in dazzling light, quickly fading to normal.

"You okay?" Ginny asked. She reached for him again, but he had stepped too far away for her to take his arm.

Harry continued to look around—at the lighting,

the people, Ginny. Everything appeared normal. No one seemed to have noticed the blackout.

"Didn't you see?" Harry asked her.

"See what?" She touched his arm, and he jumped in response, but nothing happened. "My brother doesn't bite. No reason to be nervous."

"I'm not. I mean—"

"Better not keep Agnes waiting."

Harry nodded and swept his eyes across the dining room one last time, deciding he must be hungrier than he thought.

****

Harry caught up with Jones just before he entered the darkly paneled library, falling in behind as they stepped among the floor-to-ceiling bookcases rising fifteen feet along three walls. Jones stopped them just beyond the door.

Agnes sat in the far corner at her ornate desk, Senator Rankin standing behind her, bending over her shoulder to stare at the open laptop. Jones coughed, alerting those already in the room to their presence.

"Over here," Agnes called out, motioning for Harry to join her and the senator.

Harry walked to his grandmother, Jones following. The senator looked up from Agnes's laptop, his steely, blue-gray eyes cutting an unforgiving swath through Harry. They were precisely like Ginny's, just as intelligent, but with none of her warmth.

Bill Rankin extended his hand, and Harry took it, acting on automatic pilot. "This moment has been a long time coming," Rankin said.

Harry nodded. The moment on the porch apparently didn't count, which meant Agnes had something up her sleeve, never a good sign.

Rankin cleared his throat. "I want you to know I appreciate everything you've done."

"You mean what my grandmother has done."

Agnes scowled at him. "Don't be disrespectful, boy."

"It's okay, Mrs. Black. He's right. I do mean your family and I do know, through Agnes, about the family's situation once she's—" Rankin hesitated.

"You can say it, Bill. My time's short. This meeting's important, so don't mince words."

"It's just that it seems so self-serving of me to be here right now." Rankin placed a hand on Agnes's shoulder. "Your condition is so delicate."

Agnes patted his hand. "I've planned so hard for this day. It's a wonder I've lived long enough to finally manage it. I *have* to see it through or at least the start of it."

Rankin nodded his understanding and turned his eyes to Harry as if to say, *the boss has spoken.*

So, this was to be a rehash of her failed attempt. He looked at his grandmother who suddenly seemed tiny in her chair at the desk, the vigor she'd shown on the porch only a few minutes before now gone.

He sighed, resigned to the inevitable. "I know the scheme my grandmother's planned. And I know how hard she's worked to have this kind of influence in DC, though I don't know why." He looked at Agnes, but she didn't lift her eyes to him.

Hesitating, but resolved, he turned more fully to Rankin, squared up to him. "Politics isn't my thing, and I don't see that changing after she's…"

Agnes waved off his attempt to be delicate.

Bill Rankin said, "I don't expect you to follow in Agnes's footsteps and take an active role. I appreciate the differences between you. But I do need you, Harry, in the same way I needed Agnes all these years."

Harry shook his head, "Not me…my money."

Rankin's eyes grew harder, the smooth fundraiser now gone. "Our money, more like it. A delicate agreement between Agnes and me that you have no part in, I'm afraid." He put his hand on her shoulder again. "She's been respectful of you, bringing you into the loop on this, Harry. This is bigger than you and the estate."

Politicians…self-important pricks.

"I'm sure you think so." He looked at Agnes who met his eyes this time. "I'm sorry, Grandmother. I plan to fight whatever it is you've planned for the money after you're gone. Jack and I—"

Agnes cursed under her breath and Harry took a step back, mindful that she was just barely holding her temper in.

He glanced at the senator. "I have a beautiful lady waiting to eat dinner, so if you'll excuse me—"

Harry spun on his heels and marched through the door, Agnes's curses trailing behind.

Chapter 8

Harry found Ginny sitting in a lone chair at the far side of the dining room under an original painting of Theodore Roosevelt. He made his way through the crowd, all the while keeping his eyes on her. When he got close enough, she spotted him. The smile came instantly, but there was also a faint hint of worry, not enough to mar her beauty, though, if that was even possible. Ginny held her drink—brandy in a crystalline snifter—swirling it with a restless hand.

"That didn't take long."

"Long enough," Harry said, trying hard to improve his mood. He offered his hand.

She took it and stood, but nearly toppled off her heels. "Sorry." She held up the glass. "I'm not used to this stuff."

"Empty stomach," he said, looking around. "Let's fix that."

Harry led her through the crowd to a table brimming with shrimp and rare sirloin strips. He offered her a Florentine dinner plate, and they proceeded to gather generous portions. They went to a quiet corner. Harry found himself staring at his food, unable to do more than replay in his head the meeting with Jones and his grandmother.

"You look upset. Was it that bad?"

Harry considered his response before speaking,

given the revelation he'd inadvertently yielded to her on the porch. "My grandmother is easy to predict sometimes, but I didn't see this one coming. Should have known something serious was up."

"What did she say?"

Harry bit through a shrimp and dropped the tail onto his plate. He chased it down with a swallow of red wine. "Let's just say she's treating your brother more like the family heir than me."

"Oh, Harry, you don't really mean that. Agnes has funded him, yes, but it's her right, after all. She just wants to know you'll back his future campaigns."

"So…you knew about her plans already."

"No, not really, but—" Ginny rested her fork on the china plate and turned more fully to him. "I do know what she wants for Bill, and that she won't live to see it. This is Bill's way of asking you himself. That's all."

Harry nodded, trying to find some indication she had been trying to mislead him, but she seemed genuine. "Do you know what happens if I say no?"

"I gathered from what you said on the porch, you might say that. It's your right." She gave his arm a light squeeze and smiled. "Bill will just have to find another major donor."

Harry nodded, looking down.

"Something tells me this isn't all you're worried about."

Psychologists, a perceptive lot. Harry drained his glass and put it down, swallowing hard.

"Grandmother's trying to tie the estate to your brother, make him the equivalent of a co-heir so I'll be forced to fund him for as long as *he* wants. It takes me right out of the decision-making process. Pretty much neuters me with the estate. It's a slap in the face."

Ginny cringed and leaned back in her chair. "I had no idea."

"Really?" He'd put as much skepticism into the word as he could.

She set her half-eaten plate of food down on the intricately-carved Reginelli drum table near her and turned toward him. "I understand how you feel about politicians and politics in general, but my brother is different. I'm not just saying this because I'm his sister." She took a deep breath. "Look, I'm not involved anymore in his campaigns. I don't have time because of my practice. I didn't have any ulterior motives in coming here tonight. Other than—"

"What?"

"Oh, never mind." She got up to leave, but he put a gentle hand on her arm, and she sat back down, eyes narrowing.

Harry looked at her, some of the tension draining from him. "I really didn't mean to insinuate anything. I—" He glanced at Jones as the old boy began gathering the crowd together for some type of announcement from Agnes. Rankin was near her, holding her arm. He would probably also make a statement. Harry didn't want to hear it.

Hand still on Ginny's arm, Harry said, "I need to get out of here. Want to come for a drive?"

She placed her free hand on his. "Sure."

****

They drove the country roads, talking, laughing, before ending at her place. Late into the night, they covered everything except politics and Harry's problems. Ginny was able to compartmentalize things in a way he admired, unlike the single-minded obsession of his grandmother and Ginny's brother. The night had been for fun, not business, despite Agnes's motives.

Later, when Harry finally made it to bed, he had the nightmare again—a screaming woman held captive in a deep forest. He'd been searching for hours, the screams guiding him. And there she was, being tortured by people whose faces were hidden, doing unspeakable things to her. As usual, he woke before rescuing her, his breath rasping through clenched teeth. He sat up, looked at the glowing red numbers on his bedside clock. He'd been asleep for less than an hour. He flopped back down, his head slapping the wet pillowcase.

The shadows appeared to him then, quivering. He was too tired to be afraid. If they wanted to murder him, he wouldn't be able to do a damn thing about it, so he lay there until dawn, wondering why this dream had come, what it might mean. But he thought more often of his real-world problems—his grandmother's schemes, the fortune that now might never be his. And then there was Ginny Rankin, the psychologist. She'd come to the party for a reason other than politics. She might be able to help him in more ways than one.

****

Harry wanted to call Ginny, but a week later, he still hadn't. He didn't know why, and each passing day made it harder. He wasn't like this with women, but she was different than anyone he had ever known—classy, intelligent, accomplished. Maybe it was the specter of the political ties his grandmother had wound so firmly around him. Did he really believe what Ginny said that she wasn't there to help reel him in? That her motives were as pure as the driven snow. Maybe…maybe not.

Not calling was irrational. Ginny was her own person and not some appendage of her brother. He knew that much from checking up on her career since school. But each time he picked up his phone, the specter of Agnes's decision crashed through his mind, forcing him to put it down.

To make matters worse, Agnes's health had taken a bad turn. Harry stood at her bedside. She looked like hell—a yellowish, blue tinge settling in around her lips and sunken eyes, her skeletal frame wrapped in a pink nightgown and matching silk robe. She could hardly breathe as she lay there on plush bedding, studying him through half-open eyes.

Her precious journals were scattered across the bed, waiting for a sudden memory that might need recording, though she didn't have the strength left to write in the heavy books, much less lift one. Her nurse caretakers had been told to be ready with pen and paper.

Agnes mumbled something, and Harry leaned in closer.

"Memories," she said, coughing. "Must get more down…"

Harry frowned. Even now, with her life slipping away, all she could think about were those damn journals. Fretting over fairy tales, never mind that they were supposed to keep him alive in battles she insisted would come, as if writing them down would actually benefit him some way.

Over the last few years, she'd grown more and

more obsessed with the diaries of Clan Black. They contained old family stories, legends of mysterious events and people, but they were rambling bullshit.

Through the years, when Agnes hadn't been berating him about some stupid crap she thought important, she could be found writing in her "books," scribbling footnotes to expound on the historical record. According to Agnes, the oldest of the Black diaries had survived more than a thousand years.

Her death would bring an end to the rants about the Black family, how important they were, how Harry was the last. If he never heard another one of these stories again, it would be okay with him.

He hoped that would be the case, but it probably wouldn't be so. There was Strom Jones to think about. He and Agnes shared like-minded lunacy. Jones would see to it that the so-called *extraordinary matters* in the will would forever keep Harry from controlling the estate.

Agnes had been able to train the old lawyer in Black family lore, as she called it. Jones was now a true believer, a crusader for the glorious cause, something Harry promised himself he would never become.

Air crackled through Agnes's lungs as she struggled to take a normal breath. Impossibly, some spark ignited her. She raised her head and considered Jones first, then locked eyes with Harry.

Harry and Jones had barely acknowledged the other's presence until that moment. Harry was tired of the conflict that, for years, had hung over the house. He'd had enough. Over the last few hours, his anger had slipped away, replaced by what he supposed healthy should feel like. But reading Jones's face just now, Harry knew the fight would still be on, even after her death. He couldn't forget Jones's part in Agnes's attempted legal high jacking of Harry's inheritance. Jones had sat across the desk from Jack while his friend and lawyer studied the document Agnes wanted Harry to sign. His signature would have guaranteed William Rankin a significant portion of the estate, effectively making him co-heir. While Agnes lived, Rankin very nearly enjoyed that status anyway. Once Agnes died, there would be nothing for Rankin unless Agnes could make it legally binding. That document would do the trick if Harry signed it, but that was not going to happen.

He had won one small battle; there would be more. But for now, he had let go of his bitterness.

His grandmother pointed at him. "You need each other, boy."

Jones bent forward and cradled her fragile fingers in his wrinkled palm. "Madam, shouldn't Tommy be here?"

Her face softened, but she shook her head. "And see me like this? *Never*!" She hesitated, glanced at Harry, but spoke to Jones. "Do you have it?" Her voice had suddenly regained some of its strength.

Jones nodded and cocked his head at Harry.

Harry stuck his hands in the pockets of his jeans and waited.

"Are you sure you want to do this, madam? It won't make any difference to him, and you're much too weak for any further aggravation."

"I'll be dead soon. I want to see how Harry takes it." She struggled with the next breath. "It's up to you now, Jonesy. Promise me you'll stay to help when I'm gone. Promise me."

Jones placed the back of her hand to his lips and nodded, a single tear sliding down his lined cheek. "I have already. I'm the executor, remember?"

"Oh, yes." She gave Jones a weak smile and sank back into her pillows, a calm expression coming over her as though the weight of the world had been lifted with the old lawyer's vow.

Harry sighed. Jones would succeed in making his life miserable. It was a crappy deal, but as much as it aggravated him to admit it, he knew he needed the old man, at least for some time. The mansion, the grounds, the money—it could all become overwhelming. He needed someone, but he wished it was anyone other than Strom Jones.

Jones held her hand, patting it. Harry flashed on a vision of his future, on what should have been a peaceful life free of his grandmother's particular brand of crazy. Jones would replace Agnes; he would be just as unrelenting, just as insane. Jones was ten years younger than Agnes and far healthier. Harry still had years left of living with her lunacy about how he was the only remaining member of Clan Black, about how important he was, and about some bullshit war he knew would never come.

"Read it," Agnes whispered.

Jones narrowed his eyes. "So that's why you dismissed everyone."

The corners of Jones's mouth had curled up ever so slightly. Harry knew the look well.

A tired little quarter smile appeared on Agnes's face, a hint of the devious fire left in her eyes.

Jones straightened and retrieved an envelope from

the pocket of his white suit coat. The envelope contained two pages. He unfolded them, and read, "The last will and testament of Agnes Delores Black."

Harry pulled his hands from his pockets, resisting the urge to round the bed and snatch the document from the old man. He and Jack had been talking for years what the death of his grandmother would someday mean. Harry could still hear Jones and Agnes laughing at the expense of two boys scheming to spend a fortune. That seemed to him now the only times he'd ever seen her lighter side, content instead to immerse herself in macabre stories too strong for a boy barely old enough to ride a bicycle. So many times, he'd reacted like any normal kid would, with nightmares real enough to make him cry out in the dark.

"Can't be helped, boy," she would say, her words echoing in the back of his mind. "You're a Black. You can handle the horrors. It's time to prepare for what's coming."

There were also stories about the money, but Harry didn't have a clue how vast the fortune was. His skin prickled in anticipation. He would finally know.

"…regular employment, good income, no arrests…" Jones had been saying, reading from a section of the will he'd been told some things about.

So far so good, but as Harry continued to listen, his face began burning.

"So you see," Jones continued, "the will is provisional. The last inheritor will not receive anything immediately."

Harry tried to swallow, but his throat tightened. The words Jones had first used at the party sprang up in his mind.

Extraordinary matters.

Harry already knew the will to be only two pages. What he had already heard, while galling, wasn't the crux. "Go on," he choked out.

Jones flipped to the second page. "Now then, what comes next is most important and concerns more directly the provisional nature of the will."

Jones hesitated before reading on, but a glare from Agnes forced him to clear his throat. He continued in a slow, Southern drawl. "The estate can only be transferred for use upon certain extraordinary stipulations. One Joseph Harry Black, Jr. must be shown to have met and be willing to accept these stipulations."

Harry was silent as Jones read on, but he could feel the heat rising in his face. This was complete bullshit. He kept his eyes on Agnes, seeing the domineering old lady clearly, maybe for the first time. The will, the damn will, was just reinforcement of her control over him even after her death, even beyond those pages she had tried to get him to sign.

Agnes must have read Harry's reaction on his face. "For your own good, boy. You'll see that one day and thank me."

Jones would be the sole judge of when Harry met the stipulations on the second page. The extraordinary matters could be well off into the future, or they could happen much sooner, even within the hour. No one knew for sure because, according to Agnes, no one had any control of such things.

Harry held the bedspread with both hands, his knuckles turning white.

"The legacy will come to you when it is needed

and not before," Agnes said.

Harry stared hard at his grandmother. Her strange stories were clearly fantasies, legends of a family with a history of mental illness. They had to be. Here she was, not even a blood relative of the Blacks, but a believer, nevertheless. A believer in all the myths that had been passed down—of sorcery, of the supernatural. She hadn't made it into the modern world where people no longer needed those kinds of explanations for things science could explain. She was stuck in the so-called Black family lore, too stuck to see how out of touch she'd become.

"Sit down, Joey," she said with as much breath as she could muster. She'd reverted to using her preferred name for him, the one she used for his father.

Harry didn't sit. "How could you tie my inheritance to something like this? You know what you've done, don't you? You've set it to where I'll never get the estate because this thing you say will happen one day, well, it won't. It won't because the stories aren't true. There is no legacy, no such thing as sorcery. I won't change into some kind of freak." He threw up his arms and let out an angry growl. "This is the twenty-first century, Grandmother. Who in their right mind still believes this kind of thing?"

Agnes sighed and took in a long rattling breath, but try as she might, more air wouldn't come. "I know what you think, but I also know the truth. I will not abdicate my duties to you or those who have gone before. The legacy demands more of our family." She stopped to draw more air. "The family has never been about the money. It's there for the work, not to live in luxury like pampered fools. You didn't expect to receive it now before you could even demonstrate—"

"Demonstrate? Grandmother, you've been duped. You have to know that. All the stuff in those loony diaries. Jack will be able to tear through it before a judge." He gave Jones a nasty look. "It'll be easy."

"Oh, you think so, do you?" Jones growled.

"Piece of cake."

Agnes shook her head. "Stop!" She met Harry's eyes. "Your father and I had a plan."

"What, some goofy bullshit about ghosts and legends and…What did you call them?"

"Do not interrupt me, son."

"I'm not your son. I'll fight it—Jack and me. We'll fight this."

Harry threw aside the bed linen he'd been clutching and stalked to the door, but stopped, hands on either side of the doorframe, head down. He turned, fighting to keep his anger in check, and managed a calmer voice. He didn't want to end it with her like this.

"I don't believe any of it, and I bet my father didn't either. You did the same thing to him when he was growing up, didn't you?" When she didn't answer, he looked at Jones. "You're insane. Both of you."

"Look at me, Joey," Agnes said, struggling to rise. She made it to one elbow. "Your father, God rest him, believed it all too well, and you will too—one day." She fell back to the bed and tried to take a deep breath but couldn't. When she finally had enough air sucked in, she continued. "You haven't earned a dime of it, so why should you enjoy it until you can use it for the work?"

"I've earned every single penny of the family fortune for putting up with your insanity and not having you locked away." He sneered at Jones. "Make her see. What she keeps talking about, this supernatural stuff, it's all phony, made up just to make the family seem more important. It's not real."

Jones grunted something and turned away, obviously still attached to Agnes's leash.

"You have an obligation, boy," she said. "Your ancestors lived their lives for others, many nobly dying to make the world free of *them*."

Harry rolled his eyes at another one of her mysterious references.

"Selfish brat, Black Manor will *never* be yours unless you do as I say."

Those words seared him because she could very well make it happen.

She made it to the second elbow. "Things will get dangerous for you."

Her sudden surge of strength surprised him, but all he could do was stare at her.

"Don't you see? Haven't I told you often enough? It won't ever leave you alone until you accept who you are. You'll be haunted by…by…" She hesitated and stared into the distance, as if searching for some bit of information she should have written down. Her hand shook. She reached for a sheet of paper and fumbled with a pen, but it was no use.

A look of fear struck her, and her eyes began darting about. "Terrible dreams. Wild nightmares—unending—" She coughed again and nearly choked. Jones rushed to help her. "You'll see what I mean, boy. You'll—" She gasped for breath, and said, "It's yours, n-no doubt. You're the last. Forget your rights and take up your burden."

Falling into a fit of spluttering, growing paler by the second, she clutched at Jones. When she finally quieted, she reached for Harry. "I'm sorry," she said at last, "for the way I've had to be. I forgive your stubborn streak." She sucked in more air. "You forgive me too, Harry, won't you?"

For the first time, she'd used the name he preferred since he adopted it after high school, her eyes brightening as she searched his face. She strained to touch him. Reaching up, she stared into the distance as though recalling something more.

He took a halting step closer, but before he could take her outstretched hand, it fell to the bed, and her last breath rattled free of her thin, worn frame.

Chapter 9

Harry still hadn't talked to Ginny twelve days after the party. They had driven off together, laughed, and enjoyed each other's company well into the morning. He'd picked up the phone so many times since then, and each time he set it down again. And now his grandmother was dead.

At Agnes's funeral the day before, Harry felt the loss of his grandmother more acutely even than when his parents had died, when he'd been too young to understand what had happened. Now, he simply wanted to be left alone with his emotions, puzzling as they were. He never realized he loved the old woman so much, never realized that even a few short hours after her passing, he would miss her with an ache in his chest as painful as anything physical.

He endured the funeral, not wanting to see Jones or Jack or anyone. He didn't want to talk to them or shake their hands and thank them for being so kind, and all the other meaningless bullshit people say at times like that.

Agnes had been right. To deny it now would be his own brand of insanity. A dead body is as tangible as things get, no matter that the man at the diner had been killed by free-forming shadows. He hadn't been able to bring himself to admit it to Agnes in those last few days of her life. It was cruel to her. It would have possibly given her some relief to know her work had somehow succeeded. That's how she would have seen it. But after years of fighting, of denying, after weeks of no sleep and enduring the woman's screams, he knew she had been right. Harry had been furious at her and Jones. He'd wanted to strike back rather than admit the strange world she inhabited could be real after all. And if so, what of the woman he heard every night? Could she be real, too? Could that torture scene at the fire be real?

He finally had to admit something was happening, but he was still of a mind to fight Jones. For that, he needed Ginny Rankin. He had seen the disappointment in Ginny's eyes when she came to him at the wake and again at the family plot on the grounds of Black Manor. He'd barely said a word. Her questioning look settling into hurt made him cringe every time her face popped up in his mind, and it often did over the last twenty-four hours.

Harry needed her opinion on the dreams, to be cured of them, for them to be out of his life, even if everything his grandmother said proved to be true.

His heart thumped in anticipation of hearing her voice. Feeling like a heel, he let the phone ring and ring. Finally, the line opened.

"Hello."

Maybe she had known it was him and had debated answering. He had it coming. "Forgive me for not calling sooner and for the way I acted yesterday."

There was a long pause. "It did puzzle me. And then at the funeral when you…well, you weren't yourself. You were obviously grieving. Are you okay?"

"No, not at all. I need help, Ginny. Listen, can we meet somewhere? I have to talk to you."

"What is it?"

"Not on the phone."

"And not at my office. I have a full patient load today. If I show up there, I'll get swamped. I could cancel the first couple."

Just hearing her voice made him feel better. She was willing to at least talk to him. "It shouldn't take long, but I really need to see you. Something's happening I can't explain. How about coffee?" He glanced at his watch. "It's still pretty early. Breakfast somewhere?"

"Sonny's Café. It's close to my office building at the corner of Decker and Brightside."

"I'll be waiting," Harry said.

****

Rush hour traffic on the I-55 Expressway flowed as languidly as the Pearl River through Jackson. Harry drove to the medical district and past the neat row of red brick buildings surrounded by pink crepe myrtle in full bloom. He located her corner and sped north, wanting to be there before she arrived. He didn't know what she could do for him other than recommend a specialist, something that could have been settled on the phone. So why the meeting?

The answer was obvious. Harry wanted to see her again, regardless of what she may be able to do to cure him. He didn't know why he hadn't called or why he avoided her at the funeral. He couldn't explain what he had been feeling, a mixture of anger at the way his life had gone with Agnes and sadness that she had now left him alone. And Ginny complicated things. He needed her professional expertise. He needed help, and whether he could ever hope for something beyond friendship with her was something he had to put aside for now.

Harry parked the Mustang across the street. The smell of frying bacon hit him as he entered Sonny's. He chose a booth in front to see her approaching and ordered a coffee. Television sets blared the morning news from their erected spots near the ceiling at both ends of the small diner. Everyone at the counter craned their necks watching a White House press conference, but he was too distracted to make out much of what was being said. He glanced at his watch; the waitress turned up both TV volumes with a remote. The talking heads had switched to another urgent topic. Harry could hear a reporter effusing about the latest economic summit in DC. William Rankin was on now, in what was apparently an earlier interview.

Bill Rankin was a natural—affable, intelligent, attractive. Agnes had anticipated a time when Harry's money could make friends for him, allies he would need in his fight, as she put it. As always, Harry had tuned her out. She told him his money could also make enemies. Either way, the better part of his life would still be about the money. Better to know how to spend it and who to spend it on, she always said.

But the days of fawning over politicians were over.

He kept telling himself that. Jones had pestered him at the funeral to maintain the political connections. Harry hated those kinds of attachments and how they would obligate him. Jones had tried to reinforce Agnes's concerns by saying bonds formed now would be needed later when it really mattered. Harry shot back some retort laced with a few well-chosen words. When the money was his, he'd correct lots of things he didn't like, including his family's dalliance in the political arena.

He studied the people entering the café but avoided eye contact. When Ginny stepped through the door, his heart leaped at the sight of her, but as she walked toward him, there was no indication on her face that she shared his anxiety. Men stared at her, creating a twinge of jealousy in him.

"Traffic was awful." She took in the diner with one sweeping glance before sitting. "I'm afraid I don't have time to eat. Have you ordered?"

"Just coffee." He got the attention of the waitress by holding up his cup. Harry took another sip for courage as she settled in. "Wish I had my flask."

"Nervous, are we?" The corner of her mouth had turned up.

"Yeah, I mean, you look nice."

"So why haven't you called?"

"There are things I have to talk to someone about, Ginny. I've been struggling, and I haven't had time to hardly…" He let the thought die, not knowing just yet where to take this.

Her green eyes were penetrating, large and exotic, the lavender-colored blouse complementing them well. It was damned distracting. Harry maintained eye contact but finally had to turn away, which was a rarity.

"I understand if you're seeing someone," Ginny said. "We don't have to be involved. Not if you're—"

"I'm not. I did want to call, but—"

She waited, but he didn't say more. "Okay. You finally did, and here I am. What's the matter? Why are we here?"

"I'm having trouble sleeping. In fact, I can count the hours on one hand over the last ten days. I think it's an indication of a larger problem, a problem I couldn't really divulge over the phone."

Over the next few minutes, he explained his nights to her, keeping the legacy part out of it. She nodded often, asked pointed questions when necessary, but mostly stared a hole in him with eyes threatening to swallow him.

"Nearly seven weeks is an impossibly long time to endure almost no sleep." She shook her head. "How do you feel?"

"Like a billion bucks."

"You look it." She caught herself, her milky skin flushing a bit. "Oh, I-I simply mean you look fresh, alert. You're telling me there has been hardly any effect."

"I haven't slept at all the last five nights. I don't count the dreaming, which always seems like a workout. When it forces me awake, that's it for the night. No more sleep."

She thought a moment. "You should probably see a neurologist."

"The problem's not physical, Ginny. It's the damn nightmares caused by all the stories my grandmother fed me. I want them to go away."

"You think Agnes caused this?"

Harry told her how, as a small boy, he'd been forced to listen as she read from her journals. He now included the bit about the screaming woman of his nightmare, but he left out the particulars of his grandmother's ultimate motivation—the legacy and all the supernatural crap. And he didn't mention those murderous shadows he'd been seeing regularly now since that night at the diner.

She straightened at the mention of the woman and the torture scene. "And this happens early after you've gone to bed."

He didn't say anything, so she continued.

"It's curious because nightmares usually occur later." Her eyes never left his. "Most nightmares are a normal reaction to stress. You've just lost the only family you have, and there's the problem with the inheritance."

Harry began shaking his head.

"Let me finish. Some believe nightmares help people work through traumatic events. But when they become frequent like you're having, and they affect your life, they become a disorder. You understand what I'm saying, Harry?"

"Go on."

"Usually, nightmares are easy to understand if you relate their symbols to the recent events taking place in your life."

"And the screaming woman is supposed to be a symbol of what?"

"Well, I don't know. It's not for me to say. One theory states that nightmares are the result of the work of the subconscious mind when it stores events that happened on a certain day in its long-term memory."

"A certain day? How about hundreds and hundreds of days having to put up with Agnes since the age of four? Does that qualify?"

"Sure, yeah, the nightmares might be the representation of those collective bad days decoded into a format understood by the subconscious mind. Agnes's death and the problems with the will could have been a trigger."

"Except they began weeks before her death."

"Okay, but still—"

"You're saying solving my real-life problems could prevent the nightmares."

"It could work that way, yes."

"You willing to explain that to Jones?"

Her eyes narrowed. "This is about the money, isn't it?"

He reached out to grab her hand, meaning to say his life wasn't just about the money, that he needed a normal life to damn well enjoy his inheritance. She had given him a ray of hope and the ammunition he would need to fight Jones. But an equally important part was that she had given up her busy morning to see him. He focused on Virginia Rankin, her delicate face, scarlet lips, flowing red hair, but when he touched her, the light in the café dimmed, just for a moment. Like at the party when this had last happened, she didn't seem to notice.

But was it the light? He squeezed her hand harder, and his head pounded in response. He stole quick glances around. His throat tightened, dampness soaking the back of his neck.

He tried to say something but couldn't.

She put her other hand on top of his, which only worsened things. "Are you okay?"

The pressure to speak was unbearable, but he resisted the thoughts demanding to escape his brain. They were gibberish to him like something had taken over his mind, putting words there that weren't his own, controlling him, opening his mouth. He gritted his teeth, but the words pushed through them anyway.

"Trolley forgives Bill," Harry blurted out, his voice

loud enough to be heard throughout the café. The force of the sentence threw him back into his seat, breaking the handhold. But there was more. "She says it wasn't his fault. Says—"

He jerked away from her and nearly bit his tongue in two, the taste of his own blood making him nauseous. He sprang from the booth and, in a few quick strides, stood at another window overlooking a side street.

A mother strolled along the walk outside, a child holding her hand. A young woman, dressed in a jogging bra and baggy shorts, ran by. Ginny came up behind him. He could feel her stare, so he turned to her.

Dr. Virginia Rankin bore down on him with rounded, incredulous eyes, her face having turned two shades paler. "How could you know?"

There was no damn reason he should know, but it had all come spilling out. He'd managed to close the flood gates, or he would have said more, but how could this vital information about her brother get into his brain. In the wrong hands, it would surely ruin the senator's political career. It made no sense, but getting the words out relieved him like a weight had been lifted. The thumping in his head eased, but the look on her face, a sternness, like a teacher who'd resolved not to take any more bullshit from a particularly troublesome student, made him wish he hadn't come.

Ginny's color returned, and now the pale surprise was replaced with raw anger. "You better explain yourself," she said in a cold voice. "How could you *possibly* know?"

His teeth clenched, he wanted even now to rail against that hypocrite brother of hers, but all he said was, "She loved him…deeply, and he didn't give a shit."

Ginny's eyes widened, but Harry had control of himself now. He swept past her and threw a twenty-dollar bill on the counter. Picking up momentum, he crashed through the door as though hell hounds were chasing him.

Chapter 10

Harry drove through the morning and into the afternoon, ignoring his growling stomach as lunchtime came and went. He finally headed north on I-55, thinking to escape to Memphis or even to St. Louis for a few days. Peggy, his secretary, nixed that idea and told him to take the rest of the day off, but there was no way in hell she would cover his ass tomorrow. He took the not-so-subtle hint and got back on the interstate heading south and home.

At four in the afternoon, the lowering sky had grown so dark with thunderheads dusk had fallen over Black Manor. He slammed the kitchen door and headed straight for the phone. He needed to call Ginny with the lame explanation he'd cooked up. The blinking message light on the answering machine brought him up short. There were two calls from Jack, wondering where the hell he was and demanding that he answer the damn phone.

The message from Ginny had been placed a half-hour earlier. He pulled his cell phone out of his pocket. He'd forgotten to take it off silent, so Ginny had dialed his house line.

He sat at the desk in the gathering room, just off the kitchen, and listened to her frantic voice.

"Harry! Have you seen the reports on TV?"

He paused her message, found the remote, clicked

on the sixty-inch Samsung. A Fox News report appeared.

Something about a bombing in DC. Two senators killed. Delaware and Illinois. Several others connected to the economic summit that had been meeting all week. All slaughtered. Thirty-seven dead bodies sprawled out in grisly detail. The nation's capital locked down hard.

He started the message again and could detect a note of relief in her voice.

"What was that this morning? How could you possibly know about Trolley and Bill? Wait—never mind."

Soft crying. Incoherent words.

Harry wiped the sweat from his forehead with his free hand.

"If you hadn't said what you said, I-I wouldn't have called Bill—wouldn't have distracted him—and-and he would be dead right now, like those other senators.

He could hear her struggle to regain control.

"H-how did you know? How could you know?" A long pause. "Listen, I don't know where you are. Your office wasn't helpful. I'm coming to your house. I'll wait there all night if I have to." A moment's silence. "You saved my brother's life."

There was no more. Harry stared down at the phone, her words reverberating through his mind, but banging on the front door startled him out of his thoughts.

Ginny's eyes were bloodshot. Mascara smudged her cheeks.

"I want an explanation," she said, pushing past him

and entering the house. “What the *hell* is going on?”

“Calm down, okay?”

He tried to take her elbow to usher her to a couch, but she yanked her arm away.

“No!” Ginny said. “How could you know that personal stuff about my brother? Not even my girlfriends know it. No one does. No one but Bill and me, and my dead parents.”

Harry ran a shaking hand through his hair and began pacing. “You don’t understand. That stuff just—”

“Bullshit,” she said, hands on hips. “Don’t give me that crap. Who are you now, Harry Black? Who have you become since you were that boy who ran away all those years ago? I must admit, you had me pulled in. You said you’d checked up on me. You had someone dig that up from my past to get to my brother somehow. Who are you working for?”

Harry started to deny again, but a look of understanding rocked her, and she plopped down on one of the seats Agnes had scattered about the foyer.

“Of course. I should have realized. This has to be tied to the summit in Washington. What, has the Black fortune taken a hit?” Her eyes rounded in sudden realization, and her hands shot to her mouth. She jumped to her feet. “The bombing—you’re connected.”

“*What*? Hell no! You can’t believe that.”

Harry reached for her hand, but she pulled it away, turning, searching for something. Ginny grabbed an antique Tiffany lamp off a nearby table and yanked the cord from the wall socket. “Don’t come closer.” With her free hand, she had her cell phone out, dialing.

“Wait! You’re right, I haven’t told you everything,

but I will now if you'll listen."

"I'm calling the police."

Ginny held the lamp at arm's length, warding him off, but Harry lunged past it and managed to take the phone from her. "I can explain if you'll just calm down."

"How do you know about Trolley and Bill?" Her face had become scarlet, veins bulging at her neck.

Harry had his arms out as if to soothe a mad dog, but the sound of the doorbell spun them both around, someone in uniform at the sidelight, peering in. He held up her phone. How had they responded so fast?

"I'm just going to the door, okay? I'll explain when you put down the lamp."

Sheriff Thomas Boone limped in on his bad knee, all six feet six of him, Glock in holster. He was way past seventy and had been around Rankin County for most of that time in some official capacity. Ginny had followed Harry to the door, minus the lamp.

Boone wore a frown on his face. "Afternoon, folks." He tipped his hat to Ginny and grimaced when he noticed the smudges on her face. "Don't think I've had the pleasure." He offered his hand. She stared at it and didn't move.

"Here, this might help." He took a clean handkerchief from his breast pocket and offered it to her.

Ginny thanked him. She turned to a mirror hanging just inside the door and began patting at her eyes.

"This is Dr. Virginia Rankin, Sheriff," Harry said.

"Bill's sister, yeah. Know your brother well. Very fortunate, what happened today, or what failed to happen to him. Course those other two senators weren't so lucky. Been trackin' the reports. Sure looks like terrorism, domestic or otherwise. Fact is, that's why I'm here."

Ginny gave Harry an accusing stare, anticipating his imminent incarceration.

"What?" Harry asked Boone.

"That fella at the Cold Fish. You're an eyewitness, you and Jack Hallowell."

"Eyewitness to what?" Ginny said, giving them both hard looks.

Harry ignored her. "That's right, Sheriff, but what does that—"

Boone waved him off and turned to Ginny, his face a mask. "This won't take too long, Dr. Rankin." He hesitated. "Matter of fact, I have a question or two you might be able to answer." Not giving her time to respond, he said to Harry, "Was this fella acting unusual?"

"Just walking to the diner. Collapsed hard." Harry hesitated because he knew he had to lie. "We all assumed it was a heart attack."

The sheriff fumbled with his note pad. "That's what other folks said. We wouldn't normally be involved. Paramedics would take him right to UMMC, but when they rolled him over, a .45 revolver fell out of his jacket pocket, loaded for bear."

"So? Not all that unusual around here."

"True, but this fella didn't have a holster. No permit, either."

"Okay, so why are you here telling me this?" Harry said. "Everyone in the place witnessed it. I don't think I can give any more details than what's already been given."

Boone nodded. "Took us days to ID the guy." He gave Ginny a mysterious look, causing her to squirm. "No wallet," Boone went on. "Had to track his hotel key down. Slow work. Finally found the room where he was holed up. Found pictures of you." He pointed a long meaty finger at Harry.

"Come again?" Harry looked up into Boone's droopy eyes, but couldn't focus on the man's familiar, lined face. Pictures? Of him? The words seemed to echo inside his skull.

Boone pulled out of his shirt pocket a three-by-five picture. "Recognized you right off and the place. That's your office building there, Schuster and Howard."

Harry took the photo. The picture was recent, probably taken in the morning while he had been arriving at work, his black leather briefcase in hand. There was nothing there that would indicate a date.

The sheriff cleared his throat. "He had others, but I didn't bother bringing them. They show you on different days, mostly entering your place of business. Some from around here."

"Around the mansion?"

"Yeah. Nice camera work too. Taken at a distance so as not to set off the alarms Agnes placed around the grounds."

Good old Agnes. God bless her paranoia.

"Do you have any enemies, son?"

Harry and Ginny exchanged knowing looks. He begged her with his eyes to keep her mouth shut, but she just gave him a defiant look.

"First theory, one of my boys thought was someone is after your money."

"They'd be in for a big surprise because none of it

is mine. I live here, receive a modest stipend, but other people control the estate. I'm a working stiff just like everyone else. You know Strom Jones, I think."

"Old lawyer. Lives in Madison. He still works for you?"

Harry shrugged. "I see my grandmother's arrangement isn't common knowledge."

"Enlighten me."

"He's the executor of the estate. I'll inherit, but only under certain conditions I haven't fulfilled yet and can't talk about."

Boone nodded. "The gun he had, the picture, he obviously followed you there. I'll ask it again. Do you have enemies?"

"No, Sheriff. Not even anyone who's pissed at me. I've been terrific lately to my clients. Excellent return on their investments." He glanced at Ginny.

"The only thing that's puzzling is the identity of this man. Do you know anyone from Senator Rankin's staff?"

Harry had turned to Sheriff Boone, but now he gave Ginny a quick glance. "Why?"

The sheriff pulled out another picture, one of the dead man lying on his back outside the diner. Ginny Rankin's hands flew to her mouth. "Carl?" She turned shocked eyes to the sheriff. "Carl's dead?" She turned to Harry. "He was in Mississippi, but on a fishing vacation, he said. That's why he missed the party."

Boone frowned. "He's your brother's chief-of-staff, isn't he?"

"Yes," Ginny said.

"We called the senator's office to inform them. Dunbar was supposed to be back in Washington today.

We called after the bombing. I talked to the senator personally. Mixed day for your brother. He could have easily been in the car with the other senators. News of Mr. Dunbar here hit him real hard."

Ginny lowered her arms. "But why would Carl be at that diner? Why was he in that motel? Why did he have Harry's pictures?"

"No one knows. We checked the flights. The man left Washington around eight the night before he died. The vacation was a ploy. Checked with his wife in Brookhaven. He'd told her the same thing. But she was getting mighty worried because he hadn't contacted her, though it wasn't unusual for him and Mrs. Dunbar not to talk for days when he got real busy with the senator. She thought he might have slipped back into work mode. Maybe he planned to be back and call before anyone noticed anything unusual."

Boone waited for a response, but Harry and Ginny just looked at him. "Anyway, your brother's office tells me he wouldn't be carrying a weapon, wouldn't know how to use one if it was placed in his hand. He must have gotten it here in Mississippi. Hard to trace though with the numbers filed away."

"I don't know about all that, Sheriff," Ginny said, staring at the picture. "But they're right. He doesn't know how to use a gun. He's very close to us. He couldn't do this."

"Then why was he after Harry?" the sheriff asked. "A man he didn't know?"

"You don't know what he was doing," Ginny said.

Sheriff Boone shook his massive head. "Looks bad, though, you gotta admit. And now you're here."

Ginny's head shot up. "You think I'm involved in

this?"

"I don't know what to think. The only thing I know is that Harry would be dead right now if Dunbar hadn't died on that walkway. That's my theory anyway."

Ginny seemed to be having a hard time recovering from Boone's insinuation, but Harry stepped in between them. "Sheriff, you're barking up the wrong tree here."

"Am I? I'd like to think so, but I know, or suspected, some of what Agnes was doing with your inheritance. Knew the old girl pretty well."

Harry swallowed hard and gave Ginny Rankin a long, searching look. But then he shook his head. "I can't believe the Rankins—any of them—are involved in this."

"Thank you," Ginny said, noticeably relieved.

"We're looking at all the angles, son. You understand?"

Harry nodded and walked back into the living room. Ginny followed and sat next to him on the couch, but not too close. The sheriff loomed over them both.

"He must have been here that night," Harry said, "at the mansion at some point, waiting. I hadn't been to The Cold Fish in months. I went there to meet a friend."

"Jack Hallowell."

"He's also my attorney. We were discussing my legal problems with the estate. We had coffee, talked a while. I planned to be gone only a short time."

"Unusual hour to do business," Sheriff Boone said, looking dubious. "What problems you having?"

Harry gave Ginny a quick glance and said, "That's private."

Boone's skepticism was evident. "Is Dr. Rankin your friend too?"

Ginny sat up. “We’re only acquaintances, really, but our families are obviously connected through Bill and Agnes.” She glanced at Harry. “Harry asked me to help him with—” She hesitated. “—certain issues. That’s why I’m here. I-I can’t believe Carl Dunbar was out to murder Harry, and I certainly am not, nor is my brother.”

“You always make house calls?”

She blushed, but Harry suspected it was more from anger at the multi-level insinuation.

Harry got to his feet. “Look, this whole day has been one coincidence after another. My relationship with Ginny—Dr. Rankin—is professional. If you’re implying something else—”

“Now hold on, son. It’s just that her brother’s right-hand man, who had a gun with filed-off numbers, and no history of owning a legal one, seems to have been stalking you for a reason we can only guess wasn’t related to your good health. We wanna know why. Coincidences are working here—” He nodded in Ginny’s direction. “—that are real hard to explain.”

“Believe me,” Harry said, “I want to know why, too, but leave the Rankins out of it—” He hesitated. “At least for now.” He walked off and poured a drink at the wet bar.

“Bit early for that, son.”

Harry grunted something to Boone and downed the brandy.

“It doesn’t look good,” Boone said. “This guy has no priors. You wouldn’t suspect him for something like this. It’s odd, a real puzzle.”

Harry nodded.

Boone gave Ginny an appraising look, her paleness

threatening to become a permanent fixture. “Hope your brother’s okay. Voted for him myself. And I hope my words today haven’t upset you too much.” He glanced around the room. “I’ve been here before. Knew Agnes well. She’d called about a prowler fifteen years ago. I told her who to call about a security system. You were just a youngster, Harry. Sat right there staring wide-eyed at my holster.”

“I remember.”

Boone nodded, and a look more sullen than usual fell on him. “We were friends of a sort then, Agnes and me.” He cut his eyes away from Harry as though the admission had embarrassed him. “Anyway, sorry about her passing. I attended the funeral but stayed at the back.” Boone took another long look around the place, apparently deciding that he’d asked enough questions. He tipped his hat. “You folks have a good evening despite all that’s happened.”

Chapter 11

Washington, DC

The city was in lockdown mode. Flights had been diverted, the central government district shut down. From the exact point of detonation, the bomb had left a thirty-yard crater in the broad avenue and adjoining property. Windows had been shattered on both sides of the street. Miraculously, every one of the buildings in the blast radius remained upright, although inspections and repairs would keep them empty for months to come.

The platform for the bomb had been a red van parked curbside. From the beginning of the economic summit, the series of limousines carrying the three US senators had preceded the arrival of the treasury secretary's party by minutes, a pattern that, as it turned out, had apparently been noticed by the bombers. Eyewitnesses would report that the nearest car had stopped about twenty yards from the red van, which had its left rear wheel jacked up next to the curb. The van had been pointed in the wrong direction from where it sat at curbside to change out that left side wheel, an oddity lost in the aftermath of the bombing.

The red van had disintegrated in the massive explosion, as had most of the three-car motorcade carrying a portion of the US contingent. Two senators had been killed, but another had escaped the calamity. Through chance occurrence, he'd been late that morning and had missed the ride over.

When the dust cleared, the story had come together. It was obviously a targeted attack. The red van had been planted at the spot the bombers knew would put it close to the senators' motorcade. People clearly remembered seeing a man changing a tire. Then the explosion had wiped out both the van and the person. The convoy carrying the unlucky politicians was taken out. There had been no survivors within that three-car contingent, and passing traffic had not been light. Several cars were flipped, others torn in half, some twisted and blackened in the fireball. Information was still flowing in, but the death toll had reached forty, and most expected it to climb higher. People in the nearby buildings hadn't been spared.

The setup was straightforward. It was obviously a suicide bombing. Islamic jihadists had claimed responsibility an hour later with three separate phone calls to local media. FBI and CIA analysts were busy dissecting the calls, gleaning from them any detail that might contain useful information, no matter how minute.

Nothing had been found yet of the red van—not a piece of the license plate, not a chip of engine that could identify car and owner. But there was a more complicated puzzle. The splatter as they call it, the human remains of such a destructive force, was concentrated at the curbside where the three-car senate contingent had stopped. That was, of course, expected, but there was nothing at the actual bomb location twenty yards from the senators' lead car. The spot where that bomb had been should have shown its own splatter evidence. Where were the remains of the tire guy, the supposed suicide?

Roger Trower sat in his office, running these facts through his mind when he got the call at eleven o'clock, roughly two hours after the bombing. The call was from his boss, F. F. Bartlett, Director of the United States Secret Service. They were needed at the White House immediately, which puzzled him. Trower wasn't part of the presidential detail any longer. He'd been pulled off after last year's election. A grave mistake in judgment had cost him the coveted stint at the White House. He hadn't seen the inside of the Oval Office in more than a year. So why was he being summoned now?

Trower's office was just down the hall from Bartlett's in the Executive Office building across the street from the West Wing of the White House. Fifteen minutes later, the two men entered the nearly five-thousand square foot intelligence management center, a complex known as the Woodshed. They were headed for the Situation Room, a conference facility secured for high-level meetings. They found two spots at the table opposite the end where they knew the president would sit. After running the facts through his head once more, Trower watched the president stride into the room, quickly meeting eyes and nodding at those already seated, his rotund chief-of-staff following closely at his heels.

It was easy to see that Hackett and President Franklin had been arguing. Trower noted the tight lines around the president's famously smiling mouth. The president's chief-of-staff, however, looked positively giddy, almost as if he enjoyed the sudden conflict that had been leveled on the city and nation. It was a well-known trait of his. While Franklin didn't like argumentation, his chief aid liked it too much. How the two had come together as an effective political team was the talk of Washington following the election. The president had reined Hackett in for meetings like this. But today was going to be a problem, thanks to the heightened tension the terrorists had caused.

The president's secret service detail had ramped up immediately, over one hundred agents on the highest alert protocol. The White House compound was in lockdown. The president and the other principals had been moved downstairs to the command center, where the national security contingent could monitor the crisis. The Secret Service Counter Assault Team had been deployed around the executive mansion. Stinger surface-to-air missiles were readied, and the presidential limousine was waiting on the south lawn to evacuate the president if necessary. But over the last hour, it had dawned on them that the White House was not a target, so evacuation plans were scuttled.

President Franklin remained standing at his high-backed leather chair. Along one side of the table sat the chairman of the joint chiefs and the director of the CIA. On the other side sat the secretary of defense and farther down the FBI chief sat next to Trower's boss. The last person present was a surprise to Trower. He sat just off the head of the table at the president's left hand.

Common knowledge was that Senator William Rankin of Mississippi had missed the bombing. When it became clear to Rankin's office that their caravan had been hit, they issued a statement telling the press the senior senator from Mississippi had been late, a very fortunate mistake. No one knew why, but from the preliminary information that had come to Trower in the two-hour interim, it looked like the usually punctual senator had simply missed the pick up at the senate office building. That saved him, and Trower could see the relief on the president's face as he addressed Rankin in a private moment at the end of the long table. Senator Rankin, though of a different political party, was the president's right hand in a bipartisan effort to resuscitate the weak US and world economy.

The president cleared his throat, and the muted chatter died an instant death. "What do we make of the three claims of responsibility? Can they be believed?"

The chatter commenced at once, but Director Stott of the CIA spoke over everyone. "Sir, working with the FBI, we've been able to confirm those calls were indeed from the leaders of Hezbollah, Hamas, and al-Qaeda. We're working on the particulars of the setup, how they might have gotten the explosives into the country or if they acquired them here. It's early yet, but we'll pinpoint it."

"Some of the usual characters, then?"

"Afraid so, sir," Director Stott said.

The president folded his arms across his chest. "The intelligence I have says those groups have been largely inactive of late. How the hell did they suddenly escalate to this scale? Why now, and here of all places? They're known to have few resources and haven't worked that well together. How could they have gotten into this country and planted themselves at that curbside at that exact moment?" The president looked at one of the generals. "What do you think, Vinny?"

General Paul Van Housen, Chairman of the Joint

Chiefs, frowned when the president addressed him by his nickname. The moniker had been attached to him during his Harvard days. The blue blood New Englander liked to tinker with cars and had a peculiar fondness for vehicle identification numbers. The nickname, Vin, came soon after. He and Franklin had been unlikely roommates at Harvard. After Vin Van Housen had somehow relocated a stripped-down engine block into their dorm room, Vin became Vinny, because, as Franklin had informed him, only someone connected to the Italian mob could have accomplished that feat. Of course, the sandy blond general didn't look Italian, but that iteration of his old nickname stuck. When Franklin was elected last year, the first Jewish president in American history, he quickly elevated his old buddy, turned warrior, to his current position.

"Sir, if one of these is our perp, they've obviously acquired new financing," General Vinny Van Housen said.

"If," Hackett said with some disdain in his voice. "Is there some doubt about that, General? In my book, it's one of these groups, but not all three." He looked at Director Stott. "They're known to compete with each other, is that right?"

Stott nodded.

"Right, then we have to assume one of these admissions is real. It's up to the CIA and FBI to sort out who's lying and bring the bastards responsible to justice."

"Let's not jump the gun," Stott said. "We're still analyzing the tapes of those calls. For all we know, it could be another group altogether, and they're just slow to call in to claim responsibility."

President Franklin nodded once, unfolded his arms, and sat down. "It feels right, gentlemen. The groups are known to use suicide bombers. My bet is it's one of the three." The president stopped. He locked eyes with Bartlett. "Frank, if your man has something to say, by all means, he should speak his mind."

Bartlett turned shocked eyes to Trower. It was a lapse in the protocol for Trower to have worn his views on his sleeves. "Well?"

All heads turned to the special agent. "Sir," Trower said, looking directly at the president, "it's just that there's something that doesn't fit. It's been bugging me for the last hour."

"Let's hear it."

Trower cleared his throat. "The eyewitnesses reported that the red van was parked a ways off, and—"

"We know that," Hackett said harshly, "get to the point."

Trower slowly moved his gaze from Hackett back to the president. "Mr. President, it's something I'm sure Director Brumford will be familiar with." He looked briefly at Ned Brumford. The FBI chief had started out two decades earlier in forensic investigation and would be well-versed in what Trower was about to say. "It's the splatter record, the human remains of the bombing. There was none for the suicide. That's quite unusual and leads me to think it may not have been a suicide at all."

Hackett laughed and turned to the president. "That's an asinine theory, given the eyewitness accounts."

Franklin turned to Brumford, who hadn't removed his eyes from Trower. "Ned?"

He didn't hesitate. "I'm inclined to believe the eyewitnesses. Too many people noticed the tire guy moments before. We even have corroborating accounts of his description, which is pretty unusual in itself when you think of it." He hesitated. "But what the special agent says is an interesting piece of forensic inconsistency."

"Is it inconsistent enough to matter?" President Franklin asked.

There was a long pause before Brumford answered. "I'd say no. My bet is that we have a suicide. One of three Islamic groups is our target, or maybe they're working together."

"Unlikely," Stott said.

The president stood and turned his back on the group.

Which was it? They had their confessed group, three of them. Still, this new piece of information was potentially troubling if other evidence could point them in a different direction, a direction that led away from jihadists, but to where?

Trower was deep in thought as the president turned back to them, arms folded again.

"I'd say that's an alternate theory you have, Agent Trower." He looked at Ned Brumford. "And I'm not ready to discount it just yet without new evidence."

Everyone nodded as they scribbled on their notepads. President Franklin walked around the corner of the conference table and placed a hand on the shoulder of Senator Bill Rankin.

"We haven't yet discussed what seems obvious to the media—that they were targeting the senators' motorcade. The question I've been asking myself is, why the senators' motorcade. The information I have is that they settled into a nice pattern—the senators' arrival, followed by the treasury secretary's party, then some aids from my office."

"It's damn clear to me, sir," Ned Brumford said, "that they were specifically targeting the senators. They could have taken out Secretary Stokes's party by waiting a scant few minutes."

"Why the senators then?" the president asked.

"I wouldn't put too much stock in this," Hackett said. "These guys aren't that smart. The senators were high profile enough. They took the first guys to arrive."

"That simple?" Franklin said.

Hackett shrugged. "Hell, yes."

Bartlett shook his head. "It would embarrass the administration more to strike a blow at the executive branch."

"You and I know that," Hackett said with a snort. "Like I said, these guys are clueless."

Ned Brumford had his eyes on Trower, who had sunk back in his chair after his earlier gaff, but now he turned back to the president. "I have to disagree, sir. They're apparently smart enough to pull off something like this."

The president nodded. "I agree, and that's why I have the secret service at this meeting. You all know the news from Senator Rankin's office about his chief-of-staff dying back home in Mississippi." He looked down at Rankin.

"The funeral's tomorrow," Senator Rankin said. "I fly out in three hours. I'll be back as soon as I can. Tentatively that's the day after, but I'm available if you need me to come back earlier." He gave the president a furtive glance, who nodded and went back to his chair.

"This mess has stalled the summit, gentlemen, but I'm committed to its continuation here and now. We need to keep the momentum going and send a message that these important matters can't be halted or even stalled by terrorism." He stopped and looked pointedly at Rankin. "But the restart can wait until you get back. We'll try to keep the new location in town secret until then."

"Won't be possible," Hackett said.

Franklin ignored him and addressed Bartlett. "I'm sending the secret service on a detail they usually don't undertake. Have Special Agent Trower select his best men and accompany Senator Rankin to Mississippi."

Hackett groaned, giving Trower the distinct impression he and the president had been arguing about this very thing earlier.

"Sir," Bartlett said, ignoring Hackett, "our mandate protects the executive branch only, and—"

"I know, Frank, I know. I'll issue an executive order authorizing it."

"But for what purpose?" Hackett asked. "It's not like we know he's being targeted." He looked at Senator Rankin. Trower knew he hated members of the other party more than generals. "Are you telling us you believe this bull that they were specifically after those senators?"

"I think it's a smart move," Director Brumford said. "It's clear to me the senators *were* targeted. They clearly weren't interested in the treasury's motorcade."

"Wait a minute," Trower said. "You're saying the senator is a target apart from the bombing. That he's still in danger." He looked at Rankin. "You think they'll come after him down in Mississippi, Mr. President?"

Franklin shook his head. "I'm saying I don't know, but I'm not willing to take that chance. The summit is too important, and Senator Rankin is my lead there. No offense to the secretary of the treasury, but Rankin is a bigger cog in my plans. I'll put that order out right now, Frank. Get your team together. You leave in three hours."

Hackett was full-blown pissed off by now, his face redder than it had been even a moment earlier. "Think of the political fallout, Gabe. This won't play well with your base, sending a detail out to guard a member of the opposite party. And issuing an executive order to do it—" Hackett got up and started pacing. "Shit, it's a damn nightmare I'll have to deal with here."

"And you'll deal with it because that's your job. I'm keeping politics out of this one."

"No, my real job is to get you reelected. Think what you want, but politics play a role in every decision you make as a first-term president."

Gabriel Franklin gave Hackett a sharp look. "Maybe." He hesitated a moment then abruptly turned, all eyes following him as he stepped through the doorway.

Chapter 12

"That was a hell of a way to get back in the mix," Bartlett said as he and Trower rushed through the underground tunnel system connecting the White House to the Executive Office Building next door.

Trower tried to keep up beside the frenetic Bartlett but had fallen a step behind. "Did you know about this ahead of time?"

Director Bartlett gave him a sideways glance as they made it to the elevator that would take them back to their offices. He didn't answer the question, and Trower wished he hadn't asked it the moment it left his mouth.

They entered the elevator, and instead of punching the floor number, Bartlett let the doors slide shut and hit the stop button. "The president made a personal call to me earlier, yes, but he didn't ask for you. I made that decision. You want back in, right?"

Trower nodded. Driving a desk was about to drive him crazy. Every hour spent sitting in that damn chair felt like another day in hell. The worst thing was, he'd done it to himself. It had been a shitty deal. Trower had thrown himself under the bus for the sake of the service, but Bartlett's predecessor hadn't seen it like that. Instead, his demotion last year hadn't blown over, and he was beginning to think it would hound him through to the end of his career.

"Good, then don't blow it." Barlett's finger hovered over the button marked eight, but he didn't push it. "That was some display in there. Your first visit to the Situation Room, and you start spouting theories running counter to the obvious."

"The obvious? We're trained to think, and I brought up an inconsistency, that's all. And I still think I'm right. That was no suicide."

"Suppose it wasn't. What does that prove?"

"It proves we don't know shit about what went down. It may prove that we aren't dealing with radical Islamists and that how they approach the investigation may be skewed from the start."

"Whoa—that's a mouthful in the face of those claims of responsibility."

"I know, but it had to be said."

"Maybe, but you just can't lay it out there like that. If none of those groups did it, what explains the eyewitness reports?"

"What explains the lack of physical evidence for suicide?"

Bartlett shrugged. "The Fibbies are still gathering evidence. It was a big blast. I don't know, maybe it took out all the evidence."

"Not likely."

"You haven't answered my question. You throw out a bombshell like that you better have an alternative explanation."

Trower shook his head. His boss had a point. He'd spoken too soon, got the runs of the mouth as his father used to say. He didn't have a clue as to what could explain the missing splatter record.

There was no alternative other than what seemed

obvious to him—that this wasn't a suicide bombing.

"Well," Bartlett said, filling in the silence, "you've got some balls, Trower. I guess that's why I like you." He punched the button, and the elevator jerked into motion. "But investigating a bombing is not our job. I want your selection of personnel pronto. I know the senator booked a flight for himself and his family, but that was before the president gave us our marching orders."

Trower glanced at his boss as the elevator glided to a smooth stop. "You've got a bird selected? Is it ours or the FBI?"

"Neither. Stott's personal bird. Leaves at about the same time as the commercial flight Rankin had set up."

"CIA. The president's pulling out all the stops for this guy."

Bartlett smirked. "Anything for the Messiah, right?"

"Guess so. It's a pretty risky political move by the president, though, working so closely with someone of that profile and of the opposite party on such a hot button issue as economics is right now. Could backfire."

"Not our concern. We just protect them. Remember."

Trower rolled his eyes. "I think I still know how to do it."

Bartlett gave him a pat on the shoulder. "Good, then go round up the guys you want and be in my office within the hour."

Chapter 13

Black Manor, Near Jackson, Mississippi

Harry walked with Sheriff Boone onto the porch and would have preferred a quick goodbye, but Boone had other ideas. He turned to Harry before continuing down the front steps.

"This whole mess don't sit well with me, son." Boone stared over the expansive front acreage.

"The alarms still work," Harry said, anticipating his thoughts. "Jones takes good care of me here."

"Jones, yeah, he always did." Boone hovered over Harry with those baggy eyes that had seen all the crap Rankin County had dished up for him over the years. "This thing going on in DC, I don't see how there's a connection, but my gut's doin' flips. I don't like it, don't like it at all." Rubbing his stubble, Boone sighed. "Keep that little lady close by. Maybe that way you can figure out if she's lying to you."

"Listen, she's not lying, and neither is she my—"

"Yeah, you said it earlier. Just do as I say and keep an eye out. I'll put a patrol through here twice a day till my nerves settle."

"Thanks, Sheriff."

"No problem. Here." Boone handed Harry his business card and noticed the dark clouds rolling in. "The sumbitches who did DC are bigger'n we local boys can handle. You know that." He started off the porch but hesitated again and turned back to Harry. "You got lucky, son. Damned lucky. You ought to be in the ground right now. What are the odds of that man having a heart attack seconds away from blowing your head clean off?" The sheriff's hand went reflexively to his holster as he said those words. "Anyway, I'd better get going before the storm whips up a fury."

Harry watched Boone amble down the steps and to his patrol car with the picture of his brains splattered across the booth of some crappy diner popping up in his head. His skin dampened, and his sight dimmed. He recovered by pacing the veranda, scanning the perimeter of the place. It was peaceful, luxurious, kept that way by an expensive grounds crew, but he knew looks were deceiving. There could be someone hiding there now, watching. He backed through the door and returned to the living room where Ginny stood, stone-faced, pouring a drink.

She set down the bottle and clicked the cap into place. Sighing, she sipped the heavy treacle-colored brandy. "My God, Harry," she said in a dazed voice. "Carl Dunbar—dead."

"Yeah, well, no offense, but better him than me."

She took another sip with a shaking hand. "I'm their oldest boy's godmother." She put the glass down and covered her mouth with her hand, tears welling up. Crying softly, she put her head to his chest but jerked back, realizing what she'd done. She stepped back, looking embarrassed, and stifled the tears.

He put a gentle hand on her shoulder. "It's okay."

"I'm fine." She cleared her throat and glanced at her watch. "Here I am accusing you of something terrible, and it turns out you have reason to doubt me."

"I don't."

"That's kind of you, but not very smart."

"I'm a good judge of people. Always have been. Your brother wants my money, but he's not going to kill to get it."

Ginny nodded, a look of relief settling in. "I need to call Margaret, Carl's wife." But, instead of acting on it, she picked up the glass and gulped the remaining brandy without a single wince, even though Harry knew the brandy had one hell of a kick. "You must think I'm a lush. I don't ever drink this stuff."

"I'll pour another. It'll relax you a bit."

He handed her the glass. She tried to smile, but it came out crooked. "I don't care what Sheriff Boone thinks. Carl couldn't be mixed up in a plot to kill you. It makes no sense. What would be his motive? There's simply no reason. Carl's no murderer. He was a sweet—sweet—" She choked down another mouthful of brandy.

"Take it easy." He took the glass, led her to the sofa, and settled in beside her.

"I can't believe this."

A thunderclap slammed against the mansion, rattling the windows. The rain beat down like drums, and the house was suddenly cast in shadows. They were both silent a moment, then Harry sighed. "I believe you. It's time you believe me too. I had nothing to do with the bombing. I'm not interested in politics. I've never contacted your brother and don't know anyone connected to him other than the man who tried to kill me."

"Allegedly."

"Whatever."

"I know it looks damning, but it's so out of character. He's been close to our family for years. He's like a brother to Bill and me. He just wouldn't."

"You can't deny the evidence. Maybe it's an insurance policy to get my money. I'm not saying the senator had anything to do with it. But maybe Dunbar tried to do it for him without his knowledge. He must know I'm not going through with Agnes's plan."

Ginny sagged, her beauty diminishing with the weight of what they'd learned. She began to shake her head as if stubbornness would make the nightmare go away. "I don't believe Carl would do something like that."

Harry sighed again and got up. He walked clear of the marble coffee table and turned to her. She was staring into the empty glass, both hands grasping it hard enough for her knuckles to have gone white. It was Dunbar who had died at the diner, after all, not some crazed Dunbar clone. But why would the senator's closest confidant be gunning for Harry? It was senseless. There wasn't a convincing connection. There was only the money, but Dunbar didn't fit the model of a cold-blooded killer. The senator was hot enough politically to attract other significant donors.

"He was there, Ginny, with a gun, with my pictures, and he died before he could get to me and pull that damn trigger. How do you explain it?"

She held sorrowful, searching eyes on him, but there was nowhere for her to go, the logic behind the harsh reality of his words too hard to escape. More tears cascaded down her cheeks.

"Okay," she said reluctantly, wiping her face, "you

win. I believe you, Harry, and I'm sorry about what I said earlier. I guess you aren't involved in the bombing. But why would someone like Carl want you dead?"

Harry walked to the center of the room. The rain was beating harder now, the wind gusting. The trees out front swished in sudden fury. Had a tornado warning been issued? Another thunderclap rattled the windows. Though the house was comfortably cool, his shirt collar had dampened against the nape of his neck. He had a sudden urge to run to his Mustang, and this time keep driving, but the need to get his story out was stronger. He figured she needed to hear what he had to say, and he sure as hell needed to say it.

"I haven't been candid with you." He gave her a tentative look. "You won't believe what I'm about to say, but I swear to you, it's all true. I'm not making any of it up. I wouldn't do that, especially now that things have become so serious."

She sat in shadows on the couch while Harry paced before her, sometimes calmly, then more animated, arms flailing, hands saying nearly as much as his mouth. She listened in silence. When he broached areas of his family's story she would find hard to swallow, he tried to find in her any sign that she might believe some small part of what he'd been saying, but she remained quiet.

When he finished the story, she followed his movement to the sofa with those magnificent eyes that defied him to lie, to obfuscate the details just to cover his ass. He knew he couldn't count on her understanding. He just wanted to know she believed him, believed he wasn't making any of it up.

"I know you think I'm nuts, but that's the story my

crazy grandmother fed me. That's why I think I'm having these dreams. As incredible as it seems, I think what she fed me all those years was the truth." He paced in front of her a few more times, stopped, and threw the glass he'd been holding, smashing it against the far wall of the room. Ginny jumped back into the couch. "Sorry, this thing is just…" He looked at her. Her mouth was open, eyes wide. "I need your help."

Ginny got up and went to him, took his hand. "Does anyone else know this?"

"Strom Jones—"

"Oh, yes."

"And my friend, Jack Hallowell, more or less. He's like a brother, so we've been having fun with this for years. They're the only ones. I have no family. If I die without a male heir, the so-called legacy dies as well, at least according to my grandmother. The money goes to charity. I was ready for you to help, to try and cure me of this…this…"

"I think shit would be the right word."

Harry tried to laugh, but it came out as a groan. "It's the perfect word. Jack has a file on me, labeled that way."

"But it's no laughing matter. People are dying. People I love. And Bill nearly—" She began to choke up.

Harry put a hand on her shoulder.

"Somebody wants you out of the way, Harry, but for what reason? And what's Carl's involvement?"

"Forget Carl. I'm in no one's way. I live far removed from anything. I'm not a danger to anyone. I don't have enemies. I'm an all-around decent guy."

She shook her head. "You might believe that, but

it's obvious some people don't."

"Some people," Harry said in a whisper, staring up into the crystal chandelier sparkling from the ceiling. "You know, if this thing is true, it's obvious they've made the first move."

"And it's equally obvious my brother and his work are linked somehow."

Harry nodded. "And your brother is very well-connected, isn't he? I mean apart from being a US Senator. He's the president's right-hand man on the economy, right? I've kept up with this a little, because of my job as a financial consultant."

Her eyes rounded with something other than fear. "My brother isn't of the president's party, but yes, President Franklin relies on him and has taken heat for it."

"So, the Summit's off for the time being, obviously what the terrorist wanted. Was your brother about to strike a deal for the president?"

"I don't know," she said. "We don't talk about his work."

"It has to be the reason for the bombing. That's no coincidence."

"They wanted high profile deaths."

Harry nodded.

"And my brother just missed being there because of my call. A call I made because of what you said."

It sent a parade of goosebumps dancing down his spine. "Let's leave that for a while. You think Carl Dunbar was compromised in some way? Forced to act on behalf of my enemies, whoever they are?"

"You mean forced to murder you. Aside from why you're important in all that's happening, I can't believe

Carl would murder, no matter the pressure. He was too close to us. We would know if Carl got mixed up with the wrong people." She gave him a piercing look. "And another thing. You couldn't have known about Trolley and Bill. No way could you have dug that up because there is nothing to dig up. No one else knows about it, but my brother."

"And he didn't tell me."

"No way."

"So leave my lamps alone." He got a weak smile from her.

"You saved his life with whatever it is you did. But why? Why not words to spare the others as well? Those other senators were as important as Bill."

Harry hesitated. "Were they?"

Ginny's eyes rounded. "No. I don't think so." She gasped. "He was the real target? The others were just—"

"It looks like it. It would stop the president's plan, take his best agent away, probably set him back a good bit."

She nodded. "Bill's the brains behind the administration's plans. This summit is a big deal on the world stage since the recession has lasted so long. But all those poor people, why not spare the others too?"

"Think about it. The others were beyond my reach or something like that."

She pursed her lips.

"Hell, I don't know, Ginny."

She reached out and touched his arm. "I suppose you're right. But what is this thing you have?"

Harry didn't answer her question. "It's time for me to see Strom Jones."

Chapter 14

Before leaving, Harry and Ginny hovered together over the kitchen island, eating sandwiches while maintaining separate phone conversations. Jack agreed to drop some appointments and meet them at Jones's house in Madison, a suburb just north of Jackson. Ginny cried again, talking to Carl Dunbar's widow.

When the storm subsided thirty minutes later, they left the mansion in Harry's Mustang.

They arrived in Madison at six p.m. and parked on the street in front of a white picket fence. Jack's road bike wasn't out front. Harry checked his watch. There was still time. Maybe he had a late client meeting or something.

"You think he's home?" Ginny asked.

"Jones is always home, except for two weeks out of the year when he goes to the Big Island in Hawaii. Been doing that way longer than I've been alive. He's never married, so when Jack and I were kids, we'd accuse him of stalking island women in grass skirts."

Ginny lifted an elegant eyebrow at that.

"He's so old now he wouldn't know the difference between a grass skirt and a bush."

Ginny laughed as they walked to the porch. Harry detected a strain in her voice with the events of the day hovering over them. They ducked under trumpet vines branching between two columns, offsetting the steps. A white swing moved lazily in the breeze. White wicker furniture adorned the farthest end of the porch. Hummingbirds darted about. This place had been the site of countless arguments with Jones.

Harry knocked on the door—no response. He stepped back to the front of the porch and considered the sky, the air sweet-smelling after the rainstorm. "Come on, he may be tending his roses after the drenching they just got."

They walked on flagstone blocks, flecked with mica, and rounded the side of the house. The expansive backyard was dotted with islands of rose bushes throughout. A Labrador barked and ran to Harry at the gate. Jones's call out to them followed a moment later.

"Buster!" Harry bent over the gate to pet the black retriever. "Take me to the old boy." The dog trotted off toward the back of the property.

"Must not be very busy in his law practice," Ginny said, "if he takes care of these without help. They're beautiful."

"The only work he's had for years is as Agnes's assistant and now executor of the estate. Pays him a bundle. He still does some pro bono work on the side, but not much."

Harry took her hand and led her down some steps rough-hewn out of the sloping yard and formed up with railroad cross ties. They arrived at the back fence where Jones was on all fours, working with mulch.

"Storm do any damage?" Harry asked.

"Not much. How bad was it your way?"

"Seen worse. You know, you can get hired help to do your grunt work."

Jones groaned as he rose to his knees and struggled

to stand. "Never considered it."

"You remember Virginia Rankin from the party."

Jones pulled his gloves off and cupped her hand in both of his. "It certainly was good news today that your brother missed the calamity." He winked at Harry. "Glad to see you've improved your taste in female company."

Harry cleared his throat. "Never mind the bullshit, Strom. She knows. I've told her everything."

Jones glared at Ginny, a shadow of disapproval lowering over his black eyes almost hidden behind his stringy gray strands. "You mean *everything*?"

Harry nodded.

"Damn, boy, unwise of you, very unwise. It isn't enough your friend Hallowell knows something of your true identity, now this woman. And she has very substantial connections."

"It was necessary."

"Oh, it's *never* necessary." His eyes swept over Ginny. "You know you won't ever be able to have a normal relationship with him."

"I'm afraid you've misunderstood, Mr. Jones. We haven't spoken since the party. He came to me this morning for help."

Jones glanced at Harry then turned a nasty scowl back to Ginny. "Psychological help for his problem, no doubt. Well, now, this is a great turn of events. You'll just have to live with the danger. Anyone close to Harry will be a target to get to him." He turned in a huff, cut a wild vine, and pricked his thumb in the process. "You believe you can solve the problem of the sleepless nights, the dreaming. You seek a cure to convince the courts to do away with certain stipulations in the will."

He sucked his thumb, dabbed at it with a clean handkerchief. "Well, it won't work."

"If it'll make you feel better, I'm beginning to believe you."

Jones's eyes narrowed at Harry's admission, his forehead furrowing in the process. "What's happened?"

Harry absently pulled at a vine of the darkest roses he'd ever seen, but like a hen protecting her chicks Jones grabbed his wrist before Harry could snap a stem. For a man closing in fast on eighty, he was surprisingly agile and robust. "Be careful with that bush. It was Agnes's favorite. She was delighted when we succeeded in breeding it. See how I've perfected it, made it ever so dark." He clipped a single rose off the vine and stripped the thorns. "The blackest parts are much darker now than when this rose was first introduced. It's called Black Velvet." He handed it to Ginny.

"It's lovely," she said.

"It's become the symbol of the Black family. Mind you, black isn't a color found much in nature, especially of something as beautiful as this rose. Of course, it isn't truly black, just a very dark red, very disease resistant, flourishes at night." He turned to Harry with a devious look. "It was just a matter of time before you saw the light. You Blacks are a persistent bunch, but seven weeks of little sleep is a bit much."

"I'm pig-headed, I guess."

"More like a horse's ass."

A laugh broke from Ginny, but she quickly quelled it.

Jones turned back to the bush he'd been tending and finished spreading a small mound of mulch with a rake. “You haven’t said what’s happened.”

“There’s a guy who nearly got murdered a few days ago, and one today.”

“I know about the senator. Who else almost bought it?”

“Me,” Harry said. “At the diner.”

Jones gave Ginny a quick glance. “We’ll discuss the senator in a moment.” He scowled at Harry. “How did you manage to stay alive? With everything Agnes tried to teach you, apparently failing miserably, I’d have thought you would’ve been a goner years ago.”

“Thanks for the vote of confidence.”

“Oh, I’m confident. You see, you’ve really had no choice in this matter. You chosen Blacks are always dragged in, kicking and screaming mostly, but dragged in all the same.”

“Into what, Mr. Jones?” Ginny asked.

“My dear, into a life you want nothing of, believe me.”

Ginny gave Harry a questioning look.

He turned away.

“That’s not a proper answer, Mr. Jones, and I need one. Harry saved my brother’s life today.”

Jones dropped his rake and wiped his sweaty brow with the back of his hand. “Did he now? Explain.”

“It was during our talk,” Ginny said.

Jones smirked and shook his head, but she went on.

“Harry just…well, he gave what I could only describe as an ecstatic utterance.”

Jones’s eyes widened. “So, it’s finally happened.” He grabbed Harry’s shoulders, looking eye to eye with him, and slapped him on the arm. “Congratulations, my boy.”

"What?" Harry said, rubbing his arm.

"You know your family's history. How they moved to America nearly two hundred years ago. It's been that long since the last outbreak and the need for a Protector."

"A Protector?" Ginny said. "What kind of outbreak?"

"Like I've been telling this hard-headed jackass here, it isn't really a matter of accepting the inheritance or not accepting it. You can't decide who your parents are. The legacy is yours, whether you want it or not." He poked Harry's chest with a wrinkled finger. "You just have to go with it once it grabs you. You really have no choice."

"Just like that?" Harry said. "What about the dreams, the insomnia?"

"Oh, you'll sleep now and dream only when it's necessary."

"And the money?" Harry asked.

Jones grunted. "I knew you'd be getting to that." He hesitated before saying, "I'll sign the papers tomorrow. My job's done—finally. The estate's yours." He poked Harry's chest again. "But you'll be surprised how you use it."

Harry plopped down on a rickety cypress bench standing along the picket fence encircling the property. "It's mine?"

"To use for the legacy. To free you for where the work takes you."

"Nearly eight hundred million." Harry almost choked on the words.

"Oh, it's more than that now…twenty billion, more or less."

"Even with that last market crash?" Ginny asked.

"Amazing, isn't it? Supernatural, you might say. The Black fortune has always been there for them. Always."

Harry hadn't moved or uttered a sound, and now he felt their eyes on him.

Jones sat down beside him. "It's what you wanted, after all, but it all comes at a very high price."

"That's why we came over," Harry said. "What's going on? How am I supposed to—"

"Gracious, boy, didn't you learn *anything* from Agnes?"

"Didn't listen very well, but I'm all ears now. Someone tried to kill me, but these two black shadows—"

Jones jumped from the bench like a kid who'd sat on a nail. "You've seen them?"

"For weeks now. They killed the senator's chief-of-staff."

"Wait!" Ginny shouted. A neighbor in the next yard looked at them, but Jones waved the woman off. "What are you two talking about?" Ginny whispered. "You said he had a heart attack."

Harry stood to face her. "Not exactly. This is the last of it, I swear."

Jones shook his head. "Oh, not the last, I'm afraid. You should have listened more attentively to Agnes. It fell to her to keep the family legends alive since it had been nearly two centuries since a Black had acquired the legacy. She knew, of course, that you were the chosen one. The family had almost been decimated in Europe before fleeing to America. The castle in England had been destroyed, forcing Clan Black to disperse. They sustained heavy losses during America's civil war and the two world wars. There is no other branch. It's just you that's left. There hadn't been an outbreak until now, so a Protector wasn't needed." He threw his hands up. "Imagine that. A new Protector, and it's the scruffy boy Agnes could never rein in."

"What outbreak?" Ginny asked again. "And what's a Protector?"

"A Warder, someone who keeps prisoners in check. Harry here will do the same for sorcerers, my dear. The Blacks check sorcerous outbreaks."

Her laugh had more than a tinge of incredulity in it. "Oh, you can't be serious. We're in the twenty-first century, Mr. Jones."

Jones shrugged as if to say, *so what*, and went back to his rose bush.

"How, exactly, did Carl die?" Ginny asked, gripping Harry's arm.

Jones placed a wrinkled hand on her shoulder. "What Harry saw were Grigori."

Harry and Ginny turned slowly to him, but Jones had walked off several steps to the picket fence. He stared over the hillside descending from his yard. When he spoke again, it was more softly, almost reverently. "Of course, I've never seen them. Neither had Agnes." He turned back. "They're thought forms, autonomous psychic entities comprised of the thoughts of a group of people. At least that's the way Agnes described them."

"What people?" Harry said.

"Why, your people, of course, who happen to all be dead. You're linked to them. Had you listened to your grandmother, you would have known this."

"I can't believe I'm actually going to say this."

Ginny turned to Harry. "You *conjured* them, and they killed Carl. That means *you* killed Carl."

"Oh, hell no," Harry retorted.

"You both are right and both wrong. The shadows are linked to Harry, but they're intelligences, and, as such, are beyond any real control. It's not like he can turn them off and on, or conjure them, Ms. Rankin. Harry's not a sorcerer, for goodness sake. Sorcerers are who the Black family has been fighting for over a thousand years. The Grigori help, they watch, they protect Harry. And Harry protects everything else, including you and your brother."

"They give me the creeps," Harry said. "What did they do to Carl Dunbar?"

Jones shook his head and turned away. "I wish I could have seen it." He noticed the horrified look Ginny gave him and sighed. "It's terrible, my dear, I know, but they have a useful purpose as Harry saw. Was that man carrying a weapon?"

"A .45 revolver. Sheriff Boone told us today."

Jones whistled through his teeth. "Would've taken your head right off."

Harry sat back down, suddenly weak.

"You're not invincible, you know. The stories of the Blacks are rife with the gruesome murders of Black Protectors. Why ole Meriodoc Black had his eyelids sliced off and boiling oil fried his living eyeballs right in their sockets. Only then did they tear his entrails out with such precision he lingered for days having to fend off rats and other vermin in their dungeon." Jones stopped and gave Harry a lingering look. "Meriodoc was the last. Now there's you."

Harry choked down the bile rising from his

stomach. "She never explained it like that."

"No, she wouldn't. She didn't spare you, but describing what she knew of certain unfortunate members of your family would have been excessively cruel."

"I can't believe what I'm hearing," Ginny said. "Carl was a good man."

"Good, yes, but controlled. They got to Carl, but why use someone close to your brother?"

"You think my brother's the target."

"Looks like it. Your brother is a powerful member of the senate, but that wouldn't necessarily…" Jones trailed off, thinking.

"Wouldn't necessarily what?" Ginny asked, grabbing his arm.

Jones stroked his chin. "He's just a cog. There are larger geopolitical issues than what your brother has been involved with." He stalked around a nearby rose bush. "They're shooting for higher game, but he might have been the initial target because of his background in economics and his closeness to the president. You've got to get to your brother."

Ginny looked doubtful. "This is too sensational, too crazy. He won't believe a word."

"Yes, but tell me, how did Harry save him?"

Without giving any details, she told him about the personal information there was no way Harry could have known.

Jones nodded throughout, looking impressed. "No two Black Protectors are the same. Agnes stressed that point. Everything depends on the circumstances of the outbreak. What Harry did ought to convince your brother, at least make him pause." He turned to Harry.

"Well, my boy, you're in the thick of things now. It's been a struggle pulling you in with your stubbornness, but what you did today sealed the deal." He held his hand out. "Let me be the first to welcome a Black Protector into the twenty-first century."

Chapter 15

32,000 Feet Over the Southern US

Trower had his team selected, a group of four agents he had personally trained, all comprised of his old detail tasked with protecting the previous president. He didn't like to think that he owed any man anything, but Bartlett had really stuck his neck out for him this time when others would have considered him persona non grata after that fiasco. Due to a miscommunication, a private citizen had run right up to President Miles during one of his last vacations before leaving office. This wouldn't have been so bad, except for the fact that this citizen had been carrying a revolver. He had a permit to carry, but that wasn't the point. The idiot had forgotten he had it on him and had insisted his only guilt was being overly enthusiastic. It wasn't an assassination attempt, but the damage had already been done. Trower and his detail had been summarily shipped to the secret service version of Siberia.

Bartlett had been the assistant to the retiring director and had argued against such a harsh demotion. Trower would never be able to repay the man for putting him back in the game, giving him a second chance. This little venture, then, was all about redemption for all of them. It was what each of the five men had joined the U.S. Secret Service to do. They weren't office guys. They weren't suited to the investigative mission like catching counterfeiters or running down bad checks. Each craved action, and what could be better than butting heads with terrorists hell-bent on murdering America's elite?

Trower looked around the sleek plane from his position at the back row, port side. The CIA Director had been able to secure the agency's Gulfstream V long-range jet. It was outfitted with a VIP package: plush leather seats, galley, bedroom, and, best of all, a secure communications system. They wouldn't have to fear their chatter being intercepted.

They had collected their passengers, the senator, his wife, and two young kids, and had driven them to Langley an hour earlier. Rankin's new chief-of-staff had also tagged along, bitching the entire way. He was a skinny prick named Fred Savage.

The VIPs were safely tucked away, but Trower still wasn't satisfied. He checked his watch. They had taken off a half-hour ahead of schedule. That would put them in Mississippi around four in the afternoon with the change in time zone. They would then reconnoiter at the airport where Trower would make it clear to everyone the need to remain on schedule and follow protocol exactly. He had arranged local police backup in Brookhaven, Mississippi, the site of the funeral. Trower liked to run a tight ship on protective details and could care less about the ideas some of these politician types inevitably came up with. He would listen courteously and then do his job his own way.

But it was a nervous business, and he was still on edge about that bit of forensic inconsistency in the aftermath of the bombing. Something stunk about the whole thing, but he couldn't put his finger on it. He averted his eyes from the window in time to see Senator Rankin making his way down the aisle to the back of the plane.

"May I?" Rankin asked, nodding to the seat.

Trower grabbed a notepad he'd been using, and Rankin settled in.

Both men were quiet. Like most people in law enforcement, Trower was a quick study when it came to people. He didn't know much about the man, but over the last hour, he'd found out enough to know he didn't like Mississippi's senior senator. Rankin's superior attitude had activated Trower's old working-class bias. The senator was an elitist, and it wasn't hard to see. It was that usual Washington political class snobbery toward the hired help. Trower braced himself for the inevitable.

"You've done a good job so far, Mr. Trower. The president will be pleased, especially after all the publicity from last year."

Trower nodded but kept his face blank at the insincere compliment.

"I went along with what the president felt was a prudent measure, even though we all know it is completely unnecessary."

"I don't think it's unnecessary."

"Yes, I know. As it turns out, your theory has put more fuel on the fire of the president's suspicions." Rankin looked back toward the front of the plane, where his family sat huddled together. "I was hoping to go mourn my friend and then give what little time I could afford to my family and try to relax for a few hours, but now that we're in the bubble, that's impossible. My wife and kids are feeling stressed already."

"It can't be helped, Senator."

He nodded. "No sense crying about it now. Gives you a taste, though, of what their lives are like, doesn't it—presidents, I mean?"

"Like I said, Senator, it's necessary. And it wasn't my theory that put us together today. The president had already decided on the issue. That's why he called Bartlett and me to that meeting."

Rankin gave him a perfect smile, his teeth overly white. "True, but I was hoping to escape the president's hook. You made that impossible."

Trower shook his head. "The evidence made that impossible. I only pointed it out." He glanced around the plane and lowered his voice. "That's not why you came back into the cheap seats. What can I do for you now? We land in an hour."

"My wife has decided to stay in Mississippi for at least two weeks. She wants to comfort Carl Dunbar's widow. I hope that won't be a problem."

Always the changes with these guys, but, as changes go, this was pretty mild. "I'll have to inform my boss and the White House."

"Go right ahead, but that's the way it's going to be."

Not if the president says otherwise, Trower wanted to say, but he kept his mouth shut. "Anything else?"

"Just one thing—you do know the FBI forensics team has yet to find the remains of the suicide."

Trower nodded, unsure of why Rankin was mentioning this. He didn't seem the type for small talk. "They'll just have to look closer. Jihadists aren't involved, Senator. Mark my words."

"Then why would they claim responsibility?"

"No idea, other than—"

Rankin turned more in his seat. "Other than what?"

"No other group uses suicide bombers, and none of the other terrorist groups are religious. There are no virgins waiting in heaven for the bastards that did this."

"Meaning?"

"It's a misdirection. The terrorists are obviously leading us in the direction they want us to go. Have they finished analyzing those tapes?"

"Nothing."

"Nothing *yet*."

"So what are you thinking, some home-grown group calling in and claiming to be Islamic? The FBI claims otherwise. They've confirmed that at least."

Trower nodded. "Senator, I don't know what to say about that, but I do know that when a suicide bomber blows up, they leave a record. There was no record. If these aren't jihadists we're dealing with, then we have a drastically different playing field."

Rankin thought about that. "But to what end? Seems to me both kinds of groups end up accomplishing the same thing—disruption."

"You forgot one thing," Trower said. "You see, I kind of agree with Hackett. Jihadists wouldn't necessarily care which motorcade—yours or the secretary's—just so long as they hit something big enough to cause some serious disruption. If I'm right, if this is more than a jihadist group with a hard-on for the Great Satan, there was a reason they hit your motorcade and not the one transporting the treasury secretary."

The senator's eyes widened. "To get at me."
Trower nodded. "And they missed."

Chapter 16

Madison, Mississippi

Jones walked Harry and Ginny to the gate but didn't follow them out. He grabbed Harry's arm instead, delaying him while Ginny continued on to the car.

"Remember to keep your wits about you. And I would develop a first-class bullshit antenna if I were you. The chance of you dying a horrible death drops off with each day you manage to keep your carcass alive. The learning curve is steep and slippery. Remember that. Pick very carefully who you trust. If there's a change in behavior of any of your friends or acquaintances, take note. Anyone, even that pretty lady there, can be turned easily enough."

Harry wanted to thank him but wasn't sure the gruff bit of advice didn't warrant a curse instead. Jones must have read his thoughts because he softened.

"I know all this comes as a shock. Look within yourself for strength. It's there." He placed a hand on Harry's shoulder. "And take care of those you choose to keep close." He gave a furtive glance at Ginny, who had stopped short of the car, phone to her ear. "It won't be easy for them either."

Harry said a quick thank you but hesitated as he turned to leave. He spun back to Jones. "Look, how are you going to handle the transfer of the estate?"

"Don't worry, it'll be seamless. And believe you me, I'm glad to be rid of the responsibility."

"Once we sign the papers, I'll want the account numbers. I'm taking over immediately."

"Don't you think you ought to devote your full attention to the senator first? There are forces in play you have to get a handle on. You have enough to think about without having to—"

"Just do it, Strom. I'm putting Jack Hallowell in charge, basically taking your job." He patted Jones on the back. "You'll even get a generous severance package." Jones raised a silver eyebrow, but Harry turned serious. "I'll try not to screw up too bad in this fight, whatever the hell I'm supposed to do. I guess what I'm saying is, I'm a believer now. I'd be nuts not to be after what's happened." Harry hesitated and glanced at the car. He could see Ginny still talking on the phone. "My life's on the line here, Strom. How in the hell did that happen?"

The old man shook his shaggy head and didn't answer Harry's question. "It's not just your life. I told you she's in danger now." He nodded toward the car. "And so are your old friends. Your enemies seem to be attempting to influence world affairs. You think they'll let a few locals stand in their way?"

The gravity of Jones's words hit Harry like a heavy blow to the gut, but he managed to say, "You have my word. I'll do my best."

Jones's gray eyebrows furrowed together. "And the word of a Black is supposed to be as good as gold."

The insinuation hurt, but Harry didn't care what Jones thought of his ability to carry the burden of the

Black family legacy. "If that's what they say, I guess it's still true."

"We'll see," Jones huffed but became somber as he glanced at Ginny, now sitting in the car. "The pieces on the chessboard are already moving, and you're horribly behind. Try to remember your grandmother's lessons. They're buried deep within you, boy." He put his palm flat upon Harry's chest. "They'll come back to you as needed." He sighed and sagged a little. "I've been handling your family's affairs for forty years. I knew the time would come, the day I would be handing everything over, but old habits die hard. I suppose I have to trust you with the estate."

Trust you with the estate. Harry swallowed hard at those last words. He and Jack had schemed and planned for this day. Now Harry would be able to move out from under Agnes's shadow, call the shots himself with no arguments from anyone. He'd be able to remake the Black name into his image. The day had finally come, but at what cost? Incredibly, Agnes's warnings were coming true. He'd always kept his head down and shouldn't have enemies, but, of course, they weren't his personal enemies. How could they be? It was the family, the old stories, older hatreds. Had he listened more closely, he might have known who the hell it was trying to kill him. As it stood, he didn't have a clue.

For the first time, his heart filled with gratitude for the old lawyer. "Agnes always appreciated you, Strom, you know that, and I do too, the way you stayed with her, helping her with me."

Jones nodded and looked away.

"But it's my problem now. You have no choice in the matter. You're out, and Jack's in." Harry gave him a soft punch on the arm. “You deserve a good, long Hawaiian vacation.” He turned and left Jones at the gate.

“Be at the bank at nine in the morning,” Jones called out.

Harry acknowledged him with a wave and got behind the wheel of the Mustang. He checked his cell phone while pulling away, but Jack hadn’t left any messages, which puzzled him. Why had he failed to meet them?

****

Harry drove away with no immediate destination in mind. Neither of them said a word, which suited him. He knew Ginny would have questions he couldn’t answer and was glad for the silence. He needed direction, a plan, but most of all, he needed Jack to call.

He redialed his friend’s cell. No answer. He’d just about had enough of the silence when Ginny finally spoke up.

“Why didn’t he show?”

“No idea.”

“I just called my brother. He’ll be in tonight for the funeral tomorrow. I want you to come with me and talk to him before he goes back to Washington.”

“I don’t know if that’s a good idea.”

“Mr. Jones is right. We have to make him see. You need to tell Bill what you told me in the diner. That’ll keep him here until we figure out a plan. I think he’ll be safer if he stays in Mississippi a few days until the authorities in Washington get a handle on who was responsible for the bombing.”

Harry glanced down at his watch again. Jack would have called or texted him if he couldn’t make it to

Jones's.

"Are you listening, Harry?"

He started to apologize, but a patrol car, lights blazing, no sirens, pulled even with the Mustang, almost sideswiping it. The deputy took a hard right and skidded to a stop, blocking Harry from entering the onramp to I-55. Harry stomped the brakes and spun the car to the right. The Mustang's rear swung around and slammed into the side of the patrol car, pinning the driver's door against the maroon and white sedan, trapping him. Ginny flew into Harry, the force of the impact jamming his left shoulder into the driver's door window. Harry cursed as the officer rounded the front of the Mustang, pistol drawn, arm rising.

"Do something!" Ginny screamed.

Harry recognized the deputy as Brick Taylor, but what the hell was he doing, stopping them like this and drawing his gun. Finally, his mind clicked, and he slammed the car in reverse just as the first shot ricocheted off the top of the windshield. The Mustang barreled across the road as the next shot rammed through the windshield and smashed into the bucket passenger seat Ginny occupied, barely missing her left shoulder. Harry spun the wheel, drove the stick shift to the first position, and peeled away, tires screeching as the officer ran back to his car after firing two more rounds into the back passenger side door.

"I'll never outrun him," Harry yelled as they sped away.

The cruiser's siren blazed behind them. Ginny searched inside her purse. "Why is he shooting at us?"

Harry floored the Mustang and flipped his phone to her. "Shirt pocket," he yelled as the Mustang went airborne over a sharp rise in the road. They plunged to the street, and two hubcaps pinged off the wheels, sailing through the air on opposite sides of the car. Harry and Ginny bounced like puppets, their heads driving into the headliner.

"Sheriff Boone's card. Can't take my hands off the wheel."

The back window exploded with more gunshots. Ginny screamed as she climbed over Harry and managed to get the card from his pocket.

"Get down."

Ginny shrank to the floor of the car and fumbled with the cell phone. "Help!" she yelled into it as the Mustang took two more gunshots.

Harry hit the brakes in a sharp turn, which wedged Ginny farther under the glove compartment. "Put it on speaker!"

Ginny did so and held it out in front of her.

"I'm on Broadway going east." Harry barely dodged a kid on a bike. "A deputy is trying to kill us. Get me Boone. We need help."

He hit the brakes again, and the car screamed to a stop. He jumped out, ran to the passenger door, and helped Ginny unravel from the floorboard. When she exited, their heads spun to the sound of screeching tires. The rogue cop was nearly on them.

"Why did we stop?"

"We can't outrun him." Harry grabbed the phone.

"Boone here," the sheriff yelled into Harry's ear.

"Brick Taylor's after us!"

The patrol car stopped twenty yards from them. Harry and Ginny ran toward the nearest store, shoppers shying from them as though they were dangerous street thugs.

"Taylor?" Boone yelled. "Why's he—"

"We've taken half a dozen hits or more, and he's getting out of his car. We're at Brignac's Jewelry, the branch at the Sweet Time Mall, and on foot."

Harry grabbed Ginny's arm, and together they sprinted past storefronts and away from the deputy. Harry considered one shop after another, but each one was either too crowded or too small. Anywhere he entered, others were sure to be in danger.

"Right now would be a good time to do that thing you do," Ginny yelled as they raced down the walk and away from the murderous deputy.

"I didn't conjure those things last night, dammit. They just appeared."

By the time they made it to the clothing store at the end of the strip, they had a good fifty yards on Taylor. He hadn't fired at them again, but the way Brick now pursued them, so methodically, so determined, like a cat confident his prey would be cornered, unnerved Harry. They needed to hide, remain in one place, and let the cavalry come to them. Sirens had begun to blare in the distance.

"We're in the department store at the end of the mall now," Harry said into the cell phone, trying to keep his voice down with his heart beating in his throat. "Get the hell over here—now!"

They stumbled into the women's lingerie section, ducking through clothing racks, trying to hide as they moved. Harry got tangled in a row of burgundy double Ds. Ginny grabbed his arm, shaking off the bras, and they darted to the changing room. They made it to the farthest stall, forcing a plump lady in new slacks and an old bra to run out, screaming.

"We're loud enough to lead a blind man to us."

"Just stay down." Harry couldn't help the commotion. If it led Brick to them, it would also do the same for Boone and his troops. He put his ear to the door and could hear muffled voices, then abrupt silence. Taylor must have entered the store.

Ginny crouched in the corner of the stall, trembling. Harry couldn't stay with her. It was too late to escape, but if they were together when Taylor found them, she wouldn't survive. Seeming to read his mind, she stood and grabbed his arm, but before she could protest, he said, "You'll be safe here. I can't let him find us together."

"Don't go. Give Sheriff Boone time."

He grabbed her shoulders. "There's no time. Brick's been told where we are by now. I'm going to the first stall and try to surprise him as he passes. Here." He handed her the phone. "Contact Boone again and lead him to us."

Harry left their stall and hurried to the one closest to the entrance of the changing area. He left the door open a crack and had a direct line of sight to a row of mirrors. Reflected in the mirror was the door now being slowly pushed open by the barrel of a gun.

Chapter 17

Harry held his breath as Brick Taylor stood in the doorway. The nickname fit the ex-star lineman to a tee. Harry had known him briefly, but Taylor went on to play at Mississippi State and flunked out in his third year while Harry had gone off to Ole Miss, the party school. The words of Strom Jones flooded his mind as he stared at the reflection of the man hunting him. Something in the eyes nearly froze Harry's beating heart, something more animal than human. Raw, naked blood lust, an absolute need to kill.

They were cornered here in this changing area, and Brick knew it. He wanted Harry, that much was clear, but why Brick Taylor, a local yokel who'd barely made it onto the sheriff's squad of deputies? It made no sense.

Those eyes again, animalistic, strange. Harry's survival instinct kicked in so intense, he nearly bolted on the spot, but if he did that, death would come in an instant.

The thought of Ginny saved him. Taylor wouldn't stop with his death. He would find her, wipe out the witness, and fabricate something when Sheriff Boone confronted him.

Harry couldn't let the bastard get off that easy. He took a slow step backward while fighting the tension building in his shoulders and neck.

The step took him away from his line of sight, but he didn't need the mirrors any longer; he could hear Taylor's ragged breathing.

"Black." There was no malice to the voice. It was merely an acknowledgment, a salutation. "I know you're here with the redhead. She can leave now, you know. No need for any collateral damage as we say in law enforcement." He laughed. "This is just a little misunderstanding between you and me. It was a mistake earlier, firing those shots. I've straightened it out with my—" He hesitated. "—employer. I got different orders now. They just want to talk to you, make you understand. Get you to stand down and forget those silly things your grandma taught you. Take your millions and live the good life. Buy yourself a few dozen women." He chuckled again. "You do that, and they'll back off. You got my word on it, buddy."

Sweat poured down Harry's face. He swept the back of his hand over his eyes as Taylor stepped closer to the stall Harry occupied. To answer him would have been madness. His mind spun with questions. How had Brick become involved in this thing? How could he know about his grandmother and the Black family legacy?

The sirens had grown progressively louder, and now they stopped right outside. Taylor cursed under his breath.

"Too late," Taylor said, almost serenely. "I guess it has to be the hard way. It always is with Clan Black." His voice had suddenly changed. It was now throaty, the Mississippi drawl gone. Definitely not Taylor's voice any longer.

The door to the stall Harry stood in creaked and

started opening. Taylor had selected right the first time.

Harry got ready to hurl himself at Brick, and he would have done it, except for Ginny calling out and Brick releasing the door to Harry's stall.

She tried to put some courage into her words but failed miserably. Her voice shook when she said, "If you really mean it, put the gun down and slide it over. We'll leave with you. We're in the back stall. Harry's hurt. He's bleeding."

Ginny had just increased his element of surprise ten-fold. If they were lucky. If Taylor would just move his big ass beyond this stall. Harry could almost hear the gears grinding in Brick's thick skull as he stood there, considering her words.

"Hurt, uh. Why ain't there no blood around? Floor's cleaner'n shit."

The door to Ginny's stall opened and banged close.

"Well, now, you're a brave one. Gonna save your man? You better come here and—"

Harry threw himself against the door and rammed into Brick. But Taylor had spun at the last moment in an attempt to bring the gun around. It fired not two inches from Harry's head—twice—which set off resonant gongs inside his skull threatening to shatter his senses.

Harry had mustered enough force to send both of them crashing into the opposite row of changing booths. Over five hundred pounds of men shook the flimsy structure. The two of them went down with Harry on top of the deputy.

Brick earned his nickname well, because each forearm was the size of Harry's thigh, and though he tried, Harry couldn't punch his way through them, or dislodge the gun. Another shot bore a hole in the stall door next to Ginny. She screamed, which distracted Harry long enough to get thrown to the side. For a huge man, Brick was surprisingly quick. He was on his feet and raising the gun.

"Watch out!"

Another shot rang out, and an eternity passed before Harry realized he wasn't hit. Taylor had dropped to one knee, blood soaking his pant leg and flowing onto the floor. He still held the gun at his side, the fake smile Taylor had worn a moment before replaced by a murderous look. He didn't seem to realize he'd been hit.

"Deputy Taylor."

Harry's head jerked to Boone's booming voice of authority. He'd been staring at Brick in such focused disbelief he hadn't seen the cavalry enter. For a brief moment, recognition dawned through Brick's narrow eyes as the sheriff's voice settled into the room. His expression dissolved into doubt, but in a flash, the sneer came back.

Boone crept around to Brick's right side, a crimson puddle the size of a platter forming around Brick's bent knee, color draining from his face. Boone held the gun high in both hands. A no-nonsense sneer marred his face.

"Dammit, Taylor, what the fuck are you doing? Stand down. You don't want this, son. Let me get you some help." He was now nearly in front of Taylor, inching his way slowly. "Whatever this thing's about, we'll try and fix it, make it right."

Harry knew Boone hadn't gotten through. Brick's murderous eyes never left his. In answer, Brick croaked, “Black, you insolent bastard,” in a strange voice that wasn’t his, and in one sweeping upward motion fired his gun at Harry’s head.

Chapter 18

So this was how dying felt. A muzzle flash. Body jerking. Falling. A smorgasbord of color. Impressions from his dream. His life passing before him. An eternity in a blink. He'd read that bullshit somewhere and almost laughed at the clichéd ending of it all.

Agnes's ranting echoed through his memory. Pain. Then stillness. Life, precious life draining away through one circling moment.

Except for Ginny crying in his ear, red hair draping his face, tears dripping into his eyes.

Pain.

His head shouldn't be pounding. His ass shouldn't be hurting where he'd landed on it.

Harry raised his head. Brick's brains and pieces of hair and bone had been blown all over two doors of the changing stalls. Harry let his head fall back to the floor. "Owww…"

"Lie still," Ginny said next to his ear. "Sorry, I pulled you too hard. Are you okay?"

Harry focused on the lovely upside-down face hovering above his—red lips quivering, wild eyes searching his. "Not dead," he managed to say.

Ginny's face dissolved into a puzzled look. "What? Of course, he is. Didn't you see?"

The throbbing in the back of Harry's head went into overdrive. He groaned and tried to lift his arm, which had the effect of turning Ginny's eyes into vast pools of worry. Her hands flew over his chest, his stomach.

"You're *shot*?" Ginny looked up at the men milling around Taylor's body when Harry grabbed her searching hands.

"This tile floor isn't exactly soft."

She burst into one long sob. "Oh, thank God." She helped him to a seated position against the stall. "You scared me. I thought maybe—"

"Me too, for a moment, at least." Harry rubbed the back of his head and rolled onto his side, facing her. He reached up and wiped the tears trickling down her cheek. "Thanks for coming out when you did. That was incredibly brave."

She blushed and started to say something but stopped when Boone stepped closer. He had questions Harry couldn't answer. There was no explanation for what Taylor had done, but Boone managed to fill in some of the gaps.

They knew a side business deal of Brick's had soured at the loss of a quarter-million dollars, a princely sum for someone on a deputy sheriff's salary. It had eventually cost him his marriage. Of course, Harry couldn't see how a bad business deal had anything to do with wanting him dead, but no one seemed the least interested in pursuing that simple inconsistency. He sat there, content to let Boone generate all the questions.

Carl Dunbar's name came up, but there was more than a little irregularity in putting those two together. The men were different, Taylor and Dunbar, and they both wanted Harry dead. It seemed incomprehensible. They were of opposite worlds, and as far as Ginny knew, Dunbar didn't know Taylor or anyone that could even be remotely connected with him. And that's that, as they say, except they both had tried to kill Harry, Taylor very nearly getting the job done. There must be some kind of connection, a link to the business in DC, but he wasn't about to mention it now.

Toward the end of the questioning, the coroner's men came and took away Taylor's body. Harry could see the grief on Boone's face. The shock of having to put down one of his own had already etched another worry line through Boone's creviced forehead. Harry stared at the soles of Brick's huge boots as they rolled him away on the gurney.

Harry thought about Brick Taylor, about their high school days, and what he had become after. His two kids had just lost a father, and all because of him, Harry Black, Protector, whatever the hell that was.

How had Brick become entangled in this mess? *Who wants me dead, and for what reason*? As Harry sat, absorbed in his thoughts, Boone turned to Ginny. "Sorry for the language back there."

Ginny sat in one of the stalls, sipping coffee someone had brought her. She had a dazed, faraway look, and wasn't listening.

"Forget it, Sheriff," Harry said. He stood and found his balance as the shock of the fall, and those gunshots near his ear wore off. "You saved both our lives today."

Boone shook his head and glanced back as the gurney finally left the changing area. "This is one fine mess, son. Two dead men and both of them after you. How do you explain it? What do I tell the press when they find out about a rogue deputy nearly gunning down innocent citizens?"

"Believe me, I wish I could explain it."

Boone merely nodded. "Things don't add up, but there's a connection. I just have to find it."

Harry had never been a good liar, and now his reaction betrayed him. He glanced at Ginny but quickly snapped back to Boone.

"You got something, son."

"I'm just as puzzled by this thing as you are. Listen, if I think of something, I'll call you."

Boone's heavy brown eyes bore down on Harry from several inches above him. "You do just that, you hear? And don't take any chances."

"Yeah, I know." Harry glanced at her again and turned back to Boone. "There *is* one thing. How did Brick find us? I mean, we were visiting with Strom Jones, discussing business, and the next thing I know, I'm getting shot at as we were getting on the interstate. How could he have known where we were?"

Boone shrugged. "More puzzles. We'll have to establish Brick's timeline and try to piece things together. I know he had personal problems with the divorce and all." Boone looked at his men doing their job. "I just don't understand it." He turned back to Harry. "Why would he do this?"

Harry wished he could say something to help Boone out. It was obvious. Either someone had tipped Taylor off, or he had been following Harry all along. Either way, people were watching his every move.

Ginny stirred behind him and took his arm. "We have a meeting with your lawyer, remember, and I haven't eaten for hours."

"You sure? I mean, after all the—" Harry turned to the people cleaning up the gore.

She pulled Harry close, which surprised him. “I’ve seen worse in anatomy labs in school. Nothing kills my appetite. Guess I’m macabre that way. I want to see where Carl died. Maybe I can help Margaret get some kind of closure somehow.”

Boone looked from one to the other. “Past twenty-four hours been a gutbuster for you, son.” He nodded to Ginny. “And now she’s involved. I’d feel better if you folks got off the street. Go home, get some sleep, or…” He cleared his throat and looked to the side.

Ginny released Harry’s arm. “It’s not like that, Sheriff.”

“What I mean to say is don’t stray too far tomorrow. I might have more questions.”

“Sure thing, Sheriff Boone,” Harry said.

A deputy with a blond crew cut came up to them and stood silently by. Deke Pelgram, according to the name tag, Boone’s chief deputy. He broke into the conversation by speaking into Boone’s ear. The sheriff turned to Harry. “Seems Brick had himself a lawyer because of his problems. Name Paula Grisham, ring a bell with you?”

“Yeah, she’s Jack’s—” Harry caught himself. “She works in the same firm as my attorney. She’s supposed to be good.”

“And expensive,” Boone said. “How does a good ole boy like Brick hire a former DC hotshot like her?”

“Don’t know, but I’ll make damn sure I ask Jack about it.”

“Yeah, you do that, and remember what I said.” Boone turned away and barked some orders for his men to clear out and give them some privacy. Turning back, he pulled a pistol from his belt. “It’s a nine-millimeter

Beretta. Got plenty of stopping power. It'll put anyone down with a body shot." He gave Harry a stern look. "You know how to use it?"

It was heavy in his hand, but it wasn't an altogether unfamiliar feeling. "I'll pass in a pinch, but I don't have a permit. If I get caught with this thing—"

"Not a problem. Keep it on or near you at all times. I'll be out to your place tomorrow around lunch to make sure you have the basics down. Until then, keep your head good and low."

Harry stopped Boone as he turned. "Don't you want a formal statement or something?"

"No need, son. I've got a clear picture." Boone nodded once to Ginny and gave a last glance at the death scene before ambling out of the changing room.

Harry and Ginny followed the sheriff past the place where Brick Taylor had lain moments before, the stench of blood drifting up to him. He'd never smelled this much of the foul odor before, but somehow he knew it wouldn't be the last time.

Chapter 19

Harry and Ginny ignored the stares of the department store's employees as they hurried through the store. Pushing open the glass doors, they walked into the parking lot. They were disoriented, but it wasn't difficult to find the car. It was the only Mustang riddled with bullet holes.

"Bastard," Harry cursed. "Why'd he have to shoot up my car?"

It had ten holes and a couple of shattered windows. The interior was a mess of fluffy cushion stuffing.

"I think you've got enough money now to buy a thousand of these."

"That's not the point. I've had this car for ten years. It's a classic '65 Shelby, mint condition. You don't find these around every corner. Now, look at it."

Ginny stared at him and shook her head. "I'll hold my opinion of you until I see if the money goes to your head." She placed her hand on his arm and gave him a smile that sent shivers down his spine, and through other parts of his anatomy, but he didn't have time to think about it right now. "Thanks for what you did back there," she added.

"What, nearly getting my head shot off?"

"No, tackling that monster. That saved us more than anything."

Harry glanced sideways at her. "He was coming in

my stall, gun first when you called out. That's what saved our asses." Her mouth turned up into a charming half-smile. "So, no, thank *you*."

She squeezed his arm, and he relaxed a little. "You don't have any intention of going home, do you?"

"And you aren't starving, are you?"

"Actually, I am. And I really do want to see that diner."

"I need to see Jack." Harry pulled out his iPhone and clicked on the Google search box. He gave Ginny another sideways glance and hesitated a moment before saying, "Paula Grisham is Jack's girlfriend."

She jerked her head to him. "What?"

"Brick's lawyer is Jack's girlfriend."

"I understood you. It's just—" Ginny turned her head back, staring forward. "All that's happened, do you think it means something? She's from DC, right? Could it just be a coincidence?"

"I don't know."

"How long have you known her?" Ginny asked.

"I don't. We met once at a party. Paula and Jack have been together for about six months."

"Is it serious?"

Harry shrugged. Jack never had a relationship he would call serious. He went through women by the box full. They both had been carefree, playing a pretty broad field, Jack more so than Harry. "She monopolizes his time more than anyone ever has, and he lets her, which tells me it's serious. Sleeps at his place more than hers, and he seems content with the whole thing. I think he's planning to settle down, which is surprising, considering."

"Considering what?"

Harry turned to her with a shy smile. "His appetite."

She rolled her eyes and turned back in her seat.

"What are you thinking?"

"Remember what Strom said about people being turned?"

Harry shook his head. "Jack's not, and neither is his girlfriend."

"How do you know that?"

"I just do."

"But how? Where is he anyway?"

"Listen, if someone wanted to get to me, if people around me are vulnerable, Jack would be perfect. I haven't seen a change in him. We talk almost every day. He's not turned, or whatever the hell they're supposed to do with people. It would've been too easy. I know he's not." Harry felt her eyes on him, but he wouldn't return the stare. "Someone wants me dead. Tried twice already. But I'm telling you they could have gotten to me every which way and twice on Sunday by now through Jack. He has access to the mansion—keys, codes—you name it."

"Okay, I believe you, but why haven't they moved through him? If you're part of some grand scheme, some obstacle that has to be removed, why not get to you the easiest way possible?" She took a deep breath. "Don't you know *anything* about these people your grandmother warned you about?"

Harry almost said no, but he stopped short. His grandmother had told him hundreds of stories, starting at a very young age. He'd absorbed some things, the more horrific stories in particular, but specifics like names were difficult to remember. He slowed the car and stared off into the distance, past the traffic and buildings, past the bustle of life, pulling Agnes's face from his memory, her gravelly voice.

A name came to him. "Ausberg."

"What?"

He repeated it, more confident now of his memory. "They're an old family from the Netherlands. Big in the banking world."

"I've heard of them. The World Bank. That sort of thing. Bill talked about them. The European Union, a single currency, one-world government. But why would one of the world's wealthiest families be—"

"I don't know. All I have are Agnes's stories, and this family name had been front and center."

"They're power brokers, have been for decades."

"Longer," Harry said.

"Okay…and they have all the money in the world. Let's say this prominent family is involved. What else might they want?"

"More influence, control."

"Over what, politicians?"

Harry shook his head. "Countries, maybe."

Ginny nodded, but he couldn't tell how it might be sounding to her, like some crazy take-over-the-world plot. There wasn't much else to go on.

"So, suppose they're connected to the bombing in Washington. Trying to…to…" She stopped, but nothing came to her. "Help me out here."

"Connect the dots. The bombing disrupted an economic summit. Your brother was a key player from his position as the ranking minority member of the Senate Finance Committee and newly-elected minority leader."

"And the president's confidant," Ginny said.

"Right, they definitely meant for him to die as well."

"It all points to economics. I can see why they would want these senators killed, but it doesn't seem enough to me. How can a single bombing disrupt America's economic engine when bringing down the Twin Towers didn't do it? Something just doesn't fit."

"It's still evolving. But think about it, maybe there is another way to weaken the country."

Her eyes widened. "You mean there could be more bombs?"

Harry nodded. "And something like subterfuge. They're trying to take out the important players for reasons connected to their goals, whatever they are."

"And you?"

"If my grandmother's stories are true, I'm the wild card they can't control, like a computer virus running amok, fouling the system. They have to defeat it along the way, or they're screwed. Only I don't know what I'm supposed to do. Where do I fit in?"

"But you've done a lot already. You saved my brother."

Harry turned in his seat. "Yeah, and your brother could be a bigger cog in all this than we think. We said it before. He could be their prime target still."

Her eyes widened, and she fumbled for her cell phone. Harry placed a hand on hers. "He's not in Washington anymore, which means he could actually be a little safer. Let's wait until we see him tomorrow."

She reluctantly put her phone away and took a look around as Harry eased the car along the curb. "Why are we here?"

They had sped south on I-55, eventually pulling off to enter some nondescript North Jackson neighborhood after consulting the address shown on the phone. They were parked in front of a ranch-style house with tall, blooming white oleanders in the front yard.

He killed the lights but didn't release the steering wheel. "Look, we'll get to your brother." His head was starting to throb between his eyes. "But I want you to know I don't have any answers yet. I need to see Jack. I need to ask him about Paula. I need to settle the estate tomorrow and have another talk with Jones and try to sort some of this shit out, and we have to see your brother."

"And you need to stay alive until then."

"Yeah, that too." Harry took her hand. "I should take you home right now. There's no need for you to be part of this crap. These people know things, so they'll know you and I aren't involved and that they can't get to me through you." Harry cringed at the hurt look in her eyes. "Oh, hell, Ginny, I only meant I'm sure you'll be safer if you aren't involved. They have to know we aren't a couple."

"Funny, I don't feel safe, and what you just said is no consolation. If it's all the same, I'll see this thing through. I feel safer with you anyway, as crazy as it may sound."

Harry gripped the wheel harder. Someone close to her family had already died, and they had gone after her brother. He hadn't caused those things, but letting her edge closer to the precipice of this cliff Harry seemed to be on was dangerous for her. But, dammit, it felt good to have her with him, helping him. He needed her, so he just gave her a stiff nod.

She pulled her hand away. “You didn’t answer me. Why are we here? I thought we were heading to the diner where Carl died.”

He nodded, not really listening. The front yard was cast in shadows from a lone lamp just up the street.

“Harry?”

A car passed them, driving slowly. The male driver turned his head ever so slightly and accelerated when he noticed Harry staring back. Harry’s hands tightened on the wheel. When the car continued around the bend and out to another street, he turned toward her.

“We’re paying a visit to Brick’s ex-wife before the cops do.”

Chapter 20

Ginny shook her head. “What do you hope to gain by visiting her? You’re going to tell her what a monster her ex was that he tried to kill us? What good would it do?”

“I knew Taylor in high school. Whoever got to him must have known that. Brick screwed it up when he came out shooting like a wild man.” He stopped talking to the steering wheel and looked at her. “I knew Sheila, too. She’ll talk to me. She may know something about what he’s been up to, who he must have met.”

“This is about Jack’s girlfriend, isn’t it? Taylor’s lawyer.”

“Maybe.” He checked the rearview mirror. The street was dark and deserted. “Come with me. I’ll feel better not leaving you in the car alone.”

Ginny followed his gaze and spoke softer. “You think someone’s following us?”

He shrugged and turned back to look at the dark front of the house.

She turned to face him. “What are you planning?”

“Can you tell when someone’s lying to you?”

“I’ve developed a knack. Most therapists have. Earlier, when your story came spilling out, I knew it was the truth.

“Good. I doubt Sheila knows you.” He became more thoughtful. “It’s been a long time since she’s seen me. She'll remember me, though." Ginny's eyebrows arched. He sighed. "I just need to ask her about Brick."

He got a sharper look from her. "Don't you think she ought to find out from the authorities?"

"No, actually, I don't." Lights came on in the front room, and a shadow passed across the window. Harry noted the new Chevy Impala sitting in the driveway. "She's home and she's about to get some company. She just doesn't know it yet. I don't think they would tell her by phone." He turned back to her. "I want to be gone before Boone shows up." He opened the door.

"Hold on, we need to—"

He didn't wait for any more arguments. He got out of the car but waited for her before crossing the street. She grabbed his arm to slow him down.

"Okay, Harry, but go easy on her. I know they're divorced, but he *was* the father of her children."

"I won't say anything stupid."

They were at the windowed door and staring through it when Taylor's ex-wife passed through the foyer to another room. Harry knocked hard, and she poked her head from around the corner with a puzzled look. Recognition dawned on her face, and a broad smile broke out. It faded when she opened the door and noticed the tall redhead standing behind him.

"Joey, what are you doing here?"

Ginny stepped out from around Harry and gave him a quizzical look.

Harry shrugged. "No one's called me that since high school except for my grandmother." There was an awkward silence before Harry cleared his throat. "Sheila, this is a friend of mine, Dr. Virginia Rankin. Do you mind if we have a word with you? Sorry for not calling first, but it's essential."

Sheila glanced from Ginny to Harry and hesitated a moment. "You go by Harry now, don't you? I heard you changed over for college." She hesitated again. "Well, anyway, y'all can come in for a minute. The kids are playing in their room. Since Brick left, it's just me and them anyway." She gave Harry a weak smile, pulled the rubber band out from her ponytail, and ran her fingers through bleached hair.

She stepped aside, led them into the living room, and excused herself. The place was nicer than expected, tastefully decorated with a mixture of antiques that went well together but wouldn't bring much on the market. She came back with a tray of lemonade. She'd quickly brushed her hair, but the puzzled look hadn't left her.

Harry's heart sank at the thought of what he needed to do. He hadn't let on to Ginny that he and Shelia had been more than acquaintances in high school. There was a brief fling, but Harry had broken it off the summer after graduation. She had taken up with Taylor at State later that fall. Harry figured the last few years hadn't worked out so well, but at least the house was decent enough. She had aged but was still as beautiful as ever.

Sheila sat opposite them in a wing chair and stared at her guests.

"Something's happened you need to know about, and I—"

"It's Brick, isn't it? What's he done now? You're a financial man, aren't you, Harry? Did he miss a payment on that stupid venture that went south? Lord knows he already missed a bunch of child support.

Makes it kinda tough for us here."

Her face had suddenly turned to stone like she couldn't take one more ounce of bad news about the man who continued to cause problems in her life, even after he'd left.

Thankfully, Ginny broke the awkward silence. "Maybe it'll be better if you sat over here when you hear what Harry has to say." She nodded to Harry, and before Sheila had time to think, Ginny was up and offering her seat.

Sheila sat next to Harry, her knee almost touching his, and glanced back at Ginny. "He said you're a doctor. What kind?"

"It's not important." Harry cleared his throat. "Look, something bad has happened. In fact, I don't have much time before Sheriff Boone or someone else gets here with the news."

"What? Has Brick been arrested? And why are you involved in this? Why are you here?"

"I'll tell you everything, Sheila, I promise, but first I need you to tell me something. Someone's tried to kill me twice now. One a few mornings ago at the Cold Fish Diner and once more about an hour ago at the strip mall in Madison."

"Murder," Sheila whispered in a shocked tone. "Are you all right?" She grabbed his arm with both hands. "Did Brick help? He's one of Boone's best, you know."

Harry shook his head and took her hand in his. "Tell me what happened to you and Brick."

"Well, Jackson's big, but in many ways, it's a small town. Why do you want to know?"

"I promise I'll tell you in a moment, but I have to

find out about Brick first. It's important. You can trust me."

"I know I can."

He was counting on the old connection. "Ginny's a friend, but we aren't involved." He glanced at Ginny again, and she rolled her eyes.

Sheila's face lit up. She smiled at him and planted her knee firmly against his. "What's this all about?"

"Just start off by telling me why you and Brick divorced."

"Oh, the usual. Money problems, of course. Brick lost a lot in that stupid, hare-brained business he got himself into. But the worst was the lady lawyer he took up with a few months ago." She turned pink, and the hard look came back. "I figured he was spending an awful lot of time with her trying to get out of his financial fix. But I knew this was different. A wife always knows." She glanced at Ginny, her eyes narrowing and edged closer to Harry. "Well, sad to say, I caught them."

A tear rolled down her face. Harry took her hand.

"I'm not crying for me. It wasn't the first time Brick cheated, you know, but I couldn't look away this time because of the way I caught them in my own bed. That was four months ago, but I still remember that smug look she gave me. Like I was just some trailer trash. Looking back, I could tell a change had come over him. He'd gotten real quiet like he had more on his mind than a deputy ought to have. But it was somehow more than that. He really changed." She sniffed again. "When I caught them and saw her for the first time. You know that haughty look? Well, shit, I wasn't gonna take it no more. The kids are bigger now and, thank the

Lord, I have a good job. So I said to hell with it. I kicked him out." More tears fell. "Aw, Harry, he even seemed happy about it." The dam broke then, and it was a moment before she was able to control herself. "Anyway, you're sweet for coming to me like this, but you haven't said why yet. Why would someone want to kill you? And what does Brick have to do with it?"

Part of him didn't want to ask the next question, but he knew he had to, not for his own safety as much as for Jack's. "What was his lawyer's name?"

"Let's see…I never knew Brick's lawyer's first name." She stared up at the ceiling. "That big writer who used to live up in Oxford. What's his name again? Writes about lawyers and stuff."

Harry sighed and sagged a little in his seat, eyes closed. Grisham. Paula Grisham. And now she had her hands on Jack.

Sheila's breath caught. "Oh, Harry, she's not your woman, is she? And she and Brick—"

"No, no, it's not that."

"Goodness, it would be a coincidence, wouldn't it? Especially after what we had in high school and me ending up with Brick then him turning around and doing you like that again. You know, taking someone else from you." She took his hand. "Maybe it's worked out for the best." She tightened her grip, and those eager brown eyes filled with renewed hope.

But a sense of foreboding crept over Harry like a looming storm. Jack was in danger, maybe even turned like Brick and Dunbar probably had been. Paula was implicated in this mess, certainly through Brick, but maybe in other ways too. The evidence was flimsy, but it was starting to point in her direction. Paula had worked in Washington where Carl Dunbar was a fixture on a senator's staff, a senator who should be dead right now. She had moved to Jackson of all places. Not exactly a step up from a big DC firm. More like two steps down. Not long after her move to Jackson, Dunbar had come for him with a .45 revolver in hand. And now, Taylor. It could have all been a coincidence, but he didn't think so. It was pretty damn clear; Paula could easily be the common denominator. He was sure of it. It could mean only one thing for his friend. He needed to find Jack, and he had to find him quickly.

"Tell me what's got you so upset, Harry."

"You'll find out soon enough, but what I have to tell you I wanted to come from me." He retook her hand. "Brick's dead, Sheila. Killed about an hour ago."

Chapter 21

Harry couldn't tell Sheila what really had him upset. As it was, the news had stunned her. He was thankful for Ginny's presence and training, but there was little she could do. It took ten minutes to calm Sheila down and another five to convince her she shouldn't be alone. She held on tight as he dialed the number to her mother, only breaking down when her two young girls came out, hair wet from their baths, to check on the commotion. After Sheila's mother arrived, Harry and Ginny left, promising Sheila he would check in on her tomorrow.

"A high school fling, huh," Ginny said as they settled in the Mustang.

"A long time ago."

"Not so long for her."

Harry pulled the car keys from the pocket of his jeans. "She's just hurt over the divorce and feeling lonesome. The bastard may have been a terrible husband, but he could have been a decent enough father to their kids. Anyway, Brick's gone now, so she has other things to think about."

Ginny shook her head.

"I know it was pretty shitty of me, but I was counting on revving up some old feelings to get her to talk. We had a pretty intense thing going. Lasted a few months. We were two kids without much supervision.

I'm just glad no long-lasting entanglements came out of it." He glanced at her, sitting there, hanging on his every word. He shrugged. "She wanted something I couldn't give her because all I wanted was to be free of Black Manor and Agnes. I ended it pretty abruptly after graduation. I spent the summer with Jack in Hawaii, chasing skirts compliments of Jones and the estate." He sensed her irritation but didn't say more.

"I'm just saying she won't forget the hand holding. It meant something to her. She'll expect you to return and comfort her, and then she'll expect something more."

"Yeah, well, maybe what she really needs right now is a good psychologist, and I know just the one." He didn't give Ginny a chance to answer him before turning the ignition and pulling out just as a patrol car turned the corner behind them. He didn't think they'd been spotted.

"Think she'll let on she knows Brick is dead?" Ginny asked, looking through the smashed rear window. The patrol car had stopped on the exact spot they had left.

"It doesn't make a bit of difference."

Harry pulled his cell phone out and hit redial to Jack's cell. Again, no answer. He pounded a fist on the steering wheel. Had they turned Jack, right under his nose? He wanted to scream and bust some heads open, and maybe not in that order, but he held these feelings back so as not to alarm Ginny any more than he had already.

"Better run by his place," Ginny said with strain in her voice.

He gave her a stiff nod, gripping the wheel so hard

his hands hurt. "Yeah, doing it now."

The car sped toward the nearest on-ramp to I-55. He glanced at Ginny, his chest tightening, thinking of the danger Jack was in, danger Harry had caused just by being who he was.

"Jack and I were everything to each other while we were growing up. His parents were detached and power-hungry. They worked all the time and were not there for him. They owned a small specialty press and kicked out a politically charged newspaper, the *Jackson Gazette*. The innocuous name didn't fool anyone. It was really a liberal attack rag buried in staunchly conservative Mississippi. Agnes put up with me being friends with Jack because she could use him to stick it to his parents. She hated them, people with a plan to turn Neanderthal conservatives like her into liberals or something worse, real leftists. Jack loved to bait them with my grandmother. There were plenty of clashes. They finally stopped caring when we graduated. They knew they'd lost their son to an ideology they loathed."

"And you? Did you have anyone besides Agnes and Jack?"

Harry slowed as they came up behind a state trooper on the interstate. "Just her loony sidekick to keep me on the right track."

They remained silent a while longer, his thoughts drifting more and more to Jack and whether he, Harry Black, Protector, could at least manage to protect the only friend he had.

"We better find him. I think that woman—"

He cut her off. "I'm on it. He lives in the Parkview condominium complex."

"There's a pattern developing here. Paula Grisham

obviously used sex to lure Deputy Taylor in and somehow turn him. And it doesn't have to mean something fanciful, like sorcery, as Mr. Jones claims. Sex is a powerful attraction. Taylor could have had a controlling delusion operating just from being manipulated sexually. He was hurting, in financial difficulty. Couple it with an unsympathetic wife…"

She let Harry draw the conclusion. It was evident that she hadn't bought into the whole sorcery bit Jones had spouted. Harry had to admit it was one hell of a pill to swallow, but something weird and unaccounted for was happening, and not just with him. Taylor hadn't been himself; it was plain to see—the change in voice, the wild look, the hatred emanating from him. Harry hadn't seen Brick in years, had never crossed paths, or made an enemy with anyone connected to him. There was no motive for the attempted murder. A little sex wouldn't change him so completely. It didn't flip someone's personality profile in a manner of months.

"And now she's with your friend," Ginny continued.

"It's different with Jack, okay? They've been together for months and have been intimate almost from the first day they met. There hasn't been the slightest change in him other than—"

"Than what?"

"It's just that he's serious about her. You know…in love."

"Whereas, before, he was a player, right? Don't you think that's enough of a change, as it is?"

"Hell no, because I would've known it. Besides, everyone falls in love. I just thought it would be a little later with Jack."

"I hope you're right for your friend's sake. If what Sheila just said is correct, Jack's been had."

Harry cringed, but he couldn't deny it was pretty clear that Jack's girlfriend had a secret life. "What about Dunbar? She might have known him in DC before moving to Jackson."

"And manipulated him through sex—turned him," Ginny said. "No way can I see that scenario happening with Carl."

"He was coming after me, remember?"

She nodded. The strain in her admission was hard to miss. "Carl had always been such a strong family man. That he would take up with another woman and turn into a monster—"

"You're just a touch naïve, aren't you? No one's perfect. She could have gotten to him, too."

"*And* your friend."

"That's why I have to find him. But something stronger than sex is working here. What if Jones is right about this sorcery thing?"

Cars sped by as they drove on. Ginny shifted in her seat, looking straight ahead. She crossed her arms, obviously not wanting to concede the point about sorcery. He knew it was a wild idea, but there were no other explanations for what had been happening to him.

Harry exited the interstate just as Hinds County and Jackson sprawled into Madison County to the north. He quickly found Noble Street, where Jack's condo was located. They parked the car.

Harry sat there and stared at the two-story building overlooking the wide, tree-lined avenue. "His condo is just ahead," he said, pointing, "the one with no lights on." He searched the parking lot. "I don't think his car is here, and he's paranoid about the road bike, so he keeps it inside."

"Do you know where Paula lives?"

"Not a clue." He hit the wheel again. "Dammit. I wish I'd seen it earlier. But this shit is just too crazy. How could I have known?" He turned to Ginny. "She keeps such tight tabs on him. Too tight."

"A sex freak," she said. "It's an addiction."

"Maybe, maybe not, but let's hope it's an addiction that doesn't get him killed." He turned back and stared at the condo. "At this hour, my guess is he's with her. At dinner probably, then back here, or her place. They stay in for most of their entertainment."

He killed the Mustang and held up his chain by a single key. "I've got this, though. Come on."

Harry tucked the gun Sheriff Boone had given him into the waistband at the small of his back, and they quickly walked to Jack's unit. The day had been far too long, and exhaustion was creeping up.

He checked both directions to make sure they hadn't been followed. But when he turned the key and swung the door open, a presence filled his mind, stopping him cold. He released the doorknob. Something was here in Jack's place, or rather, had been here. Somehow he knew the apartment was now empty, the presence having left only a memory of itself.

Harry ran his hand over the door frame. Something reached out to him, alerting senses he didn't know he possessed. His hand tingled with a tiny electric current. He doubted something as mundane as electricity had anything to do with what met his touch. A putrid odor made him gag, but Ginny didn't seem to notice it.

What the hell?

The presence increased in strength as Harry lingered. Raw emotions flooded his mind, memories of moaning, faint cries, wailing. There was a distinct absence of anything normal as if nothing good had ever inhabited this place. Harry knew it to be false. Jack lived here, and his friend was good.

But the scent of something evil remained as a warning. Harry chose to ignore it. He tried to cross the threshold, but the strange electric current bit back hard. His skin crawled, tingled, jumped with the heebie-jeebies. It halted him momentarily as if something had pushed back against his chest, something invisible. He gritted his teeth against the unseen force and pushed through the doorway. Breathing as though he'd just done a bang-up job with a set of dumbbells, he stopped to examine Ginny, but apparently, whatever hit him hadn't affected her.

"What's wrong?" she said, stopping at his side.

Inside the doorway, everything he could see appeared normal except for two shadows flickering into being on the far wall. He pointed to them, and Ginny's breath caught. She reached out for Harry's hand.

"Stay alert and stay by my side. They aren't the problem." He reached around to the small of his back for the Beretta.

"Be careful with that thing," she hissed and turned back to the Grigori. "They're what killed Carl?"

He nodded. "But they're helpers, remember?" As if to reassure her, he turned to the flickering shadows and said, "She's with me."

No response, so she clung tighter to Harry's arm.

The place seemed to be in order. Jack had always taken a minimalist approach that would have made the

Spartans proud. There wasn't the slightest feminine touch. Maybe Paula's reach hadn't been quite so long after all. The thought comforted him, but he knew it was basically meaningless. Paula could still be some sort of witch, ready to pounce.

He walked deeper into the condo. The air was dense, making his lungs work extra hard. He began to sweat, but it was nothing compared to the voices that started to taunt him, calling his name, laughing. They were in his head because Ginny seemed oblivious to them. And it couldn't be the Grigori. He hadn't felt anything like this in their presence at Black Manor. What he'd felt at the door left a nasty, sickening stench permeating the place, but not something ordinary people could actually smell.

Ginny clung to him tighter in the presence of the Grigori. Jones said the shadows were sentient, meaning they were alive somehow, part of his family and, therefore, allies. This thought would have been beyond crazy twenty-four hours ago. Precisely what they were, he hadn't a clue, but, like Harry, they were affected by this place. Their usual sharp flickering was dull as they moved languidly over the wall and onto the ceiling.

Then he caught a smell with his nose this time. Metallic, with the onset of decay, much more potent than Taylor's drying blood had been. He turned, inhaling softly with the motion. The smell was more robust when he faced the stairs. It—whatever it was—was coming from upstairs.

"There," he said, pointing to the steps.

They climbed the stairs and entered a short hallway, which led to two bedrooms and a bath. The pressure grew worse, causing Ginny to shudder beside him. Dread permeated the very air they breathed. The closer they came to the far bedroom, the colder the place grew as though death stalked this place, sucking all the warmth and goodwill from these walls.

His heart beat in his throat. A haze clouded his mind. He began to tremble next to Ginny, afraid to look beyond the far door. That was Jack's bedroom, and something was in there, a semblance of evil placed as a guard. He stopped just short of the door.

Ginny squeezed his hand, giving him the confidence to continue. They crept to the open door, but beyond the threshold, the room was utterly black, the light of the hallway failing to penetrate into the room.

He reached for the light switch and flipped it. Nothing happened at first, but as if struggling to obey the laws of electrical conductivity, the light blinked, fluttered, flickered in an oddly pulsating fashion. It finally came on with a faint whining noise but never intensified as it should.

Harry blinked. What had happened was all around them—on the bedsheets, over the carpet, smeared on the walls—decaying blood. The stench filled his nostrils. He swept his head left to right as faint screams came to him. As in his nightmare, it was the screams of a woman, the person whose blood lay splattered about. He pulled Ginny closer, but she couldn't hear it. No one was here now, only the evidence of a murder, and there was plenty of it.

"Good Lord!" Ginny gasped as she took in the scene. She had to turn away to gain control of her stomach. Bloody handprints every foot or so marred the nine-foot white wall. They continued onto the ceiling as though the person had been the cousin of Spiderman.

She pointed to it. "How could they have done that?"

It was a scientific curiosity Harry didn't share just now. He replaced the Beretta in the back waistline of his pants and held his hand out to one of the prints, fingers spread. They were much smaller than his. "They're not Jack's." He said it with relief in his voice as he surveyed the rest of the room, careful of where he stepped. "Don't touch anything."

Ginny nodded. "There's enough blood here for someone to have been—"

"Yeah."

He took one more look around, and said, "We should leave now," just as the lights dimmed and nearly blinked out. His body arched erect. His head jerked up to the ceiling.

It wasn't exactly what he'd felt in the café the day he had almost been shot, but it was close. His head thumped like someone was trapped inside his skull, using a jackhammer to try and break out. He shut his eyes tight, but the pounding didn't last long. He opened them to an eerie silence. Ginny was still there, or was she? Her movements looked oddly out of the moment, as though she existed in another sliver of time, a gray world transposed over the time frame Harry now inhabited.

And they weren't alone.

There was a woman he knew all too well, pulling herself up the wall and onto the ceiling, clinging with bloody hands and feet, her slit throat leaving a steady stream of life trailing behind.

Chapter 22

Peggy Cox hadn't entered Harry's mind since the day he'd called for her to cancel his remaining appointments. She'd warned him to be back soon, using that in-your-face style she could get away with because she was so damn cute and perky. There was something about the portfolio of a new big-shot client the boss needed him to coddle. He'd meant to call and tell their thankless employer he no longer needed the crummy job. For some reason, after watching a naked Peggy crawl up the wall and onto the ceiling like a bloody ant, he couldn't remember anything about the client or even his own last name.

Something flung Peggy through the air. She landed prone on the bed, spread eagle for all the world to see the petite body parts he'd only dreamt about in a previous life, a life as alien to him now as an Alpha Centaurian might find earth to be. She arched her back and turned toward Harry. Terror on Peggy's face fell away, replaced by narrow, sinister eyes. They were eyes he'd never seen during all the hours they'd worked closely together over the past four years. These eyes held dark contempt, a cold calculation measuring him from head to foot.

In a voice that was damn well not her own, she said, "Black, see how you've murdered this little pretty one you care so much about? Others will fall in short order, unless you submit yourself to us. But, as always with you stubborn Blacks, you'll try to save them. You'll utterly fail and your cursed line will be no more."

Peggy convulsed and lay still, whiter than he had ever seen the blonde-haired beauty.

A sudden throttling sensation brought the present back in an instant. Peggy vanished. Harry swayed where he stood. When he collected his senses, he could hear Ginny muttering as she moved about the room. Had someone really been murdered? When had it occurred? Why in Jack's condo? And where the hell was he anyway? She wondered about motive, who the victim could be, where had they taken the dead body because obviously with all this blood around the person couldn't still be alive.

He chalked up her frantic chatter to nerves and listened with a detached demeanor. Ginny, here, with him—so alive, so beautiful—surveying this ugly scene. A moment before he had been in the time of the killing. It couldn't have been more than a couple of hours old. How did that work? How could he have seen these things, Peggy in the throes of death, her young life snuffed out?

Harry must have looked like he felt, because Ginny took his arm in an urgent grip. "Are you okay?"

He shook his head, his tongue glued to the roof of his dry mouth. He opened it with difficulty but couldn't get the words out so he sat on the bed, careful to avoid the blood.

She stroked his hand. "You said yourself the prints are too small to be Jack's."

She was only trying to reassure him. Jack might

still be alive, so he nodded and tried to get up. He had to get out of this room. Only then would the image of Peggy—naked, bloodied, dead—be pushed to the back of his mind, but never erased.

He let Ginny pull him up, but he halted in the doorway. The pressure he'd felt upon entering the apartment completely vanished. The shadows knew it too; both were in the hall flickering more excitedly than ever.

"Listen, I understand now," Harry said to the shadows. "I never got the chance to thank you for saving me."

They seemed to understand him because their flickering grew even more manic as they moved off down the stairs. Harry pulled Ginny along after them.

The Grigori glided to the living room and came to rest on the ceiling over the sofa.

"Can you communicate with them?"

"No." He ran his hands through his hair. "I don't know…maybe." Turning back to the shadows, he said, "We're leaving now."

"But what about Jack? Someone was murdered here today. We have to warn him or, oh God, maybe he's involved. We have to call Sheriff Boone."

Her insinuation aggravated Harry. "No, we don't," he said as calmly as he could. "I already know who they murdered. They meant for me to find out about her. Somehow they knew I would come looking for Jack."

"You know who the victim is? How?"

He had his hand flat on his forehead now, stalking around the room as though he could channel the answer out of each corner. How could he explain to her what he'd seen? "They're toying with me and people are dying."

"What people?"

He spun toward Ginny, thinking her voice had magically deepened, but she was staring at the open door of the condo. They had failed to close it. Chief Deputy Deke Pelgram stood there gawking at them. He entered the apartment with one hand on the grip of his holstered handgun. Harry recognized another deputy as the one who helped remove Brick's body.

Harry and Ginny exchanged a quick glance that didn't go unnoticed. "You the ones made the call?" Pelgram said.

"No," Harry said. He glanced at the ceiling, but thankfully the Grigori didn't seem to enjoy too much company. They'd vanished. "Someone else must have."

"What are you doing here? Caller said there's been a murder." Hand still on the pistol's grip, Pelgram nodded toward the other man and jerked his head toward the stairs. The deputy pulled his gun and began climbing, taking each step slow and easy.

"There's no need for alarm," Harry said. "He'll find a death scene up there all right, but the body's gone."

"Mind telling me how you know that and who this place belongs to."

"Jack Hallowell, a friend of mine and a local lawyer. We came here looking for him. He's been missing since late afternoon. I have a key. We searched the place and found the—"

"Place is clear," the deputy said, bounding into the living room, "plenty of blood, though. Better get forensics here."

Pelgram nodded. "Make the call outside while I

question these two."

"Look, Deputy, I'm worried about my friend. I have to find him. Something's obviously happened to him."

"Where is he?"

"I have a good idea, but I don't know where she lives."

"Who?"

"Paula Grisham."

"Brick's lawyer?"

"She works at the same firm as Jack. They're involved so I think they might be at her place right now." Harry placed a hand on Ginny's arm. "We need to get over there."

Pelgram held up his hand. "You still haven't said how you know someone was murdered here."

Harry tried to keep fear from his voice but couldn't do it. "Look, I don't really know anything. The amount of blood up there means only one thing."

The deputy came in. "Team's on the way. And someone was murdered all right. Like he said, blood's everywhere."

Pelgram nodded again. "Don't necessarily mean someone died, though." He turned back to Harry. "Afraid your search will have to wait a bit." He said to the young deputy. "Boone's been notified?"

"He said to let Metro handle it seein' it's their jurisdiction. I told him Black and that lady doctor were here, too."

"What'd he say?" Pelgram asked.

"Not much for a long time, then he said for you to call him."

Pelgram scowled. "Might as well take a seat. We'll

let Metro sort this out." He left the condo while talking to Sheriff Boone via his radio.

The deputy stood off to the side, stoic. If the scene in the bedroom had affected him, he didn't let on. A thought came to Harry.

"Listen, Deputy Billings, I have to find where Paula Grisham lives. Why don't you help me out by calling your dispatcher for the information? Her number's not in the phone book."

The deputy reached for his radio, but Pelgram walked back in shaking his head, his scowl worse than before, if possible. "Boone said to get your statements. You'll be likely questioned again by Metro. Then you can leave." He hesitated and pulled a notepad out. "Anything you want to add to what you said earlier?"

Harry sighed in frustration and Ginny shook her head.

"There's one thing," Harry said. "You better get to Peggy Cox's place out on Slater Road. She lives there with her folks, or used to."

Pelgram stopped writing. "Why?"

"Because she's the murder victim."

Ginny grabbed Harry's arm and gave him a questioning look.

Pelgram stopped writing and turned skeptical eyes to Harry. "And how would you know that?"

"Because that's her purse under the coffee table. I hadn't seen it before. I recognize it because I work with her. She's my assistant. Or was. The handbag's too unusual for there to be many of them around."

The deputy retrieved the purse and pulled out a wallet with Peggy's ID in it. Pelgram turned away from them and dispatched a unit to the Cox residence.

Shortly after, the Metro police forensic team arrived along with two homicide detectives. After telling their story again they were allowed to leave, but before they made it to the door Pelgram pulled them aside.

"You know, Black, Brick Taylor was a good man. I don't claim to know what sent him over the edge today, but I do know he was one of my best deputies, probably the best I ever had." He held Harry's steady gaze, silent a moment, as if contemplating his next words. "I'd take guys like him any day over rich boys who don't have a clue how the rest of us live." He poked Harry in the chest with a finger. "I don't like it that you're here right now. I don't like it that Brick's dead because of you." He paused and glanced around the apartment. "Fact is, everywhere you go people seem to end up dead. Why is that, Black?" It was clear Pelgram didn't want an answer. "I guess you're not a suspect here, but I have my doubts. Something ain't right. We'll find your friend Hallowell, and we'll damn well find out what happened here. Word of warning, best you stay away from this thing. Let *us* find your lawyer friend. Don't go poking your nose where it don't belong. Boone won't be able to protect your ass forever." He stopped and took a step away from Harry when a detective came back down the stairs.

Harry's jaw clenched and he took a step toward Pelgram. But Ginny had him by the arm and wouldn't let him get closer. "Is that all?" Harry said, not giving an inch.

Pelgram nodded, his brown eyes narrowing even more. Harry considered him a moment longer but knew better than to make some smartass remark. Instead, he spun Ginny around and they left the apartment.

Chapter 23

"Thanks for not throwing a punch at him and landing in jail," Ginny said as they made it back to the bullet-ridden Mustang. "It was obvious that's just what he wanted you to do. After all that's happened and what we have to do tomorrow, I'd rather not spend part of it bailing you out."

Harry shrugged, his concern for Jack outweighing his anger at the unfairness of it all. Pelgram had one thing right, though. Everywhere he went lately, people turned up dead.

He slumped into the driver's seat and laid his head back, exhaustion rolling over him in waves.

"You sure you can drive?" Ginny asked.

Harry nodded, but he honestly didn't know if he could. He sat there a moment, pulled out his cell phone, dialed Jack's number. No answer. He gritted his teeth and turned to Ginny.

"Listen," Ginny said, "we're accomplishing nothing here. Let's go back to your place. I'll fix up something for us. Finding Jack is out of our hands now anyway. The authorities will do a much better job of it unless you know of some hiding place he would go to."

"You mean to run from what he did—from murder."

"I didn't say that."

"He didn't kill anyone in his bedroom, Ginny.

That's just stupid. Odds are he doesn't even know what's happened."

"I know it doesn't make sense unless they've turned him already and he's become one of them."

He shook his head. "I don't believe it. Don't you see? This is all for my benefit. They lured me to the condo to find this shit. I bet Brick wasn't supposed to kill me, though he tried awfully hard. They sent him to self-destruct and deliver a message. He was *meant* to die to make things messy, cause suspicion. Like I said, they're toying with me, showing me the kind of power they have to use people like puppets. They want me to back down, or else. Trouble is, I don't even know what I'm doing, but I don't think they know that."

"You haven't said how you know it was your co-worker's blood up there. They could have stolen her purse and used it as a misdirection or something. For all we know the blood isn't even human."

"Plausible, but trust me on this one, it's hers." He turned more fully to her. "Look, I know you're trained to find the rational explanation in everything. Magic and sorcery are way off your radar. I get it. But you have to remember what I did in the coffee shop that morning has no rational explanation. This sex theory of yours is possible if this were a normal situation, but it doesn't really explain what's going on."

Ginny leaned in to him. "How do you know that?"

"Because Peggy was up there in that bedroom—dead."

She looked at him like he'd lost his mind.

"She climbed that damn wall and ceiling like a freaking bug. I don't know how she did it, but she did. She had an inch wide gash across her throat and other wounds on her thighs and chest. She couldn't have been alive at the time, but there she was, climbing the damn wall. I mean, how does that work?" He stopped and hung his head, his breathing coming in spurts.

"Slow down, okay, you're hyperventilating." She placed a hand on his shoulder. "You'll pass out."

He forced himself to breathe more easily. "It was like a film reel playing in the room. I was a bystander observing the real life action. You were there, but in a gray world, like two snippets of time had been superimposed over the bedroom. I *saw* her, Ginny. I saw her get flung from the ceiling to the bed. And in another voice, a man's voice, she spoke to me, told me I would die too. It was the same voice Brick had used."

Harry turned away, embarrassed by the tears welling in his eyes. "How could she be speaking?" he said, his voice weak. "She was already dead."

He waited for a response, and when he didn't get one, he turned back, wiping his face. Ginny sat there frowning, looking into her lap. "Shit, Harry."

Harry groaned out a short laugh. "Still think you want to hang with me at my place tonight? It might be better if you leave right now and forget about today, forget about all this. Pretend I never called you."

Ginny closed her eyes. When she opened them, Harry could tell what her answer would be because a stern resolve had turned her lovely face into a stolid mask. "I can't do that." She touched his leg. "I don't want to abandon you. You're in trouble. You saved my brother. I'm not sure how I can help, but I'm not leaving your side."

"They'll keep coming. Today was just the beginning."

She brought her hand up to his face, just a light touch. "I know. There must be a way to find whoever's watching you, turning people who should be on our side."

"Might be hard to do, don't you think?" He took her hand in his and held on tight. "We don't even know where to start."

He needed a friend in the worst way. He sure as hell didn't want to be alone with thoughts of what could be happening to Jack after seeing Peggy Cox die.

Ginny put her other hand on top his. "I'm staying the night at Black Manor and that's final. Tomorrow there's the funeral in Brookhaven where you'll meet my brother. Together, we'll formulate a plan. Okay?"

Harry pulled his hand away. She was beautiful and smart—too smart to get involved in this mess, but he was grateful for her loyalty. "You don't believe me, do you?"

"Of course, I do. I mean, part of me does. But the trained part tells me you were hallucinating."

"The purse," he said, defiantly. "Explain that. They didn't steal it. It proves she'd been there. And don't tell me I noticed it and knew who it belonged to before I walked upstairs where I had some kind of psychic event because of all the blood. That would be a good theory too, except for the fact that I hadn't discovered the purse until we were back down and sat on the couch with a good view underneath the coffee table." When Ginny didn't answer, he continued, "And how do you explain the Grigori? You saw them, the way they move, how they respond to me. They were scared shitless until things normalized. There was something in the condo. I don't know what it was."

She opened her mouth, paused in the sudden bright light shining into the rear of the Mustang. She squinted into the glare for a second then turned to settle into the seat. Harry quickly put the Mustang in gear and drove away as a metro cruiser came up behind them and pulled up at the curb.

Chapter 24

It was nearing midnight when Harry turned the Mustang into the long drive and past the wrought-iron gate and massive twin gargoyles standing guard at Black Manor. He noticed the cruiser Boone had dispatched at the spot where the winding drive left the county road. He gave the patrolman an uneasy glance. Brick Taylor had driven an identical vehicle, which wasn't a comforting thought, but there wasn't anything he could do about it.

They walked to the veranda, a cacophony of katydids singing in the heat of the Mississippi night. In the last few days it had barely cooled twenty degrees after sundown, which placed the nighttime low temperature around eighty. The earlier downpour had the humidity hovering near maximum. To make matters worse, the Mustang's air conditioning was on the blink—probably one of Brick's damn bullets.

Harry had called off hunting for Jack and Paula. He couldn't shake the feeling that he'd overlooked something important, some memory stuck in his thick skull, put there by his crazy grandmother who had turned out to be as sane as anyone.

His friends were either missing or dying. He wasn't protecting them and didn't seem able to. He needed to get Jones alone and wring out every last drop of information stored in his old brain. It was all from

Agnes, of course, but Jones represented a font of knowledge that was bound to be invaluable. If Harry wanted to live another day, knowledge was what he needed, especially knowledge of his family. He knew something of their failings, but what he needed now were success stories, what they did right, something he could use to combat this thing, this voice that had spoken through Brick and Peggy.

Who were these people? Why did they bomb Washington? Was Senator Rankin really their only target? He knew in bloody detail what they were capable of, but he needed to know about *them*. What made them tick? And most importantly, what options he might have to counter them and protect the people who mattered most? Did he have anything he could wield besides the Grigori and some weird sixth sense that would let him watch a movie of his secretary who had been slaughtered?

The shadows were there only to protect him. He didn't know if he could command them as a weapon against these cowards who used innocent people while they remained ephemeral, fleeting ghosts. *How do you fight someone who isn't there?*

His anger over what Pelgram said began to dissipate and out of it came a new wariness, a disquiet arising from a sense that something of great significance was just out of his reach. He'd made a critical mistake in not listening to Agnes. Now that rebellious streak would likely be his ruination. He should have been different growing up, should have listened, paid attention to the old woman. It had all been so hard. But she'd been right all along. He knew that now and it ate at him.

Something Jones said sent a cold shiver dancing over the nape of his neck. He couldn't trust anyone. He gave Ginny a furtive glance. He would have to force himself to remember the warning.

They went straight to the kitchen and scrounged up some late-night breakfast food. He tried to remember more of Agnes's stories as they talked. Ginny used her training to maximum effect, drawing out information where she could, but there wasn't much.

Ginny took a bite of omelet while standing across the counter from him. She briefly stared past him. "A family this old, with this kind of purpose, there must be books, diaries perhaps, and records. There must be…I don't know…some family relics around here Agnes preserved."

"There are," Harry said without thinking beyond the piece of bacon he'd just stuffed in his mouth. He dropped his fork and felt about as stupid as he always knew Brick Taylor to be. He nearly choked on the bacon. "Actually, there are dozens of them. Diaries. Her books as she called them."

Ginny's eyes widened. "Why didn't you say so before?"

"I told you about the books she used to read to me, remember?"

"Yes, but I presumed they were—Oh, it doesn't matter now. Show me." She grabbed his hand and pulled him away from the counter.

The library was a huge room behind the main staircase. Three high walls were covered floor to ceiling in bookcases filled to the brim. Agnes Black's reading tastes had been varied. The shelves contained biographies of world leaders, horror novels, spy thrillers, political treatises, and children's literature, among others.

He flipped the light switch turning on three lamps sitting at strategic reading areas around the room. He wasn't much of a reader aside from the occasional glance at the newspaper and some financial journals at the office.

"Is that your computer?" Ginny pointed to the laptop on an ornate desk in a far corner.

"It was Agnes's." He studied the bookcases. "The diaries are there."

He led her to the largest of the bookcases. Bound in ancient, cracking leather were perhaps a hundred volumes, some in good enough shape, but most looked as if they would fall apart if handled. Each had a year range Agnes had conveniently stamped on the spine of the newer volumes, or had hand-placed a piece of tape with the year written on it in the case of the oldest.

"Where do we start?" Ginny said.

He didn't know, but then he ran his hand along the stack and began walking, stopping at the nineteenth century.

"Yes," she said, with growing excitement. "Meriodoc Black. Strom's story, your immediate predecessor. Why haven't you examined these before?"

"Would you have?" he said, aggravation rising in his voice. "You and Strom should compare notes on my psyche. On second thought, try being hounded every day of your life into being something you don't want to be, something you're damn sure can't exist." He knew he had gone overboard. Feeling like a heel, he said, "Look, I didn't mean to—"

"Don't apologize. I'm the one who's sorry. You're

right. I might have run away, too, had I been in your shoes."

He pulled the volume and turned to her. "Damn straight."

She grinned. "But maybe I would also have *listened* just a teensy bit to my grandmother who deserved some respect."

Harry didn't think so, but he nodded anyway. "I'm listening now. You want to help, or what?"

She gave him another crooked smile and took the heavy book from him. They sat on a nearby loveseat and placed the big diary on the coffee table in front of them. It appeared in good order—dated entries, fairly legible script. Was this Meriodoc's own hand they were seeing or had it been dictated? It wasn't important, so Harry searched for another entry, and found a promising one marked July, 1834, Oxford, England.

" 'My thoughts are hard put, my words difficult to come by, to write down. I am so sorry they have involved her. How could I have avoided it? What could I have done differently? It is too difficult to go on. How do I live with her loss? I would have asked her to marry and now she is gone, and I am to—' "

Meriodoc Black hadn't continued the thought. Ginny glanced up from the book. "This is sad. What could he have been talking about?"

"Let's go back in time a bit to an earlier date."

She flipped the pages to an entry recorded a few months prior and began reading the passage out loud.

" 'The idea someone like me could be called into the family task was quite amusing to the others, especially cousin Hubert who is a real believer, not like me at all, though I have seen things lately that have shaken my conviction. I know now He must have a sense of humor, but I don't share it. What am I to do? How am I to face this? I am terrified of my prospects. I am a scholar, not a fighter, a theologian, not a…' "

The text was hard to read here, so she skipped down.

" 'They all laughed when it became obvious the mantle—this legacy—had passed to someone so undeserving. I cannot say as I blame them. However they chose, I'd have to question the sanity of the chooser.

" 'But no one knows, do they? The whole thing is quite inscrutable, left up to Providence, as they say. But I never knew Providence could have such a wicked sense of humor.' "

Ginny stopped.

Harry leaned back against the cushion. "Is he talking about what I think he's talking about?"

"Someone in the church must have picked him?"

Harry shook his head. "I don't think it works like that."

"Not in your case, no, but remember you're the last. If the family was larger then, there would have been a choice."

"By whom?" Harry asked.

"Providence…meaning God, I suppose."

"Oh, boy." He stood and walked off to the center of the room.

"He was some kind of theologian. I wonder what church."

"Episcopal, or Anglican in England. That's what it would have to be, because that's what we, I mean, my grandmother and parents, were."

"And you?"

"Not so much, I'm afraid."

She nodded. "What does it mean?"

"Nothing helpful." He went back to the couch and pulled the book closer to him. "It would make these sorcerers be against whatever the Black family stood for. If the Blacks were religious, the sorcerers would be the opposite." He stopped, thinking hard. "If there's a church connection, maybe there's also something there we can use."

"What do you mean?"

"Hell if I know. It depends on what it is we find. Listen, let's look for information on the sorcerers."

He got up and quickly pulled a much older volume, but it was no good. They couldn't read Middle English.

"These have to be translated as soon as you can," Ginny said.

"Sure, as soon as I get a spare moment in between running for my life, I'll commission it."

"I'm not kidding. Could Agnes read these?"

"I don't know. Maybe. I don't remember. She might have been translating as she read these to me for all I know."

She went back to the book they had first grabbed off the shelf. "Let's see if Meriodoc mentions the bad guys." She began thumbing, scanning fast.

"Here." She began reading again.

" 'If we only knew how they draw their power, our counter might be more effective. The writings are vague on this point. Of course, light counters darkness. It's as true metaphysically as much as it is in the natural realm. But what does it mean? How do I use this knowledge?

“ ‘Light—there are several sources of it in nature, but metaphysically there is only one source. Reading others’ thoughts in the writings there seems to be quite a lot of speculation into the natural realm and the Black mantle, our power base as it were. But I am a theologian, not a scientist like our Cambridge friend, Whewell, who coined last year that curious term.’ ”

Ginny pointed to the next section. “He’s getting to something here.” She read on.

“ ‘But our enemies are not interested in the natural realm, in light. They seem to manifest the darkness, the vast emptiness beyond or maybe the *dark* as in the metaphysical sense.’ ”

She stopped. “Is there anything here we can use?”

Harry shrugged. “Vague. It’s enough to give me a headache.”

“I wish Agnes were here to tell us.”

“Me too.” Harry stared at the antique grandfather clock stationed near them. “Almost one thirty.” He yawned. “Looks like we can spend days searching through these and only scratch the surface.”

“And we have to. They’re important. You have to read every one of these that you can and get the others translated. There’s something here. I know it.”

“As soon as I can, I’ll start.”

She closed the book, careful to mark the spot she had been reading. They marched up the stairs holding hands. He showed her to the spare bedroom in his wing. It had its own bath and was fully stocked with all the things she would need. He went back to the door, Ginny close on his heels.

“You’ll be okay?” he asked, turning to her.

“I think so.”

"Call if you need help, but we're safe here."

"You sure?"

"Yeah, but there's a couch in my room." He hesitated. "You can have the bed if it will make you feel safer. I promise to be a perfect gentleman."

She gave him a tired smile. "I'm fine."

They had been through so much in such a short time it was a wonder she still looked so magnificent. He turned to leave, but stopped when she touched his arm.

"It's just that—" She hesitated. "All those years ago when we first met, I didn't think much of you."

"I don't blame you. I was pretty self-absorbed. Still am, you might say, but the events of the last few hours ought to straighten me out, don't you think?"

She chuckled at his small joke. "I know now how hard you had it. It's just…I'm sorry for what I said today, the accusations I made. You're a lot different now than the kid I met, or even the man I met at the party a few short weeks ago."

He thought about it a moment. "Yeah, I suppose I am."

"I know that now. Thanks for everything you've done for us." Her eyes widened. Harry expected her to come closer, but she pulled herself together. "You saved Bill. I'll never forget that."

She lifted her face to his and lightly kissed his lips.

He closed his eyes and when she withdrew he lingered that way for a moment. Opening them, he found Ginny examining him, her eyes searching, as if she could see his soul. What she might find there, he couldn't be sure, but it didn't seem to repulse her. He figured she hadn't expected him to respond to the kiss, not tonight. That wasn't the purpose of it, but it felt like the start of something between them. Embarrassed for the first time after a woman's kiss, all he could do was look down at his shoes.

He found her eyes again, but Harry and Ginny just stared at each other for what seemed like minutes. Finally, she took a step back. "Goodnight, Harry," she said simply.

As she did, he reached out for her hand and gave it a moment's squeeze before stepping backward into the corridor as she gently closed the door.

Before entering his room a few doors down, Harry walked to the end of the corridor where the grand window allowed a view to the back of the property. The waxing moon hung low over the woods. He remembered those screams from the nightmare he'd been having. The screams originated in those woods. He didn't know if it was his new senses developing, but he felt certain of it. He still didn't know if the woman was real. How could she be? It was only a dream.

Meriodoc Black's words came to him, strangely disconnected as the thoughts were. Light and darkness, an age-old juxtaposition. Good and evil. The power base of the Black Protectors versus that of the sorcerers. He hadn't mentioned it to Ginny, but he'd grasped something of what Meriodoc said in his writings.

Stars crowned the night sky in a sea of sparkle. They would have been brighter if not for the light of the waxing moon. Did Clan Black really draw from these sources as Meriodoc suggested? Harry rubbed the back of his neck thinking about it, exhaustion eating at him. He had no real understanding what the hell Meriodoc Black, the last Protector, had been trying to say, but Harry knew his life depended on finding out.

Chapter 25

Sometime between the last bite of omelet they had whipped up after midnight and the moment his head rose off the pillow at seven the next morning, he had forgotten a beautiful guest resided in the bedroom down the hall. Despite the horrors of the previous day, he slept well. Maybe it was the kiss that settled him. Maybe it was the promise of more to come.

As usual, there had been a dream, but nothing to do with a screaming woman and people engaged in orgies of sadomasochism. Instead, in his dream, he was four years old again, flying in a plane when a face appeared in the clouds, laughing, taunting him. Unlike his usual nightmare, he knew what this one must be about. It was strange. He'd never dreamt of that fateful day when the plane crash on the Mississippi coast killed his parents. Agnes had informed him years later how terrible the crash had been. His parents' decimated bodies couldn't be identified. How had a scrawny kid survived?

He finally remembered Ginny when she poked her head in, announcing breakfast. Wrapped in one of Agnes's old robes, she reminded him of his meeting with Jones, something about becoming the newest billionaire in the western hemisphere. And if that wasn't enough to jog his brain into action, those long legs she couldn't fully cover did the trick.

Those legs had woken other parts of him too, but it

was something he couldn't deal with just yet, especially when Jones's lined face popped up in his mind.

No relationships for you, boy. You'll just get her killed.

People turning up dead or missing had a sobering effect on any such thoughts. The one woman he could be interested in and he should be pushing her away. The alternative wouldn't be the same slit throat Peggy received, a relatively quick death for her, but not for someone who had saved his life. It would be much worse.

He walked to his window buttoning a shirt, Ginny and his missing friend on his mind. He'd called Jack's cell earlier and didn't receive an answer. He contacted Jack's office, but he wasn't expected until later. Calling Boone right after, he'd been told that they had an APB out on Jack, standard procedure for a missing murder suspect.

Peggy's body had been found in a dumpster next to Jack's complex. The blood proved a match. Three dead bodies in Mississippi, many more in Washington, and it was apparently up to him to stop it. And the only thing the local boys could contribute to solving this mess was to hound one homegrown lawyer.

****

Harry had on his best dark-gray suit with a red power tie as they left the mansion. They made a detour to Ginny's house. She needed a fresh change of clothes. When she appeared in a sleek, black dress appropriate for the funeral, his heart nearly stopped.

Her red lips parted into a shy smile when she noticed how awkward he'd become.

Driving her new granite-colored Lexus LS 460,

because the Mustang was no longer capable of keeping them fresh in this Mississippi heat, they arrived at First National at nine o'clock. Thirty minutes later the sum total of the estate, including all real property and holdings, passed legally and fully binding into the hands of one Joseph Harry Black, Jr., now the richest man in Mississippi.

Harry sat mute during the whole affair, thinking about Jack and whether he could still be alive, silently willing the clock to tick faster. He needed to get back to the work the legacy had dumped on him, find his friend, and stop whoever had planted those bombs in Washington, setting in motion this whole mess. The transfer of the estate had become only one more thing to be squeezed in, as though your bank account swelling to billions was just another mundane transaction in an otherwise ho-hum morning.

Without Ginny, it would have been worse. She reminded him he had an ally in this game of life and death. He knew she was vulnerable, knew he shouldn't expose her to more danger, but Ginny needed him in Brookhaven within the hour. If she felt loyal to him, it was his duty to respond in kind. After all, it was his stupid ecstatic utterance that had gotten her into this mess.

With the documents signed and all the accounts under his control, there was one last thing for him to do before they left for the funeral and the meeting with her brother. Harry told her he needed a few minutes with Jones so she made herself comfortable in a leather chair in the anteroom and gave Harry's hand a reassuring squeeze.

He reentered the boardroom where the transfer had

taken place. Jones was still there, talking to the banker, one old friend to another. Stanley Smith gave Harry a look that spoke volumes. How would this upstart handle the estate now that Jones, that old war horse, was out of the picture?

Harry didn't waste any time. "Thanks for your help, Stan. Couldn't have done it without you." It wasn't true, and they all knew it. "So far I've lived a pretty quiet life." Jones's eyebrows shot up. Harry had yet to tell him any of the events of the previous day from the time they'd left his house, but Jones knew someone had tried to kill him the night before. "I'd like to keep it that way as much as possible. So I'd appreciate it if what just occurred remained out of the press."

Stanley Smith gave Strom a quick glance. "But surely you don't expect to remain anonymous with your newfound wealth."

"I will if you keep your mouth shut. And if you can't, I'll take my accounts elsewhere, all of them. I promise. That's 300 million from this bank alone. I don't want to see my name in the *Financial Times*, or *Wall Street Journal*, or even the local papers."

"Do you even plan to remain in the area?" Smith asked.

Harry turned to Jones. "I feel safe at the mansion, for now." Jones gave him a small, knowing nod. "The setup we have will remain in the short term. I'll let you know through my attorney, Jack Hallowell, if we'll be using your institution over the long haul. Until then, I have to clear up some things—" He glanced at Jones again. "—and then we'll see."

Smith's head swiveled from Jones to Harry and

back again, apparently not knowing whether to thank Harry or lecture him about sound banking practices and why First National was the only choice for him, dammit.

"I need a word with Strom," Harry said dismissively, "so if you don't mind."

Smith nodded stiffly and left.

The moment the door closed Jones spun on him. "Damn, boy, that man has been good to your family for many years. Show him a little respect."

"I don't like condescension, okay? And he was full of it. Besides, I meant what I said. Jack and I will decide the final disposition of the accounts."

"Just like that, huh?"

"Just like that."

Jones walked back to the table and sat with some effort. "Where is Hallowell anyway? He should have been here this morning, gloating."

"He's tied up."

Jones gave him the little smirk he used when he knew Harry was lying. "Hope you know what you're doing." He nodded toward the door. "And drop the girl. You'll get her hurt, or worse."

"Believe me when I say I fully agree with you." He ran his hand through his hair. "What I need now is for you to explain a few things."

"What things?" Jones glanced at his watch. "My plane leaves for Hawaii in an hour."

Harry sighed heavily. "To hell with Hawaii. I might need you."

Jones shrugged as if to say, so what? Harry could see the amusement dancing at the corners of his mouth. "Sure doesn't sound like you need me. You seem to have it all worked out."

"Yeah, well, this has nothing to do with the money. There are some developments from overnight."

Jones glanced at the door and his smile widened.

"Take your mind out of the gutter. I'm talking about the Black family legacy. Brick Taylor, one of Boone's boys, tried to murder Ginny and me after we left your place. We barely escaped. Peggy Cox—you know my assistant—was murdered in Jack's apartment sometime yesterday. Jack's a suspect and now he's missing."

During his recounting of this story, Jones watched Harry with unwavering eyes. For the amount of concern he displayed for Jack, Harry could have been reciting a grocery list.

"What do you want from me that I haven't spent the better part of my life doing for your family? I can't help you with this. You have to find your own way." Jones stopped, took out a large white handkerchief, and began wiping his forehead. "You should have listened more, boy. Now you're in a real pickle."

"I'm not asking you to take an active part. You know things about other Protectors, things I should have been thinking about all these years to prepare myself better. I need to know what you know, everything you know. Maybe there's something that'll help me stay alive one more day. They're looking for Jack now as a suspect in the murder, but I know he didn't do it."

Jones eyebrows arched. "How do you know?"

"I can't go into it right now." Harry shifted and hesitated a moment, not knowing how to proceed. "Listen, the Grigori showed themselves to Ginny and me, and—"

"Damn, boy, she's involved way more than she ought to be, and this involves her brother and larger issues neither you nor I can fathom right now. If you drag her in any further, they'll surely use it to their advantage." He stopped and his scowl worsened. "Odds are she's as good as dead already."

Harry's throat suddenly went dry. He knew Jones was probably right. "It's a little late for that. She's involved. I tried to get her to go home last night, to pull out, but she wants to help." Harry stared at the closed door, thinking of Ginny. "Look, I see your point. Now they're attacking people I care about who had no part in this thing, murdering them. I'm not going to let that happen to her."

"You like her. If you want to protect her, make her see that she needs to end this thing with you before it starts."

"It's already started, Strom. I need help. My predecessors must have had something they used to protect people with this supernatural crap going on. I don't know, maybe some kind of offensive weapon."

"And you think I know what it is?"

"You listened to Agnes. She knew, right?"

Jones sagged a little and shook his head. "My boy, the last Protector operated way back in the early nineteenth century. Yes, stories got passed down, but they get changed over time until they resemble legend more than actual fact. There's a semblance of truth, yes, but who is to know for sure? Certainly not Agnes. She was born ninety years after poor Meriodoc died a horrible death."

This time it was Harry's turn to sit down.

"Of course, she had most of the history right, but you have to remember Black Protectors acted alone. Very few people actually observed them at work, knew what they did, how they fought. And not all of them were alike. For example, not all of them had the Grigori. You should take heart in that. They've kept you alive once; they'll do it again. Of course, on the flip side, they're probably only here because this will be a particularly bad outbreak."

"Thanks for the rosy picture."

"My pleasure." Jones walked around the end of the table where Harry was sitting and placed a hand on his shoulder. "There is something you should know, though I can't know how it might prove useful. Remember when I told you the story of Meriodoc Black. How he died? The person who arranged the whole thing was his brother, your great, great grandfather."

Harry's chest tightened.

"Oh, he wasn't a traitor. He did it to save the family. Meriodoc, bless him, went along willingly, something Black Protectors have been known to do from time to time. For the greater good, you understand. As memory serves, a truce had been called. The sorcerers were nearly beaten, but the Blacks were no better off, and by some accounts worse off. The two sides called it quits rather than have their clans utterly destroyed. To make sure it would be final, the principals gave their lives so the age-old conflict could end. That was the plan anyway, but we know it wasn't to be. The truce lasted until yesterday when those bombs went off in Washington."

Harry stood and squared off with Jones, eye to eye. "How the hell is this story supposed to help me?"

Jones shrugged and walked to the door. Instead of leaving, he turned back to Harry. “I picked up on what you told Stan earlier, about feeling safe at the mansion. You ought to, you know. It’s holy ground.”

Jones pierced him with those dark eyes, but before Harry could blurt out any more questions, the old lawyer left the room.

Chapter 26

Harry found Ginny sitting as patiently as she could in the anteroom, looking at her watch and tapping her sleek, black shoes on the thick carpet. After he apologized for making them late, they hit the road. Luckily, the state troopers were scarce, so Ginny zipped the Lexus over the expressway and transitioned to I-55 where she gunned it to ninety miles an hour.

They sped south toward Brookhaven, a sleepy little community with the railroad that gave it birth running right through the town. It had once delivered Mississippi cotton and timber to markets up north, but that was many decades ago. Ginny drove them through the downtown area in search of Carl Dunbar's mother's residence in a quaint section noted for a sprinkling of Victorian houses. The Dunbars were an old Brookhaven family, and the matriarch of the family wouldn't have her youngest boy laid out in some nondescript parlor at some fancy funeral home for what those directors charged.

Ginny located South Chippewa Street and stopped on the opposite side in front of a large white house with a wrap-around porch and six square columns, each stretching to the ceiling beneath lifelike floral carvings. Harry stared at the house. It wasn't Black Manor, but it had its charms. Azaleas grew thick and colorful along the tall porch and flanked both sides of the wide steps.

A huge, centered gable provided focus to the place. Three bay windows upstairs opened onto a small balcony overlooking the street. At the center window stood a big man in a dark suit watching over them and the houses beyond. Guards of some sort, here to protect the senator from terrorists stalking Mississippi. The thought of terrorists in Mississippi would have seemed silly a short time ago, but not now. The hairs on the back of his neck prickled. As they crossed the street, he searched the yard only to find the requisite activity for this type of gathering—somber-looking people dressed in their Sunday best.

Ginny had been on the phone with her brother and Carl Dunbar's widow during most of the trip down. At her urging and using his clout as a United States Senator, Bill Rankin had gotten Sheriff Boone to keep quiet on the ongoing investigation concerning the circumstances of Dunbar's death. She hadn't disclosed to her brother why this was important. All the senator knew was that Carl had had a heart attack. He trusted his sister and she convinced him that she had a good reason to be cryptic. Apparently, Sheriff Boone hadn't confided in the senator his suspicions that Dunbar had planned to murder Harry Black. It was Harry's doing, a favor he collected from Boone to remain quiet on the Brick Taylor affair.

The sheriff had jumped at the chance to keep that bit of bad press away from his department. Harry in turn would be able to keep the senator in the dark until he and Ginny had a chance to speak to him.

Since he was stepping right into the heart of the Dunbar family to meet the senator, Harry wanted everyone to remain ignorant of what had been happening in Mississippi—things he suspected were tied to the bombing. No sense making this meeting any more difficult than it had to be. For all the Dunbars knew, he was Dr. Virginia Rankin's latest flame. He'd picked up some whispers advocating this hypothesis as he and Ginny walked through the front yard. Curious onlookers directed their gaze his way. The speculation made him smile.

A man in a dark suit and dark glasses wearing an earpiece stood at the front door passing a wand metal detector over everyone entering the house. Two teenage girls were giggling, pointing at the secret service agent who looked to be in his mid-twenties. These weren't just hired help. The president must have felt the senator needed protection, even here.

Ginny slowed their walk. She knew Harry had the Beretta stuck in the back waistband of his slacks hidden by the coat.

"This won't work," she said under her breath as they climbed the steps. She fumbled with her purse and pressed the lock release on her key chain. Across the street the Lexus chirped. "I'll wait here while you stash it in the car."

Harry didn't answer. He'd spotted two shadows on the ceiling of the porch. He nodded toward them.

"Here?" she said. "In daylight?"

"I guess it's not a problem for them."

He stopped on the top step when a younger couple sprinted up. After a quick exchange, she grabbed his arm. "I need you inside with me. Get rid of it."

"I'm not about to leave the gun, especially after yesterday. I have a plan."

Her eyes were pools of questions. She tried to pull

him closer, but he was already moving toward the Grigori where they had slithered to the far end of the porch. He stood under them and looked around. No one was watching so he craned his neck and stared directly up at the two quivering shadows.

He had no idea if his plan would work, but it was the only way to get past the guard with the gun. The night before, after his experience in Jack's bedroom and the sickening pall that had been cast over the place had lifted, he'd tried to communicate with them, and it seemed to have worked. They responded to him, and now he had a thought along those lines.

They were essences of his ancestors. Sentient, intelligent souls glued together and manifested somehow to help him in his role as Protector. But were they connected to him on a plane beyond the physical? Could there be some kind of psychic link that would allow communication?

Since entering the property his senses had been on high alert. Something unknown, something new told him he needed his gun inside the house. The only way to get it inside was for the Grigori to help. Thinking of them now sent a cold shiver down his spine. They could inflict physical damage on a person, damage enough to kill, but could they do other things?

He lifted his head to the ceiling and stared into the deep black shadows, trying to clear his mind. It wasn't easy, but when he finally settled and closed his eyes, his breathing and pulse rate slowed. He could sense the thoughts he had wanted to project leaving him as though a conduit had suddenly been opened, a bond between his mind and the Grigori. They were absorbing what he needed them to know, absorbing one idea. Get him in the house with the gun. This was a new day, and he didn't plan to be defenseless again, not with Brick's brains splattered over the doors of that changing room etched in his memory.

He relaxed and turned to find Ginny standing next to him with a puzzled look on her face.

"What are you doing?"

"You'll see."

There was no one at the door now, so he ambled over and stood before the guard. Harry raised his eyes to the porch ceiling in time to find the Grigori hovering above the agent.

The young guard, a big fella with shoulders impossibly broad, stood there bored and yawning. He began to lift the wand but wavered and put his arm back down. The Grigori had made a sudden move and were now streaming down in one long slither of shadow to the top of the man's head where they disappeared into his skull. Harry looked beyond the man into the house, but no one was watching.

He had expected something like this because of what they had done to Carl Dunbar. He didn't want them to kill this man and had tried to communicate that as well. The man's pupils dilated and he swayed a bit. His eyes closed for a full five second count. When he opened them they had changed color from sky blue to a dull gray.

It was like they had opened to a world the agent had never seen before. He dropped the wand he'd been loosely holding and snapped back to Harry with obvious recognition.

"The world has changed since my day, lad."

It was a British accent Harry knew this secret

service agent didn't possess. He'd caught snippets of the man's conversation earlier.

"Thy dai…" Another voice spoke from the mouth of the agent, a much older man, but speaking in a thick accent, some form of early English. "Assaie thou eft fro thousand yeres slep to comen."

Harry glanced at Ginny as the agent grew conflicted, as though an internal war had ensued.

"You're speaking gibberish to his ear, man," another voice said. "This be the twenty-first century we're standing in."

The agent's eyes widened as the older persona took charge again. "Right…quite right. I forget myself. Sorry, my boy. I can converse in the modern tongue, you know, but the words of my day sound so good after a thousand year sleep."

Harry wanted to say something to Ginny standing beside him, but another voice stopped him.

"My, I'd forgotten already how lovely Ginny is, Joey dear." Agnes's voice now issued from the young agent. "I approve wholeheartedly."

A scowl formed on the agent's face. "Of course, that's just the mother in me talking. Your relationships must always remain superficial. Calm your lust if you will and move on for your safety and hers." The agent shook his finger at him. "No long term attachments for Black Protectors. That's the rule and you ought to follow it."

The agent stepped toward Ginny, took her hand, and began stroking it.

"Agnes?" Ginny said. "I can't believe this is happening."

"I hear my grandson saved Bill. Excellent. I told

the boy it would happen, didn't I, son?"

Harry could only nod.

The guard frowned and turned to look inside the house. "To move again, to feel, to *breathe*." He took a deep breath and turned back to Harry. "Can you slip me a cigarette?"

"You know I don't smoke, Grandmother."

"No? Well…" The agent licked his lips and sighed. "Back to business then. Now that you've discovered how we work, you don't have to waste any more time. This guard is asleep while we're here, so just move on through."

Harry hesitated. "Grandmother, I have so many—"

"Not now. Time to buck up and make us proud. Stop these sorcerous hooligans before they get started, you hear? We'll be close by, always. Now go before we damage this man. His nervous system won't handle much more. Oh, and tell Jonesy I think he's done an *excellent* job of things."

"Right," Harry said, embarrassed at the mention of Jones. He hadn't exactly treated him with much respect over the years.

They rushed past him and through the door before the agent regained his senses. Once in the foyer, Harry glanced back at the guard who was busy trying to bum a smoke off an older gentleman. He got one, lit it, and threw back his head with the first deep draw.

"Still think I'm hallucinating?" Harry asked Ginny. They were standing next to a granite-topped table where a guest book lay open ready for their signatures.

"It's unbelievable," Ginny whispered. "I'd know that voice anywhere. It was really her."

He glanced at the ceiling, but the Grigori were

nowhere to be seen. He turned back to face the opening of the spacious room. Dozens of people were milling about, the atmosphere somber, but not morbid. Being from good Episcopal stock, Gladys Dunbar wouldn't let the house sink into a morose state. Good Christian decorum was called for, Southern style. There would be no wailing here today, only silent tears and cheerful thoughts for her son going off to meet his maker. A happy time.

Harry bent over and signed the guest book after Ginny, and together they merged with the crowd.

"Oh, there you are, sweet thing," a plump lady said, rushing up to Ginny. "And who is this young man you have here?"

"This is Harry Black, a friend." As Gladys Dunbar took his hand, her grip weak, Ginny continued. "It was such a shock to learn about Carl. You know how much he meant to Bill and me."

"Yes, yes, we all knew. It's too bad, but he's in a better place now, so no frowns today. Lord knows I'll see my boy again soon enough. Anyway, enough of that. I never approved of his avocation into politics. I think that killed him more than anything. But don't take me the wrong way, dear. He cherished Bill and was happier for it, though it was undoubtedly a rough business. And Washington—oh, don't get me started. I knew his constitution wasn't good. I certainly knew he wouldn't hold up well."

Ginny nodded dutifully through all this while Harry eyed the long table beyond the arched entry to the large dining room. Two more men in dark suits and earpieces stood there eating and watching the crowd, their heads on a swivel. More guards.

Harry had counted four so far. He knew they wouldn't normally be accompanying senators on trips back to the home state, but this senator had been a target. And by the number of agents sent to Mississippi to protect him, someone obviously believed him to still be in danger. Would four even be enough? The people after him had demonstrated a very long reach, assuming they were also responsible for the bombing, which he didn't doubt. The ingenuity of his enemies was foreign to anything the US Government would expect. There wouldn't be any secret service protocol to combat sorcery. That put Harry in good company. He didn't have the slightest clue how to fight them either. But at least now he could communicate with the Grigori, and that gave him a sense of hope.

Harry and Ginny had managed to catch up on the news late last night while eating before collapsing into their respective beds. Speculation as to the source of the bombing had been rampant, but everyone agreed it had been a Jihadist group. No less than three had already claimed responsibility. Harry figured their claims were lies, but he couldn't be absolutely sure. In the meantime, though, the government was busy expending resources tracking down these bogus confessions. A pretty good trick the bastards had played to sidetrack any suspicions the authorities may have been able to rightly place on the real perpetrators. Bottom line—the administration was being led to look in the wrong direction.

Ginny wrapped her long fingers around the fat hand of Gladys Dunbar. "I'm so sorry for your loss. Carl will be greatly missed."

The old lady patted her eye but grew cheerful again

as though putting on a mask. She offered them a cookie from a tray on a nearby table. "By all of us, dear, by all of us. I'm just glad I was able to rescue his body from the medical examiner. Something about an autopsy and an investigation. Dear me, I couldn't understand why since he'd only had a heart attack, so I convinced them it wasn't necessary, that I wanted his wake done as soon as possible. God was with me, because they relented." She stopped and bit into a cookie, looking off into the distance. "Bill is with Margaret right now, you know, in the room we've set up for viewing. He's been wondering where you are."

God could take the credit for Carl Dunbar's escape from the examiner's table, but Senator Bill Rankin was likely the immediate cause. Washington schedules didn't often wait for local technicalities, not when it involved one of their own.

Ginny nodded. "I'll go to him now."

When they entered the room where Dunbar's body lay, Harry scanned the space in one quick sweep. The open casket was on the far wall. He didn't spot any men in dark suits and serious looks. A blonde-haired lady sat to the right side of the room on the front row of fold-out chairs. A boy and a girl sat on either side of her. A man, taller than Harry, stood holding her hand—an older, male version of Virginia Rankin. It was her brother, Bill.

Senator Rankin lifted his head and spotted Harry and Ginny making their way down one side of the column of fifty or more chairs sparsely taken by guests. He kissed Dunbar's wife on the cheek. After whispering something in her ear, he straightened and met Ginny as they made it to the front row, near the casket.

Ginny gave her brother a long hug, fighting to hold back tears. There wasn't time for them while running for her life as the ugly events unfolded the previous day. When they separated, Bill Rankin held her at arm's length, checking her out.

She tried to explain to him over the phone on the car ride down what had taken place after she and Harry met with Strom Jones. She kept important details back, details like the fact that they both could be dead right now.

Senator Rankin searched Harry's face over her shoulder, but his gaze didn't carry the gravity it should have.

"Mr. Black," Rankin said. He stepped closer to Harry, just like an old chum would. "Ginny seems awfully anxious for us to meet today. We must have a serious discussion one day soon about the state of affairs in this country. Maybe take back up where we left off at the party. Agnes would have wanted us to become friends and maybe get as close as she and I were."

Harry nodded. He wasn't here to be glad-handed by a politician. They hadn't divulged anything to Rankin, fearing he wouldn't take them seriously. Now it was time to make him see. Harry was hopeful he might learn something in the process that would help him make sense of the events unfolding.

But they had to get Rankin alone first and away from his handlers.

"Good to see you again, sir," Harry said, holding out his hand.

The senator took it and Harry nearly collapsed. The stench of death met him like a thick, ugly cloud.

Chapter 27

Death crept upon Harry, nearly choking him, followed by a strong static charge. Harry jerked his hand away as an electric jolt hit him square in the chest. Ginny yelped and jumped back.

“What the hell was that?” Bill Rankin said, rubbing his hands and face.

The hairs at the back of Harry’s neck prickled. He spun back to the room and noticed a man in a white dress shirt, no tie. Harry hadn’t seen him before.

The man in the white shirt rose calmly from the back row and walked to the doorway where he stopped and looked back at Harry.

“Who is that man?” Harry said, ignoring the senator’s question.

Bill Rankin followed his gaze. “Fred Savage, my new chief-of-staff.” There was a thin man sitting on the back row near the door writing furiously on a note pad. “He’s replacing Carl and insists on working on the speech I was to give yesterday.”

Harry followed the senator’s stare, but Bill Rankin wasn’t looking at the man standing behind Savage. “Not him,” he said. “The man in the doorway.”

The man was now smiling at Harry, and when he turned to leave, he shimmered and was gone. He’d simply vanished. Harry nearly choked as he tried to swallow.

"Are you okay?" Ginny said, touching his arm.

They hadn't seen what just happened. He wiped away a bead of sweat running down his brow. "No, I'm not. Look." He pulled Ginny's arm into an urgent grasp, making her focus. "Brief your brother about what's been happening. And don't leave this room. I'll tell those two agents stuffing themselves at the table to get their asses in here."

He turned to leave, but Ginny stopped him. "What's this about?"

Harry shook his head. "Trouble. Just stay put. When they get here, tell the agents to do their job and protect your brother. He's in danger." He gave the senator a brief look. "And don't let him wander from this spot. I'll be right back—I hope."

Harry spotted the man walking casually through the front door and onto the porch. He followed him, but the man had already rounded the side of the house. Harry quickly scanned the front yard. Kids were tossing a football. He turned the corner of the house where a thick stand of crepe myrtle had showered the rich lawn with pink petals.

He cleared the last of the branches and almost ran into the man's raised hand. He had his palm out. Distorted air seemed to be emanating from it. The wave hit Harry square in the chest, stopping him.

"There," the man said. "Close enough."

He still had the stupid smile on his face. There was the beginning of a tattoo, a web design starting high on both sides of his neck. And Harry noticed something else. Evil. He could "smell" the same stench he'd picked up in Jack's apartment and, again, just a moment ago on the senator. It saturated the man. Harry grimaced, wishing he had a drink to wash away the stink, so thick he could taste it like a sour burning menagerie of oils.

Harry's hand went reflexively to the gun at the small of his back.

"No, no," the man said, shaking a finger. "I am only a messenger, and you must not shoot the messenger."

The pressure lifted and Harry let his arm fall to his side. "Who are you and how the hell are you doing that? You don't belong here. You have to leave."

"You do not need to know my name, but you are right when you say I do not belong here." He batted at a mosquito. "Damnable heat."

The accent was definitely northern European, probably Dutch from the Flemish region of Belgium. Harry had been there on more than one occasion for his job. The man pulled at the collar of his shirt. He was stocky without being overweight and wore his blond hair in a buzz cut.

"I know you have a gun stuck back there. I cannot help but wonder how you cleared security with it."

"I could ask the same of you."

"But I carry no visible weapon, only my skill in simple veils and some slight talent at other forms of aeromancy." He shrugged. "It is a small matter. But you," he shook his finger again, "be careful or I will gladly enlarge my role in this to your detriment and claim self-defense. My master will understand."

"Master?" Harry said. His fists clenched. He took a step toward the man. "Where have you taken Jack?"

"They said you had half a brain. Worked it out on your own, have you?" He chuckled and gave Harry a small bow. “I must beg off supplying any details of the capture. It is not for me to say since I am only a foot soldier.”

“If you lay a finger on him, I’ll—”

“Come now, Mr. Black, you have been on the job for all of a day while we have bided our time for more than a century. What will you do? Your skills are fledgling. You are a pup yet, a mere babe that has been warned twice already. This is your third time. Consider the very personal nature of this warning a compliment.”

“For what?”

“For the past. For the respect other Protectors have earned for themselves. We do them honor now by talking directly to you. Just this once. My master wishes to tell you that we can be civil. This is, after all, the twenty-first century. The playing field is much more subtle than before, less need for bloodshed.”

“Tell that to the bomb victims and their families in DC.”

“So you have made that connection, too.” His smile faded. “Well, connect this. This matter is none of your affair. There need be no more unnecessary deaths. The time has come for the silly differences between our clans to be put aside. You live your life and we go about our business.”

“What is your business…exactly?”

He waved his hand as if the question wasn’t important. “The world has gotten far too complicated. We want to make it less so. To do that, the big players must be taken down a notch or two. You are being given a choice, Black. We have shown you what we can do. If you want to see your friend again, do what we say.”

What they could do? Harry knew the answer to that. Turn people. Rape and murder women. Kidnap his friends. His heart beat faster, thinking of Peggy's slit throat.

"And the senator?" Harry nodded toward the house. "You tried to kill him in the bombing, didn't you?"

The smile left the man's face altogether. He stiffened. "A job to be completed at a later date, I assure you."

Harry tried to swallow, but his mouth and throat were dry. "I thought so."

"You are a very wealthy man now, thanks to your family. Live—enjoy it. Stay out of our way."

Harry glanced at the house. The information he somehow knew about Senator Rankin meant Rankin was a first class jerk. But, dammit, Ginny loved her brother and she had not only saved Harry, she wanted to keep helping him. He wanted to talk to Bill Rankin, needed to take the measure of the man. Worthy or not, Harry intended to help Rankin for Ginny's sake.

These bastards were also attempting some kind of takedown of the American Government. Details were scarce, but some answers were likely inside with the senator. If Harry could help in this sphere, he would try to stop these sonsofbitches.

"Don't think I can do that," Harry said. 'You can't take down our government so easily."

"Oh, we do not want to take it down. We want to change it. There will be a United States when we are through, just not one quite so strong." He laughed. "The world will be better for it."

"Doubt it."

The man laughed. "You forget your friend. He and others you know will be dead unless you back off."

Harry glared at him.

"What is it with your cursed clan? We have seen this obstinate trait before, but in your case it is—"

He stopped and stared past Harry.

"You recognize them, don't you?" Harry glanced back over his shoulder. The twin shadows hovered ten feet above his head; a dark flickering that could almost be dismissed as a trick of the sun shining over a tree limb. "I'm told it's been some time since your kind has seen them?"

The man's cockiness wilted. He took a step back. "We were told they were here."

"Told? By who?"

He sneered and muttered something in a language Harry didn't understand. "You are too weak to control them, Black. You will regret this decision, mark my word."

"Don't think that's true either."

"Fool, we will see about that."

As he said it, the man's voice took on a hollow quality, as though emanating from a deep well. He began to shimmer and fade, but the Grigori were too quick. They flashed over to him, and before the man could become wholly invisible, he solidified. His eyes widened before he collapsed.

Don't kill him. Confident now in his ability to communicate with the shadows, another idea popped into his head. *Can you move him*? The answer came immediately and he nodded. *How far?* He smiled. *Good, take the bastard to Black Manor. Holy ground should take the bite out of him. Put him in the basement and watch him closely. I'll be back in a couple of hours, and we'll find out if he's lying about not knowing where Jack is.*

Chapter 28

Harry hurried back to the house and noticed Bill Rankin conferring with his chief-of-staff in the viewing room. They were removed from the Dunbar family who had congregated near the casket. Two secret service agents stood on both ends of Rankin's row, watching the door and the steady stream of visitors entering and leaving.

Ginny stood next to Dunbar's widow and her children, their heads bent together, both shedding silent tears. She noticed Harry first. Margaret Dunbar stared up at Ginny, but quickly wiped at her tears when Harry drew close.

"Maggie, this is my friend, Harry Black—Agnes's grandson."

"Oh, yes," Margaret Dunbar said. "It was good of you to accompany Ginny all the way to Brookhaven."

Harry took her hand, but before he could say anything Gladys Dunbar burst into the little group with Bill Rankin on her arm. She pulled Margaret and her children aside, explaining that they were nearly ready for a brief service to begin.

Harry motioned for Ginny and her brother to follow him. He led them to the left side of the room far away from the nearest of the Dunbars. "Where did you go?" Ginny whispered as her brother's chief-of-staff drew near.

Harry knew the questions would start, but this wasn't the place to ask them. "Is there anywhere we can talk, away from all these people?" He gave a conspiratorial nod in the senator's direction. "We were being watched, and I can't tell who else might be around."

Rankin exchanged a quick glance with his sister then turned to the agent who had been following him. "Sir, there's a huge back porch. Special Agent Trower's stationed in the upstairs bedroom at the rear of the house. He just reported in"—he tapped his earpiece to emphasize the point—"and says all's clear out back. That area might work best. I think it's empty right now."

Rankin nodded. "Tell Agent Trower and the rest of the team."

The agent named Piper turned away and began speaking into his lapel. He also notified Agent Shultz and the young agent at the front door.

Four ceiling fans made the screened-in porch bearable for short periods of time. The men quickly rid themselves of their coats, except for Harry who would have trouble explaining how he'd gotten the Beretta past security.

Shultz positioned himself in the doorway leading to the house with Piper at the screen door leading from the porch, both far enough removed to keep private the words spoken by Rankin and Savage, most of them anyway. The big men were wiping sweat away in seconds.

Rankin's new chief-of-staff, Fred Savage, had followed them to the porch. He was a nervous sort, about five feet ten with not enough weight to remain standing in a stiff wind. He had a red nose, probably from heavy drinking. Harry could tell he wasn't the kind of man to let just anyone have time with this prime piece of political commodity that was Senator William Rankin.

A black iron patio table with four matching chairs sat at one end of the porch. Savage took the chair with his back to the sun, glowering at Harry sitting across from him. "What's this nonsense about someone watching us?" he said. "This place is obviously secure." He gave a sharp, aggravated look at Rankin and threw his hands up. "I'm too busy for this shit, you know. I've had to rewrite the speech entirely due to the damn bombing and it still needs some work."

"I know, Fred, but Ginny thinks this is important so—"

"Ginny thinks—" Savage took a deep breath. "Look, with all due respect to your sister—" He cut his eyes to her and rolled them back to the senator. "—I make your schedule. Our time is too valuable to be giving conspiracy nuts an ear, family friend or not. We'll be here about an hour longer." He checked his watch. "Then we're off. The Dunbars want a private gravesite service anyway, so it'll give us an extra hour, tops." He turned his attention to Harry. "You can have ten minutes, Mr. Black. Let's hear your story."

Oh, boy. Harry needed a private hearing with the senator, because the information he knew about his personal life was just too sensitive. And according to Ginny, only the two of them knew what Harry now knew. That left this blow-hard Savage out of the loop.

By the look on Ginny's face, she was thinking the same thing, and for that matter so was Senator Rankin, because he said, "Fred, I promised my sister some personal time here and it seems she wants her friend in on it. I'm afraid you're going to have to leave."

"But—"

"Sorry, that's the way it has to be. Why don't you go check on the progress being made with the ceremony and call me when they're ready? We shouldn't be long."

Savage's face turned as red as his nose. He gave Harry a sharp look and slid his chair back. He glanced at his watch. "Ten minutes, no longer."

They watched him stride off and Rankin suppressed a chuckle. "He wasn't my first choice to replace Carl, but he knows a ton of people in Washington and knows how to keep me on time. I apologize for that performance. Now tell me. What's going on?"

Rankin sat back in the chair, waiting. Harry kept folding and unfolding his hands on the table. He had no idea how to convince this man of the danger he was in. It was far more complicated than anyone suspected, not as simple as identifying a group of terrorists intent on disrupting government business using bombs. The more ordinary tools of the trade they could handle, but not sorcery. And that angle was a nonstarter. The senator wouldn't believe any of it. How could he and his handlers be convinced of something so far-fetched?

Ginny finally got right to the point. "Do you believe the reports identifying the bombing as the work of Islamic fundamentalists?"

Rankin waved his hand in a dismissive manner as though the answer was obvious. "Of course, I do. We have three groups claiming responsibility. It's just a matter of time before we narrow the list. Then we hit them where it hurts." He pounded his fist on the table. "Take the fight to them just like after Nine/Eleven. The president has promised me that much. He knows I was targeted along with poor Joe Russell and Samantha Pierce."

Harry and Ginny exchanged looks.

"Come on, Sis. I know you think it was Mr. Black who—"

"The name's Harry, Senator, just Harry. My father was Mr. Black. I figure I have a least twenty more years before Mr. will fit comfortably on me."

"Okay, Harry. Look, I don't doubt something happened that caused Ginny to make a phone call that delayed me. I'm a believer in providence, in God, if you will. I'm grateful for whatever part you played. Maybe it just wasn't my time, but to say that—"

"I know about you and Trolley, Senator."

Everyone froze as this bit of unwelcomed news sank in. Ginny sighed and put her face in her hands. Rankin's face paled, but he regained his composure like a seasoned politician who'd just been blindsided. His eyes narrowed to twin daggers, focusing on Harry as though he'd suddenly sprouted a second head.

"I see this level of betrayal in politics all the time," Rankin said to his sister, his words icy, "but for it to come from you? How could you do something like this? How could you tell him about Trolley?"

"Bill, you don't understand. You know I would *never*—"

"She never said a word to me about this, Senator. I can't hope to explain how I know things about your personal life, but I think you'd better listen, because this thing is bigger than you and your political career."

"You're blackmailing me, is that it?"

Harry wanted to laugh in his face at the ludicrous assertion. "Just this morning my bank account swelled to something north of twenty billion dollars." He noticed the look of surprise on Rankin's face. "That's right. I'm in control of the estate now. So if I wanted influence in the political arena all I'd have to do is spread a tiny fraction of it around."

The senator stood, the iron chair making an angry grating noise on the floorboards of the porch. His hand went to his forehead as he considered Ginny again. "If it wasn't you—" He stopped. "You said Trolley had kept quiet. Who could she have told?" He turned back to Harry. "Good Lord, who else knows? Where did you hear this?"

"Oh, Bill, how could you suspect Trolley? She loved you. She took her secret with her when she died in the abortion clinic."

"How the hell does he know something only you and I should know if Trolley kept it secret and you never told him? She had a fake ID for that clinic. No one knew her."

"Yesterday morning I wouldn't have thought it possible for anyone else to know, much less Agnes Black's grandson. Harry came to me for help. He'd been having trouble sleeping and horrible nightmares. We were talking—just talking. Then Harry sat up straight. His face lost all expression, and he looked like he was seeing into…into…I don't know…into infinity. Then he looked back at me, his eyes snapped into focus and he—this information about Trolley just came out. He *knew*, Bill, without learning it anywhere. He just knew."

"Just out of the blue, huh?"

Ginny reached out and grabbed his hand. "Please sit back down. You have to believe me. He knew about you and Trolley without having been told by anyone, without having read about it somewhere because no one else knows about it. No one knows this secret. Don't you see? Something beyond our control is happening here, maybe something supernatural. I've seen things in the past twenty-four hours that seem impossible to explain by reason or logic or science."

The senator pulled his hand away and turned his back on her.

Ginny continued talking. "I placed the call that saved you. Thanks to Harry, you're alive right now." She stood, grabbed his shoulders, and spun him to her. She locked her green eyes onto her brother's, struggling to make him understand. "What's happening now isn't isolated to DC. These people are here in Mississippi. Twice in the last twenty-four hours someone has tried to murder Harry and almost killed me. These aren't isolated incidents, and we're almost positive it's tied to the bombing. You need to make the president understand something else is happening here and it had nothing to do with radical fundamentalist groups."

She hesitated, having discussed her next words with Harry on the ride down from Jackson. They both knew this part was tricky. Her voice grew quieter. "Bill, it was Carl. He tried to kill Harry, and I was almost murdered, too, by a deputy sheriff when I became involved accidentally. They were being controlled."

At the mention of Carl Dunbar, her brother very nearly snarled out his next words. "What does this have to do with Carl? He never tried to kill anyone. What the hell are you talking about?"

Ginny grabbed both his shoulders and shook him. Harry rose from his seat and walked around the table to them. He placed a hand on her arm, and she broke off.

"It's too complicated to get into right now, Senator," Harry said. "But you have to know that Carl was compromised."

"All I know is something must have happened for him to leave Washington. I heard they found a gun. Are you say—"

"They got to him in some way, Senator. As far as we know, he might have been in on the bombing too, maybe passing information on to the people who did it."

"The bombing." Rankin studied the two people before him as though they weren't worthy of his attention. "You two are serious?" He broke off from them and started to turn but stopped short. "Carl, a terrorist? That's the craziest thing I've ever heard."

"I wish it weren't true, but it is," Ginny said. "Maybe not the terrorist part, but he's connected in some way."

Harry nodded. "Don't believe for a second they're Middle Eastern. The man I spotted earlier, the accent was Dutch."

Rankin just kept shaking his head. "The hell, they aren't. And what man are you talking about?"

Time was short now. The best way to move her brother was to make the matter most urgent with Ginny. "The Grigori took him to Black Manor—holy ground—understand?" Harry asked. She nodded. "He's one of them. I have to get back home and interrogate the bastard to find out where they've taken Jack and try to get to the bottom of the rest of it."

Harry looked at Rankin and could tell all of this was just insane talk to him. He was used to being in control and this new information had him as far out in left field as he could possibly go.

"What's he mumbling about, Ginny?" Rankin glanced at the door leading to the house. "I think it's time we got back inside."

Her face had turned red. "You have to listen to him before it's too late. I think you're their prime target. It was never about the others."

"Listen to what, some garbage about Carl being a murderer? Are you nuts?"

Ginny slapped him and both agents ran over to them. Unsure of the proper protocol to diffuse a brother/sister fight, they stood there like rabid dogs ready to pounce on the next thing that moved. Luckily, the slap had shocked Rankin into slowing things down. He stood there rubbing his face, staring at his sister, but that she would do such a thing unnerved him.

"Remember the night I became pregnant? I'd fallen in love with you months earlier."

The words, spoken softly, had come to them as though it had trickled down from a cloud, but something was terribly wrong. The voice didn't belong on this porch or even among the living for many years now. Ginny and her brother turned to Harry. It was illogical. Impossible. Ginny's hands shot to her mouth and color drained from Rankin's face.

"I wanted the baby, Bill, but you convinced me not to. Of course, your life was set—married five years, two kids already, bright political future. It was at our place in Bay St. Louis where you convinced me, remember? Far away from prying eyes. I listened and loved you. So I tried to have it done. I tried."

When Harry finished speaking, he stumbled into a chair, breathing heavily. Rankin backed away from him, trying to get as far away from his past as possible.

"Our place," Ginny said, latching onto the meaning in those words. "You mean the house on the bay her aunt had left her?"

Rankin nodded. "Not even you knew that."

Harry could see disappointment in Ginny's eyes. She lowered her head. Her brother had let her down all those years ago by not doing the right thing by her friend, by dismissing his cherished conservative principles and having the affair, then pushing her friend toward that abortion. Now a fresh wound had opened. Harry believed she'd forgiven her brother's indiscretion, but the senator wasn't making the situation better with his blatant self-preservation kicking in.

"Do you believe us now?" Ginny whispered.

Rankin didn't answer her question. Instead, he asked in a hard voice, "What *is* he?" Before either of them could answer, he growled to the agents. "Not a word of this or I'll have your badges." They reluctantly walked back to their previous positions.

Harry's breathing finally slowed and he was able to talk again. "What I am isn't important right now, but believe me when I say you're in danger. They're coming for you."

Harry pointed to the agents staring back at him. "Round up the others. We have to get the senator back to Jackson. I want a car in front and behind Ginny's car the entire way there."

The agents just stood there. Without taking his eyes off Harry, the senator nodded his approval. “Tell Trower we’ve got to move as soon as I’m done here. Twenty minutes—tops.”

That was enough for them to jump into action.

Chapter 29

The ceremony took about twenty minutes, as predicted. Harry kept watch at the door to the viewing room along with Shultz and Piper who weren't happy to be standing next to him. The senator's words were few but filled with emotion for his lost friend. Afterward, he politely said his goodbyes. They all filed out of the house to let the close-knit family grieve on their own. Rankin explained to his wife that something had come up. The best thing would be for her to remain with Dunbar's widow. Luckily, she didn't question him.

On the way back to Black Manor, Ginny told Bill everything. Harry listened from the backseat, still fuzzy-headed from the bit of crazy speech he'd exhibited earlier. He caught Rankin looking at him more than once through the vanity mirror above the dash. He wasn't surprised that Rankin hadn't bought much of the story even after the little display he had pulled off.

Rankin did ask plenty of questions, though, and more than once Harry could see him shaking his head as though it would help him make sense of what he was hearing. Things grew quiet during the last forty-five minutes of their trip to Black Manor. The senator seemed unconvinced by the story, and because Ginny had become a full-fledged believer in Harry, he sensed the senator had lost respect for her. Very quickly, Harry had become *persona non grata*. Placing herself at his side made her guilty by association.

Harry bristled, watching his reactions. Rankin was wrong. Given his moral failures, he didn't have a right to think less of her. But worse than that, Ginny didn't deserve any negative judgment because of what Harry was.

Rankin had been targeted by the blast. The feds obviously believed it; dispatching the secret service to guard him proved that point. Rankin had no idea of his vulnerability. His cocksure attitude was bolstered by the attention the president had provided in casting over him the aura of secret service protection. It was a kick in the old ego, being on the national stage like this.

But Harry was privy to information none of the good guys knew about. It was now certain the bomb had been meant for Rankin. White Shirt had told him as much. Harry knew Rankin was only the beginning, a small piece of a bigger pie, and that pie was the whole country. Their angle was the economy. Where Nine/Eleven had failed to bring it down, this bunch seemed to be attempting the same thing one small piece at a time, starting with the senior senator from Mississippi and the economic summit. The other casualties were collateral damage, a necessary waste to get the job done.

The long trip back to Black Manor was meant to change Rankin's attitude in the most dramatic way possible, bring him down from the clouds, make a believer out of him. It hadn't worked. Harry would have to introduce the good senator to his new house guest—the terrorist—part of this family of sorcerers the Black clan had been battling for over a millennium.

But he needed local support to do it, an ally of sorts, one with enough clout to help make Savage and Rankin listen. Sheriff Boone was just the man.

A simple text message to the sheriff's cell phone guaranteed all the players would be ready by the time they made it back to the mansion.

****

It was nearly six p.m. when three cars rolled to a stop in the circular drive. The sheriff's sedan was already situated directly in front of the broad steps leading to Black Manor. Boone paced at the front of his patrol car, sweating in the heat, his right hand resting on the holstered revolver. Five agents made smooth exits from the lead and rear cars followed by a jostled Fred Savage who Harry could hear spewing curse words in all directions. He had reluctantly agreed to ride with the agents in the front car, which was like pulling a mother from her infant son. The special agent in charge, Roger Trower, trotted back to the Lexus as Harry exited the backseat.

"I'm still unclear of the situation, sir," Trower said to Rankin. He was even larger than Sheriff Boone, and a lot younger and more muscled. Trower looked at Harry, unsure of what to make of him, no doubt due to the reports of Piper and Shultz.

The senator held up his hand. "There's apparently been some kind of threat. I gave the order to take us to this location. It's my responsibility."

Trower's face remained passive as he gave the place a quick scan. It was obvious he didn't like it one bit.

"With all due respect, sir, it's *my* responsibility. I realize we wouldn't normally be expected to secure this location as well as if we were on detail with the president." Trower looked from Rankin to the sheriff. "Considering his orders to keep the senator protected, I don't think this is a very good idea." He stopped and gave the mansion another once-over. "What is this place anyway?"

"My home," Harry said, coming around the end of the car after a quick conference with Boone. "It's the best place to be right now until we develop a plan."

"A plan?" Trower glanced back at Rankin. "Sir, I don't take orders from private citizens. And they sure as hell don't plan security details for me."

Harry watched the senator closely as Rankin paced off several steps. The agent had a point, but he hardly had all the information he needed to create a fully informed plan, information like the fact that certain nameless people could become invisible and sneak up on the senator, put a knife in his back, and be gone while the agents in charge of protecting him were busy staring off into the distance. For what they were up against, this place was probably more secure than the White House. Harry hoped so anyway.

Rankin spun back with a no-nonsense look Trower couldn't miss. "We're here for a reason I don't understand, but I promised my sister I would give her and Mr. Black some time."

"Listen, folks," Sheriff Boone said, "if it'll help, I can have a small contingent of deputies here in ten minutes to lend a hand. I'll be damned if I'm gonna let anything happen to Senator Rankin in my county."

After hesitating, Trower nodded. He barked off orders for his four men to check the perimeter of the place and fall back to the house to secure all entrances.

If there was a threat, he would damn well make sure it wouldn't be easy to get to the senate minority leader.

****

With the entrance to the drive secured with a parked patrol car and several deputies on constant watch roaming the grounds, Special Agent Trower, Sheriff Boone, Senator Rankin, Fred Savage, Ginny, and Harry entered the house with another thunderhead brewing in the distance.

With the storm rolling in fast, a disquieting note of precognition grew in Harry's soul. He was only one person. What could he do to stop this steamroller coming for them? The answer was nothing, but now at least he had plenty of guns at his disposal.

A muffled scream resounded through the mansion and everyone stopped walking. All heads turned to the house's owner.

Trower drew his gun, spun in a half-turn toward the sound, and began barking instructions over his lapel mic to his team outside. Seconds later, two agents burst through the front door. Silence greeted them.

Everyone stopped moving to listen, but Savage sneered at Harry. "Tell me there's a TV on, playing some damn horror movie."

Ginny drew close. "Was that the man you mentioned?" she whispered.

"He's in the basement."

Sheriff Boone dislodged the thumb break on his holster and kept his hand in place. "Son, I suppose you wanted me here for a reason. You said the senator was in danger. Might as well give it to us straight. Now would be a good time."

"One of the terrorists responsible for the bombing

is in the basement. That must've been him."

This was straight enough to start an unintended avalanche. Trower drew his pistol again and leveled it on Harry. "Keep your hands where I can see them." He nodded to Shultz who holstered his firearm.

Boone stepped up and put a hand on Trower's shoulder. "Son, there's no call to get carried away. Just lower your weapon and let's talk this thing through."

Trower gave Boone a slow once over, but he didn't back down. "Search him," he told Shultz.

The Baretta came out an instant later. Shultz wrapped a thick paw around Harry's wrist.

"Dammit, I can explain."

"Let me see that." Boone snatched the gun from Shultz. "I can vouch for this. I gave it to him yesterday for protection. The man's life hasn't been worth shit."

Harry's prisoner screamed again, and every head turned in a different direction as the eerie wail echoed through the walls.

"I wanted you all here so you'll know Ginny and I have been telling the truth. Sheriff, I do know more than I've been letting on and I'll explain, but you've got to promise me you'll find Jack Hallowell. They've kidnapped him."

"Why?" Boone asked.

"To make me stand down, stop pursuing them, disappear. Take my money and forget my family's business is fighting these creeps."

Boone stroked his stubbly chin with his free hand. "I sense an 'or else' in there somewhere."

"Or else, Jack's dead, and maybe others." Harry glanced reflexively at Ginny, but her worried eyes were all for her brother.

Boone considered this for a long moment and met the eyes of each person gathered in the entry hall of the mansion. Another scream washed over them. Ginny pulled Harry close. Thunder pounded in the distance.

"Wait a minute," Trower said. "You're telling us one of the people responsible for the bombing yesterday is here—being held captive."

"Yeah," Harry said.

"How could you possibly know that? Wait, scratch that." Trower searched everyone's face as Boone had done. "This is just too much. I've heard of people going to extremes to draw attention to themselves, but this is bullshit. He's probably hidden a recording somewhere."

"You know I'm right, don't you, Senator?" Harry said.

Rankin cleared his throat, obviously reluctant to side with a madman, but he was stuck. "I think we should go down and see for ourselves." He turned to Boone. "Sheriff, if this man—" He pointed a slender finger at Harry. "—has broken any laws, he should be arrested." He hesitated and gave his sister an apologetic look. "But something tells me he's not lying, however farfetched it may seem to us."

Boone nodded. "It's time we found out. Son, I think we need to have a look at this fella."

Chapter 30

I can't believe we're just going to play into his hands like this," Savage said. No one turned to listen to him as the group continued toward the kitchen. "Right." Savage pulled his cell phone out. "You go along with this charade, Bill, but I have work to do. I'll see you back at your place. I'm calling a cab."

Savage had begun walking back to the front door, but Boone spun him around with a flick of his mitt-sized hand. "I suggest you put that away and get your butt back to the group. We stay together until we have a handle on this situation. Is that clear?"

Savage tried to work up a retort, but Boone's massive size made him wilt. He stuck the phone back in his pocket and returned to his boss's side, grumbling.

Harry took the point position through the kitchen and led them past the wall of windows in the breakfast area to the door leading to the cellar. It was already cracked open, but he knew the screams weren't escaping through the stairwell. More likely, the mansion's air ducts had conducted the eerie sounds, making it seem like the very walls had protested their arrival.

The cellar was one of the oldest parts of the mansion, which had undergone a complete renovation three times during the last hundred and fifty years. They descended the narrow stairway single file to the tiled floor far below.

Harry flipped the light switch as another scream assaulted his senses. Seeing Harry, White Shirt turned his frustration into a filthy diatribe against Clan Black that must have included every important member of the family over the last two centuries. It impressed Harry, though ninety-nine percent of the names were new to him. The sonofabitch must have been studying Harry's family tree.

Harry found the sorcerer, or whatever he was, cringing next to three oversized water heaters servicing the massive dwelling. After the inky blackness of the cellar, White Shirt's eyes adjusted slowly to the light, but his tongue hadn't been affected.

"Shut it," Harry said.

"Keep them away from me," White Shirt yelled, pointing and looking past Harry.

Harry glanced over his shoulder at the group, just catching up with him. "No one's going to harm you."

"Not them, you idiot." White Shirt backed farther into the corner. "Those things have been toying with my mind since they dropped me on my head in this…Where the hell am I anyway?"

Harry could only guess what the Grigori had been doing to the bastard in the two hours since they had made him their prisoner. "Black Manor."

The words hit White Shirt like a concussive force. He stumbled back a few feet more and began stuttering, fear stringing out his voice into discordant notes. "The old witch kept that cursed name? My master hadn't told me."

"Holy ground's a bitch for you guys, isn't it?" Harry said.

White Shirt snarled and lifted his right hand, palm out. Harry flinched, but nothing happened. The sorcerer howled. "You bastard. If I had my powers right now, I'd cut off your balls and make you eat them. I'd grab that fucking neck of yours and choke the fucking life from you."

White Shirt suddenly stopped his diatribe and glanced above Harry's head. He turned two shades paler and sagged to the floor. "Keep them away." He covered his head with his arms.

Hovering on the white plastered ceiling interspersed with massive oak beams were the Grigori.

"What's wrong with him?" Rankin asked. He tried to draw nearer, but the sheriff prevented him.

In answer, White Shirt rose to his full height and addressed the senator with a short, formal bow. "Why, if it isn't Dr. William Rankin, MIT genius, the boy wonder of the fucking U-fucking-S Senate, and anointed savior of the failed economic policies of the idiot from Idaho."

Rankin stepped closer. "Who the hell are you?"

"We make it a point to know the people we target. I could write your biography, complete with an exclamation mark at the end—'died violently at the hands of'—" He stopped short with a sheepish look on his face.

"Finish it," Harry said. "Who do you work for?"

"You'll know soon enough, Black. Your end will be the same as his."

White Shirt lunged at the senator. Rankin yelped and jumped back but tripped and fell hard to the floor. The agents yanked him to his feet and pulled him farther away from the madman.

White Shirt had intended it as a feint. He howled with laughter. "There is your economic savior, Black. You sure you want to give your life, protecting this pampered asshole?"

Harry was on him instantly. He grabbed the front of his starched shirt with both hands and rammed him into one of the water heaters, eliciting a loud grunt.

"Listen to me, prick."

The Grigori appeared again, inches above the man's head, overshadowing both of them. White Shirt began spluttering. His legs went limp. Harry had to struggle to hold him up.

"I asked you a question. If I don't get an answer right now, you'll have very little brain left in that skull of yours when they finish with you."

His eyes, red and full of fright, darted between Harry's face, inches from his own, and the flickering shadows hovering not more than a foot above them. "Don't," White Shirt whimpered, "don't let them. You have no idea, Black. You're just a boy, really. No offense, mate, but you really have no clue what you're getting involved in."

"Oh, I think I do." Harry glanced up at the quivering shadows and smiled. "You're gonna start talking now, and you're not going to stop until I'm satisfied."

The man hesitated then nodded.

"First things first. What's your name?"

"Arie…Arie Peeters."

"Okay, Mr. Peeters. That was easy enough, now for some real answers. Where are Jack Hallowell and Paula Grisham?"

"The lawyers? I don't know, man. I swear, I

don't."

"Okay, the hard way."

He released the terrorist, and the Grigori engulfed him. Peeters went semitransparent. Harry glanced at the group standing behind him. Every one of them had taken a keen interest in what Peeters had been saying, but just now, as the Grigori had him in some kind of stasis, he wasn't sure just what it was they were seeing. The water heaters were in a corner away from direct light. With the Grigori hanging over him, the place became even dimmer. Peeters began screaming again, but this time they were muffled as though he stood hundreds of yards away.

Harry turned back to Peeters. The shadows had left him with a silent scream plastered on his face. Harry grabbed Peeters by the shirt and waited while the bastard recovered coherent speech.

"I'll talk. Just keep those things away. There's a warehouse on Front Street, real shitty part of town."

Harry glanced at Boone, who was already speaking into his lapel mic. He turned back to Peeters. "Is he dead?"

"No." Peeters wiped the sweat from his face. "Not yet, anyway."

"And the woman?"

"With him."

"You better not be lying." Harry glanced at the shadows, which made Peeters shudder.

"I swear."

"By the way," Harry said, releasing him, "you should really consider using mouth wash." Harry stepped back while Peeters composed himself. "Who murdered my assistant, Peggy Cox?"

Peeters appeared puzzled at first, but then his eyes widened. "Not me, mate. That was Vogels. Not me. He did her. She liked part of it if you know what I mean. But not me, I swear."

The insinuation of rape sent Harry over the edge. He punched Peeters square on the nose, twice. Blood spurted out on the second punch.

Trower rushed up and pulled Harry off Peeters before he could do more damage. Someone located a towel and used it to stop the bleeding.

"Dammit, Black," Trower said, "we won't be able to explain his injuries."

Harry whispered into Peeters' ear. "You better swear by everything you hold dear, because the Grigori are staying right where they are and if you so much as burp—"

Trower grabbed Harry's shoulder. "Enough. I need him alert to verify details of the bombing before I'll believe him. Specifics he wouldn't be able to get just anywhere. I'll take over."

Eventually, Peeters gave Trower what he wanted, except for names. They tried hard to get the names of his handlers, but it didn't work. Harry wondered if some sort of mental block had been placed on Peeters. Each time they requested a name, he'd start sweating even more, and gibberish would flow from his tongue. The Grigori entered Peeters but could pull nothing out of him. There was a lock on his brain nothing could undo.

A half-hour later, Boone came back down to tell Harry the warehouse had been cleared out. Plenty of evidence had been left behind. They were having some blood analyzed, but there wasn't enough of it around to make them think someone had been executed. No bodies were found. Jack Hallowell and Paula Grisham were still missing. Neither had shown up for work.

"Pelgram found Hallowell's cell phone," Boone said. "Has a bunch of messages you recently sent."

Harry nodded and turned back to Trower and Peeters, who had been having a conversation about the explosives: type, where they were purchased, exact amounts. One of Trower's men had the FBI on the line, and the small details were checking out.

Harry got up into Peeters's face. "You didn't lie, but you didn't tell the truth either. Where *is* he?"

Peeters laughed and wheezed. He spat out some blood. "You've made a mistake, pup. You should have never brought me here, especially now that you've spilt my blood."

Harry grabbed his stained shirt. "What are you talking about?"

"It's on me, Black, you'll see. You'll damn well see." Peeters cackled louder, but stopped and sank to the floor, trembling and stuttering. The Grigori had reappeared.

Harry wanted to kick the bastard in the nuts, but instead punched the wall and turned away. He couldn't get any more information out of him this way and doubted Peeters knew where they had taken Jack or what their ultimate plans were for him. One thing was clear. They wanted to make Harry relent and go away, but he had made it clear he wasn't going to do that. The shadows disappeared again, and Peeters craned his neck to look up at the men standing over him, all the fight now gone.

"He's getting weak," Trower said. "We probably

ought to give him some water and a little food. I still have a long way to go with him."

"The weaker, the better," Harry said. "Maybe then, we'll get somewhere."

Trower overruled him. Harry turned away in disgust and marched up the stairs to find Ginny. They had a long way to go, but how much more could they get out of Peeters before time ran out and Jack was dead?

****

At some point during Harry's interrogation of Peeters, Ginny and her brother had gone upstairs where Fred Savage was still whining about needing to leave. The president expected Rankin to be back in Washington tomorrow. Trower had his orders. He wanted to leave immediately, arguing the place wasn't safe.

Harry knew it would be a mistake without more information on what they were facing. Peeters had grown more confident throughout the questioning by the secret service, even with the threat of the Grigori. Harry believed there was a plan, but he hadn't figured it out, and the president's men hadn't a clue.

What had Peeters meant when he said *it* was on him? The agents had searched him and found nothing.

While Trower and Rankin argued over their next move, Harry motioned for Ginny to follow him to the library where they had researched Agnes's diaries the night before.

"How are you holding up?" Ginny asked as they made it to the nearest shelves. She didn't wait for an answer. "We'll find Jack, you'll see. And we'll stop them."

Harry took a deep breath and lowered his tense shoulders. "You're an optimist. Or is that part of your psychology training?" He turned away and thumbed absently through the pages of one of the books lying open on a nearby table. "I don't feel very optimistic right now."

"You'll feel better on a full stomach," Ginny said. "One of the agents left for takeout. Everyone's starved. No one wants to leave. Well, no one except that weasel Savage."

The last two days had been unbearably tense for both of them. There didn't appear to be any relief in sight, so Harry welcomed the levity in her eyes.

"Listen, sorry I got a little carried away in there."

"A little?" Ginny asked.

"Yeah, well, in my mind, he's a bloody pulp right now, so yeah, I managed to pull back." He hesitated. "I wish you hadn't seen it, though."

She shrugged. "His nose will be fine, but not Peggy Cox. I can't imagine what her family must be going through right now." Her face grew stern. "You keep doing whatever it takes to catch the murdering bastards and keep them from getting to Bill."

Harry smiled. "What are they all saying? I haven't had a chance to gauge their reaction to…well, you know."

"My brother is badly shaken. You've proven your point effectively. All we can do is extract as much information from Peeters as possible. The agents have been in touch with the White House. The CIA ran his name through their data banks."

"And?"

"So far, nothing."

He nodded. "There won't be anything either. These people are off the grid."

"How do you mean?"

"They have billions, and a contingent of them is sorcerers. Why else would the legacy have come to me in time to save your brother? I saw what Peeters could do in Brookhaven, and he said he wasn't particularly talented, only a foot soldier. They'll have ways to remain hidden from such things as computer searches and databases."

"Are you sure about the family you mentioned, the Ausbergs?"

"That part's sketchy. I know some of what Agnes thought, but I have no idea how to get to them or implicate the family she focused on in her stories. And I'm pretty sure Agnes didn't have a clue how to do it either. If she was right about this one family, how do I separate out the sorcerers from the rest of them?"

Ginny nodded. "I see your point. They may not all be involved. But they have a family head, the person who holds the purse strings. That's the person we need." She went to the laptop computer on Agnes's desk.

"I know Agnes was savvy with technology. You think she could have found something on them? She probably has years of research built up."

"Now that you mention it, she did spend most of her free time in here until she got too sick. I haven't touched the place." He turned slowly. "It's pretty much the same as it always has been. Jones must have told the housekeepers to leave this area alone."

Ginny sat down at the computer. "Do you mind?"

"Go ahead."

It booted right up and luckily wasn't password protected. "Agnes has a ton of files. This will take a while. This old laptop is slow." She glanced at Harry and frowned. "What are you thinking?"

He shook his head. "It's just that, so far, we've got a bombing and threats against your brother. Ordinary terrorist stuff. I haven't seen any magic that could be a threat other than what Peeters can do and, of course, Dunbar and Brick being controlled."

"Don't forget what they did to your friend Peggy."

"Wish I could forget that."

"So you're thinking, what's your purpose in all this?"

"Good question." Harry hesitated. "The fact that the legacy came to me at this time is pretty meaningful. But why, exactly?"

Her eyes widened. "Are you saying something more is coming, something they know you'll be a major threat to stop?"

Harry nodded. "Everyone's focusing on identifying these terrorists. I've been working under the assumption they're also the sorcerers. It's why I'm needed now." He shook his head. "The assumption may not be true. The real threat, the sorcerers, may not have played their hand yet in a major way, except to put Carl Dunbar and Brick Taylor under compulsion to try and take me out."

"But we do know Agnes has been right about many things." Ginny stood and put a hand on his shoulder. "You have to remember more of the stories. Look, here's where we stand." She ticked off the facts with her fingers. "One—we know they're rich and powerful and have an economic agenda going. They disrupted the summit. And two—they're threatening my brother who is leading the way on that front for the president."

"Exactly, and Peeters let it slip what they're really after is to weaken our government. They intend to take us down a notch, so the world isn't as complicated anymore, whatever he means by that."

She tapped her fingers on the laptop. "We have to find a way to connect the bombers to the rest of the family, the money people, and find out what else the sorcerers are doing. Then we tie it together and bring the bastards down."

He smiled at her.

"What?"

"You've never cursed like that before."

"Well, I'm mad as hell."

Harry stopped smiling. "Problem is I'm supposed to be fighting sorcery, right? What we've just described is mostly a job for the CIA and maybe the FBI. How do I fit in? I need to find a way to check out the rest of this family of sorcerers, go all the way to the top, follow the money people. They're the key to all this, but something tells me they're one and the same."

"I think our fight is on two fronts."

"Come again?" Harry asked.

"War analogy. We need to recruit an ally, someone from the CIA, a little covert action to free you up for the more important fight to come—the sorcerers." She stopped a moment, thinking. "I heard what Peeters said down there. How does this place cut their power?"

"No idea. Jones referred to Black Manor as holy ground, but I don't know what that means other than some kind of safe haven."

"At least you know you'll have a place of sanctuary when you need it. You think it's connected to the church in some way?"

Harry cringed. He'd been inundated over the years with stories that had all run together in one gigantic hodge-podge. "I suppose…" He stopped and shook his head. "…I don't know. It would be pretty embarrassing if it were true since I'm not very religious."

An agent poked his head in. "Food's here."

"In a second," Harry said.

He turned back to find that Ginny had stepped into his personal space. She reached up and placed a hand around his head, entangling her fingers in his hair.

"What are you—"

She pulled him to her and kissed him, and despite Jones's protests about getting involved, he responded. He lost himself in the kiss, a respite from the horrors of the last two days.

When they finally broke, he stared into her eyes. "Remember what Jones said—and Agnes?"

"Is that what you think too? Can't you ever—"

"Not this way, not when it matters."

She leaned into him again, and the kiss was far more urgent this time.

He didn't want it to end. He wanted it to progress to other, more needful things. By Ginny's response, she wanted it too, but he had to stop it here. He caught his breath. "I think you know what I want, Ginny." A tear fell onto her cheek. He brushed it away with the back of a finger. "With you, it would be something I've never had before, but that's selfish. You would be in danger. I can't do that to you. I won't."

"I *am* in danger, and I don't think it's because of you. These people could get to Bill through me. Anyway, don't I get a say in this?" Her eyes were brimming with tears.

He took her trembling hand. “I didn’t mean to suggest you couldn’t handle it, but you don’t know the cost.”

“I do.” She hesitated. “You may not realize it, but you saved my brother again today when you convinced him to come here. Listening to that crazy man made me realize how much danger Bill is in. The bomb was meant for him. The terrorists didn’t even care about the others, even those two senators who died. They wanted Bill.”

The tears were flowing now. Harry pulled her to him. She started sobbing onto his shoulder, trembling. After a minute, she said, “I can’t.” She pulled away and wiped at her tears with both hands. “I can’t fall apart. Bill needs me to be strong because he’s—”

“I know.”

“It’s not that he’s weak. This just isn’t his—”

“I know what you mean. He’s a power player, and this is down and dirty in the primal jungle sense.”

“But Washington is where he’ll be most vulnerable,” Ginny said. “We can’t let him go back there. He’ll be dead before he has a chance to board the plane.”

“I’ve never followed politics much. I take it from what Peeters said your brother is some sort of wonder boy.”

She shrugged, as though this was old news. “Doctorate in economics from MIT at twenty-six. He went straight to Princeton for two years of teaching and more research before deciding to come back home to enter politics. I suppose his seminal paper will receive the Nobel one day. He’s that good.”

Harry gave out a low whistle and turned away, surveying the massive bookcases. It was apparent the senator was essential to the plans of the terrorists. He turned back to her. “Bill’s a threat to their agenda.”

“The president needs him in Washington to jumpstart the economic summit again. Bill told me that before you came back upstairs. The administration isn’t letting the bombing deter their plans.”

“We can’t force him to stay, Ginny.”

“I know.”

“What’ll we do?”

“I don’t know, Harry. I don’t know.”

Chapter 31

Harry headed to the basement to check things and found Peeters cuffed to a one-inch diameter pipe running exposed up the wall. Across from him at the same makeshift table, Agent Piper sat hunched over a box of fried chicken. Together Peeters and the agent practically snarled over their food.

Peeters nearly shit his pants at the sight of Harry, who merely smiled and marched back upstairs. As he looked out through the massive kitchen window, the backyard and the woods beyond were darkening in the last minutes of twilight. The storm had blown over, leaving only a light sprinkling. The others were sitting around the large breakfast table, eating in silence. Only then did Harry begin satisfying his gnawing hunger. He hadn't eaten since Ginny's breakfast.

Trower pushed his chair back, scraping it noisily on the Macassar ebony wood floor. Harry gave him a look, and Trower lifted the chair the rest of the way and gently set it back down. "Nice place you have here, Black."

Harry grunted through another bite of a chicken leg.

"Listen," Trower said, "I'm not going to ask how you gained possession of Peeters. It's not really my jurisdiction, but the FBI will want to hear about it in detail. They'll be here soon."

"They won't like my answer," Harry said, staring into his box of chicken. He lifted his head and studied Trower. "How much longer do you guys think you'll need to interrogate him?"

"Never mind about that. The terrorists won't try anything here anyway."

Harry thought about that. "You're moving him?"

"Unless this mansion is also a jail, I think it's best, don't you?"

Harry sat back, looking from Trower to Boone. "Actually," Harry said, "I think you should let him go. Put a locator on him and track his movements. He'll take you to his bosses."

Trower snorted. "That stuff's for spy novels." He pointed a finger at Harry. "And I wouldn't stray too far from the plantation. The FBI wants a word with you. Downtown."

Harry stood. "Why?"

Sheriff Boone groaned and placed a heavy hand on Harry's shoulder. "Now look here, Trower. Harry's done you boys a favor, giving you this prick. Just take Peeters and leave."

"If he's innocent, it'll come out. But they *will* question Black—in custody."

"You honestly think I'm part of this?" Harry said. "Why would I bring you guys here? It doesn't make sense."

"Not for me to decide. Just come clean on how this joker came to be in your house."

"You saw them, Trower." Harry turned to everyone at the table. "You all saw the shadows." All he got for this revelation were some incoherent grumbling.

Morons.

"You know this isn't a normal situation. We're dealing with something here you won't be able to contain or explain. If you try to bring Peeters in, people will die." He pointed to Trower. "Your people." He swung to Sheriff Boone. "And yours."

Trower bit through his biscuit. "What the hell are you talking about?"

"I think we're being watched."

All heads turned to the wall of windows. The tree line was dark now, the yard just a little brighter. Boone brought a nervous hand to rest on the grip of his gun.

Trower snorted again, spewing pieces of biscuit. He grabbed a napkin, covered his mouth, and coughed. "We've had no indication of that," he said, choking the words out. "Sheriff Boone's boys have walked every square inch of this place for the last two hours. They haven't heard a peep or seen anything."

"I'm telling you," Harry said with mounting fury, "if he leaves Black Manor, his people will know, and it won't end well for whoever you send to guard him. Didn't you see what went on down in the cellar?"

Trower gave him a puzzled look. Harry knew then no one had perceived the things that had occurred in the basement in the exact way it had happened. "I didn't see anything—" He gave each of the others sitting around the table an appraising look. Bill lowered his head to stay out of the crossfire. "—but a frightened sonofabitch being mistreated by you."

"You've got to be kidding me. Are you blind?" Harry waited for an answer, but Trower merely glared at him. "Let me spell it out for you so you secret agent boys will get it. We're dealing with *supernatural* forces here. Stuff you aren't equipped to handle."

Trower laughed, but he was the only one. The others seemed either too puzzled to laugh along, or maybe they all understood more clearly than Harry had given them credit for and weren't willing to step out on any limb where a supernatural explanation was the most logical choice. So they remained quiet.

Trower stood slowly and leaned over the table, trying to get as close to Harry as possible. "I don't know what kind of game you're playing here, and I'm still not convinced you aren't directly involved with this shit, but I'm willing to let the FBI handle it from here. They're taking Peeters. That's final. We have to get the senator back tonight. He'll be well protected, believe you me."

Ginny nearly knocked over her chair, jumping to her feet. "No. Bill, make them see you can't go. Tell them Harry's right."

Her brother lifted his head and cleared his throat. "We should all remain calm."

Harry growled something incoherent and stomped away from the table, but then turned back to Trower. "Look, at least stay here with Senator Rankin long enough to prove me wrong about moving Peeters. If you guys get him out of here clean and lock him down, we'll talk about the senator. But if there's trouble—" He motioned for Boone to help. "—Sheriff, it's your men they'll use for the delivery. I'm telling you, you shouldn't let them." He jabbed a finger at Trower. "Make *him* use his men if the FBI doesn't bring enough help. Don't sacrifice your boys."

"You feel that strongly about it, son?" Bone asked.

"They've already murdered three of yours, Sheriff, counting Brick."

Boone's eyes widened at the mention of Taylor.

"Yeah, it was their doing. Brick was under some kind of compulsion. I'm sure of it."

That was enough for Boone. He marched off to the backdoor, stepped onto the porch, and yelled to the two deputies patrolling the tree line. He had them get the others and wait at the front of the house for further orders.

****

Trower had been clutching his biscuit so tightly it reduced to crumbles. He threw the pieces on the table and wiped his hands.

"Black, I'd like a word with you." Trower scanned the others. "The rest of you stay here."

He led Harry to the foyer, where the two men stood facing each other like boxers before the start of a match.

"You must think I'm some kind of fool," Trower spit out.

"Not a fool, just blind."

"Well, I'm neither."

Trower hesitated. Harry could tell he was trying to keep his voice even. Something was obviously on Trower's mind, and Harry was curious to know what.

"You're right. I saw what happened down there."

Harry straightened in response, but he didn't say anything.

"Listen, you need to think this thing through."

"Why'd you call the FBI if you believe me?"

"Because this situation falls under the jurisdiction of the Bureau and they *need* to be brought in. I can't handle Rankin and a prisoner at the same time. If he's one of the terrorists, it's the FBI's jurisdiction. They *will* talk to you, Mr. Black. You need to face it. Just answer their questions."

Harry began shaking his head before Trower finished. "I don't have time for it. They have my friend. They want the senator too. If you leave with him, you're going to have trouble."

Trower simply nodded. When he spoke again, it was in an even softer voice, a more reasonable tone. "You believe the senator was specifically targeted. That's what Peeters said. The president believes it, too. It's why he put a secret service detail on him. That in itself is highly unusual. I believe there are some irregularities with how we believe the bombing went down. You know anything about it?"

"The only thing I know is Islamic Jihadists had nothing to do with it. The news reports are bullshit."

"It's not what the FBI and CIA say. They've confirmed all the claims of responsibility. The one from Hamas seems more solid, at least that's what I've been hearing. The CIA managed to trace the call. It originated from the Gaza strip—from fucking Khaled Mashaal himself, Hamas's supreme leader."

"And the others?"

"They haven't been able to make a definitive connection. Hamas is their group. The CIA has made a positive ID of the caller, so they are pretty set with it."

"So what are they planning, an attack in the Middle East?"

"The president's a dove. He wouldn't normally take military action, but with something like this, he'll have to respond."

Harry let out a low groan and pushed his hair back with both hands. He looked down, thinking. "It's a ruse.

Tell them that. They're about to start another war on faulty information. You know it, don't you? You have to tell them."

Trower turned away and walked to the front door, where he stared through the sidelight. This was a critical moment. Harry couldn't push him on the issue. He had to let Trower work things out for himself. Two of Trower's men were stationed out front, another on the back porch, and the last in the cellar with Peeters. They appeared safe for now. Harry knew it had to be Trower's primary concern, along with protecting Senator Rankin.

Trower spoke without turning back to him. "My gut tells me we have one of the terrorists, and there's no way this guy is a Muslim. He has a visible tattoo, something forbidden in Islam. I tried to tell them the bombing doesn't follow the suicide pattern. They think they can explain away the lack of splatter evidence from the guy changing the tire at the van that blew up. We have eyewitness reports. There was definitely someone there changing a tire. That's convinced them it was a suicide from an Islamic fundamentalist group."

Harry snorted. "You know better than that now. People like Peeters are cunning. It's what they want you to believe. It's a misdirection. They have ways to make things seem other than what they really are."

Trower turned back to him. "I can't just go to them with this shit, Black. It's too crazy." He rubbed his eyes with both hands, obviously conflicted. "I'll tell you something." He took a deep breath. "You're an odd character, Black. Well, not odd, per se." He stopped to collect his thoughts again. "It's the situation. There's no training protocol for something like this. I believe you have the senator's well-being in mind. You're right about what happened in the cellar, but the others...I don't know...it's too strange. The others saw what they wanted to see, but I had a better view of things."

Trower stepped closer, his square jaw set firm, and poked Harry in the chest with a finger. "We could make a real difference here if we get this right, but if you're part of this thing somehow and merely playing me, I'll hound your ass. You hear me? You won't escape me."

"You're in a real quandary," Harry said, not backing up an inch, "but you can't take Rankin from here. This place is protected."

"In what way?"

"You won't believe me."

"I've already seen some weird shit, okay? Just say what's on your mind."

Harry gave him a long look before answering. "I think the group is from the Netherlands. They're after Rankin. He's the first bite of pie. Once he's out, they have other plans to disrupt the country. I just don't know how they'll go about doing it. But they aren't terrorists, not in the conventional sense anyway. The bombing was meant to kill Rankin. But more than that, the way it was done was meant to deflect us. You're right. There was no suicide. But...I don't know...maybe they thought eyewitness sightings of the tire guy present at the time of the bombing would be enough to convince people it was a suicide. And it would be enough to deflect opinion, to turn attention to the usual suspects. They probably should have planted some blood to make it more definitive."

Trower nodded. "The blood would have nailed it. It was a stupid oversight, but it hasn't yet sunken in with the people in charge. They're convinced they have the right terrorist group. So tell me something, how in the hell did the tire guy get away so fast? No one reported seeing him running from the scene before the explosion."

Harry shrugged. "Part of their tricks. I'm not an expert on this stuff. That was my grandmother, but she's dead. You need to know Hamas's leader is probably being controlled. They can get to anyone."

"How?"

"Same way. Through some kind of sorcery." Harry gave Trower a look that defied him to argue the point, but Trower merely nodded, accepting Harry's explanation. "My family has a history with these people, and…"

Harry stopped.

"What is it?"

"Listen, I don't know what their plan is other than to take Rankin out. That implies they're going for some kind of economic disruption on the political front. The timing of the bomb was too obvious. They've already tried to kill me twice and missed. I've just managed to stay one step ahead. Ginny said something earlier that made sense. We need to find out what's going on. We need to get someone inside their organization."

"You haven't said who they are."

"The Ausbergs of The Netherlands."

Trower whistled his surprise.

"I know what you're thinking."

"No, you don't," Trower said. "You have no idea how big they are."

"Actually, I do. I know the world of finance. I've had some dealings in Northern Europe before. That name is sprinkled throughout my grandmother's stories."

"Are you sure they're involved?"

"As sure as I am about any of this." Harry hesitated. "I'm positive they're the people behind this. We have to implicate them, but that's not really my fight." Harry walked off a few paces, his steps clicking off the marble floor. "We need help."

"What kind of help?" Trower asked.

"Something covert."

Now the special agent was the one who hesitated. His hand went reflexively to his chin. "You're talking CIA."

"You know anyone there we can count on?"

Trower smiled. "Actually, I do, but tell me this first." He lifted his head to the massive chandelier and swept it toward the elegant stairs. "Tell me about this place. Why do you think it's safer here?"

Harry didn't know how to explain it and didn't really want to. "You know, all this crap is almost as new to me as it is to you. I have no idea what this place means to these people. It's all tied up in my family's history. My grandmother probably knew. The best thing I could do is read her writings. What I do know is—this will sound strange. The house is holy ground. Sorcery can't function here."

Trower crossed himself.

"You religious?"

"Catholic," Trower said. "You a churchgoer, Black?"

"Not since I was a kid."

"Well, you better start back up." Trower hesitated, conflicted about something. "I have to get Rankin back.

The president dropped him in my lap, which was surprising after my screw-up last year."

Harry waited for him to explain, but Trower let it go. Both men turned to the sound of Boone's voice booming out orders and heard their names being called. Trower and Harry spent a moment longer reaching an uneasy truce, but Trower made it clear the FBI would arrive, and they liked to do things their way. Bottom line. Harry was on his own. Trower wasn't about to be seen as an obstructionist backing a demented outsider, but he would help where he could.

A minute after the two men made it back to the kitchen area, Special Agent Shultz lumbered in, followed by a slender man in dark glasses and dark suit. A tall, pudgy black man dressed the same way walked in beside him. The FBI had arrived.

Introductions were made. Hands were shaken, or at least acknowledgments grunted. The taller and darker of the two, Special Agent Duffy, went into the cellar and came back with Peeters. Both hands were cuffed behind him, Piper holding on tight to the handcuffs.

"And the other detainee?" the older man, Special Agent McKeen, said, "Where is he?"

Everyone turned to Harry.

"You Black?" McKeen said,

Harry nodded.

Duffy drew out a spare set of cuffs.

"No fucking way," Harry sneered.

Before anyone could react, everything got quiet, and everyone seemed to be moving in slow motion. Trower rounded the table with a determined look on his face. Shultz came at Harry with thick, reaching fingers set to put him in a vise grip. Boone's voice boomed out an obscenity. Ginny shrieked, “No!”

Savage and Senator Rankin shrank against the windowed wall, which shattered as a decapitated head came smashing into the kitchen.

Chapter 32

The head bounced with a blood-splattering thud off the table, scattering half-empty boxes of fried chicken. It landed on the floor at McKeen's feet, and Peeters let loose with a barrage of laughter until Harry punched him senseless with one blow to the jaw.

Chaos ensued. Guns were drawn. Orders shouted.

Boone recognized who the head belonged to. "Dammit, it's one of my boys. Billings."

Harry recognized the mangled head as the young deputy who had accompanied Deke Pelgram into Jack's apartment following the call meant to embarrass him. Another sheriff's deputy entered the kitchen to report that Billings had gone missing. Everyone turned from the deputy to the bloody and smashed head on the floor. The deputy leaned against a wall to steady himself when he recognized who the head belonged to.

A burst of words suddenly blossomed in Harry's mind.

"*You see, Harry Black, another avoidable death, placed squarely on your shoulders. Is this how you protect the innocent?*"

The words had been placed there with searing pain, doubling Harry over.

"*Oh, I do feel for you, young Harry, but you must forgive me. I forget how inexperienced you are, which is remarkable when you consider what you have managed to accomplish in such a short time. Of course, you will fail in the end."*

Harry gritted his teeth. "*You won't get away with this.*"

The apparition laughed. "*Good...good, you are learning, but to no avail, for in the end, we will be victorious. I have foreseen it. Just as your courageous grandmother knew after the death of your mother and father.*"

The mention of his parents stunned Harry. For a moment, he forgot where he was. He turned to the destroyed windows. "*What do you mean? What do you know about it?"*

There was no reply, only fading laughter while his mind cleared. Turning back to the room, he made eye contact with Ginny, which drew her to his side. At the moment she moved, an arrow with plumed, yellow feathers at the fletching flew through the smashed windows. It pierced Piper between the eyes, nailing him to the wall. A blast of semi-automatic fire disintegrated the remaining parts of the window. Everyone dove for the floor.

Crouching at Harry's side, Peeters said, "Payback's a bitch, isn't it, Black?"

Cackling like a hyena, he flung himself onto the table. The bullets stopped long enough for him to jump through the window, broken glass raining down around him.

Harry lifted his head enough to watch in stunned silence as Peeters broke into a dead run toward the dark trees, his hands still bound behind him. As he approached the woods, Harry noticed a glow of bluish-white light forming around his hands. A moment later, the cuffs fell cleanly away.

Harry cursed and turned to survey the mess as McKeen cried out. More gunfire erupted. McKeen went down, grabbing his knee.

Blood flowed freely down the white wall where Piper stood, impaled. Duffy crawled over to his boss. Everyone else scooted on their bellies as best they could to the central part of the kitchen, where a solid wall would give them better protection. Harry helped Duffy drag McKeen out of the line of fire and went to Ginny, bent over her brother. The senator was unharmed, but Rankin glanced back to the breakfast area. Savage lay near the table, unmoving, a pool of blood collecting under him.

"Fred," the senator moaned.

"Fuck!" Trower screamed. "Boone!"

The sheriff was well ahead of him, speaking into his lapel. They could hear more gunfire coming from outside, but none directed at them. Boone's boys had begun returning fire into the woods.

Harry knew it was too late. They could search all they wanted. Peeters was already gone.

Moments after the blast of bullets had erupted, the other two agents had come running in from the front of the house. They moved Rankin to the library. Harry ran to his kitchen phone and called an ambulance for McKeen, who had already lost a fair amount of blood.

"Metro's sending a chopper," Boone said to everyone, "and an army. We'll flush out whoever's in those woods."

"Don't bother," Harry said, "they're gone."

"How the hell do you know that?" McKeen said through gritted teeth.

"You wouldn't believe me." Harry glanced at Ginny and saw the same question in her frightened eyes. How had they known where to find Peeters? And how had they mobilized so fast?

Duffy worked as best he could on McKeen's blown-out knee, but the pain was too much. McKeen gritted his teeth so hard Harry wouldn't be surprised to see cracks form in the enamel. He spat at Duffy through the pain, "Keep Black where you can see him."

"Oh—come—on," Harry growled.

Duffy gave him an angry look. "How do we know you hadn't planned the escape all along?"

"Dammit, you idiots!" Boone yelled. "Call off the hounds, McKeen. I'm vouching for Harry. No one's laying a finger on him." He stopped for a moment, his nostrils flaring like a raging bull. "My office and metro police have twenty bodies out there right now, scouring Johnson's woods. The chopper's made a couple of passes already. Nothing. It's like the sumbitches just up and disappeared."

"It hasn't been five minutes," Trower said. "How's that possible? Those woods must cover a small area."

"They're huge," Boone shot back.

Harry had been examining the ruined wall. "Dammit, it's possible." He smashed a hand down on the table.

"More magic, I suppose," Trower whispered sarcastically to Harry.

Harry knew better than to argue the point. He exchanged a knowing look with Trower and walked over to Sheriff Boone. Without a word of exchange, only a brief hand on the big man's shoulder, he thanked the sheriff for his help.

"Son, let me handle these guys, okay?" Boone whispered. He gave Harry a concerned look with those hooded eyes. "The FBI don't have shit on you. But it would be mighty nice if I had a decent explanation of how Peeters came to be here."

"The truth, I suppose."

"That would be best."

Harry let out an exasperated sigh. "Okay, you asked for it. I had the spirits of my ancestors transport him from Brookhaven, where we captured him after he delivered a message to me. He told me to back off, or Jack was a dead man, and he threatened the senator. He said they would get him too. So what could I do? I got him instead."

Boone arched a thick eyebrow. "With spirits, huh?"

"You didn't see much in the cellar, I take it."

"About like Trower said."

Harry looked for Trower, but he had walked back to where they were keeping Rankin. No doubt that's where Ginny was, arguing with them about leaving. McKeen was being worked on by the medics who had arrived. Both dead bodies were in the process of being moved after pictures had been snapped, documenting everything. They had found Billings's body about fifty yards into the woods. Two metro detectives were in the house to help with Boone's dwindling resources. Boone's deputies had taken up their guard duty again, stalking the perimeter of the property.

Harry knew it was a futile effort. They were pawns in this game. All the firepower at their disposal hadn't aided them in keeping one lousy prisoner under lock and key. He turned back to Boone. "I know it's a lot to ask, Sheriff, but you have to trust me on this. It happened just as I said."

Boone scanned the death scene and cursed something under his breath. "Show me."

"What?"

"You can't ask me for that kind of trust, son. People are dying. All I've seen so far is one crazy sumbitch who was scared out of his mind of you. I want to know why. So show me."

Harry stiffened as the Grigori made themselves known to him. Someone within them said to his mind. *"Tis often helpful to have a lawman on our side. We consent."*

They materialized above Harry's head. Boone's eyes widened as the shadows flickered to Duffy and entered the black man's skull through his right ear. Duffy blinked twice and turned slowly to Boone.

"Any questions, Sheriff?"

It was the younger British accent again. Boone stared at the FBI agent, dumbfounded, but McKeen had noticed Duffy's distraction and howled a profanity in his direction. Duffy, possessed now by the Grigori, ignored him. He turned his round eyes onto Harry, and in the voice of Agnes Black, said, "We've done all we can here, my boy. You need to leave if Jack is to be saved. Prepare yourself."

Before he could answer, the Grigori streamed out of Duffy's head, making him stagger. McKeen must have interpreted this action as an assault, because he brushed aside one of the medics, and drew his gun from his shoulder holster.

The report of the Glock exploded in the room, but blackness had surrounded Harry, and everything vanished in a swirling phantasmagoria.

Chapter 33

The penetrating blackness lasted only a moment as Harry hit solid ground. A star-filled sky stretched out over him. He noticed the dilapidated warehouses up and down the dark street and knew instantly where the Grigori had taken him. Someone moaned. Harry spun to find Duffy rising to one knee, then standing.

"Why'd you bring him along?"

"His badge, son," Agnes Black said through Duffy as he dusted off his pants. "You heard what Meriodoc said about how useful lawmen can be on your journey. Plus, it's easier to communicate with you this way."

"Won't he…you know…be damaged?"

"He has a strong mind. He'll hold up, but we'll be careful."

Harry nodded as Agent Duffy surveyed the area. They were on Front Street, a good fifteen miles west of Black Manor as the crow flies. Harry shuddered as he relived the experience. Duffy noticed.

"First time's difficult." It was Meriodoc Black this time. "But it's only what I've been told. Never had them helping me."

"Yeah, so I've heard." Harry tilted his head left and right as though trying to clear water out of his ear canals. "Disorienting as hell. How's it even possible?"

"The void? Don't know. Just is. You held up well, I must say."

"I'm not so sure." Harry kept shaking his head, trying to clear up the aftereffects of the ride through the void.

"Better than the magus Peeters who screamed like a stuck pig."

Nausea churned through Harry's stomach. "Was that a gunshot back there?"

Scanning the empty street, Duffy's mouth quirked up at one corner, and he nodded. "The bullet would have gone right through your heart."

The matter-of-fact way in which he said it didn't help the shock factor. Harry fought to keep his legs under him as he held Duffy's stare and those black eyes that had become hazel in the presence of the Grigori. "I'm losing count how often you guys have saved my ass. Thanks again."

"Don't mention it."

"Bastard, McKeen, taking a pot shot at me. What do you think is happening back home now?"

"Besides a lot of cursing and lewd anecdotes about your parentage?"

"Yeah."

"Nothing much. Boone was the only one really paying attention, so he would have noticed your sudden disappearance. McKeen was in a lot of pain and not seeing clearly. He's probably been moved by now. I'm surprised he had enough strength to pull the trigger as much blood as he lost. I don't believe anyone noticed you and Duffy blink out."

Harry nodded.

A blank look came over Duffy's face. "We'll have to do something, though, to make it right by this one. I'd hate to see Agent Duffy lose his job—or worse."

"Get thrown in jail for helping me escape? Good point."

"Actually, I think his brain might turn to mush if we stay too long."

Harry cringed at the thought as he scanned the street again. Gang graffiti decorated every building he could see. They had long ago taken over this section of Jackson. Nearly every building had broken out windows. All of them were missing light or curtains, staring like the blank eyes of a corpse.

"I can't believe they could trash my place like that so easily. I thought the holy ground thing protected it from assault."

"Assault by sorcery, yes. You did notice Peeters was powerless. My boy, they know where it is now, so it's entirely open to ordinary attack."

"Bullets, bombs, regular people."

"Correct."

"Shit, they're still in danger, especially since we've gone."

"Quite right again."

Harry cursed and turned away from Duffy. "Bill Rankin and Ginny." His shoulders tensed in the realization. "I need to get back. Take me home!"

"No. We need to retrieve your friend while the lawmen battle the others at Black Manor. They can at least assure the house isn't overrun. Our enemies wouldn't have expected you to catch them lying about Jack and abandon Black Manor. Chances are they're still in the woods but veiled from ordinary detection. We go for Jack and hopefully find some useful information to bring them down."

Harry rubbed the back of his neck, not liking much

the sound of the word abandoned, and stalked off several paces. Jack or Ginny—why did it have to come down to that choice? "You sure about this plan?" he asked.

Duffy caught up with him and placed a gentle hand on Harry's shoulder. When he spoke again, it was quiet. "We have to outsmart them. It's often the only course in our fight. We're usually outmanned, so we have to be smarter."

"How do I do that when they've been toying with me all along?"

Meriodoc didn't answer.

"I'm puzzled by something," Harry said. "How did they find Black Manor?"

"We've been wondering about it ourselves. Our place has always served us as a sanctuary, even in the earliest days. That was a gift bestowed to make lighter the burden of the legacy. Part of that gift was the place had its own veil, a nonmagical one, you see, but one much more powerful. We don't really understand it. The mages couldn't attack us there, but better than that, they couldn't even locate it. And they never have…until now. It seems they've solved the problem."

"But how?"

"Yes, well…" He paused as if listening to his own thoughts. "Chauncey is the scholar among us. He seems to think we may have…uh…blundered."

"Yeah? Welcome to the club. How so?"

Meriodoc cleared Duffy's throat. "Yes, well, we should have been a little more direct with you when we noticed you catching on to us so quickly. Bringing Peeters to the house, you see, gave them a huge advantage. It seems his purpose may have been more than to deliver the message." He paused to collect his thoughts. "Harry, they *wanted* him to be taken. It provided a type of—" Duffy stared over Harry's shoulder as though talking to someone behind him. "Yes, yes, Chauncey, I understand the concept." He focused on Harry again. "Forgive us, but we have a debate going on as we speak."

"Just tell me."

"The best explanation is that Peeters was needed as a type of metaphysical anchor for the sorcerers to locate Black Manor. Agnes tells us it would be analogous to a homing beacon in your day. Once they had their man in Black Manor, it became a simple matter to locate him and stage an attack."

"Shit."

"Quite. I am sorry, Harry. We'd hoped to have some freedom in this contest. There is still nothing they can do to it by magical means, but we will need to locate them and, by force of arms, remove them."

"Does it work both ways?"

"How do you mean?

"Can we home in on them as well and trace their location in the woods to the exact spot they're being veiled?"

Duffy's eyes widened. "Chauncey's working on it."

They were silent for a while, and Duffy asked, "You know where we are?"

"Yeah, but we need to find the building they held him in. Couldn't you have just deposited me at the front door?"

Duffy gave him an aggravated look. "We can't be expected to do it all, you know. We have no idea which is the correct building."

Harry supposed they were right. "The sheriff's people said they've moved him anyway. So why'd you bring me here? You think they might have missed something? Some clue?"

"Remember when Agnes's man, Jones, said not to trust anyone? He meant *anyone*. Well, except us, of course."

"Getting a little paranoid, don't you think?" Harry said.

"Can't afford not to be unless you want your eyeballs fried out of their sockets like mine were."

Harry tried to swallow, but his throat seized.

Duffy produced a wry smile. "Better develop a healthy bit of skepticism, my boy, if you want to live another year."

Harry reached out, grabbed Duffy's arm, and pulled him to a stop. "This is Sheriff Boone we're talking about. You think he lied? You think he's been turned, don't you?"

Duffy shook himself loose. "Don't get physical with us," Meriodoc said.

"I'm telling you Boone's too solid. They can't get to him."

"The sheriff has a strong psyche, yes, but anyone can be turned. You'll do well to remember that, or it'll bite you in the arse someday. Boone does seem legitimate enough but think for a moment. Can you trust the information he gets and passes on?"

Harry lifted his hand to his eyes. "Damn, I'm an idiot."

"A fair assessment." It was Agnes speaking this time.

"You have any idea who reported to Boone after Peeters gave us the location?"

Duffy shook his head, and Meriodoc spoke. "You'll have to ask him yourself. But I must caution you. Chances are it was meant to mislead you."

"That can't be right. You just said Boone was okay."

"We're not omniscient. I said Boone seems so. But he was *given* that information, wasn't he?"

Harry had to face the logic of Meriodoc's words. He pulled his cell phone out, meaning to call Boone, but reconsidered. If Boone wasn't what he seemed to be, an ally, all he needed to do was lie again. He turned to look up the street in the direction they had been walking. Who to trust? Jack could still be on this street somewhere in one of these neglected warehouses, but which one? There was at least a dozen stretched over a mile with smaller buildings interspersed. His heart began to pound as he tried to remember who had given the report to Boone. Suddenly, he had it. Deke Pelgram, the chief deputy. He remembered the bravado and bluster Pelgram had spat at him in Jack's apartment. What was it really about? It could very well have been a smokescreen. Maybe he hadn't even gotten a call to show up there in the first place. Perhaps he had set the whole damn thing up. Maybe Pelgram was Peggy's real killer. And now the young deputy who had shown up in Jack's apartment with him was dead, his head brutally ripped from his shoulders. Could it have been merely to erase a potential witness against him?

Duffy must have seen the confusion on Harry's face. "Got something?"

"I think you might be right, but I don't suspect

Boone. Not yet. He was too surprised by the Grigori. Genuine surprise. He'd have known all along about you guys if he'd been compromised in some way." Harry hesitated. "And he's got my cell number. If he wanted to sell me some bullshit, send me off on a false trail, he would have by now. But he hasn't. He's turned us loose." He glanced over the street again. "I think he was lied to. Jack might not have been moved after all, but there are so many to check."

Duffy smiled. "You've been developing quite nicely. Use those new senses you have. Reach out and feel where they were—where they still might be."

Harry nodded and paced off in one direction, but stopped. A pressure developed in front of him as though the air had thickened to prevent further progress. He tried to continue, but it was harder to breathe.

"Right, it must be this way." He did an about-face, and they started off toward the ugliest part of an already nasty section of Jackson.

They'd walked nearly two hundred yards when Harry said, "So those stories of how Meriodoc…how you died…are true."

Duffy stopped and stared off into the distance as though remembering something long lost. "You have to understand my people didn't have first-hand knowledge. There weren't any witnesses from the family. But it was obvious how bad it had been when they were allowed to recover my body."

"I see. Sorry about that."

Agent Duffy gave him a sideways glance. "Our job is to keep it from happening to you." He started walking again. "Picking up anything yet?"

"Actually, yes."

Harry's ears had been ringing since making that about-face, and the ringing had grown louder the closer they came to one of the warehouses standing like an old derelict on the opposite side of the street. A group of street hoods stood at the corner of the building in question, eyeing the white man and his black partner dressed in a conservative business suit. No doubt, Harry and Duffy smelled of cop, and the locals were wary.

These boys were here for no good reason. But it was way too late to turn back and try to approach the building from a different angle. They'd been spotted. The boys stood at the only discernable doorway to the building they needed to enter.

As they crossed the street, the group began to stir, murmuring among themselves. Harry searched the area for any sign of imminent danger. Nothing was there, nothing that he could see anyway.

"Ignore them," Meriodoc said. "They may not be involved. They aren't even old enough to buy liquor in your world. I don't want to hurt children."

Harry slowed his walk as they neared the other side. "One of these *children* has a gun." He nodded toward a big punk in cutoffs and a leather overcoat twirling an angular Colt .45 on his index finger.

"Pay no heed to them," Meriodoc repeated and led Harry in a circuitous route to avoid the group.

It didn't work.

Short Pants was still showing off with the gun. "Wasup B? You cops lost or somethin'?"

Duffy scowled. Using a rough British accent, he said in a clear baritone, "Hand it over, and I won't run your arse in for possession of stolen works and loitering and a couple of other things I can dig up."

"Good job," Harry said. "Pretty authentic."

"Picked that right out of Duffy's brain," Meriodoc whispered back.

The group of boys had a good laugh. "Black cop's a frickin' Brit," Short Pants said. "What chew doin' he'ah wid whitey. Cops ain't allowed down he'ah no way, 'specially not dis corner. You boys jus' go on and leave."

Duffy glowered at him, his expression as jovial as a rocky crag. "Stop spinning the barker, sonny, before it fires and kills someone."

Short Pants bared his teeth but did as Meriodoc said.

"That's better. Proves there's a brain up there. Now—" Meriodoc examined the group of boys. "Tell me who posted you here."

The big kid, maybe eighteen at most, squared his shoulders and stepped away from the rest of the gang. "Now, why we wanna go spoil the best bank we evah made?"

Duffy was a big man, bigger than the smart-mouthed kid who didn't have enough sense to be afraid. In an instant, he was on the kid and had stripped him of the gun, his other meaty hand around the kid's thick neck. "I won't waste words on your kind. You're lost in more ways than one, not long for this world, and believe me, the next one isn't any more pleasant than you've had it here, and far worse if you ask me. And I do know about the next world." He pulled Short Pants closer, practically growling into his face. "So, Mr. Lewis—they call you Blink." The kid's eyes widened in surprise. "Yeah, I know who you are. A real tough sport, but you'll always find someone tougher. Me, for instance."

By the end of Duffy's little speech, he had lifted the kid off his feet with one hand, dangling him like a ragdoll. The others took a step away from Duffy.

"Stop."

A squirrelly kid about the size of an eighth-grader, but obviously closing in fast on his post-teen years, had stepped forward.

"Put my little brother down. They was here all right."

Duffy let go of the nearly asphyxiated Blink who collapsed to the pavement in a heap.

"This dude told us to stand right here all night. Gave us five Benjamins. Promised another five if we didn't run off."

"Okay, what are you supposed to be doing for him?"

"Checking out the street. Tell 'em if anything goes down."

"Like cops showing up."

He nodded.

Harry had been holding back, but now he stepped forward. "We ain't cops, kid. So you better consider the five hundred pure profit and run off."

The spokes kid stared at Harry with shrewd eyes and must have thought his suggestion made sense. He snapped his fingers. "You boys get Blink up." They did, and the group turned to leave.

Duffy spun to Harry. "Got any money?"

Harry gave him a quizzical look but pulled his wallet anyway and yanked two bills out, which Duffy took without so much as a thank you. He waved it like a flag, and the runty kid turned on his heels as though he could smell them. “Two more Benjamins for some information.”

The kid eyed Duffy suspiciously.

“Tell me everything that went down here. How many men? What they looked like? Even the number of nose hairs the bastards had.”

There were muffled giggles from the younger ones, but they stopped when the runt in charge glared at them.

“Your choice,” Meriodoc said, and he folded the bills and stuck them in his front shirt pocket.

The runt’s eyes shot from the pocket and back up to lock onto Duffy’s. “Dey was badass muthafuckas, who don’ give a shit ’bout nuthin’, ya know? Hardcore gangstas, we ain’t neva seen before. You bes watch your back. Know what I’m sayin’?”

The kid stopped, focusing on Duffy’s pocket again.

“Nearly there,” Meriodoc said, “got any more?”

“Only dat dey was foreigners. Said we be in serious shit if we didn’t do it right. One ov ’em lifted his hand and picked up Lil C right off his damn feet widout touchin’ the boy.”

The smallest kid with cornrows shuffled his feet as though he’d done something wrong. “Both of dem foreigners laughed, but not dis other dude or his chick clinging to him like she was scared shitless.”

Harry knew he had the right place, but, beyond that, his senses had failed him. The building could have contained a hundred people or no one. Something was blocking him. “Did anyone leave? Are they still in there?”

“Hell, that was six, maybe seven hours ago. I didn’t see no one come or go.”

Harry considered the kid at length and nodded. "One thing more. Tell me about the guy who didn't laugh."

"Sharp looking dude. Light brown hair. But he was ragged out, man, like he been on a binge for days."

"Did he look hurt or injured?"

"Busted up, yeah. And his shorty was worse off."

"Shorty?" Harry said.

"His woman."

"Really?" Harry gave Duffy an unsure look, and said, "Sounds like Jack and Paula, but I can't be sure. I'm not picking up anything in the building."

Duffy nodded and handed over the money to the chief runt. The kid snatched it and gave Duffy a two-bill salute with the cash. As a group, they turned to go, but the runt hesitated.

"Guess I just remembered somethin'." He gave Harry an expectant look and hesitated.

"I'm broke now, kid. That's all I had on me. Tell me all you know or so help me I'll—" Harry stepped forward, and the kid held up his hands, palms out.

"Okay, okay. I hear ya. There was dis old fart, about a hundred, come strolling up smart ass like. About two hours ago. Guy had on dis white suit and yella tie. We tried to stop 'em, but he had a cane. We didn't want to bust him up, so we let him be. Just as well, told us he had business with da fucker who hired us. We let him pass figuring, you know, he must be one of dem."

Harry could only stare at him, the runt's words having temporarily stalled out his brain.

"You okay, mister? You don't look so good."

Another kid pulled on the runt's arm. "C'mon,

Buck, we gotta go."

Before Meriodoc could stop them, they turned and ran off.

Chapter 34

"I know what you're thinking, my boy," Agnes said, "but you can't be sure it was Strom that riff-raff saw."

In his confusion, Harry wasn't ready for the sound of Agnes's voice once again coming out of the surly FBI man. He did a double take, but the big agent with the round face and doughy black eyes kept staring at him. It couldn't be right what the runt had just said, but what if it was? The implications were apparent.

"I'm telling you it isn't true," Agnes said again. Duffy stamped his size thirteen foot on the cracked pavement. "Are you listening to me, Joey?"

Harry turned to Agent Duffy. "I know, Grandmother, I hear you, but the description—"

"Could have been anyone. You don't know for sure. You don't have anything that would implicate him, do you? I trusted Jonesy all those years, and I see no reason to stop trusting him now."

Harry had nothing to go on except the word of a street punk, but something came flooding into his memory. Jones had always disliked Jack Hallowell, the impertinent boy who insisted on befriending Harry. The dislike grew when Jack became a lawyer, and the two friends, now young, ambitious men, began making plans for the future of the estate. It was Harry who had convinced Jack to go with him to Ole Miss and stay for law school. It was Harry's vision of what their future could be. He trusted Jack like a brother, and he needed someone his age by his side. Strom Jones was ancient even when Harry was a kid. He could die any day, and if he did, what then? The only reasonable course was something his grandmother couldn't foresee, a future well beyond her and Jones's death. He had a plan, and Jack was in it, despite Jones's grumblings.

The history between Strom Jones and Jack could have colored Jones's reaction when Harry gave him the news of Peggy Cox's murder and the fact that Jack was now missing and the lead suspect. Maybe it was a completely innocent reaction, but perhaps it was something else entirely, something more sinister. Jones's response earlier in the day to the news that Jack was missing didn't seem to fit. He hadn't expressed surprise befitting the report, hadn't shown much at all. And now the street runt claimed to have seen Jones at the very spot the terrorists were holding Jack and Paula prisoner. But Paula was supposed to be one of the bad guys if Ginny's theory was correct. Was she? He was no longer sure of that if what the kid said was right, that she had been beaten worse than Jack. If Paula was part of this thing, if she had recruited Brick with sex to be a murderer on her behalf, why had they brutalized her?

"Do you, boy?" Agnes said, more insistent this time.

Harry didn't answer the question. "If you don't mind, get Meriodoc back for me. We need to plan our next move."

Duffy's expression grew perplexed, and Agnes started to argue. It made Duffy appear to have a split personality as the two voices competed for dominance.

Meriodoc finally gained control and started to say something, but Harry's cell phone chirped. He pulled it from his pocket and stared at the number being displayed.

"Yeah," Harry said into the phone, failing to keep his growing agitation out of his voice.

"Harry—oh, Harry, you're okay. I've been frantic—"

"Ginny?" He turned and paced off a few steps. "Listen, how's everything? This is a terrible time to talk. I've got to—"

"They've taken Bill. I couldn't stop them."

"Tell me you mean Trower and not the—"

"Yes, yes, it was the secret service. They wouldn't listen to me."

Harry breathed a sigh of relief and noticed Duffy standing at the door to the building, his hand out as though he might be trying to find his way in the dark. Meriodoc was studying the structure, testing something in the air. Harry concentrated his newly acquired senses and could see patterns of undulating colors near Duffy's outstretched hand. The colors flowed alongside the building in both directions but were most energetic in front of the door.

Ginny said something in his ear, pulling him back from his distraction. "Dammit, sorry I wasn't there to stop them."

"I tried to make them take me with Bill, but they said they weren't responsible for me. I'm about out of my mind. Where are you?"

He lowered his voice so Duffy wouldn't hear. "The Grigori snatched me up when things got rough in the kitchen. I didn't want to leave you. They took me against my will."

"Lowering your voice won't help, you know," Meriodoc said. Duffy turned his head to Harry but didn't seem in the least distracted from what he was doing with the colors.

Harry glowered at him.

"I know, I know," Ginny said. "McKeen had a fit after he shot at you, ranting and raving at Sheriff Boone and anyone else who would listen. The pain finally shut him up. There's an all-points out on you now. Boone had to go along with it. McKeen thinks you gave the agent something to make him do what they think happened."

"What *do* they think happened?"

"They aren't sure, or at least won't say what they actually witnessed."

"Something pretty unbelievable."

"Yes, but where did they take you, and when are you returning? They're wrapping up the crime scene. I'm afraid to stay behind. The place is no longer secure."

"Where's Boone?"

"He left with most of his men. McKeen's been taken to the hospital. Metro's leaving too. Trower and his men cleared out with Bill a minute ago. They wouldn't listen to me, and Bill was powerless with their insistence. I'll be alone soon with a couple of Boone's deputies." She lowered her voice to a whisper. "I'm not sure of them. Boone told them to escort me home, but what if they're…you know?"

"Listen, go back to the library, and lock the door. Don't let them see where you are. Do not leave the house. There's a gun in the safe Agnes kept there. It's behind the big picture of Thomas Jefferson. Pull it forward. The combination is 30-8-83. Got that?"

"Yes."

"Get the gun. It's always loaded. Keep it with you. Don't let them see it."

"Harry—"

"Make sure the safety is off. Be alert. I'll be there soon."

"You sure?"

"Half hour tops. I promise. We have a bead on Jack. I think Boone was given false information. We're checking things now."

"There's something else. After you left, I had a chance to do more checking on Agnes's computer, and I found something." She hesitated.

"Tell me."

"Don't you think it's strange the way Agnes trusted Jones so much? I mean, he's had an enormous amount of influence for years, and now he has complete control."

"There has never been anything unusual. And the transfer went off without a hitch."

"Do you know that for sure?" Ginny asked.

This time Harry hesitated. He was missing Jack now more than ever. In truth, he wasn't sure of the legalities.

"You should read through her personal journals. They're all on the computer. She has things dating from the 1950s when she became head of the family. She was suspicious of Jones early on. Did you know she wasn't sure Jones was even his real name?"

"No, I didn't, but look," Harry turned to Duffy and knew Agnes would hear, "turns out Jones may be up to his elbows in this thing. Stay there, don't talk to anyone, keep the gun handy, and shoot if you have to."

"One thing more. Agnes suspected Jones was tied to the Ausbergs in some way, maybe even part of the family."

Duffy made eye contact, but Harry turned away. "Grandmother was always suspicious of everything, but he obviously won her over. She still trusts him, but she may have blundered."

Duffy gave him another sharp look.

"The old bastard could have been playing her all these years. It makes sense with what we just learned."

Meriodoc grunted. "The mage's work is particularly strong here. It won't be easy to cross this threshold. We need to concentrate, so end the conversation and get over here."

"Hold on." Harry lowered the phone. "Can you enter as the Grigori…as pure energy or spirit or whatever you guys are?"

"No problem, but there's Duffy to contend with. He'll be a handful for you."

"Let me worry about Duffy. Get into the building. We need to know what's in there."

Duffy stiffened as the Grigori left him. The big man staggered but didn't fall. Momentarily, he noticed Harry, who put his hands behind his back to hide the phone, managing to keep the connection open.

"Black." Duffy addressed him with frantic, almost feral, eyes. "Where are we? What is this place?" He began pacing like a cornered lion.

"Calm down, Duffy. You're the one who brought me here."

"What?" He grabbed the front of Harry's shirt.

"When? How'd we get here anyway? Where's my car?"

"It's around the corner. Don't you remember the kidnapping? Boone mentioned he needed to check out this warehouse but didn't have the men to spare. You agreed to have a look on our way downtown. I'm cooperating with you. It's that simple."

"No shit?" Duffy said. He noticed Harry's hands. "You cuffed?"

"Nope, but I—" Harry brought the cell phone from around his back. "I'll just be a minute longer with Dr. Rankin. We were kind of in the middle of something."

"Hurry up. The building seems…I don't know…different."

Harry felt it too—a kind of vibrating energy around it. Meriodoc had mentioned a threshold, but Harry didn't know what it meant other than crossing through those big double doors not twenty feet away.

Duffy suddenly turned back to the building. "If we're here to inspect this place, we better go ahead. I figure McKeen is anxious to get you in for some questioning." And without another word, he drew the Glock from his shoulder holster and entered through the double doors with the crumbling glass panels.

Harry expected some kind of response and blew out a nervous breath when there was none. He lifted the phone to the sound of laughter. A man's sardonic cackle.

Harry stiffened. "If you harm her, I'll let them have your ass next time…completely. If you thought the void was tough in the short time you spent there, you have no idea what the next ten years will do to you."

Peeters stopped laughing.

"Put her back on the phone and clear out of my

house."

"Can't do that, mate. She's already gone. And as far as your little threats are concerned, you won't be in a position to make good on them."

"Bring her back!" Harry screamed.

"You have one chance, Black, and one only. Tonight, midnight, be back here at your lovely place. We'll have instructions stuck to the dead bodies of those two fine deputies the sheriff so kindly left to guard the little pretty. They made good target practice. Precisely twelve. We're watching, so don't be late."

Chapter 35

Harry stood there a moment longer looking down at the cell phone, the connection now dead, the realization of what had happened sinking in. He had failed to protect her.

A cold shiver ran through him, making him hunch over like an old man. And that's when the shame hit him and the realization that she was gone, possibly forever.

Harry struggled for the next breath as his mind calculated what would surely be her reward for helping him. She would be brutally tortured and summarily executed, all because of his ineptitude. Suddenly, the memory of Peggy Cox, dead and climbing that bedroom wall, came to him in one sickening flash—the cruel cuts covering her body, the disjointed way in which she moved, impossibly defying gravity. Sorcery put her there, but it was Harry's own weird ability that allowed him to glimpse the vision of what had happened to her.

In a new vision, the insectile woman turned her head to him, but this time it was no longer Peggy Cox, his assistant. Instead, Ginny leered at him from that bloody perch with sorrowful, longing eyes, the same eyes that had held onto his as they embraced not more than two hours earlier. But now they were haunted, pleading. She spoke to him words he didn't want to hear.

"Why did you leave me?"

He knew the Grigori had taken him to save his miserable life—always *his* life. With disgust, he tore himself from the tragic bedroom scene, hoping it was just a strange twist of memory and not a vision of Ginny's actual fate. She couldn't be lost to him, not now when the two of them had just begun. She was gone, but maybe not forever. Those words became a mantra to be repeated over and over, a repetition that could become a reality if he only believed it enough.

He examined the doorway where Duffy had entered. They were ordinary doors, a simple entrance, not some kind of metaphysical threshold. He remembered to look more closely, as Duffy, possessed of the Grigori, had been doing. The undulating currents of colors vibrated strongest just before the door, its pulsating, rasping energy crackling in his new hearing.

Agent Duffy called out to him again from somewhere inside the building. He had expected to hear him being mutilated, but nothing of the sort was happening. What did come to him were Meriodoc's words. Finding Jack was his next mission. The Grigori had brought him here for that singular purpose—to find him. Hopefully, a clue would turn up to help them conclude this business more effectively.

Experimenting, he ignored the buzzing energy and stepped toward the door to no discernable effect until he reached out for the brass handle. The shock of the touch was light, smaller than the static charge he and Rankin had received when shaking hands earlier in the day. The simple act of touching Rankin had presented to him a preternatural warning. At that touch, Rankin had suddenly smelled of death, but death in the purely metaphysical sense, not literal as in rotting flesh. More strongly than what Peeters had been able to declare, Harry knew Rankin had a death sentence hanging over him, and for all he now knew it had already been carried out. He had saved Rankin's life once, twice according to Ginny, but now he knew it could have all been for naught.

The door.

Harry reached out and touched the handle again, and in the simple act, a new message came. It made him pause, for this was a positive note. Jack was still alive, maybe even in this building, though Harry couldn't be sure of it. He held onto the handle as the sense of life wafted over him in something akin to a minty aroma. It flooded him with emotion and purpose, a surge of hope, lifting him to the task at hand.

He doubted the sorcerers had meant for him to receive this message. More to the point, they probably didn't realize he had such ability. Jones had said each Protector was different. He could use that knowledge and strike back hard with it.

Duffy called for him again. In response, Harry put more pressure on the door, and in response, more static charge erupted against him. He grabbed the handle tighter and pushed, looking closely at the buzzing colors. Harry moved an inch more onto the threshold, and the vibrations pulsed in a wash of aurora-like splendor. He kept advancing, and whatever this was resisting him began to feel like a gelatinous substance. It enveloped him, suffocating, oozing. He stopped, sweat dripping into his eyes. The door had opened only a couple of inches. He started again—grunting, his breaths coming in spurts—the gelatinous force sliding past little by little.

"Calm yourself."

It was Meriodoc. Harry tried to comply. *"Is it safe?"*

"Duffy is well within the building and should be safe."

"Dammit, what about me?"

Ignoring Harry's worry, Meriodoc simply answered, *"Continue."*

The pressure slid around him, but it had been building, too. Behind him, the force grew as he slowly displaced the barrier in front of him. If it blew, the building was history, and so was he.

How the hell did Duffy enter? Then Harry remembered the Grigori no longer possessed the big agent. The shadows simply entered the building through means beyond his reckoning, leaving Duffy free to follow by natural means. Yet, Harry could not easily overcome the barrier.

"If you don't gather yourself, I assure you, you won't like the outcome of violating this magical boundary. Now remain calm and, when the trigger snaps, the sorcery will not touch you."

"How?" Harry could feel the power behind him, growing to gigantic proportions.

"Concentrate."

"On what?" No answer, so he gritted his teeth and pressed forward, leaning into the barrier. The substance continued to slide past, the pressure growing like a monstrous bulwark.

"You must hold your concentration. Avoid your natural senses. Disregard them. This is critical to your

survival. Become one with the magic."

Harry rolled his eyes. This was obviously Agnes speaking through Meriodoc. He remembered all the sci-fi flicks she'd been so fond of. All he needed now was for Meriodoc to begin parroting some weird theory Agnes might whisper into his ear.

"You heard me," Meriodoc said with not a little agitation. *"When it blows, the explosion will be away from you in the opposite direction and quite ineffectual in the natural realm if you've been successful."*

"And if not?"

"You, Duffy, and the couple walking past on the opposite side of the street will be disintegrated."

Harry's heart clutched at his ribs. He would have stopped right there if he hadn't been so terrified of making a mistake. So he gave himself up to thoughts of Ginny and Jack. They needed him, and so did others, maybe countless others, if he had accurately assessed the ramifications of his failure.

Concentrating on his friends saved him because when he took another step, the pent-up force behind him ignited into an explosion which shook the ground like a magnitude ten earthquake or a shitload of TNT. He cringed as the earth quaked. The building trembled and began to crumble. His eyes had momentarily snapped shut, but when he opened them, nothing of the sort had happened. The floor was still intact, as were the doors and the entire building.

"Good boy, you did splendidly. I hope the bastards felt the bloody hell out of that on the other end of this metaphysical link."

"What was that explosion? Why am I still alive?"

Meriodoc uttered a sigh of relief that Harry felt like

a tickle in the back of his mind. *"Usually, but not always, Protectors can turn magical currents away, to short-circuit them as you would say in your day."*

Harry zeroed in on the critical part of what Meriodoc had just said—not always. *"Suppose I didn't have that ability. What then?"*

"It had to be tested, my boy. It seems you've been given a full complement of powers that many of your predecessors never possessed."

Harry said nothing, choosing instead to let his racing heart calm. He wiped the sweat from his face and sat down on a nearby bench, his legs too shaky to keep him standing.

"When overcoming the sorcery as you just did, the effect is not produced on the physical plane. Of course, if you had been unsuccessful, you really wouldn't have noticed it either because you would have been dead. This whole block would have gone up in one gigantic fireball. Our enemies really wanted to keep you out of this building, my boy."

"You couldn't have warned me of all this ahead of time?"

"If we had, you would have failed. Far better this way, don't you think? Now, let's get to work. I've rejoined Duffy."

The building stank of sorcery, but not a stench he could simply pick up with his nose, something almost too subtle to notice. With his new senses, he could peer into an aspect of the world formerly unknown to him, a plane the sorcerers could access, a kind of undertow of emotion, of threat, entirely malicious, something that could overwhelm him and cut his will to continue. The warning came with silent voices, laid down in the building as one might record music on a tape, there to mock and challenge him. They meant to turn him away from the course he'd already chosen. In response, Harry continued to focus on his friends. Their need was greater than his safety, so he kept moving forward.

He met Duffy at the entrance to an enormous central storeroom that opened up through two large doors onto loading docks at the back of the building. He found Duffy in a wistful mood as though Meriodoc had remembered some detail from his past.

"I was never good with thresholds, and, of course, I never had the Grigori to advise me."

Relieved to finally be with him again, Harry nodded.

"You're young and stronger than I was." Duffy stared off into the distance. "I was middle-aged when I got recruited into the legacy. Philip Black, my first cousin, died fighting them, and suddenly it all fell to me. There were no others."

"I can sympathize with you on that one."

"I was a scholar." Duffy turned to him with a forlorn smile on his face. "A fellow at Oxford, aware of my family's unique role, but removed from it, or so I thought. So very wrong I was. My quiet life of books and teaching, enjoying women, drinking in the pubs, was soon shattered. Fifteen months is all I lasted before the agreement was struck, and, of course, you know something of the rest of my fate. The exchange was made. That would be the end of the conflict, there would never again be the need for a Black Protector, because, of course, the other side would perform a similar sacrifice and end all the strife. There would never be sorcery in the world again. A noble duty my family called it, one I was bound to take up. A bitter end for me, though." Duffy shuddered. "And painful."

"Why didn't the conflict die?" Harry asked.

Duffy turned to him, an equal amount of puzzlement in his own eyes. "The dead don't know anything of the world, Harry, but I did wonder about it when I found myself part of the Grigori some weeks back, and we could access the living world. Chauncey doesn't know either."

Harry put a hand on Duffy's shoulder. "We have about an hour to get back, but I want to return sooner than that."

Duffy leveled a knowing look onto him, and Harry couldn't keep his thoughts private.

"Ah, the woman. I see. They've captured her. Listen, my boy, I know you've been warned about these kinds of attachments. In this awful business, there often is much suffering of others you can't avoid. You have primary goals to achieve, and running off to save a lovely damsel is not something—"

"I don't give a damn what you or the others think about this, okay?" Harry checked himself and lowered his voice. "I just don't, so enough with the shitty advice."

Meriodoc placed Duffy's big hand on his shoulder. "It's a lonely life. It isn't fair to those chosen for it."

"Chosen!" Harry practically spat the word out at him. "I didn't choose this life, and I might still reject it."

Duffy gave him a surprised look. "Not likely."

"We'll see."

A wail, non-human and eerie, echoed through the large holding area, wafting over Harry and Duffy in waves of undulating fury. It was a challenge and, when it ended, Harry straightened, clenched his fists, and without looking at Duffy, entered the chamber.

Chapter 36

Harry and Duffy studied the immense space before them. It was a vast room with rails on the ceiling that supported a mobile crane. Heavy steel supports held the tracks. They stood near deep wells in the floor, which housed hydraulic mechanisms.

"What the hell was that?" Harry whispered.

"Could be several things, my boy." Duffy covered his mouth with his hand and spoke in a muted voice. "No telling how long they've kept this building, but for what purpose?" He put his hand out, sensing the place. "They've had time to make the building very secure. Not to mention the time to put in some surprises for us like that massive threshold you deftly maneuvered."

"You think it's a trap?" Harry asked.

Meriodoc closed Duffy's eyes and lifted his head as if to sniff the hot air blowing into the room from the far end where two thirty-foot steel hangar doors were partly rolled up.

"No, I don't get that feeling at all. I think it's just a well-fortified holding place. Magically fortified, you understand. A staging ground, if you will. They obviously don't want any Protectors poking around in their business."

Harry tried his sight, but for some reason, it wasn't working. "Dammit, my senses are muted in here, but earlier at the threshold, I had an overwhelming feeling that Jack was still alive."

"And now?"

"I'm over the threshold now, but something's blocking me. I can't—" Harry walked off a bit and stopped. A faint ringing had commenced within the last few moments. If his skin could have crawled off, it would have.

"They could have planted that idea for you to pick up, though I can't see why they would do it."

"Jack's alive, and Paula too." Harry checked his watch and stared at the far end of the room. It was all he could do to keep from throwing caution aside and walking straightway through those big ass doors to the docking platform beyond.

"You think they know we're here?" Harry asked.

Meriodoc was too wrapped up in his own examination of the room to answer.

"They were held here, in this room," Harry said at last. "I know that much. Part of the previous day and all of yesterday until several hours ago, Jack and Paula were there." He pointed to a small room next to the opening at the far end.

"I see it," Meriodoc said, "but let's not be hasty."

Harry nodded and pulled his cell phone out. He hesitated, itching to call Boone, solid in his conviction that the sheriff was still on his side, but he thought better of making the call himself. "Are you able to speak in Duffy's voice?"

Meriodoc thought about the question a moment. "A close approximation, I think. Why?"

"Because we need backup when we get to the house. I know where they'll be, generally."

"If we get back."

Harry gave him an aggravated look. “Dammit, Meriodoc, now’s not the time to be a smartass, okay? Has Chauncey figured out how to use Peeters as a beacon?”

Meriodoc didn’t answer, but Duffy cleared his throat and began talking in a gravelly voice of someone quite a bit older than Meriodoc Black had been at his death, and from an earlier time.

“You understand, do you not, that ours is not the way of sorcery. However—” Duffy hesitated. His eyelids lowered as though he had drifted into sleep.

“Chauncey?” Harry said, frustrated. “Would someone please wake him up?”

Duffy’s eyes opened slowly. “Right, yes…as I was saying, the principle is the same, but the means is quite different.”

“I don’t need a frickin’ lecture on weird science, Chauncey, just come out with it. Can you pinpoint the location or not?”

Duffy became quiet for a moment until Meriodoc spoke up again. “Let me have a word with him. Chauncey is a bit girlish in the feelings department, but he is, or rather *was*, a brilliant scholar. We’re lucky to have him. As mother always said, ‘Patience will out.’ ”

Harry was about to say something rude when Meriodoc interrupted. “Pardon me for a moment.”

“Great, all I need now is for a spook to go all sensitive on me.”

Meriodoc and Chauncey started arguing, and they weren’t doing so silently. “One moment,” Meriodoc said, speaking to Chauncey. Duffy turned to Harry and put a big paw on Harry’s shoulder. “Be gentle.”

Harry rolled his eyes. “Chauncey, I’m sorry, man,

for getting annoyed with you, but this is important. I know it's a new thing I'm asking. Can it be done?"

"Of course, it can. I've studied the matter thoroughly, and yes, it can be done. It is a simple matter of triangulating the—"

Harry prodded his cell phone; time was getting away from him, closing in fast on eleven-thirty. All he had was a little more than a half-hour to execute his plan.

"—that would put you squarely, rather precisely, I might add, on the exact spot next to your target. I have even made an adjustment for the small matter that two bodies cannot occupy the same space at the same time. A crucial concept, you know."

"Brilliant, Chauncey, perfect. Meriodoc and I have to see what's here first and when I give him the word, you and the others will take Duffy and me to Peeters, right?"

"It is all planned out, my boy. Trust me. But are you sure of your target? If the beacon is not where you desire him to be—"

"He's where I think he is," Harry said. "Just wait until I give you the word."

"We don't really need to know his location. I have a fix on him wherever in the world he is."

Harry waited while Meriodoc came back. "Now we make the call, but I don't want it to come from me. Its official police business and Duffy's close enough. If Boone's turned, he'll—"

Meriodoc noticed his hesitation. "What is it?"

Harry didn't answer at first. Something had just struck him, a better plan. "No, it's not Boone I need to call."

"Who then?"

"Look, I've changed my mind. Deke Pelgram's our mole. I'm sure of it. He's Boone's chief deputy, the one who reported that this place had been found. Remember, he said they'd even found Jack's cell phone."

"Yes, but why is it important?"

"I'm going to expose him to Boone. My guess is when I tell him we're on the way back, he'll have an ambush ready. I'll end up dead and Boone's none the wiser."

Duffy smiled down at him. "Bloody brilliant."

"Just trying to stay alive, Merry."

Duffy spun on him. "What did you call me?"

"Merry, like a character from a movie I saw once who had your name. They called him Merry, too, a nickname."

Duffy had tears in his eyes. "My Berta used to call me that. So long ago it was that I've forgotten how she looked."

"Sorry, man. I know it's tough. Let's go get these bastards and put them where they belong."

Duffy smiled a sad smile and nodded. In a matter of seconds, the temperature dropped at least forty degrees.

Chapter 37

Cold. In June. In Mississippi. That was a piece of sorcery neither Harry nor Meriodoc expected, but here it was smacking them in the face as if to say, "So what's keeping you guys. Let's rumble."

The vibrations Harry had felt grew stronger. Fear washed over him like cold rain, rendering him immobile. His thoughts stopped churning. His heart strained to beat against the rush of panic. It was the hardest thing he had ever done to keep from screaming like a teenager and running. The fact that his grandmother would see forced him to swallow his fear and man up.

Duffy stood beside him, staring blankly about the expansive room.

"What the hell?" Harry whispered. "What are we supposed to do now?"

"They're trying to intimidate us," Meriodoc said in barely a whisper.

"You think so? I've been thoroughly smack-on sick with intimidation for two days now."

"Me too," Meriodoc said sheepishly.

"Great, now that we've decided we're both scared shitless, what'll we do?"

Meriodoc raised Duffy's hand and scratched his chin. "Go ahead and make the call while I ponder this new situation."

Pelgram. Harry looked down and found his phone in his shaking hand. He punched the main number to the Rankin County sheriff's office and put the phone to his ear, remembering the ploy he had been about to embark on. In a moment, Deke Pelgram barked out a rough approximation of the word, hello.

"It's Harry Black."

There was a long silence. It was clear Pelgram hadn't expected this particular caller.

"You there, Deke?"

"Chief Deputy Pelgram," he finally said with venom in his words. He composed himself. "How's the FBI treating you, Black? Provide any useful answers yet following that cockamamie bullshit you tried to sell?"

"So, Boone told you I was taken in for questioning, right?"

"Sure did. Got your story straight enough yet to avoid the lockup?"

He was lying. Harry could hear it in his voice. He knew Boone hadn't informed Pelgram of anything, not after witnessing the way the Grigori had snatched him out of his kitchen before McKeen could put a bullet in him. Pelgram hadn't been there, which prompted an uneasy question. Who had informed him of Harry's departure?

"Never mind about that," Harry said. "I've got information you should take to Boone. I know where Jack Hallowell and Paula Grisham are being held. They also have Virginia Rankin now. The senator's sister. Got that? By the way, the deputies who were protecting her are dead."

Harry stopped, and there was absolutely no

response to what he'd just said, not even a sharp intake of breath over the death of his men. He wanted his message to get out loud and clear to the people controlling Pelgram.

"I need backup when I get back to the estate, plenty of it, you hear? I'll be arriving with Agent Duffy in about a half-hour. We need to be prepared to get these three people back. Tell Boone to be ready."

"Is that all, Black, or do you have more orders for me?"

Harry tried to remain calm, but it wasn't easy. "Yeah, just one, you prick, go tell your new bosses that I'll be ready. You know who I mean, Deke. I'll be ready for them."

With the curse words barely out of Pelgram's mouth, Harry broke the connection. He had to warn Boone. With the cat out of the proverbial bag, the sheriff had suddenly fallen under Harry's protection, only he didn't know it yet. It would be easy to get to Boone now, kill him, thereby throwing the department into chaos, which would effectively remove it from the equation. If that happened, Harry would soon be rotting in jail, or worse, smelling up a field or ditch somewhere.

And something else, Harry had no idea if Pelgram was operating with any more turned deputies. Pelgram hadn't been acting alone. Brick proved that. But who else might be involved? It had to be someone who had been in his kitchen at the time of Harry's departure, but probably not anyone from the sheriff's deputy corps, considering that it had been practically decimated. The theory felt right, but he wasn't confident the sheriff's other deputies hadn't been turned.

He tried Boone's cell and didn't get an answer, but it was too soon to worry. The temperature had dropped another ten degrees or so, an extraordinary thing considering the hot Mississippi night through that considerable opening on the far side of the room.

"It's Pelgram," Harry said, "he's behind some of this shit, maybe a lot of it."

Duffy turned to him and tried to answer, but before he could respond, another voice boomed through the expansive room.

"I applaud you for that less-than-brilliant deduction."

Duffy and Harry nearly jumped out of their shoes. They spun in opposite directions, trying to pinpoint its exact location. The voice seemed to be coming from all directions at once.

"Where?" Harry breathed through chattering teeth. Impossibly, it was getting colder. Duffy hadn't yet uttered a word. In fact, the big agent was cringing beside him. "Meriodoc, what the hell's the problem?"

"Oh, this is too much," the voice boomed again.

Its origin point was the docking platform, the place he'd been loath to go near for fear of what may be lurking there.

"Is that you, Meriodoc Black, Protector from my younger days? I know it is. I could always sense your fear. You've grown darker lately." The voice chuckled. "But I know it's only a borrowed body."

Harry grabbed Duffy's arm and felt him trembling. He whispered, "Do you know him?"

Duffy swallowed.

"Meriodoc," Harry said again, getting aggravated with him, "snap out of it. Who is this bastard?"

Laughter rumbled through the storage chamber like far off thunder.

Staring straight ahead, Meriodoc finally spoke. “He’s too much for us.” Duffy turned his shocked eyes to Harry. “Better to die now…quickly.”

“No one’s gonna die, Meriodoc, especially you.”

Duffy cringed again. “There are things worse than death, far worse, in fact. He can still affect me, us, the brethren whom I’m bound to. We mustn’t—”

“Oh, just let them fly off, Harry,” the voice said, “and go back to that place beyond. They can still enjoy some peace.”

“Shut up!” Harry yelled and turned back to Duffy. “We’re losing time here. People are dying. They need our help.”

Duffy was rubbing his big hands in full-on panic mode. “Go back? Yes…back.” He began to tremble harder and took a step away from the entrance to the holding room.

“Meriodoc,” Harry said again, trying to get his attention. “Agent Duffy!”

The FBI man finally turned to Harry, who slapped him with all his strength across the face.

Duffy brought his meaty hand up to his left cheek and rubbed it, the look on his face one of hurt and puzzlement.

“Why’d you do that?” Meriodoc said in an astonished voice.

“Are you okay now?”

A look of shame came across Duffy’s face. “Yes,” Meriodoc said, “Sorry, it’s just—”

Faraway laughter rumbled through the room.

“I didn’t expect…*him.*”

"Who?"

Duffy shook his head. "We can't win. I mean, somehow he's still alive, and his power must be—"

Duffy's eyes had become riveted on the far platform. A mist began to form. It organized into a shape. A flowing robe appeared first, some sort of black material forming out of dark wisps of air. A hooded form, tall and with a regal bearing, finally coalesced. Harry couldn't see the being's face. All he could see were two slits of shimmering blue where eyes should have been.

Meriodoc was muttering beside him. "Don't make me, Harry. The things he'll do to me. Don't make me."

"Get a grip and pull yourself together before this freak damages my grandson." Agnes Black's voice seethed with anger out of Duffy's mouth.

"Shut it, woman," Meriodoc said. "This is Protector business. You have no idea of his power. Better to die now and save himself from pain and us from misery."

"How did that plan work for you, Meriodoc, all those years ago?" Agnes said. There was a low grumble from Duffy. "Ah, yes, not so well. A fine pickle the family put you in then, and here we are nearly two centuries later, and he's still alive. Someone pulled a fast one, didn't they?"

"Listen," Harry said, "we can't start a family feud."

The form was moving now. It had already levitated off the platform and into the room, advancing slowly.

"Desmin…here," Meriodoc groaned, "after all this time. Chauncey, how is it possible?"

Duffy went silent as the figure got closer, the cold boring into Harry, a malevolence causing the very air to vibrate with a sound within the range of normal human hearing. Chauncey stuttered something Harry couldn't make out. The robed figure spoke.

"It's taken us all this time to make a return. The plan worked to perfection, but we didn't account for the backlash. It seems the Blacks have some clout with the universal consciousness." The thing walking toward them sighed. "We paid dearly, though I lived." He lifted a hand, and the loose robe floated along with his movement as wisps of black smoke flew momentarily away from the main body and congealed back into the figure a moment later.

"Your trickery nearly broke my power completely, but we were saved just in time by our mastery of deeper, more powerful sorcery. You weren't as lucky, though, were you, Merry?"

Duffy shook his head slowly, hesitantly.

"Of course, you never knew what we did with your woman, the whore, Berta."

Meriodoc groaned. "No more. I won't hear it." But he changed his mind. "How are you able to be here, Master Mage?"

"That is not for the likes of you or your pathetic successor to know."

"You were supposed to be dead. It was our agreement. All this was to end once and for all. I kept my part of the bargain."

Duffy paced about, speaking to the apparition one moment and to no one in particular the next.

"It was *your* agreement, never mine. I had other plans regardless of what arrangements the family had set up with you cursed lot."

He stopped. White, delicate hands appeared out of

the long sleeves of his black robe. He lowered the hood. His face was whiter than his hands, accentuated by blood-red lips. And for someone nearly two centuries old, he looked pretty good. Light brown hair without a hint of gray, face unwrinkled. He could have passed for a youngish forty-something.

"How's it possible?" Harry whispered in Duffy's ear when the big man's agitation waned. Duffy stood as still as a statue without the typical wobble most people exhibit. Then a black substance exited from Duffy's ear and slithered down the back of his dark suit. It passed to the floor and began a slow advance toward the apparition.

There were spots on the floor, dirty oil stains, and the shadow moved quickly until it reached a large stain five feet from where Desmin stood. There it stopped and didn't move again, lying invisible to all eyes.

"Now," Desmin began again, "I suppose you'll want to know why I maneuvered you here."

"I have a pretty good idea," Harry said.

Desmin continued to walk until he reached the big oil spot, maybe ten feet from where Harry stood. "You have disregarded our warnings and made yourself a nuisance. We would have let you live, let bygones be bygones, but since you seem adamant about dying, I am here to oblige you."

"It won't be that easy." But before Harry could enjoy his repartee, something hit him.

Harry would have been brave to go along with his irreverence, but the pain was too much. He doubled over and fell to his knees, clutching his chest.

"A little something for your impertinence, I think. And the thrall…"

The spooky sonofabitch glanced at Duffy, who hadn't even blinked for a couple of minutes. He considered the big agent, then he snarled and lifted a hand.

Duffy's body became more erect, straightening to his full height, chin jutted forward. Desmin twisted his hand, and Duffy's head cocked to one side.

"Interesting." Desmin suddenly began to search around the room—to the side, over his head, down to the floor. "Where are they, Black?"

Before Harry could respond, Meriodoc spoke to his mind. *"Don't answer it, Harry."*

"It? What the hell do you mean?"

"He isn't real. It's a psychogeist, a mere manifested memory, but one with considerable power. I'm in contact with it."

"What do you want me to—"

The Desmin thing let out an ear-piercing shriek and began flailing his arms as the Grigori crept up from the floor and slithered over the sorcerer's phantom body. The thing became insubstantial as it thrashed and flopped and stomped about, shrieking and cursing as the Grigori slid over it.

Rolled up into a snake-like shadow, the Grigori entered the creature's mouth and ears, but before they disappeared altogether inside the thing, Agnes's words blossomed in Harry's mind.

"Let's get him."

The creature shuddered once, struggling with itself, but as Meriodoc had said, it was powerful. It locked eyes with Harry, made some kind of gesture with its hands, and thrust them high overhead. The psychogeist mumbled a word of gibberish. A rushing wind swooshed past Harry.

Duffy took a sharp intake of breath and collapsed in a heap as the phantom creature exploded into a thousand wisps of black smoke.

Chapter 38

Harry bent over Agent Duffy. The big man's eyes were open, but he still hadn't made a sound. In fact, Duffy appeared to be…

Harry shook the agent's shoulder again, harder this time, but he didn't move.

"Harry," Meriodoc said to his mind.

"What?" Harry shot back, his nerves raw with what had just happened. He ran shaky hands over Duffy, trying to find an injury, something that would explain his condition.

"I'm afraid Duffy's dead."

Those words worked their way slowly through Harry's brain. "Dammit, Meriodoc, how?" He sensed their presence and searched the air in front of him. He found them to his right. "What the hell am I supposed to do now? How do I explain this when they find out I was with him here?"

"You won't have to explain anything. You'll just leave Duffy's body here and place a call for his compatriots to retrieve him. They'll find no marks on him, nothing that will show how he died. They will assume something natural like a heart attack or some other such mundane occurrence. They will not bother you about that. He was merely here checking a lead on the kidnapping, and he brought you along. There is nothing to indicate foul play other than the obvious fact

that he is dead."

But Harry shook his head. "Like hell. They'll bring me in."

"An inconvenience only. The authorities cannot touch you, Harry. It's unfortunate what happened, but we cannot do anything for him now."

Harry nodded and, before standing, he closed Duffy's eyes. Correct, nothing could be done, but there was so much left to do this night. A sense of hopelessness fell on him like a hundred-pound wet blanket, making his limbs lethargic. He was now truly alone except, that is, for a group of dead people who had seen fit so far to save him. And why was that when he couldn't even protect those closest to him? Jack was missing and likely dead. Likewise for Ginny. And as for Jones, Harry would never trust his sorry old ass again.

He reached out with his senses. Nothing. The place was empty now of sorcery, just an ordinary building once again.

"Can you detect anything?" Harry asked Meriodoc.

"The place is clear."

Harry noticed the time on his watch, eleven thirty-five. Soon the witching hour would be here, the real battle would begin, but he couldn't get Duffy out of his mind.

"How?" he asked Meriodoc again. "Why not kill me? That's what that thing was placed here to do."

"Truth is, Harry, we don't know how or why. Chauncey is beside himself. You were a sitting duck as they say, as vulnerable as anyone could be."

"Okay, you saved me again. Why not Duffy too?"

There was a long pause before they answered. *"We*

counted ourselves able to attack the thing, but when you say we saved you, you may be attributing too much to us. We destroyed it, but Desmin was able to get off a piece of sorcery. And it was directed at you."

"Then why am I not the one lying there with a blank face? Why is Duffy dead instead of me?"

The shadows flickered wildly and cast about. *"We don't know. Desmin obviously missed, but we don't know why."*

"Dammit, that's not good enough."

"We don't understand why, Harry. Chauncey's working on it."

"Chauncey, right, the arcane scholar." Harry wiped cold sweat off his forehead. "Let me know when he's got something. It could be important."

Harry walked to the glassed-in office, and, as he entered, the thumping inside his skull started again as the full force of what had happened there hit him. He staggered through the door and had to lean against an old wooden desk as he stepped into one of his visions. The screams of Peggy Cox assaulted his senses, her assailants laughing, knives slashing. Scene after ugly scene rolled over him—torture, rape, the slit throat. They hauled her out in a filthy canvas bag.

Harry lurched out of the room, and the vision cleared, but not from his memory. He dropped to his knees and threw up. When his head cleared, he went back to the door but didn't enter. The evidence of blood was everywhere, though someone, an indistinct gray figure lingering still in the fading memory of the vision, had tried to clean it up. Across the room, some kind of examining table had been used at one point. The instruments were still strewn about.

The cell phone lay on a counter next to an old fax machine. It was Jack's. Entering the room again, he grabbed the phone, opened it, and another horrific panorama unfolded before his eyes.

Jack, strung up and hanging by his bound hands on the loading platform like a slain deer about to be gutted. Paula Grisham, naked and gagged, hands and feet bound, lay nearby. Jack's toes barely touched the concrete floor…

****

"Do we do it now?" somebody said in the vision. The guy had a black-handled knife in his hand.

"Lord Desmin says we wait, so unless you want your balls shoved down your throat, you'll listen. He don't want no more killings just yet."

Jack moaned, and Paula cringed away from the two men, but it was apparent to Harry she wanted to stay close to Jack and aid him with her nearness. He and Ginny had been wrong about her.

"The trap is laid anyway, but just in case, he wants these alive for a while yet. The Protector will know to come here for his friend, and he'll have those damned things with him."

"So it's true, what Arie heard. They're in the game this time."

"Yeah, they're in. Should be interesting."

"And what about Black? What's he like? Dangerous, or is he a pussy like some of the others mentioned in the old stories?"

"What I heard is that he's different, but that's not much to go on. What's important is he's got them, right? The master's got it covered, though. He'll know how to handle those things." The speaker paused and turned dispassionate eyes onto Jack. "Cut him down. We've been told to move out."

With one flick of some sort of shiny, lethal blade, the heavy rope was shorn in two, and Jack crashed to the floor nearly on top of Paula. All the strength and fight had been taken out of him. He lay there groaning, barely moving, Paula sobbing over him…

****

Harry snapped Jack's cell phone shut and placed it in his pocket.

"You saw something, didn't you?" Meriodoc asked as the Grigori hovered over Harry's left shoulder.

Harry gave them an aggravated look. "Time to go," he said before storming out of the room.

"Wait. We have to tell you something first. The shadow of Desmin had power, but it was no match for what we could do to it."

"Yeah, well, you guys did good seeing as I'm still alive. So thanks again."

"But you don't understand. Before we knew what we were dealing with, we thought it was the real Desmin. It's a good thing it wasn't, or you would be dead."

That stopped him. "What are you guys trying to say?" A sound erupted in his mind. He equated it to the Grigori clearing their throats. "Just come out with it, dammit, I've got to get to the clearing."

"What we mean to say is we didn't acquit ourselves very well. We were afraid, deathly afraid. If we meet the real Desmin, the outcome will probably be different. We wanted to make sure you understand that. Really understand it."

"I'm ready to die if that's what you're getting at.

The hostages are probably dead already anyway. But listen, maybe Desmin isn't even alive. They just used him to frighten you, and it worked, but not for long."

"No, Harry, the psychogeist couldn't form without the real thing doing it. It's him—his voice—his memories, but just a small fraction of his power. He's alive and here. You have to know that and be ready."

"And so do you," Harry said as he strode out of the enormous storage room.

Chapter 39

On the Tarmac at Jackson-Evers International Airport

The three-car contingent led by Sheriff Boone made it to the airport without any problem. Trower felt lucky to have gotten everyone to this point. They had lost two men, but the senator was intact, and his family was presumably safe in Brookhaven. Savage had been one of the losses, but that didn't concern him much. He had insisted on coming, knowing the orders were for them to protect only the senator and his family. His boss cursed like a sailor when Trower called in the deaths while in transit to the airport. With all the shit that had gone down, they were lucky to have their own heads still attached. He would be forgiven those losses, regrettable as they were.

The one nagging thing was that Trower's men were now eyeing him with concern, and not a little suspicion. They were leaving one of their own in Mississippi. It was clear to them that Trower had given Harry Black a pass. He'd seemingly accepted a story that, on the face of it, was wild and beyond belief. Trower had overheard their grumbling, but decided now was not the time to discuss the crazy things happening.

None but the two agents who had overheard the conversation between Black and the Rankins on that back porch in Brookhaven knew the full extent of it, and even they had missed many things.

One of those agents was now dead, killed in a fashion that seemed unbelievable in the twenty-first century. This detail had shaped up as the weirdest Trower had ever worked. By the looks on the faces of his men, they wanted answers from their boss. Unfortunately, answers were hard to come by.

His men were well trained; the looks he now got from them were all spit and shine. Trower had told them his reasons for laying off of Black. None of them saw what he had seen, and alone in the backseat of one of the sedans with the senator, it became clear that Bill Rankin had also seen even more shit than he would readily admit. He'd given Trower his explicit approval of how he had handled his detail. That would go a long way in reclaiming the esteem they would have undoubtedly lost in the eyes of Director Bartlett and this current president after losing two men. Now they had to salvage the rest of this crappy job and get Rankin back to DC in one piece.

The cars pulled alongside the waiting jet. Twelve doors flung open simultaneously. Trower exited with Rankin and looked down the long stretch of desolate, black tarmac. He didn't waste any time instructing two of his agents to escort Rankin up the stairs to the waiting jet. He glanced up at the cockpit. The pilot who had flown them down to Mississippi waved back.

Trower turned back to Boone, who had been giving some final instructions to a deputy who'd accompanied him. "Thanks for riding shotgun from that madhouse, Sheriff."

Boone nodded as he watched the senator ascend

the steps and disappear into the fuselage. “Glad to help, but I hope you know what the hell you’re doing. My gut tells me he’d have been safer where we just left.”

“Really? Even with all the potshots we took back there?” Trower shook his head. “Just because I told Black I believed him doesn’t mean I trust him to handle this shit. Protecting Rankin is my job. He’s going back to Washington.”

“Hope you’re right, is all. Now, if you’ll excuse me, I’ve got a mess to clean up back at the mansion and my own citizens to protect.” Boone turned to go but hesitated. “Second thought, I better wait until you’re safely in the air.”

This made Trower pause. In all the commotion, they hadn’t secured anything. Truth be told, he didn’t even know who was on the plane with Rankin other than the pilot and his two agents. He cursed his sloppy work as he looked down the runway again then scanned the perimeter. They could have been followed.

He turned back to Sheriff Boone. “We better get going. The control tower’s been informed. We should be cleared.”

“Hurry, then, and I’ll watch your back.”

Boone took a step back and scanned the far tree line while Trower began talking into his sleeve to the pilot. The jet roared to life as Trower ran up the stairs. He turned at the top to signal Boone, and the grounds crew began moving the stairs away from the plane.

Just inside, a flight attendant secured the doors while Trower took in the plane with a quick glance. Everything seemed in order. Rankin was already on his cell phone, murmuring, and Trower’s remaining agents were positioned front and back in adjoining rows.

As Trower felt himself begin to relax from the constant adrenaline rush of the last few hours, the plane turned in the direction it would take taxiing down the runway. It began gathering speed, and, as happens on jets gaining altitude, the pressure inside the cabin made Trower's ears pop. This was unusual because they weren't gaining altitude. In fact, they were still in contact with the ground. He steadied himself with one hand against the ceiling, puzzling about this, then turned to the opened door of the cockpit, and blinked when he saw the terrorist, Peeters, smiling back with that same cocky, big-toothed grin.

Trower stiffened and snapped his head back to Rankin, who now seemed to have fallen asleep, and so had his men. Maybe a second passed before his brain registered the oddity of all this. In the next moment, Trower drew his gun and turned back to Peeters, who was no longer there. Instead, Bill Rankin stood in the doorway looking as handsome and standing as straight as the man who had a second before been dozing farther down the fuselage. Trower hesitated then turned back to the sleeping Rankin still there in the seat.

Before the impossibility of the situation could fully form in his mind, the lights in the cabin blinked out, Trower's knees began to buckle, and he heard the fake senator say, "Let's get to DC where the idiot from Idaho can welcome back his Messiah. From there, our Lord wants these others brought to the compound in Amsterdam and shown a little old-world hospitality."

Chapter 40

Being transported by dozens of spirits you can't see, via a void that shouldn't exist, wasn't much like flying at all, but it was the best word Harry could think of to make sense of the phenomenon. It was an almost instantaneous event.

Harry told Meriodoc to take him a block past the sheriff's office in the city of Brandon about fourteen miles south as the crow flies from the heart of Jackson. Harry didn't know how they would locate the place to make his delivery accurate. However, he had been to the sheriff's compound before, so the Grigori simply triangulated the location to make his delivery perfect. He made a mental note to ask Chauncey how it worked, but he doubted the old spook would know how to communicate it to him.

They deposited him on Timber Street. The place was quiet. There was no frantic activity, no bustle of corrupt cops making desperate plans for his murder. He didn't get any premonitions at all. Satisfied, he walked a block west to North Street, where he found a booth hidden in a dark corner of the local greasy spoon. There he waited for Sheriff Boone. Harry had connected with him before fleeing the warehouse and told Boone to come alone.

Harry didn't know yet whether he could trust him, but he knew he had to find out. He needed help in the worst way, and that help would come best from people with a shitload of guns.

Boone arrived a couple of minutes later, looking harried. Without a word, he sat and listened. Harry needed to get it all out quickly and without interruption. Time was a precious commodity.

Boone didn't take his eyes off Harry as he listened to the story. Harry had already primed the pump back at Black Manor with that disappearing act he'd pulled in the kitchen, so the fantastic elements didn't come as any surprise to the sheriff. Boone stared at Harry and sipped coffee, occasionally rubbing the gray stubble on his face.

Harry gave Boone the quick version of the dream he'd been having for weeks—the screaming woman, the woods, the clearing, and importantly, the strange people in the flowing silk robes who populated the little opening. Harry would be heading there tonight, but not in the way the sorcerer Desmin and his bunch would expect. He told him about Ginny being captured and two more of his deputies being slaughtered.

"Damn, son, I was on my way back there when you called."

"There's no one there now. Ginny's gone, and more of your men are dead."

Boone groaned and squeezed his coffee cup so hard Harry was afraid he would crack the sturdy ceramic.

Harry told Boone about Pelgram's duplicity and the conversation Harry had with him. Boone's head sagged. He put his cup down and stared at the opposite wall, more deeply troubled with this news.

"I know Deke's your chief deputy, but you can't

trust him. I'm surprised they haven't made a move against you yet."

Boone waved a hand to dismiss the thought. "It means they don't think I'm enough trouble to bother with, is all. Too old. Pelgram was a good man once, but we've had our differences about how to run things." Boone took another sip. "You think he's turned or just working for money?"

"Good point, but moot. Pelgram is bad, regardless."

"Chances are its money he's after. Supports two ex-wives, and now he's about to get the third and youngest. He does contract work whenever I can afford to release him, which isn't often enough for him. What he wants most is my job. But it's an elected position, and he couldn't get elected shit-house cleaner."

Harry chuckled. "Plus, they probably needed someone with his faculties intact. Brick hadn't exactly been all there."

"That makes Pelgram more culpable in the eyes of the law."

Harry shook his head. "None of this will ever see a courtroom. You know that, right? Who would believe it? Besides, there's no evidence. We take them out tonight, including Pelgram."

"Shit, Harry, with the deaths today, when this thing's over, I'll have to recruit. Never have done that before."

The cook turned on the TV, and a news report blared down at them, which made him remember how this whole mess had started.

"Have you heard anything about Senator Rankin?" Harry asked. "Is he okay?"

"Far as I know. Rankin is in good hands. Trower seems competent, if not a little anal."

Harry agreed with that. It was probably the thing that made Trower an excellent secret service agent. Harry was unconvinced how well Trower and his depleted crew could protect the senator until they had him under lock and key back in Washington, or if it was even possible to lock him up tight enough to keep him from the sorcerers. Harry had his doubts about it.

He was about to say what he thought about those good hands when a reporter started talking.

"The president has not been able to say definitively when the economic summit will resume. The temporary delay is a show of defiance to the terrorists and to provide the president's chief economic advisor, Senator William Rankin, time to return from the funeral of his chief-of-staff and good friend, Carl Dunbar. We can confirm he has not returned to Washington."

The reporter consulted his notes again. Boone checked his watch.

"I left them on the tarmac at nine," Boone said, "nearly three hours ago. They had the CIA Director's private jet."

"Was the flight logged in?"

"They probably have a way around those routines to remain covert, but there was no need for it. I overheard Trower speaking to air traffic control directly. They had a regular flight number and everything."

Harry nodded, understanding the implication.

The reporter was saying, "…it has been confirmed the bombing was the work of Khaled Mashaal, who we have just learned has been captured by a SEAL team.

The details of how they got him so quickly are sketchy. He has confessed to the bombing and is being held in an undisclosed location."

"Bullshit," Harry blurted out.

"There had been speculation all day as to when Senator Rankin and his new chief-of-staff would be returning to the capital. Sources in the senator's office would not confirm his expected arrival time in Washington. We do know the jet was supplied by the CIA."

During all this, Boone had been busy on his cell phone, speaking in hushed tones. He closed it and lifted his head. "I saw the plane take off, Harry. The boys in air traffic control tell me they watched it all the way to Washington. No hitches. It didn't crash. They reported a safe touchdown. He should be there."

"Maybe the DC reporters missed it."

Boone's eyes narrowed. He shook his head. "The story's too hot."

The cook flipped to another channel, and both men turned back to each other.

"Something's not right," Harry said. "Peeters kidnapped Ginny."

"That retarded bastard." Boone shook his head. "I should have brought her with me."

Harry's jaw tightened, but he said nothing.

"They've got Rankin locked down, is all." Boone opened his cell phone again and started scrolling down his number list. "Got Trower's number right here. Gave it to me on the tarmac." He dialed it, but there was no answer. "Well, shit! He told me to call if you surfaced."

"He's probably dead, Sheriff. I know they have Ginny. They probably have her brother too."

Boone's head sank lower on his shoulders. "Dammit all."

They sat silently for a moment, Harry's guts churning, his anger barely in check.

Boone kept fiddling with his cup. "Guess nothing's leaked yet about Savage being killed."

Harry nodded.

"The story's out locally, but not much detail. We were able to control what really happened by saying it was a break-in, and the deputies were gunned down when they responded. We're keeping Savage's death under wraps, for the time being, same for Trower's boy. The president knows, and he's covering it under a national security blanket."

Harry stared at the old sheriff. "That won't last long. That many deputies killed, plus the others, an FBI agent wounded, all happening while the senator was back in his home state. A reporter will pick up on it. It'll draw national attention."

"Hope Rankin's sister makes it somehow. Hate to see her end up a statistic."

"Listen, my friend is still missing, Sheriff. Everyone seems to have forgotten about him and Paula Grisham. These people are adept at taking someone of sound mind and turning them into raving maniacs just like that." Harry snapped his fingers. "Tell me you're not part of them, Sheriff, turned like Brick and maybe Deke."

Boone arched a shaggy eyebrow. "You really think I'd tell you if I were? Does a zombie know he's a zombie?"

Harry slowly shook his head but kept eye contact.

"What did you bring me here for, son? It was pretty

stupid if I'm working for the other fellas."

Harry gripped his cup hard, lifted it, but put it down again, conceding the point. "If they have the senator, why take Ginny?"

"Good question…no answer."

"Here's one. Maybe because the plan is to no longer kill Rankin."

Boone considered it, realization sinking in. "Turn him…place him in Washington as their man."

Harry nodded. "If the senator is turned, he could do more damage in Washington that way. What would achieve their goal sooner, a murdered senator, or a turned senator?"

"Turned makes more sense."

"They keep Ginny handy to control him if something goes wrong. We have to assume the senator's taken and that everyone else with him on that plane is dead right now."

"How do we get word to the president?"

Harry shook his head. "We don't, not yet. We find Jack and Paula and get them back first. That is—"

Boone straightened at Harry's hesitation.

"I probably won't make it tonight, Sheriff. I'm going to the clearing. You know that now. You may not be able to stop me right this moment if you're one of them…" Harry paused and glanced up to the ceiling above the booth where they sat. The Grigori flickered darkly against the glaring light of the diner. "I've told you about my plans and where I'll be. Maybe you'll be able to get a pot shot off at me later."

"Pretty dumb coming here, if you ask me."

"Totally."

"Except, I'm not working for them."

Harry took in a fully relaxed breath for the first time since he'd been sitting with Boone. "Yeah, I was pretty sure you weren't. I had to hear you say it."

"Smart," Boone said. "The words a man says, but more so the way he says them, speak loud and clear about that man. Better to be face to face to really know him."

Harry nodded. "Things are about to get worse. You have some men you can count on? Deke's probably not working alone."

"I know the kind of men he favors—men like Brick—big, stupid. If this was some fifty years ago, the sumbitches would be wearing those white pointy hats and setting fire to crosses."

"Any more good men around?"

Boone grunted, none too happy with the way the department's mortality statistics were trending. "I have Freddie, Fernando Rivera."

Harry nodded.

"And there's Hendricks—we call her Snap."

"She better be a big one. I got a feeling Deke has more muscle behind him."

Boone laughed. "Rowena's a tiny thing. Smart and quick and blacker than Duffy. I'll bring them."

"Come loaded for bear and be stealthy. Come in through old man Scott's farm to the south. Know where I mean?"

"Yeah."

"We'll meet at the edge of the woods behind his place and wait for the best time to surprise the bastards."

"Sounds like you got a plan," Boone said.

"Sort of…I don't know. We'll think of something."

"Is Duffy in with you?" Boone turned in his seat. "Where is he, anyway? Waiting outside? Or did you give him the slip hours ago? I did see those things grab him too, didn't I?"

Harry took a long sip of the lousy coffee, staring directly into Boone's eyes. "Duffy's dead." Boone didn't blink. "They got him too, Sheriff Boone," Harry continued. "In fact, we should leave a message at the FBI office for them to get his body. He deserves to be taken out of that shithole right away. But you should make it anonymous."

He told Boone where the warehouse was.

"I'll do it." He checked his watch. "FBI called a couple hours ago looking for him. I told them I didn't know anything. McKeen's in the hospital for a while, but he's mad as hell at the big fella."

Harry only nodded.

"Jack Hallowell's alive, you say?"

"Yeah."

"And his lawyer friend, the one Brick hired?"

"They're both alive."

"I've got to get my deputies up and armed. But answer one question before you go. You really been talking to Agnes?"

Harry sat back in his seat, caught off guard by the question, then he smiled. "You liked her, didn't you?"

Boone's shaggy brows shot up. "Yeah, yeah, guess you could say that. She was about fifteen years older. Hell, it didn't matter to me. I sparked her a little in the old days after your grandfather died and way before you were born, but of course, our stations weren't compatible. She was uncomfortable with our age difference. I told her I liked them older." He chuckled in the admission.

“She wouldn’t have cared about what you did for a living or how different your backgrounds.”

“She said as much. When her husband died young, she told me she had other things to do besides looking after another man in the house. Guess I damn well know what she meant now.”

“You want to speak to her?”

Boone’s eyes widened. “What, like in a séance?”

“No, nothing like that. Listen, if we both survive the night, I’ll ask, okay?”

“That’ll be interesting.” Boone thought a moment longer. “You’re no longer armed.” He pulled the Beretta out of his jacket and slid it across the table to Harry with an extra magazine. Boone gave one final glance at the Grigori. “Insurance,” he said, “in case you need extra help.” He got up to leave.

The big man limped away, but Harry called out, “Sheriff,” in a flash of inspiration. Boone retraced his steps to the booth.

“You want to get Pelgram red-handed, get him good, right?”

Boone rubbed at his stubble again. “We got nothing now, just what you said, and that ain’t enough. So yeah, if you have something in mind, better say so now.”

Agnes spoke to his mind. *“He’s an excellent candidate, strong mind. I approve.”*

Harry nodded. *“I’m giving him a choice, though. No more coercion.”*

“Of course.”

Harry lowered his eyes to Boone. “To catch Pelgram, you’ll have to be closer to the action, plus I wouldn't want you to be trudging through those woods on that bad knee."

"How else am I gonna—" The Grigori moved from the ceiling to Boone's line of sight, cutting out his next words. "You mean, use me like they did Duffy?"

"Exactly, but Duffy didn't have a choice. They just took him. With you, we'll cause some confusion, some doubt. Plus, the Grigori work better with a vessel. And there's the whole surprise angle. Go in like you're turned and bringing me along to the slaughter. We size up Pelgram if he's there. Take him out with the others."

"And Peeters, Harry," Chauncey said to his mind. *"We need to get him to cut their psychic connection to Black Manor. That way, it can be imperceptible again."*

Harry didn't answer him. He was too busy focusing on the sheriff, who had a devious smile on his face.

"Lots of holes in all that, son, but I like your spunk. You got some of Agnes in you all right." Boone hesitated, rubbing his chin, considering the Grigori, flickering above Harry's left ear. "Does she, I mean, *will* she know?"

Harry's only response was to return Boone's sly smile with one of his own.

Chapter 41

Boone stumbled and nearly fell into a deep ditch as the Grigori deposited them across the road from Black Manor. Harry steadied him with a hand, and they quickly hid behind a thick growth of azaleas.

"Damn," Boone said, looking like he had just taken one shot too many of Jack Daniels.

"You okay?"

"Could have warned me some, Hoss."

"The effects don't last long," Harry said, scanning the property. "You'll get used to it."

He let Boone adjust to his quick trip through the void while Harry continued to survey his surroundings. In the distance, the house rose over the manicured grounds like a foreboding castle. Harry longed to be back in there, but he couldn't just march in as if nothing had happened. They were probably watching.

A dense cloud had moved in, shielding the mansion from the intense moonlight that had bathed the estate moments before. Harry and Boone were well concealed, but they needn't have bothered. The place was cast in darkness and appeared deserted. No interior lights were on, and the exterior was pitch-black.

That was fine by Harry; the gloom safeguarded them from prying eyes.

"My boys must still be in there," Boone whispered in Harry's ear, his voice tight with anxiety.

"Dead a couple of hours now, I think."

Boone growled.

Harry gave him a questioning look. "What were you going to do, anyway? Make her stay the entire night, guarded by those two? You should've known something like this would happen after all the shit that went down. You had the chance to get her out of there, keep her safe, but didn't take it. Why?"

The criticism was too much. Boone's gaze drew in. He clenched his teeth, but just as quickly, he caught himself. His anger dissipated. He shrugged. "Hell, son, I'd feel the same if it were me, but you got to know things were happening too fast. I felt it best to escort Trower and the senator to the airport personally, halfway expecting an attack on the way over. I was gonna swing back around for his sister, but I had given my deputies orders to escort her home. I was gonna call her there to make sure she arrived, but you called first."

Harry gave him a stiff nod. They had basically abandoned Ginny, and he seemed to be feeling every bit as guilty as Boone should be feeling right now.

"Look, I had to make a quick decision. I didn't like leaving Ginny there, but at least she wasn't alone."

"Yeah, well, they weren't much help, were they?"

Boone grabbed Harry's arm. "Those boys died trying to save her. I wouldn't go mouthing off about them in front of me."

Boone's anger had been quick, but Harry didn't care. He wasn't in the mood for excuses. He jerked his arm away and took a step back but didn't retreat. "You don't know how any of that went down. The bastards had us, Sheriff. That's why you shouldn't have left her."

Boone grunted something and seemed to deflate. "You're right. I don't know what happened after I left. It was my duty to protect her brother first. I did what I thought best and escorted them to the airport." He sighed, dismissed Harry with an aggravated wave of his hand, spun in disgust, and promptly twisted his bad knee. "Dammit!" He stood to his full height, his head just showing over the top of the bushes.

"You okay?"

Boone didn't answer that. "Those two were good men, Harry, and they're dead, just like the others who are dead right now mainly because of you."

Heat rose up in Harry's face, but he fought hard not to let it bubble out and make the tension between them worse. It was the same accusation Pelgram had levied, but it hit home harder coming from the sheriff.

It was useless to argue about leaving Ginny. It wouldn't bring her back. The helplessness gnawed at him.

He turned to look at the big sheriff. Even in the dark, it was easy to tell that Harry's accusation that Boone hadn't done enough, that he had failed her, had gotten to him. But Harry had failed her too. His friends were in mortal danger. Maybe they were already dead. He'd tried not to think about them as he sat with Boone in the diner, but now back at the mansion, he couldn't help it. He had to do something, and he had to do it now, but he couldn't be reckless about it. He needed a plan, a way to win out, to make these bastards pay for ruining the life he had and giving him one he'd never wanted. And now they were taking the lives of his friends. He had to save them, or what would be the point of going on?

Harry turned, his heart beating a rapid rhythm in his throat, and searched up and down the dark road one last time. He wanted to walk straight to the front door of the house and examine the damage, but that would be stupid. Maybe he would be lucky enough to stumble upon something, anything that might help him in what must be done. Something Ginny said during that last conversation came to his mind. Agnes's personal diaries were all on the library laptop. She had found something there about Jones, something incriminating.

"Meriodoc," Harry whispered.

He switched to telepathy since they didn't have a host body. *"Scout the area. Are any of them around?"* It took less than a second for an answer.

"No one stalks the place...sorcerers or otherwise. We're alone. And Chauncey says the sorcery dampening field is still in effect, but as you know, due to our stupidity, the house has become locatable. That is the main problem right now, and we have to correct it if you're to live very long."

It was Agnes, just the person Harry needed. He had lots of questions only she could answer. *"I know. But we can talk about it later."*

Harry came out from behind the bushes, jumped the ditch, and stepped up onto the side of the road. Boone followed slowly and silently behind.

Out in the open, Harry had to act fast, so he said, using his mind, *"I don't want to be seen. Take us directly into the house."*

****

Boone handled the transport easier this time, wincing and cursing once as he hit the solid floor. Harry kept the lights off, but by now the cloud had passed, and moonlight gave the front rooms an eerie glow. Boone pulled his flashlight and began looking around. It was a mess—muddy tracks ran from the foyer to the kitchen and library. One slain deputy lay in a puddle of blood that had collected around his head and shoulders. They found the other in the library in the same condition. Both had been tapped twice in the head by small-caliber rounds.

Cursing, Boone started to call Metro police, but Harry stopped him. More crime scenes would delay them. The deputies weren't going anywhere.

"Okay, do what you have to," Boone said, "while I round up a couple of people I trust."

"Make it fast."

With Boone on the phone, Harry switched on the lamp next to the computer. The light was too feeble to penetrate into the hallway and cause anyone watching the house to notice their activity. He went to the computer, still running the file Ginny had been reading. He sat at the small desk and took up where Ginny had left off. He smiled. She had made some changes—bolding some sections to alert him to the crucial passages.

It didn't take long for him to be sucked in by his grandmother's narrative.

…Jones showed up late without much of an excuse. It was just one of many instances that made me pause.

It was something about a business trip Jones had been on for the family. One paragraph later…

I'd been playing the part of an out of touch multimillionaire, maybe just a little eccentric. It worked all too well. At least, I think it did. At the time, I felt it was necessary because I didn't fully trust him. I could never verify Jones's last employment before hiring him, but I accepted him because his references were impeccable. He'd been a good lawyer. People from around here knew him.

And, of course, there were family connections. His last name didn't fit, but he checked out with my sources in England. The old alliances still mattered it seemed. But there was the accent. It didn't fit. I would catch him in moments when he was unaware of my presence. His voice would be different. He always corrected himself after noticing me, slipping quickly back into a Mississippi drawl. Very smooth. It bothered me at first. It was such a curious thing. I could swear the accent was from Northern Europe. It sent up red flags in my mind, but I never caught him again. I just dismissed it out of hand. The helpers had convinced me of his parentage. That was a beginning I knew I could build on and make a believer of him.

To say I'd grown to trust him is an understatement. After my poor Joey died and his sweet wife, it was all I could do to hold it together. I don't know how little Joey, Jr. survived. Some call it a miracle, and it's what I believe, too, but I also knew there was a higher purpose working because of the family. When Jonesy came on board, I began laying it all out for him, all the family history. He resisted, of course. It was all too fantastic to believe, but finally, after much effort, I could see a chink in his armor. He began to weaken to my story, began to see his own family heritage, how they were always connected to the Blacks, that his coming to Black Manor wasn't just coincidence. And I thought I have him now. A true ally.

But was it really my persistence that won him

over? I remember talking to him from time to time, rambling on about this and that related to our history, and thinking surely he knows something about what I'd been saying. Of course, it could be that I'd told the stories so often. I guess I grew into the eccentric role too well.

It still gives me pause. I still question myself for trusting Jones too much. I shouldn't have trusted anyone after that so-called accident killed my son. But what was I to do? I had to trust Strom Jones. I couldn't do it alone. I had no husband to help me rear a four-year-old boy. Goodness, it's been so hard.

Harry read on, skimming sections that weren't highlighted. The passage he had just finished had obviously been written shortly after Harry had come to live with her, which was pretty recent history compared to how long Jones had been with the family. From Harry's memory, their association began after Harry's grandfather had passed away a few years after WWII. His grandfather had been a lawyer, so there had been no need for someone like Jones before that, someone who Agnes eventually put in total control of the Black fortune.

He could remember picking up bits and pieces of this critical family financial business as he came into his middle teen years and began showing a grudging interest. Jones wasn't family, but his grandmother treated him as such. Was she wrong to do so?

The question gnawed at him now. Someone on the inside as Jones had been could do lots of damage, but he hadn't stolen the money. He'd remained loyal and Harry obviously made it through to adulthood and acquired the legacy. If Jones had never been what he claimed to be, couldn't he have killed a helpless boy long ago? Jones could have arranged things to his favor with the eventual passing of the matriarch. Or he could have murdered her too for that matter, or have her killed. But maybe that thinking was too simplistic. There were legalities to follow, after all, concerning the will, regulations, and the like. It wouldn't be so easy to simply take over the estate. Maybe Jones had decided to wait. The fortune would be his eventually. But that hadn't happened either. Harry had the money, all legal and final, or so he hoped.

Harry stood at the computer, not knowing how to take all this, not knowing what to do. He wanted to believe in Jones, but he wasn't sure. Was Jones innocent? If so, what was he doing at the warehouse where Jack and Paula had been taken and tortured?

Or maybe all the strangeness that had always surrounded the Black family would have made it impossible, or nearly so, to simply take the fortune over by subterfuge. Maybe Jones had been trying for decades at it and failing. Perhaps he *had* tried to murder Agnes and Harry and hadn't been able to do it for whatever reason. Maybe the death of Harry's parents was as close as he had ever come. Perhaps Jones was a murderer after all, or complicit in the murders of his parents.

It was clear the loss of his parents hadn't stopped the legacy. Harry had been kept alive for a higher purpose. His grandmother had seen it, and Harry saw it now. The plane crash on the coast, if it was murder, was meant to destroy both Harry and his father.

Harry tried to think. It was nearing half past midnight, well past the appointed hour. It didn't matter.

The bad guys would wait for him to show, wait for him to come willingly. They knew of his friendships, knew he wouldn't simply let them die. They would remain, but perhaps not much longer.

Boone walked into the room and flipped his flashlight off. Harry sat back down and refocused on the screen. He vaguely noticed the sheriff waiting silently by the door. Then that strange phrase popped out at him as he scrolled down to the next highlighted section.

Moonlight and blood don't mix.

Suddenly the Grigori were there, flickering and quivering on the ceiling. He'd remembered those same words while standing over the body of Carl Dunbar, a man sent to murder him. At the time, he hadn't attributed the phrase to Agnes, but he'd obviously been mistaken since here it was again. Agnes had probably used it many times as he grew up, embedding it in his memory, just another instance of her brainwashing him with cryptic sayings.

"What does it mean, Grandmother?' He kept reading as he waited for an answer.

...blood represents life, the living, and flowing blood doubly so. But sacrificed blood, that's the most precious thing of all, the power in that being magnified a thousand-fold. To give one's life willingly is a noble thing and a powerful counter to dark forces. Such was the premise behind the plan they had cooked up, poor Meriodoc Black's sacrifice, but in all the intervening years the family had not been able to ascertain whether it had been effective. The plague had stopped, they all said. That was incontrovertible since there had been no more sorcerous outbreaks, and consequently, no more

Black Protectors needed, which gave the family great comfort. We've won, they said over and over down through the years.

It's all written here in the diaries. But what fools they were to think it could be so easy. I tried to tell my husband's father and his grandfather. I found myself alone with my son and his family after my husband died years later. My son felt it was over. The legacy was no longer needed. He'd obviously sided with his father in believing that, but I kept silent, not sure, not sure at all. And I grew more frightened.

Then, the accident. Joey Junior should have died that day. How did the little boy live? There could be only one reason. Harry was needed. Meriodoc had failed for some reason. It wasn't over. They would be back, and the blood of a Black Protector would be needed again.

Harry looked up at them, his body practically shaking this time. The Grigori were more agitated than usual. They knew what he had been reading, responding to it, but still, Agnes remained silent.

"Is this it?" Harry said, almost in a whisper. "I'm supposed to go quietly to my death? A sacrifice? A lamb to the slaughter? A repeat of what Meriodoc did? Or what he was supposed to have done? What makes you think it'll work this time?"

The words bloomed in Harry's mind. *"The moon. The moon is the key."*

"What the hell is that supposed to mean?"

"Whoa…who are you talking to?" Boone had crossed the room in two quick strides.

"The missing ingredient. We finally worked it out."

Harry jerked his head up to them. "Explain it,

dammit."

"Better to do it this way, I think." It was Meriodoc speaking from Boone's body. "Agnes, for all her eccentricities, has proven to be a fair scholar in these matters. Chauncey thinks so, anyway. Actually, I think he has a bit of a crush on her. It's quite charming, really. But I think that—"

"Dammit, Meriodoc, spare me the details of spook relations. Tell me what it means."

"We don't know exactly, Harry, but Agnes seems to think it was the key to my failure. It's an ancient contract, one we had forgotten about. It's the same contract with the Blacks that gives us the legacy, that protects the residence, that cuts sorcerous power here, that makes Black Manor holy ground and quite dangerous for them. Harry, it could actually work this time."

"What, some weird moon power?"

"And earth and star. The entirety of the physical universe."

Harry nodded. He'd already read some of this in Meriodoc's diary entry. "More metaphysical crap?" He got up and stalked to the center of the room. "Did she tell you all this?"

"Agnes and Chauncey have been debating for weeks now."

"Yeah?" Harry stared intently at Boone. "Why isn't she speaking to me?"

"Put yourself in her shoes, Harry. You are her direct descendent, her grandson, the last of Clan Black. She doesn't want it to be her that sends you to your death."

Harry searched Boone's saggy eyes. There was nothing he could say to that.

Chapter 42

Three men and one tiny, but tough-looking woman, stood in deep shadow at the edge of the large tract of woods due south of Black Manor. They were behind old man Scott's house, well off the beaten path, and well hidden. Five hundred acres of thick growth separated Scott's farm from the Black estate. The moon that had begun to wax full two nights previously bathed the grounds in a milky intensity Harry had never seen before. Separated from the edge of the woods by a large pasture, the farmhouse stood like a dark, silent sentinel.

It was after one in the morning. Harry hoped Peeters had been bluffing about being on time. He figured he could still pull his friends back from the brink of a horrible fate and would damn well die trying.

Death—apparently, it was part of the job description of Protectors. He stared up into the brilliant night sky. Other Protectors had willingly gone down this road. Could he? Would he have the balls to stare it in the face and smile? Maybe, if he knew his friends would be safe. He'd probably have to die anyway to stop these bastards, according to Agnes, who apparently was too ashamed to tell him so directly.

Aggravation was nearly spilling out of Harry's ears, but he couldn't blame the sheriff who was just sleeping inside his own body while these spirits had control of him. What would be the point of bickering with them or railing against their plan? Had they kept him alive only to die in these woods to finish the job Meriodoc should have accomplished long ago? Before his frustration got the better of him, he turned away from the sheriff and the new arrivals and took several steps toward the woods.

Harry had hunted here for years with Jack. He could still see the clearing in his mind's eye, the place he now knew had been part of that dream. The cult-like group was in there, waiting for him. He didn't have to physically see them to know it was true. The vision of the fire and screaming woman were seared into his memory.

From where the small party stood, Harry calculated the clearing would be no farther than a half-mile in a northeasterly direction. He could take the deputies there instantly, but that wouldn't do. Harry wanted to keep that part of his identity secret. He had explained that he and Boone would approach it using a more circuitous route and come in on the other side from the deputies' approach. He got sideways glances from them for that bit of folly. It would be almost a mile of hard walking, sometimes in thick undergrowth and at night. The deputies knew of Boone's bad knee. Both were excellent marksmen and had brought along night vision goggles to serve in a supportive role if things devolved. Correction—*when* it all went to hell, not if.

Harry had no delusion that this would end like he needed it to. Pessimism was creeping into his soul like an unwanted visitor, so he forced other thoughts to the fore. He wasn't about to simply hand over his life. Live and rescue his friends. Those were his only thoughts.

Harry would limp in with Boone on a hope and a

prayer and get out fast with the Grigori. Boone would supply the confusion by appearing to have been turned. Harry would be the lamb brought to the slaughter, an exchange, another noble gesture by a Black Protector. Once in, he figured they had a few minutes before their ruse would be undone, and this stud sorcerer started kicking some serious ass.

Boone needed to catch Pelgram in his betrayal and put him down. For his part, Harry had to get Peeters. He was the key. Chauncey had a lock on him through the weird supernatural mumbo-jumbo he knew. If need be, Chauncey and the gang could deposit Harry at Peeters's side where Harry would take him out.

Chauncey had assured them two things would happen. The veil would once again be imposed, and even this close to Black Manor, the sorcerers would be confounded in such a way they would forget its whereabouts. They wouldn't be able to find the mansion. And this meant Harry and those he protected would be safe again from attack. He could live in safety within its walls. He would have his sanctuary back and once again be able to carry out, unfettered, his duties as a Protector.

The second thing was less clear and far riskier, given the power Meriodoc assured Harry that Desmin possessed. Could Desmin be confused enough by the immediate reestablishment of the veil for a blow to be struck? Chauncey was doubtful about this part of the plan, but they had to try for some personal damage on him, or it might be touch and go for the rescue attempt.

Three people had to be taken from that clearing, and two of them were known to be in bad straits. Harry had to get himself and Boone out. Five in total. He hoped the two deputies acting as snipers could fend for themselves, but he had a pang of guilt about their involvement. Chauncey guaranteed him the twin shadows of the Grigori could work separately if necessary, but Harry wasn't so sure. He'd never seen them do it that way before.

He glanced at Boone, who looked every bit his age. The moonlight cast shadows over the furrows in his face, turning them into writhing crevices as he spoke to his deputies.

"You two can stop with the looks," Boone said. "I can make it."

The petite woman was already shaking her head. "Like hell, you can. Dammit, Sheriff, this plan sucks. I think you should stay here. Let Black go in alone and bargain for their release. Freddie and I will see to it he makes it in, and from our concealed positions, we'll be able to keep any rough shit from going down. We'll pin the fuckers down where they stand." She patted the assault rifle she carried.

Boone nodded throughout Deputy Hendricks' little speech. Harry could tell he was thankful for her support, but she didn't dissuade him. They didn't understand the variables involved. Harry was about to say as much when Boone held up his hand.

"The boy needs me there for reasons you don't know about. There's no time to get into an argument. We have three hostages. You shoot to kill anyone who threatens them."

Freddie Rivera stopped checking his equipment. "How big is that clearing anyway?"

"About thirty yards in diameter," Harry answered, "almost perfectly round."

"You'll be there before we will," Boone said, knowing full well that wouldn't be the case, but the deputies needn't have that information. The Grigori would take the two of them close to the clearing and wait for the deputies to set up. "When you're in position radio your location and we'll let you guys know when we're about to move in. We need intel on the hostages. Go in as fast and quiet as you can."

The deputies glanced at each other as though they'd heard better plans on lousy cop shows. Harry certainly had. Freddie spoke up. "Who are they holding? How are we supposed to ID them? Does this have anything to do with the shooting at Black's place earlier today?"

"Lots of good questions, son, but we can't go into it right now. You'll just have to trust me."

Rivera nodded but didn't look particularly pleased. He started examining his rifle for the tenth time.

Harry walked up to him. "Like the sheriff said, there are three hostages. At this point, the man and woman are pretty beat up and won't be standing around shooting the breeze. They're likely bound and out of commission. I don't know about the third one, a tall woman, redhead if she's even still alive."

Harry glanced at his watch. He was well over an hour late now. It would take the deputies a good twenty minutes of hard walking and jogging before they could get in position.

Boone noticed the strained look on Harry's face. "We need to go. Just make sure you find those stands."

"The numbers," Rivera said, looking up at Boone. "How many targets?"

Harry shrugged.

"That's why you're here," Boone said. "We need snipers. We need to keep the people in that clearing honest. We have no idea how many perps we're dealing with. Too many for Harry and me to handle anyway."

The deputies gave each other a quick glance and nodded to Boone before turning to the dark woods. They moved off at a good clip, considering the underbrush. Harry spoke to Boone in a strained voice. "This dream I'd been having contained some pretty wild images, things I would never have believed existed, you know, nightmare-type stuff. Trouble is, I think it's all real."

Boone nodded and stared at the receding backs of his deputies like a father watching his children take off into the dangerous world. "We better get going."

Chapter 43

The Grigori took Harry and Sheriff Boone to within fifty yards of the clearing, close enough to hear the chanting and the woman's screams. They filled Harry's senses a thousand times more intensely than they had in that damn dream. A chill snaked down his spine. His nightmare was here, alive. And he finally knew who the screaming woman must be.

Ginny Rankin.

Harry's hands balled into tight fists. Sheriff Boone had to restrain him from running headlong toward the clearing. When the sheriff spoke, it was no longer in Boone's voice.

"We must wait, Harry," Meriodoc said, "for the others to position themselves." He held on tight as Harry struggled. "We have to wait."

"Let—me—go!"

The last word came out much too loud, making Meriodoc hesitate as he turned Boone's head to the clearing. Lucky for them, the chanting simply continued unabated. Meriodoc whispered in his ear. "If you do not master yourself, you will give away our position, and everyone will die."

Harry dropped to one knee and clutched at the soggy leaves, his eyes intent on the firelight flicking through the woods. But something was different. There had been no manic running through a dense forest to get to this point, no stopping to orient himself to the screaming woman. That's how the dream had run every single night. But none of that had happened now and not nearly as much sweating. In fact, the woods were fresh by comparison and far less humid than they should be at this time of year, as they had been in the dream. These changes were comforting. Things weren't inevitable, not by a long shot.

There had also been another significant difference. Harry had been alone in his dream, and now he had a partner. "Check your radio," Harry whispered to Meriodoc. "Make sure it's on."

"Assuredly, everything is set to ready, Harry."

"And Boone's voice? Can you handle that?"

"Sure thing," Meriodoc said in that deep southern drawl. He laid Boone's big hand on Harry's shoulder. "No matter the outcome tonight, you've done well. It's been a pleasure working with you."

Harry frowned and quickly stood. "Dammit. Don't go all morose on me now. I'm not dead yet."

The attempt at a positive outlook didn't seem to deter Meriodoc's naturally cynical disposition. "You'll make a welcome addition to our group, my boy."

Aggravated by the old spook's negativism, Harry said, "Just shut it, okay. I'm the last, remember? I screw this up, and the line ends. There will be no future teaming up with a bunch of floating ghosts glued together like a fucking blob of taffy."

Meriodoc put a surprised look on Boone's face. "That's right, isn't it? I forgot. If you don't make it tonight, Clan Black will have failed." This realization sent him into an even deeper depression. He walked off, Boone's head hanging. "I will have failed again."

"Shit, Merry, get over yourself. We all fail sometimes, but this is where it really counts. The world is so different now. It's gotten tiny. If these bastards win, things really will go to hell."

"Best to be positive, I suppose," Meriodoc said. "That was never a trait of mine."

"So I've noticed."

Screams cut a sharp divide through Harry's nervous system. His head jerked to the clearing, and Boone's radio gave off a faint chirp.

It was Deputy Hendricks. They were almost in position. Five more minutes, and they would be ready.

Boone's face went taut. He nearly dropped the radio. Meriodoc said in Boone's deep drawl, "Deputy Hendricks."

Harry grabbed his arm. "What's wrong?"

"The line went dead as they were signing off."

Harry turned back to the clearing. The chanting had just ratcheted up a notch. So had Ginny's screams. He pulled the Beretta and had a sinking feeling his enemies were aware of them, that they knew their plans inside and out.

"You think they're—"

"I'm sorry," Meriodoc said. "I'm sorry." He began pacing. Harry could see sweat beading up on Boone's broad forehead. "We shouldn't have involved anyone else. Shouldn't be here at all. It's all wrong. He's too powerful, Harry. Too strong. Too—"

Harry clenched his teeth, caught up with Boone, and yanked him around. "No more, dammit. We have to get closer. You ready for this?"

"You'll have to be brave, my boy," Meriodoc said. "We have to go to plan B now. We can't let Desmin win again. He must be stopped."

"Answer my question."

Boone was suddenly still—too still—as though Meriodoc had turned him into a statue. He was obviously struggling with the question, and after a long moment, he spoke. "You really want an answer?"

Harry hesitated a moment then shook his head. "Listen, if it means anything, I'm thankful for you guys bringing me this far. You've kept my carcass alive, and maybe you'll do it again tonight, but if we can't get them out any other way, I'm ready."

Meriodoc gave a slight nod but kept his gaze on the light emanating from the clearing.

"There's one bright spot for you anyway."

Meriodoc turned Boone's head back to Harry. "How so?"

"You're dead already. No more pain, remember?"

The response on Boone's face was one of sheer incredulity. "Pain? Hell, Harry, what do you know about it? Pain is a relative, utterly metaphysical concept, and I assure you there is something completely analogous to it in my realm of existence. And, besides—"

Harry rolled his eyes. "Just shut up and let's go."

****

The last fifty yards were a thing right out of Harry's nightmare except he knew now how real it all was. Shadowy figures skirted trunk to trunk as he and Boone passed through the forest. The people were difficult to see in the gloom. In spots, the trees grew closer, but in an eerie twist of the senses, he could almost believe they were somehow creeping toward them.

He tried not to look at the strange figures, but he couldn't help it. The dream scene was upon him, so he gave himself over to it, drawn by an irresistible curiosity the dream had spawned.

The flitting bodies weren't human, but they were humanoid, with sharp talons at the end of long scaly arms. They seemed to come and go as if passing in and out of the reality Harry occupied. In the nightmare, they had raked his body before he'd made it to this point, producing bloody gashes on his arms and back. Not now, though. It was another difference, but its significance escaped him.

Whatever these things were, Harry couldn't catch sight of them properly—materializing and dematerializing as they dashed about. Evil eyes leered at Harry and Boone—scorching things, spewing hate.

The demon shapes seemed so real in the dream—the pain of their grasp, the talons so long and hard. There was nothing like that this time. These figures were insubstantial, incapable of cutting his flesh. Yet they were still a threat, something sent to intimidate and stir up primal fear in his conscious mind as they had brought to his subconscious.

It could be a psychic assault of some kind meant to dissuade him. Harry closed to within twenty yards of the clearing and dismissed the idea. They didn't want to discourage him from coming. They wanted Harry in the clearing where they would take him in exchange for his friends, his life for theirs. These things were meant to disable him, weaken his spirit to the point that all thought of winning some grand victory would be dashed.

But maybe the demons, the flitting figures, were

for Meriodoc, to confuse and incapacitate the Grigori who had already proven themselves vulnerable to fear. Harry glanced at Boone. The sheriff slowed his gait, his head on a nervous swivel as the activity of the shadowy figures doubled in the last few seconds. The woods were awash with gut-churning fear, all directed at them, but primarily for Meriodoc. It made sense.

"Fight it," Harry told him silently. *"Remember how you had me overcome the threshold back at the warehouse."*

Boone stopped and began rubbing his palms on his thighs. *"Where?"*

"You know where. Concentrate—you can fight this."

Boone turned to Harry. The look on his face made Harry want to turn away. Harry could see the struggle within, terror just under the surface. He knew the brave sheriff wouldn't have reacted this way. This was a spiritual attack on a deeper level. Meriodoc had taken over, supplanting the other members of the Grigori. This was Meriodoc's chance to redeem himself, but fear had begun to conquer him, sending him to a place where he couldn't be a useful aid. Harry knew where that place must be, a place of torture and death nearly two centuries in the past.

This would damn well get them killed before the real fight began.

Chapter 44

They stopped twenty yards from the clearing. The activity of the robed people hadn't changed. The earlier impression Harry had of them being aware of their plans had been just a momentary thing, a strong premonition that was now gone. Maybe the sorcerers weren't aware of them yet, but he doubted it was true. If they were, it didn't change anything. This wasn't going to be a surprise attack. These demon-like things were probably in constant contact with their boss anyway. Logic dictated Desmin knew they were coming and perhaps had known their exact location all along.

"Grandmother," Harry whispered. When she didn't answer, he said, "Meriodoc, maybe Agnes should head this up, considering these…" He hesitated and stared at the shapes still flitting among the trees. "What in the hell are they anyway?"

"Not important."

"No? They must be here for a reason."

"It's like you thought earlier. Intimidation. These demon figures are for *us*, not you, and they are quite dangerous when they choose to act."

"Oh?" Harry's throat tightened.

"I don't blame you for not having confidence in me," Meriodoc said.

A figure darted particularly close to them, making

Boone jump. Harry grabbed his arm. "Easy."

"Sorry, Harry, sorry."

They were under a small opening in the canopy, and moonlight bathed them enough for Harry to see Boone sweating. Meriodoc was scared. Maybe the others weren't, but that wasn't important. This wasn't their gig. It was Meriodoc who had something to prove to himself and to the others who knew his story.

"I have to do this. I *need* to do this."

"Retribution?"

"Maybe," Meriodoc said, "with some vindication mixed in."

"You don't have to be a hero. You're here for one reason. To get us out quick. Remember that."

Boone nodded. "Don't forget, plan B."

Harry couldn't help the shudder that rocked his body. "Trying not to think of that."

The cloaked individuals hadn't let up their activity. He could see them more clearly now, moving steadily around the fire, circling the woman whom he could barely make out because the nearby blaze blocked his vision. But he could see enough of her to tell she was writhing, obviously being affected by whatever they were doing, her screams sharper than ever.

He turned to Boone. "Forget about these things. I think they're harmless. They're trying to mess with your mind. Scare you off."

"Another metaphysical statement, Harry. You see, we're all mind, the whole lot of us. Pure intellect, and there is quite a lot of that special quality to mess with, as you say."

"Just stay clear-headed, okay, and—"

Something struck Harry, knocking him to the

ground. He struggled to roll to his side in time to see Boone staring at his massive left hand that had apparently just delivered the blow to the left side of Harry's face. Fighting hard to clear his head, Harry struggled to his feet, wiping blood away with the back of his hand.

"Please forgive me, but if the ruse is to work I couldn't just pretend—"

Harry held up his bloody hand. "I get it."

The chanting stopped abruptly.

"This is as good a time as any, Harry. You ready?"

Harry nodded. They neared the clearing, and the robed people turned to face them. One person moved out from the rest, beckoning to them.

Harry and Boone closed the last few yards in unwavering strides, determined to show no fear. With his heart sprinting in his chest, Harry wasn't sure he succeeded. Desmin could probably smell Harry's anxiety as the sorcerer had sensed it back in the warehouse. He wouldn't give the bastard the pleasure again, so he quickly mastered himself and urged his weak legs to move.

The clearing was unnaturally bright as he stepped into it, so much so that at first Harry thought he had moved into some type of time warp and dawn had abruptly sprung upon them. He glanced up into the star-studded sky and understood that it was still night, but one dominated now by a fiercely glowing moon. And he realized something else. A terrible new danger came with the extra brightness, a feeling of hopelessness so intense Harry nearly cried out in anguish.

Chapter 45

"Alas, you've come." The speaker lifted his arms, his billowy white robe making him look like a sail caught in the wind. "Welcome, welcome, ye Black Protector."

Those gathered burst into laughter, but it was short-lived because the speaker quieted them with a flick of his raised hand. He'd spoken in an accent similar to Peeters and nearly the same the psychogeist of Desmin had used, but there was something familiar about this person's voice. Harry strained to see within his hood, sure that he knew the man, but his face remained in shadow.

Harry glanced once at Boone to make sure Meriodoc was still in the game, that he hadn't forgotten their ruse. He needn't have bothered. Harry noticed for the first time Boone holding the Berretta that had been tucked away at the small of Harry's back. Boone had remembered just in time to take it from Harry before they entered the clearing. Harry didn't know when Meriodoc had managed to get a grip on his fear, but it was apparent he'd been thinking ahead, which meant the plan was still on.

Boone spoke up in an aggravated voice, pushing Harry forward. "There was a delay in subduing Black, but we're here now to do your bidding."

It was the sheriff's voice, but Harry couldn't tell

whether it was Meriodoc imitating him or whether the Grigori had given Boone control over his own body.

Harry resisted the urge to scan the air, looking for them. Instead, he examined the clearing, trying to pinpoint his friends. He found Jack and Paula lying bound and gagged twenty yards to the left of the fire. They appeared to be unconscious. He wanted to run to them, check to see if they still lived, but he clenched his fists, fighting the urge.

There was Ginny, her hands tied behind her. She wore a robe like those of his enemies, but hers was in tatters. It barely covered her naked body. Harry had to tell himself to remain calm. His time would come, but the thought of Ginny, raped or tortured, ate at him. He still couldn't see her face as she slowly spun before the fire. She rotated mid-air, so near the flame, Harry wondered if the bastards intended to cook her like a pig on a spit. She had no visible means of support as though gravity had refused to let her fall to the ground. There were no ropes tied to tree limbs and no other structure he could see.

"I'm here for my friends," Harry said.

Boone jammed the gun barrel into Harry's back. He let loose with a deep laugh and pistol-whipped Harry to his knees.

It was a feint, but one that hurt like hell. Harry knew Meriodoc had pulled his punch. The smack in the face he'd received earlier was for the same reason. The ruse must work, and roughing Harry up was a necessary part of it. But in his mind, he cursed Meriodoc anyway for not giving him a small warning.

"Enough! We mustn't damage him—too much." More laughter resounded around the clearing.

“Sorry,” Meriodoc said in Boone’s voice. He yanked Harry to his feet as Ginny let out another long wail that trailed off into a low moan.

“I see we have another ally.” The speaker did a half-turn, and the other robed men parted, revealing for the first time where Pelgram stood. “Did you know your sheriff was with us?”

Pelgram smirked at Boone before answering. “I didn’t.”

Two other deputies stood beside Deke, carbon copies of Brick Taylor. The robed speaker turned back to face Harry and Boone. “Hit him once again for me, won’t you? Just to be certain, but not enough to do permanent damage.”

Harry didn’t have time to react before another blow knocked him out this time. When he finally opened his eyes from where he’d fallen, ghostly figures circled roundabout, looking down at him from within their hoods as though he was a curiosity worthy of close inspection. Moonlight backlit them, giving the hooded ensemble a phosphorescent glow that swam before his eyes like wisps of smoke until his vision focused enough for him to see clearly.

“Let him rise,” someone said.

It was the same hooded man who had given Boone the order. The sheriff’s performance must have been believable enough because when he stood, Harry could see Boone standing behind the group, apparently accepted now into the cult-like fellowship.

“I wish to ask our esteemed guest what we will receive in return for our releasing the hostages and why he thinks he is in a position to bargain for their worthless lives?”

This was the moment Harry feared as he stood there wobbly, the pain in his head nearly blinding him. He rubbed at the forming knot, but it didn't help.

He knew it would probably come to this. The sacrifice was to be offered, but only if the ruse failed, and he could get the hostages out by no other means. His life would be the last recourse to save his friends. They would live because the power of his enemies would be properly cut this time, unlike what went down nearly two centuries before. The scheme would work this time because the sorcerers wouldn't be put in a position again to renege on the promise of mutual destruction. This time their magic would be shattered permanently. He hoped that would be the case, half-trusting, half-skeptical of the plan his grandmother and Chauncey had cooked up.

Harry searched the hooded figures as he fought to keep the contents of his stomach down.

"Come now, Mr. Black, speak up so I may inform Lord Desmin of your folly."

Harry was sure the man hadn't meant to let it slip that Desmin wasn't here. He needed the chief baddie present to enact the sacrifice, or it would all go for naught. The centuries-old bastard, Desmin, must be the one to die this time, along with a Protector.

Harry needed time to make sure Desmin was front and center. He didn't think they would kill him before Desmin showed. Harry hoped not anyway. He glanced at Boone, who nodded once, almost imperceptibly. Harry responded in kind and fixed Pelgram with a steady stare. The deputy answered it with a cocky smirk, clearly unconcerned about the sheriff. He'd accepted Boone into their weird little fraternity.

But Pelgram had made a critical mistake. Boone had positioned himself in a way that would allow him to act. He stood near enough to Pelgram, but slightly behind him and within striking distance.

"Boone is acting on his own now," Meriodoc said.

Harry's heart danced to the words blossoming in his mind, the telepathic communiqué from Meriodoc silent, but clear. It was good to hear from him. Damn good. To bide his time, Harry coughed and sank to his knees, his head falling nearly to the ground. It wasn't altogether an act.

"I am sorry for striking you. I didn't mean to knock you unconscious."

Harry would have answered, but his pounding head hurt too damn much to use telepathy.

"We had to keep showing Boone's sincerity, or they would have magicked the truth out of him and broken him if they discovered the ruse once we were out of his body. That would endanger plan B. I hope you understand, Harry. He should be safe now until we are ready to act."

"What now?" Harry managed to ask. *"Desmin isn't here yet. Do they know you guys are still helping me?"*

"Assuredly, but they don't know how or when, and their trust in Lord Desmin is beyond measure. They, no doubt, suppose Desmin can neutralize us, and I'm inclined to think they are correct."

Harry grimaced in the face of more pessimism from Meriodoc. *"So how do we win?"*

Meriodoc didn't answer, but there was one promising point to this message. With the twin shadows wandering about, they had doubled the units of their force. The Grigori demonstrated how lethal they could be against enemies with ordinary weapons like Carl Dunbar had been carrying, but against these sorcerers, Harry didn't know what to expect. They were free to kill the hooded people in the clearing the way they had Carl Dunbar, but the Grigori weren't doing it. Was there something working to prevent such an attack, some power giving them pause with the chief sorcerer absent? Perhaps it was fear conquering them. Desmin wasn't there, but maybe they were fearful of revealing themselves even to these lesser powers.

Harry cursed himself for not asking about this part of the plan earlier. The shadows were their only hope, and though they were formidable, they had their weaknesses too. After all, they were only human.

Harry figured Boone's deputies were dead or incapacitated in some way. They couldn't count on those guns. But why weren't the sorcerers bragging about thwarting the ill-fated attempt to gain the upper hand through force of arms? Which begged the more important question—why was the ruse he had planned working?

Over-confidence, arrogance, superiority to the point of negligence. Harry's only hope was to keep the ruse going as long as possible because this was a weakness. They now had a mole among the wolves. He needed Boone to remain that way until the crucial time to act.

Harry rose to his full height, and said in a weak voice, "Let them go. You have me now. I won't resist. My life for theirs."

They heckled him for that little speech.

"Oh? And why should we when we could simply

kill the lot of you?"

"Because, you bastard—" Harry stopped when Peeters, standing just behind the sorcerer in charge, lowered his hood. Harry's fists tightened. "Breathing all right through that crooked nose?"

Peeters's face was swollen and discolored. The scowl that remark produced must have hurt like hell. Harry returned a smile, which had the intended effect. Peeters started to move toward Harry, but his boss stopped him.

"I owe him," Peeters said with a low, malevolent growl. The words were barely out of his mouth when his feet were swept from under him by some force. He hit the ground hard.

"What you owe is obedience and nothing else." The hooded man lowered his hand and told the group milling around. "We do nothing to Black until Lord Desmin arrives. *He—is—his*."

Message received. The crowd backed away, and the man in charge turned to Harry and stuck out a hand from within the sleeve of his robe. He actually shook a finger like a schoolteacher scolding a student.

"Do not think you can simply offer up yourself. I pray those wretched things have not been telling you this, young Protector."

Harry swallowed hard. They knew the game.

"Oh, yes, I see your surprise. Once we learned of the presence of, well, shall we say, help, we foresaw this might be your stratagem. We've taken the necessary steps to protect us."

Shit, what now? An answer didn't come readily to mind, so he showed some cockiness. "Where's Desmin? What the hell's taking him so long?"

Harry meant to say more, but his throat suddenly seized, making it impossible to breathe. He clutched at his aching chest, but just as quickly, he was released.

"We've heard of your impertinence. In the old days, a Black would never have dared. They would have remembered to show respect and would have received it in return. I am afraid this narcissistic generation has made civility all but extinct."

"Tell that to the innocent victims in Washington. Tell that to Peggy Cox, my assistant, who you butchered. Tell it to the others who've died here today. We may be narcissists, but we're free narcissists. Not slaves bound by—"

The hold strangled his words once again.

"Answer me, Black. What will we receive in return?"

Harry shook his head, catching his breath. "I'm not talking to anyone but the boss."

The man straightened and stuck his chest out like a rooster on steroids. "I am Lord Desmin's viceroy. I speak for him."

"Not to me, you don't."

Harry braced himself, expecting more retaliation for his smart-ass comment, but Ginny released another scream, so loud this time, all heads turned to her.

"Free her," Harry said, his voice taking on a menacing quality that surprised even him. "Release them all, or I'll—"

His words were choked out again, but this time it wasn't by the man he'd been talking to. The air temperature in the clearing dropped so fast it affected even the raging bonfire, its flames noticeably diminishing. The robed people began mumbling and turning here and there, looking to the dark trees where dozens of red eyes glared back at them. And with these new arrivals, a voice Harry could never forget.

"Do tell, Mr. Black, what it is you have planned for us today?"

Great, these bastards were not only as powerful as hell, but they were smart. A pretty lethal blend.

Desmin Von Ausberg was as tall as his psychogeist and just as thin. He walked out of the woods in long, regal strides, his silky black robe billowing behind. But whereas his ghostly copy had the appearance of a man a little past his prime, perhaps in his early forties, the real thing appeared even younger. The bitchy part was not only hadn't this bastard died when he should have, but he'd also continued to live nearly two more centuries and hadn't aged a bit, possibly looking even younger as the decades passed. Somehow it had taken that long for his power to gather enough to trigger the Black family legacy. Another question sprang up from Harry's mind—were the two phenomena related?

If they were, Harry didn't have the time to ponder it further. He could feel the sorcerer's cold eyes bearing down on him. As he neared the group, his people shrank away, bowing and making little gestures with their arms in some kind of adulation.

Ginny apparently wasn't impressed by his arrival because with renewed vigor, she screamed again. Never looking her way, the sorcerer flicked his right hand, and all sound was simply sucked from the world. Her cries stopped, and so had the cacophony of insect noise emanating from the woods.

The sorcerer kept his eyes on Harry but spoke to his viceroy. "I see you've followed instructions and waited for my arrival. Good, it is good you did so, Herr Smit."

The viceroy bowed and lowered his hood at the same time. "As you commanded, Lord."

"Forgive my delay. I had a sudden inspiration. A slight change of plans."

"Yes, Lord Desmin, no need for explanation." The lackey said this as he rose, a smile plastered across his face and a twinkle in his eyes. Stunned into silence, Harry could only stare back as the damn traitor turned his knowing smile from Desmin and onto him. It was good old Stan Smith, Harry's banker, holder of hundreds of millions of his dollars.

Chapter 46

"Now, where were we?" The sorcerer tapped two fingers on his chin. "Oh, yes, you were about to tell us of your plans, though, of course, we already know of them. But I do want to hear it directly from you. After all, it has been so long since I spoke to a Black Protector."

He waited for Harry to answer, but there was only silence.

"We have found your residence, young Harry. That cursed mansion. I know the lore master restored the once proud name. So pretentious sounding in this American context, don't you think? You're too young to have seen Black Manor in all its glory outside Oxford, England. It was utterly destroyed, of course, as will be this new American version. A shame, isn't it?"

A cheer went up. "Kill the Protector now," someone yelled. "Do it," said another. But the sorcerer responded with a raised hand, and they quieted.

"Yes, yes, the ritual will be done, and he will surely die." Desmin cocked his head and considered Harry as though studying an ameba under a microscope. "But I care not about his friends. They are mere ancillaries in this age-old fight. You are here to free them, I know, but not on your terms. You will not be permitted that." He scanned the clearing. "Their plan won't work, young Harry." He took a more extended look around. "I know you have them here. Is Meriodoc present?" He spoke with a raised voice. "The old plan won't work, Merry. Do you hear? We cannot be broken this time. Weakened, perhaps, but I have even solved that problem. The end of Clan Black is near. We will go easier on the Protector this time if he does not cause us any difficulties and try our patience."

Desmin turned back to Harry. "You were given a chance to walk away, but now I am afraid it is too late for that. Now it ends on our terms."

Pretty easy to translate—cooperate and die or your friends don't stand a chance.

Harry did the only thing he could do. He nodded, but he wasn't looking at Desmin. He was eyeing Boone, who had slipped farther behind everyone. Their eyes locked, and when Boone nodded back, Harry did a quick scan of the clearing. Jack and Paula were still unconscious, and, with a sickening feeling, Harry knew they might be dead. Ginny, still rotating near the fire, had stopped struggling, which sent his nerves into overdrive. He put it aside for now. He had to get a fix on Peeters and found him off to the side, closer to Ginny than he had been, doodling with the same curved blade, the same one from the vision on the loading dock.

The knife. The bastard had the knife that had sliced up Peggy Cox. He was her murderer, after all. Harry fought to control himself. He wanted to beat Peeters into a pulp and stick him in a place that would make a quick end of him.

Thoughts of the knife brought that strange phrase to mind. *Moonlight and blood don't mix*. But how much blood would it take?

"You seem distracted, Harry. Come now, there is only one thing left to do, and your friends can leave. No harm will come to them."

Harry had no idea how it happened. It hadn't come from Meriodoc or Agnes or anyone else from the Grigori. An unintended thought crawled to the front of his mind. "I have other friends, just acquaintances really, but we're all working together against you. I know you have them."

After a long pause, Desmin's eyes brightened in recognition. "Ah, yes, we have speculated what might be your particular gift. The answer, I think, presents itself." He waved toward the others, forcing their attention. "You are a diviner of truth. You *see*."

"Something like that."

"And do you see your own death?"

Harry shook his head slowly. "Not tonight."

He'd no sooner gotten the words out when Ginny found her voice again, but this time it came out as a laugh. Harry turned to her but froze when whatever held her suddenly released, and she sank to the ground. Still cackling like a demented stripper, she rose to her full height.

The silk robe revealed way too much of her breasts and even more of the rest of her. The torn robe also revealed something that turned Harry's stomach. Red welts marked her breasts and thighs. She'd been whipped; her skin was broken and bleeding. As she tried to control her bizarre laughter, she lowered the hood, and a red wig came off with it.

Ginny was at least thirty yards away, but the radiance of that strange moon created a milky white haze in the clearing. Couple that with the firelight, and she was cast in an eerie reddish glow. It wasn't until she spoke that Harry finally knew it wasn't Ginny Rankin at all.

"Too long, Harry. Too long since I've been near you except of course when you paid me a little visit the other night. I've thought of you often since our teen years, since those few sexy months we shared."

It was his old girlfriend, Brick Taylor's ex-wife. "Sheila?"

"So," Desmin said, "we were right. Your *seeing* has failed you this time, young Harry. You should know it isn't wise for Protectors to get too close to people. The emotional involvement often proves fatal. Just ask poor Meriodoc. When we heard of your attachment, we knew you would come and that you would be weak in doing so."

"Where is she?" Harry said with cold dread in his voice.

"Again, you *saw* the others, but not her. Tsk, tsk. That is a serious failure."

"Tell me."

"Very well. Dr. Rankin is with the others, hidden until their use has run out. Then they will be discarded like a bitter draught."

Harry growled and charged the sorcerer, but came only within five feet of him.

Searing pain bolted through his body as if his skin was being peeled away. He doubled over and dropped to his knees.

Sheila came prancing over. With a gentle hand, she brushed his hair away from his ear, bent down, and kissed him there.

Harry glanced sideways at her large breasts

hanging free of the tattered robe. Her scent brought back old memories. He didn't care to revisit them.

"You used to like these. I remember well."

He disregarded that comment and managed to say, "Why?" Marks covered her flesh. Some sort of leather strap had been used.

"These are nothing. They'll heal. It was necessary for the magical working." She laughed again. "I volunteered for the pain. It was necessary for this clearing tonight, wasn't it, Lord Desmin? My anguish led you here, Harry, did it not? Pain and anguish had to permeate this place for the working that will be the end of Clan Black."

"A brilliant plan," Desmin said, "but I can't take credit for it. Sheila devised it. Because of the old bond you two shared, it worked. I'm sure you've wondered about the dreams that tormented you. The working was intricate. To enter another's subconscious, to plant desire there, is not an easy task. That led you back to your old flame some nights ago. It was not coincidental."

Sheila laughed as Harry stared at Desmin. His mind cleared as though a fog had been clouding it. "How did you know?"

Desmin nodded toward a robed man, who took a step away from the others and lowered his hood. It was Strom Jones.

Chapter 47

Harry had suspected as much. Strom's appearing now was not much of a surprise, but seeing him was still a shock.

Desmin turned back to Harry. "We know because we put it there. We put it there because Jones here had been privy to what the lore master foresaw." He bent to him and put a long, white finger to Harry's temple as if to emphasize the point. "An exquisite piece of sorcery I can take credit for."

Harry closed his eyes and tried to swallow down what he'd been hearing. His whole life seemed to be unraveling, and Agnes had led him to an end that wouldn't turn out to their advantage.

"You had a husband," Harry said. "And they murdered him."

Sheila laughed. "Oh, I was never Brick's or yours for that matter. He was just a job, a means to an end, and so were you."

"But your kids?"

"The little accidents will be well cared for by the family." She swept her arm toward the clearing. Harry got the point. She was all theirs, and so were her children. "See what I did for my part, Harry? The lengths I went through, but it was all a charade, a way to stay close to you, to try and find that damn house. Did you ever wonder why we never did it at your place during one of your grandmother's many absences? It was always at mine or on some stupid dirt road somewhere parked in a ratty car that old bat made you use. Oh, how those cars used to rock with you and me in them." Her expression soured. "But I couldn't get close to Black Manor. Though not a practitioner, I had too much sorcery on me."

Harry tried to say something, and she bent closer to hear.

"Cramped," he croaked out.

She threw her head back and laughed loud and long. "Yes, especially for someone as virile as you. I've been a failure all these years as I sought out the location of that cursed house, but Lord Desmin was understanding. I told him about that high-minded bitch you're seeing. That Rankin woman. We knew you would come. We knew your weakness, Protector. I could feel your concern, your love, though you tried not to let on that you were really an item. I knew better. So sweet. So pathetic."

Harry let the taunt wash over him. It didn't matter any longer. Ginny wasn't here, wasn't in any immediate danger, but according to Desmin it wouldn't last long. He could focus now on getting Jack and Paula out of this mess. But first, he had another problem—the pain pounding through his body. It had him bent and as feeble as an infant.

He tried to stand with Sheila's help and made it halfway up before yanking his arm away from her grasp, almost falling over backward in the effort as another wave of throbbing pain swept through him.

"Leave him alone," Jones said.

Desmin chuckled. "I would have thought the lore

master had taught the boy something. That he would have learned more of his role as Protector."

Jones nodded. "She taught him. It just didn't take." He put a hand on Harry's shoulder, steadying him, but Harry jerked away.

"Get off me!"

"Now, now," Desmin said, "the Blacks have always been civil and polite in our contests. We mustn't forget—"

"She trusted you, dammit," Harry said to Jones. "She gave you your life back, and now you're betraying us?"

"Yes, she rescued a lawyer in need, so to speak, and I was, that is to say, I am grateful for that. But I'm not betraying her, my boy, just you. An ingrate who is about to get what he deserves."

Desmin chuckled again. "The deception is great indeed, because the lore master, your grandmother, should have known that Jones was an impersonator. He was never part of the Pǽronemn, the helping clan you Blacks have used and abused for ages."

The pain subsided enough to allow him to think more clearly. Harry stood straighter, staring at Strom Jones. "You killed my par—"

Looking more directly at Jones just now, his appearance finally registered, making Harry pause. It *was* Jones, but it shouldn't be, not like this. It was him, the same voice, the same stringy gray hair, but darker now. The same face, but he appeared at least ten or fifteen years younger. And he now stood straighter, as though the weight of the last two decades had fallen away.

"How?" Harry managed to say.

"So," Desmin said, "you notice the reward."

"Harry," Jones tried to retake his arm, but Harry stumbled away. "I never betrayed Agnes, and I didn't murder your parents." He gave the sorcerer a furtive glance.

"Yes, yes," Desmin said, "that was my doing. I admit the unsophisticated way it was done, but as my power was yet still unfocused, the plane crash was a necessary crudity. Of course, it ultimately proved a failure as you managed to live."

Harry disregarded all this and kept his attention on Jones. "How could you look so—"

"Young…well, it's like Lord Desmin says. It was an enticement too good to pass up." Jones suddenly became more animated, and this time succeeded in grabbing Harry's arm. "I was approached weeks ago. You see, they are capable of finding us, that is, you Blacks and those associated with you. It's just the residence they're unable to locate—Black Manor."

When he said it, the group of lesser sorcerers gave out a collective groan as though the name had some kind of power over them. "So they found me. Agnes, bless her, always told me they might try to get to me. You know, being so close, but without a blood bond, I was vulnerable. She always knew it was a risk having me around. The old gal was right, of course." He pierced Harry with black eyes. "Youth, Harry, eternal youth. Why, in a year or so, I'll be your age again or very near it. Do you realize the power in that? Think of the possibilities. A life lived over and already with a lifetime worth of experience to rely upon, of knowledge. It's a wonderful gift."

The idea was so fantastic Harry couldn't focus. The

evidence was undeniable. Jones had regained much of the strength he possessed as a young man. Jones turned toward Paula and Jack lying still on the other side of the clearing.

"Their capture was your doing. You led your enemy to Jack."

"Actually, that was simple. But what you, what the Grigori did—" Jones stopped and released him. He walked about and searched the air around the clearing. "—was really stupid, you know. Something that hadn't happened in the whole history of Clan Black. You gave up Black Manor when you brought Peeters here, and now your biggest asset is lost to you. Just as well, it ends tonight. You wouldn't be able to function effectively without the sanctuary." He glanced at the group standing close by. "They would have made short work of you, son. This way, you save your friends."

"And Ginny?"

Jones spun to Harry in a sudden fury. "I tried to warn you. Didn't I try? Hardheaded, arrogant, know-it-all. As if you couldn't lower yourself to be taught anything. Well, now you've done it. It didn't have to end this way for her. There is nothing I can do."

"So, just like that, you gave us all up. Agnes, me, the family, my friends. One thousand years of fighting—all gone because you want to go on living."

"It was...*necessary.*"

"Necessary? What the hell do you mean by—"

Harry couldn't finish because Jones winked at him and flipped him a pearl-handled pocketknife with the blade pulled out from its holder. Harry caught it in his left hand and, in a flash, found himself standing behind Peeters.

"Do it now."

Meriodoc's words exploded in Harry's mind. At that moment, Harry knew Jones had been working his own ruse. The old boy dove to the ground. Desmin looked around as if searching for something, commanding his minions with angry words.

The sorcerer raised his arms overhead, but before he could utter the curses that could very well finish them all, Harry said into Peeters's right ear, "This is for Peggy Cox."

Peeters was quick. He spun, and with his arm extended, palm out, a blast of force struck Harry's chest knocking the wind from him. But Harry had been quicker. He managed to grab enough of Peeters's shirt to prevent the energy of the blast from dislodging him. Gasping for the air that had been knocked out of his lungs, in one desperate lunge, Harry drove the four-inch blade into the murderer's heart. Peeters collapsed on the spot, his eyes wide, staring up at Harry, then they were blank.

Everyone froze. The sorcery Desmin created to shut out sound abruptly ended. The August night once again crashed in upon the little clearing with a thousand subtle tones. Insects, a dog barking, a distant car horn.

There was also a gunshot. Then another. And Harry knew two things almost at once. A bullet had torn through his shoulder, spinning him around so that he now stood face to face with a laughing Sheila Taylor, and Boone had put Pelgram down by blowing away the back of his head. Pelgram's gun, still smoking from firing at Harry, went flying.

The strength left Harry's legs. He sank to his knees.

Two more reports quickly followed, and the two hulking deputies who had knocked Boone to the ground fell over. But those last two shots weren't fired by Boone because Harry could see him writhing, being tortured by some unseen assailant.

The snipers, either Deputy Rivera or Hendricks or perhaps both, had somehow made it.

"Stop!" Desmin screamed, and the chaos throughout the clearing ended at once. "So, those retched things dare oppose me this time." He turned to Jones, now being held by two robed men, and growled, "We will deal with you later."

He lifted his head again, searching for the Grigori.

Harry did the same, fighting the pain and nausea to search the clearing.

The bastard lifted his thin hands, mumbled a few words, and the twin shadows appeared near the bonfire, flickering wildly.

"No!" Harry screamed. He tried to get up and run to them, but the pain shooting down his arm drove him to his knees again. He tried his telepathy, but all he got for his trouble was an explosion of agonized voices pounding through his mind. It sent a swirl of emotions bubbling up from within him. He had to break off or go mad.

But among those voices was one that came through clearly—Agnes. Harry focused on her as more grinding pain wracked his body.

"I see what you are trying," Desmin said. He began laughing. "It won't work. Don't you see it? You may have cut our link to Black Manor, but we know where the sanctuary now resides. It is now wholly in the physical plane. It is too late."

"Now, before he realizes," Agnes said to Harry's mind.

"Strom's knife," Harry answered. *"I must have dropped it."* He searched the ground around him, but it wasn't there.

"You won't need Jonesy's knife, son. You're already bleeding aplenty." But before she could say more, she started screaming, and her tortured thoughts trailed out of Harry's mind.

It was enough. With Harry's one good arm, he ripped open his bloody shirt, swiped his hand across the wound in his left shoulder, blood still oozing from it, and raised his naked palm to the sky.

Moonlight and blood don't mix, not for a Black Protector, and not when a life is given freely for others. That was the situation Harry had resigned himself to if need be. He was prepared to die in that clearing if it meant the end of this clan of sorcerers, and especially if his friends would be safe.

In the hazy light of the huge moon, a spark shot up from his palm, then another. Soon the clearing buzzed in static-filled pyrotechnics.

Then nothing. The sparks died. An eerie silence descended on those assembled. Harry's head hung. This was it, their big play, and it had bombed.

"What the hell?"

Harry tried to lift his head to meet Desmin's stare, but his strength had left him.

"Now then," Desmin said. "That was an interesting bit of…I would say sorcery…but it doesn't apply in your case, Black. Nevertheless, it was all so very dramatic, yet quite ineffectual."

Two robed sorcerers dragged Boone to his feet. He

was now standing near the fire where Sheila had hung. Harry could tell the old sheriff was in bad shape. He hadn't been shot, but whatever they'd done to him had nearly been his end. His head hung. He could only stand with support, but Paula and Jack were worse off. They were conscious now, but still bound and trying to come out of some kind of drugged-induced or perhaps sorcery-induced stupor. They made it to their knees and were attempting to stand.

Harry noticed with gut-wrenching finality that Deputy Hendricks lay unconscious near Jack. Apparently, banker Smith and some others had slipped away to look for Boone's snipers after the traitorous deputies fell. Freddie's absence didn't exactly instill any confidence that he was still alive. Harry and his friends were on their own now; no more allies roamed freely with high powered rifles. All the sorcerers were back in the clearing, and the grand plan of Grandmother Agnes was shot to hell.

Or maybe he had missed something. Maybe there was some ritual he should have performed with his blood and the moonlight now streaming down more intensely into the little clearing. If there was, he hadn't received any instruction, nor had he read it in Agnes's diaries. Couldn't they have spelled it out more plainly for him? He grew aggravated with Meriodoc and Chauncey, and especially with Agnes. The experts had really fucked up this time.

The clatter of snickering caused by Desmin's words trailed off because something odd began, something that sent a tremor through the crowd. Wisps of smoke began streaming from the twin shadows, still flicking wildly near the bonfire. These puffs of pearly white substances were hard to see in the moonlit clearing. Yet, from what Harry could tell, each piece, maybe forty or more, settled in a circular ring around the periphery of the clearing, where the shadows hung so feebly in the air a moment before, Harry could no longer see anything. The Grigori were gone.

The puffs of smoke were taking shape. Changing, morphing into people. These people were smiling at Harry. One old spook, bent as though his muscles had forgotten they no longer were losing the fight against gravity, waved at him. Chauncey. Others were chatting among themselves, many hugging as though they hadn't seen each other for ages. As one, they turned grim-faced to look upon those in robes who were now huddling nearer to the sorcerer, Desmin.

One of these new arrivals left the spot where he'd settled. Disregarding Desmin and his bunch, he walked past them and came up to Harry, still on his knees, his left arm useless. He bent low and said in a whisper, "How are you, my boy?" He tried to take Harry's arm, but his ghost hand passed through it. "Right, should have known that would happen."

It was a pudgy man wearing a vest and knickers. "Meriodoc?"

"It's me indeed, almost in the flesh." Meriodoc stared over his shoulder at the sorcerers speaking among themselves. "This is the end game, Harry. Be patient—we're almost there. But be careful. In this form, we can no longer communicate with you except through normal means."

Harry nodded, but before Meriodoc Black could continue, Desmin sauntered over, apparently in no hurry now to see an end to this thing.

"Is that you, Merry? How in heaven's name have you managed this trick?"

"Do not presume to invoke that name so lightly, Master Mage."

"Ah…still the theologian, I see."

Desmin sneered, and with a word, demon figures entered the clearing. They began encircling the dead members of Clan Black. The ghosts turned to the new threat. They outnumbered the demons, but many of these ghosts didn't look like fighters. Some were barely older than teenagers and others, like Chauncey, were of advanced age. But there were fighters among them because Harry could see at least ten tall men and one young woman in knight's armor and a long gray sword.

She lowered her faceguard and moved forward, motioning for the others to fall behind.

More shadow than substance, the demons remained crouched, waiting for another word from their master.

"You see, I have an answer for everything. You can't win this, Merry. Not this time." Desmin glared down at Harry. "Let us make a quick end to him. He is nearly dead, regardless. His life's blood is ebbing away little-by-little."

But before Meriodoc could respond, Desmin spoke another strange word, and the demons lunged at the armed ghosts. Swords flashed in the moonlit clearing. Several demons howled and went down, but here and there, some had broken through to the unprotected spirits. They were no match. Ghostly arms were severed. One head, still screaming, flew among the chaos. More howls and the last of the demons were vanquished. They lay where they fell and soon began to fade away altogether.

The stricken ghosts were in shock, crying and lamenting their limbs and other injuries. The headless ghost walked around bumping into others until Chauncey, who had a long silver gash on his leg, carried the still-wailing head to its owner. They reformed their circle and began a low chant.

The sorcerer reached out for Harry, meaning to grab a handful of hair.

It was a mistake. Meriodoc smiled and dissolved only to be reconstituted back at the circle.

Desmin screamed something to his followers. They began their own slow, circling chant around Harry. "Disregard them," he shouted. "Let us begin." He tried to free his hand from Harry's head, but he couldn't. It was like it had been glued to it.

"Help me, you fools."

Seven or eight robed lackeys rushed to him but were thrown back by some unseen force. They hit the ground with loud grunts as Desmin let loose a blood-curdling cry.

As if answering the challenge, the ghosts began chanting louder, their voices a pale mirror of their actual appearance. They circled their enemies, slowly at first, then faster and faster until it became impossible to see them as distinct persons, and they became a silvery blur.

Desmin screamed orders, but the others cringed at the strange sight of the cloud of silver circling them at ever-increasing speeds. Only Sheila dared to move. She made it to Desmin, grabbing his hand, trying hard to yank it free of Harry's head, but it was no use.

For Harry's part, he felt nothing, not the hand, not the slightest tug. He was able to turn his head as though

Desmin wasn't connected to him like some weird appendage.

Soon the circling voices became a cacophony. A sliver of gray broke off from the circling ghosts, and Agnes stood tall and straight before her grandson. It was undoubtedly his grandmother, but he'd never seen her like this, no older than in her mid-thirties.

Agnes smiled at him. "I'm so glad I was wrong."

Harry's brain was in overload. He could only nod, unsure of what she meant. Agnes smirked at the sorcerer, struggling to free himself.

"Good and stuck, I see." She huffed at him and considered her grandson again. "Soon. It's almost over, but you have one more thing to do. You're tough. You'll make it." She turned to look at Sheriff Boone.

Harry had forgotten about him. He was now collapsed on the ground. "Is he—"

"Yes. It was his time anyway, son." She turned back to Harry with a peculiar look on her face. "I have an offer for him, but that'll wait until you return here. He may want your—"

Harry understood about half of what she'd said as another painful spasm hit him. "Offer? Return?"

No answer came. His grandmother's attention had turned to something else. The chanting stopped and so had the circling ghosts. Harry could see the various robed sorcerers blinking out, disappearing from the clearing. Desmin let loose with another gut-wrenching scream, and he too was suddenly gone.

"Listen to me," Agnes said. "You're being dragged along. Focus on the girl and that will pull you to where she is, but only if she is close to their destination. The Grigori will reform and one of the pair will follow you.

There is one more act the other needs to do before Black Manor is again safe from prying eyes."

Harry lifted his head to her. "Suppose she's not there?" But he already knew the answer. They would have to find her the hard way, capture one of them, and beat the location of the hostages out of him.

"I don't know if I'm up to this, Grandmother, my shoulder."

"For us to act, your presence is needed, my boy. A group of us will be there."

Her last words faded as a tug somewhere around his navel sucked Harry into a vortex in the wake of the sorcerer's departure.

Chapter 48

Harry crashed to a stone floor and landed on his shot-out shoulder. He cried out but managed to stifle the sound of it through gritted teeth. Using his one good arm and shaky legs, he forced himself to stand, unsure of where the hell he'd been dumped.

Dim light. A room of some sort.

When his vision cleared, he could see it was a wide corridor with rough-hewn stone walls. The pain was beginning to hit home in waves—deep, stabbing knives radiating down his arm and through his chest. He didn't know what he could do, given his condition, but if there was a chance to save Ginny, he had to try.

****

"Meriodoc," he whispered. "Grandmother." He remembered she said one of the shadows would stay behind. Maybe she hadn't even come.

The corridor was long in either direction, and there was nowhere to hide, no rooms to zip into should he hear someone coming. Fear held him in check, indecision mounting. A man's angry voice came to him from up the corridor and a woman's sobbing response. It was Ginny. They weren't close, but at least now he had a direction.

He clenched his good fist and headed off to his left, creeping along for a couple of minutes battling pain and fear. He figured he had to be in the Netherlands, the home turf of the sorcerers, but he couldn't be sure of it.

Harry whispered to the Grigori in a furious voice. "Where in the hell are you guys?"

Meriodoc's thoughts exploded in his mind a moment later. *"Sorry, the ritual took longer than we thought. The veil is soundly reestablished, Chauncey tells me. Good job back there, Harry."*

"I didn't do anything but get shot up."

"On the contrary, you—"

"Shut it, Meriodoc, and listen. Is Agnes looking after things, or is she here?"

"She's tending to Sheriff Boone's ghost."

Harry's chest tightened when he remembered what had happened to Boone. He had led the sheriff to his death, an old man clearly out of his depth.

"Ginny's here. I heard her scream. Are we too late?"

"No way to know yet."

Harry nodded his understanding. "What of Desmin and his goons?"

"We did some checking before coming to you. The sorcerers are in the main dwelling a hundred yards or so from our location. Still in this compound. They're confused as to what happened. Desmin is furious, especially at you and Agnes, and me, of course. They're unsure of themselves, Harry. We've beat them. We've won!"

"Not so fast," Harry growled. "We have to get home with the others if they're here. You understand?"

Meriodoc's nod tingled in Harry's mind.

"Good." Harry looked down the corridor. "We're in Europe, the Netherlands?"

"Of course."

Harry gulped. He'd crossed the Atlantic in a few seconds, something he would have to process later. "Locate those voices. Draw me to Ginny. Someone's with her. If she's being harmed, kill the bastard, but hold off if you can. I want to interrogate him before we leave. Got it?"

Meriodoc gave him another tingling nod.

"Go to her."

Sensing Meriodoc's lead, Harry started walking faster, his wound throbbing even worse now. The shoulder made him a sitting duck, but there was nothing for it. He had to continue.

He came to a wide turn in the rambling corridor that opened into a rough, bare-beamed common room of more gray stone. The lighting was terrible here too. Luckily, no one was guarding the place. He could see three doors besides the one that opened to the corridor where he stood. Holding rooms, he supposed. Trower could be close at hand if he was even here. If not, he and his men were probably screwed.

A woman's whimpering. A man's harsh response. Harry struck left through the large room and stopped when a man's muffled voice came through the nearest door. It was half-open.

"Hold her still. The bitch can't help squiggling, but the fight's out of her now. Grab her ankles. That's right."

Harry entered the doorway, his shadow falling across the far wall where Ginny lay on a cot, her black dress in tatters. *"Now,"* Harry shouted silently to Meriodoc.

The man had been crouching over Ginny, struggling with her, his pants down in a blatant attempt at sexual assault. He immediately fell over, bounced off the bed, and to the stone floor. Dead.

Ginny screamed, caught sight of Harry, and promptly gave away his presence. The other man spun, but it was too late. Harry closed the distance between them and drove his right fist through the man's jaw, his full weight into it, which sent the man sprawling across the foot of the bed.

He wasn't out. He groaned and tried to rise. "Hold him!"

The shadow engulfed the man, who shimmered once and lay still. Only his eyeballs were moving.

Harry pulled his coat off and went to Ginny. "You okay? They didn't—"

"No," she sobbed, "but they would have." She collapsed into Harry's arms, and the pain of trying to hold her nearly toppled him, but he held on.

It took a moment, but he was finally able to separate from her. "Are there other captives? Is your brother here?"

She nodded furiously. Harry groaned as he slipped off his coat and covered her. Ginny's torn dress revealed her state: multiple bruises. A nasty red welt covered her right cheek. She had fought hard.

"How did you get here so fast?"

"Peeters took me from the mansion. He killed those deputies." She put Harry's arm in an urgent grip. "He might be here."

"He's dead."

Ginny caught her breath and buried her face in her hands. When she removed them, tears were flowing. "He told me that he murdered your assistant, Peggy. He said he'd—"

Harry put his arm around her. “He can’t hurt anyone again.”

“Did you kill him?”

Harry nodded.

Her head sagged. “He deserved it.”

“He deserved worse than that.” Harry rechecked the door but knew Meriodoc would urge him if the company came. With the sorcerers confused, he figured he had a little time, but not much. “Tell me about how they brought you here.”

“I was brought to Jackson Metro shortly after the others arrived. They put me in the plane with Bill and Trower and his men. They were unconscious. I-I couldn’t tell whether they were still alive. I was frantic, but I couldn’t get to Bill. We flew to Washington. I know that because I overheard them talking among themselves. We landed, and one of them just…I don’t know. Whatever he did, it knocked me out. When I woke, I was next to Bill in one of the other rooms here. That’s when they started beating the agents.”

Harry nodded through all this. She must have just missed Sheriff Boone, who had escorted Trower and the senator to the tarmac. He remembered how Desmin came to the clearing. Could he have been here, turning the senator?

Harry glanced at the thug lying across the cot and said to Meriodoc, “Release him, but stay visible where he can see you.”

The shadow positioned itself directly overhead. The man’s eyeballs followed, but Harry knew he could now speak.

“If you yell, you’ll end up like your buddy there, understand?”

The man nodded once, but with an air of defiance.

Harry wanted to kick the bastard, but he calmed himself. “Are there more guards?”

“None, Harry, I could have told you that.”

Harry gritted his teeth. *“Fine, what should we ask him?”* Before Meriodoc could answer, Harry said, “What were your orders?”

The man glanced at his friend, blood running from the dead man’s ears.

“Don’t be stupid.”

The man shrugged. “To guard them, that is all.” He gave Ginny a nasty look. “And to do what we like with the woman.”

She turned away.

“See where that got your friend?” Harry said. “I’m not sure yet it won’t happen to you.”

The man paled and nodded.

“Was it just the two of you? There must have been other guards? Where are they?” These two men couldn’t have beaten Trower and Shultz alone.

“Called away afterward.”

After they administered the beating, Harry understood him to mean. “And the other prisoners. Where are they?” The man turned his head instinctively to the left, signifying to Harry that they were all here just behind those other two doors. “Are they alive?”

He nodded. “They were when last we checked.”

“When were you to kill them?”

A surprised look came over the man.

“I know you guys weren’t to hold them long. When?”

“When the master returned.”

“Even the senator?”

"Senator? I don't understand?"

"He doesn't, Harry, I heard them talking. They're just low-level trash. They don't know who they're holding."

"Bitch!" The man lunged at Ginny, and Harry laid him out cold with a solid right cross to the chin.

"Arghhh!" The blast of pain from his wound pulled him to his knees.

"You're hurt?" Ginny helped him to the cot. "Harry, you're bleeding!"

"It's nothing." Harry turned and glanced up to the ceiling. "Meriodoc."

"He's out for a while."

"If he wakes, hold him here." Harry reached out for Ginny's hand. "Are you okay? Can you help me?"

Ginny responded by nodding.

He tried to smile to reassure her, but he was starting to get cold and shivery. "This arm isn't working too well right now. I feel sick."

They went to the door, but Harry hesitated.

"They're there," she said, pointing to the left. "I think Bill must be in that room." She looked across the extensive common area to a lone room to their right. "Why are you waiting? Let's hurry."

Harry shook his head. "It's too easy. This whole thing has been."

"What? They didn't expect you to come here. That's why it seems—"

"I wouldn't be so sure. How long have you been out of contact with the others?"

"They beat the agents and threatened Bill if I didn't…you know, cooperate. Oh, Harry, I relented for his sake, but I just couldn't give in, so I fought them."

He put his right arm over her shoulders and could feel her trembling.

"If you hadn't come."

"I know." Harry looked across the way to one of the other rooms. "Did they hurt him?"

"No. The men separated us a couple of hours ago, I guess, and left me alone. When they came back, I had to listen to them argue which one would have me first. That went on for a long time. They'd just decided. Do you know what that's like?"

"No, I don't." He glanced back through the door of the room they just left. The man had lied to him, and Ginny hadn't picked up on it. If he didn't know Bill wasn't important, why hadn't they abused him too? He answered his own question—to get Ginny to submit without a struggle. Maybe that's all it was. Brother and sister looked so much alike they must have worked out the relationship. It was probably as simple as that, but maybe not. He didn't like what the lie implied.

"What are you thinking?" Ginny asked.

Groaning came from his left, but nothing from across the common room.

Ginny was more insistent this time. "Why are you hesitating?"

Harry shook his head. "You don't think this smells wrong?"

"No." She hesitated. "How did you find us anyway? I'd lost all hope." Her lip trembled, and she started crying again.

He took her hand. "That's a long story. Meriodoc says no one else is here guarding. Go to Bill's cell and gather him up. Be quiet and quick. Remember that half the Grigori is here to help. We're not alone. I'll get the others."

He saw her off and went to the agents' holding cell. The bastards who kidnapped them hadn't even bothered to lock the door. Trower and Agent Shultz, puffy-faced and ragged from a violent beating, were sprawled on the floor and coming to. He didn't know how long they were unconscious, but judging by the damage they'd sustained, it could have been for most of their time here. They needed medical attention.

He helped them to the bunk. They fought him, not knowing who it was handling them, but they soon quieted when they realized this new person wasn't going to beat them again.

"Trower, it's Harry Black. Can you get up?"

He didn't answer, but Shultz rose from the bunk. "I've got him."

"Good." Harry gave them the once over but couldn't tell much about their condition other than the obvious. "Can you walk? Anything broken?"

Shultz shook his head. "Just a couple busted ribs. The chief's bad off, though. Made the mistake of disclosing his rank. They worked him over harder." He flinched as he turned to Harry. "How'd you—"

"Never mind. When I come back through that door with the senator, stand Trower up."

Shultz seemed to understand. "Yes, sir." Harry turned to leave, but Shultz grabbed his arm. "I never expected to make it out alive."

Harry nodded and smiled inwardly at the recognition he hadn't been given earlier in the day. "Plan to move, but not like you think. Be right back."

Harry was fading fast. He stumbled across the common room and made it to Bill Rankin's cell. He stopped in the doorway, brother and sister embracing, Ginny crying softly.

The senator noticed Harry entering and broke off. There wasn't a scratch on him. He wasn't bound or otherwise restricted. Harry had his hand on the doorknob, a rickety mechanism that couldn't be locked. Rankin could have moved about at will.

"Mr. Black," Bill Rankin said, staring at Harry with dead eyes. "My sister says you've saved *her* this time."

Harry grimaced as pain moved through his shoulder and down his arm in nauseating waves. "None of us will be saved if we don't move."

Chapter 49

Harry hit the ground and would have collapsed if Ginny hadn't helped him stand.

"If we don't stop this bleeding—" Ginny started to say.

Harry pulled her closer and shook his head, waiting for Bill to move off, which he did when the disorientation caused by the void cleared. He had his cell phone out, dialing.

"In a moment."

Harry looked into the sky, searching for the twin shadows. *"Is he himself?"* he asked Meriodoc?

"Ninety-five percent certain."

"That specific, huh? Why not a hundred percent?"

"We have no way to divine the truth. We're not omniscient, for heaven's sake."

They had landed safely in the clearing. Harry knew in his gut Rankin wasn't quite himself. For one thing, there was no real reason to damage him if they had turned him. They could have faked it, roughed him up a little, made an act of it, but maybe it would have altered whatever they had done to turn him and nullified it. Or maybe not. Bottom line: Harry didn't have the experience to know, and Meriodoc didn't either.

He resigned himself to ask Ginny, but by all appearances, she believed the Bill Rankin they had brought back was the real thing, and not some sorcerer-controlled thrall.

Harry assured her he could stand on his own, freeing her to go to her brother. The Grigori had brought five people back, a pretty ragged bunch. Agent Trower's face was a bloody mess, and Shultz had been taken down a notch or two with a broken collarbone, a left arm, and some ribs. Ginny, on the other hand, hadn't fared nearly as bad, but she hadn't gotten out unscathed. She'd been slapped around hard, but at least had been spared what could have been a far worse attack.

Standing there in the light of the waxing moon, her shoulders quaking, it was apparent by the look on her brother's face that she was telling him of her narrow escape. She'd been helpless to stop them, and Harry feared that helplessness would change her. He sensed the loss of something that might be hard for her to get back—confidence and a damn-the-world attitude that made her a successful professional. He wanted to be there for her but felt his own gut-wrenching helplessness, an ache strong enough to momentarily block out the pain in his throbbing shoulder. Until Ginny, he hadn't known how much he needed someone. If she needed him too, he damned well planned to be there regardless of what Jones or his grandmother thought of the matter.

He turned away from brother and sister, frustration welling up inside. Jack and Paula had been saved, but they had also been abused to within an inch of their lives. He stole another glance at Ginny. He'd saved her but hadn't fully protected her. How would the next time play out? Would he fall short again and lose her forever?

Not long after arriving, the Grigori began disassociating, each sliver of silver streaking out of the dark, shadowy substance. Soon the space was populated by more dead people than the living, but there was only one other person Harry had been thinking about since returning with the hostages.

Ginny would keep for later. Jack and Paula had each other to console. They were pretty bad off but would make it. Sheriff Boone, however, hadn't been so lucky. Harry spotted his body in a heap near the bonfire, the blaze much smaller now than it had been.

To his surprise, when he started in that direction, Ginny came along his good side and supported him. She took his hand in hers. He gave it a reassuring squeeze.

"We have to leave soon," she said. "You need a doctor."

"I'm okay." But his voice was weak, and his left arm and shoulder were useless.

She started to argue, but he gave her hand another squeeze, and she tightened her grip.

"Empty night," she said, looking up into the sky.

He stopped and searched her eyes, trying to find the right words. She helped him by planting a small kiss on his cheek.

"Thank you for coming for us." She glanced at her brother. Standing a good twenty yards off, he had a cell phone out, punching numbers, probably to his wife. She turned back to Harry, hurt and desperation an equal mix on her face. "It's something I had to do. I'm just glad you came when you did."

Harry glanced at Rankin, and the look on Harry's face must have frightened Ginny because she frowned.

"They separated him from us. He would have fought them for me if he had known. I know it. They made it very clear to me what was at stake if I resisted them." She kept gazing into Harry's eyes, tears cascaded down her cheeks.

He pulled her close to him with his good arm. "Damn, Ginny. I'm so sorry."

She placed her hands on either side of his face. "You mustn't think less of him."

He kissed away more of her tears.

"You mustn't, Harry, for our sake. I mean if we're to—"

"I'll try."

She sighed and slumped against him.

He held her tight. "I think you're the bravest person I've ever met."

She buried her face in his chest and stifled what threatened to become a river of tears.

"Don't." He lifted her chin with two fingers. "Let's get through tonight, okay?"

She nodded. "What about Bill?"

"He's still in danger, but he has to go back to Washington. The president must be informed if he hasn't already been." Harry searched the clearing and found Trower and Shultz talking to Deputy Hendricks.

"And what about you, Harry? Is the veil back in place? Is it safe here?"

"Meriodoc assures me it's done. Listen, we have to take it slow. Trower understands all about the supernatural stuff, especially now after that little transatlantic jump we just made."

They walked to where Boone lay, and as they came near, a strange twist of moonlight playing off the shadows cast by the fire revealed Boone's pale ghost. Next to him stood Agnes, arguing with him.

"Stubborn fool," Agnes spat.

"I'm just saying, it doesn't seem right, is all."

"It's a high honor, Tommy, and a chance to serve like you never have before. That's what your life's been all about, hasn't it? Well, now's the time to make an even greater difference."

"She's right, Sheriff," Harry interjected as he approached them. "I'd be glad and proud to have you serve with the Grigori."

Boone and Agnes turned to Harry and Ginny, walking up to them.

"You can see me."

"You never looked better."

"Really?"

"About forty, I'd say."

Boone turned to Agnes with a smile on his face.

"Now, don't start getting any ideas, young man, we're well past those days."

"But you're so beautiful, Agnes."

"Oh?"

"He's right, Grandmother. You're young too. Mid-thirties."

She put a hand to her face. "Wish I had a mirror." She turned back to Boone and pointed to his dead body. "This is the afterlife if you haven't noticed."

He stared down at his body and seemed to realize again what had happened.

"I'm sorry, Sheriff," Harry said.

"We both knew it could happen, son. Only thing I'm mad about is my department. Who's gonna rebuild it and take care of it?"

Boone noticed Rowena Hendricks helping Strom Jones adjust his disheveled suit.

"I'd say you have that person right here."

"Yeah?" He hesitated. "Yeah, I think you're right." To the left of Deputy Hendricks, the body of Freddie Rivera lay sprawled out. The ghost of Sheriff Boone grimaced. "I think she'll do a good job too."

"Seems you're needed elsewhere," Harry said.

Boone searched their eyes and turned his head up to the star-filled sky. "Well, all right then."

The sound of someone clearing their throat made Harry and Ginny turn. They found Trower and Deputy Hendricks looking roughed up, but defiant.

"I've called in two helicopters for the dead and injured, and..." She noticed Boone's ghost, and her mouth dropped open.

"Easy, Deputy," Harry said.

"But, he's..." She pointed to his dead body and looked back up at him, standing there as a much younger man.

"I've got this, Harry." Boone approached his deputy. "It's me, Rowena. Or me as I once was."

She took a shaky step back.

"Listen, I know this is a tough one to swallow. Life's about to get a lot more complicated for you." Boone glanced at Harry. "There's a note pad on my desk, son. You've got some strange gifts. Don't suppose automatic writing is one of them."

Agnes understood right off. "An excellent idea, Tommy. That will smooth the transition for her into a leadership role. If they knew it was your wish that she take your place."

So it was settled. Rowena was about to get the

promotion of a lifetime.

Deputy Hendricks snorted.

"Harry will write a damn good recommendation letter," Boone said, "and I'll mean every word of it. The board will listen, or I'll haunt every one of the sumbitches. When my letter gets out, you'll get elected."

They could hear the helicopters in the distance.

"There's no more time," Agnes said. "They can't find us here."

Boone nodded and turned back to his deputy.

"Shit. Me? Sheriff? Shit."

He smiled at her, but she suddenly shifted her thoughts to her partner, who hadn't made it. "I'm sorry, Sheriff. We got hit by something out there. If I'd been quicker, maybe you and Freddie would have—" She started to choke up.

"Not your fault, honey." Sheriff Boone tried to put his arm around Rowena, but he couldn't hold her. "You have to help Freddie's family."

Trower finally spoke up. "ETA in two minutes."

Everyone arched their neck and stared into the sky.

"Is the mansion safe now?" Trower asked Harry.

"Absolutely."

Trower turned to the clearing. "Hell, Harry, there are damn ghosts everywhere, and I don't really believe in the afterlife."

"I thought you were Catholic."

"Not *that* Catholic."

Harry lifted his good arm and placed a hand on Trower's shoulder. "Guess you'll be true blue now. You're gonna help me put the bastards away, right?"

Trower nodded. "I'll brief the president. He won't

believe it, but we'll tell him everything. I owe you that."

"What did you see in the dungeon and on the plane?"

"It was Peeters. I hear he's dead now."

"Yeah."

"Good." Trower thought about it for a moment. "Soon after I got aboard, they hit us with something. I don't remember anything until we woke on the stone floor. The beatings started soon after. Two of my men were missing. They're probably dead."

"They separated the senator and didn't harm him," Harry said.

"Not one lick," Trower said and turned to look at Bill Rankin still on his cell phone.

"So, you don't really know what happened to him after they took him to that other cell?" Harry asked.

"What are you insinuating?" Ginny asked.

"I'm not sure," Harry said.

"He certainly is calm and collected," Trower said.

"I can't believe—" Ginny hesitated. "He's my brother."

"He's not immune to being turned, Ginny," Harry said. "Think about it. It would be better than killing him. Think of the damage he could do serving as a mole, doing Ausberg's will by having the president's ear on the economy."

Harry had to trust Trower. He might not get another chance to make him see. "It's like this." Harry gave the senator a quick glance. "Where'd he get that cell phone he's using now?"

Trower and Ginny looked at each other. Their phones were taken on the plane. It was inconceivable they would have overlooked Senator Rankin's. They both turned to the senator as this realization spread across their faces.

"I know this is hard to hear, but he wasn't locked in his cell. He heard you screaming across the way and did nothing. Why?"

Before she could answer, Trower said, "He'll have to be watched. But how the hell am I supposed to tell the president about this?"

"It was a smart play on their part," Harry said. "We just waltz in and bring you guys back"—Harry snapped his fingers—"just like that. I don't think so. It could have been their plan all along. Once they missed killing him, they went for this."

Bill Rankin was still talking across the way. What would his phone records show if the FBI went snooping? Who was he really talking to? Not wanting to cause Ginny further stress, Harry gave himself a mental note to ask Trower about that later.

"It feels right," Harry said. "I'm sorry, but it does. If they wanted him dead, he would be. Why fly to DC? Just kill him in the plane in Jackson? Why go to all the trouble to move you to Europe?"

Harry hated himself for the pain he was causing Ginny. Her eyes showed a glint of desperation.

"We'll have to be smart," Harry went on, "and pick the right time to tell the president. I could be wrong, but I don't think I am." He spoke to Trower. "Have one of the helicopters take you, Shultz, and Rankin to the hospital. Keep Rankin away from Black Manor, understood? Tell him it's for his own good. They have to check him out. Besides, you need the attention."

Trower nodded. "I'm on it," and walked away.

"Why not bring them to the mansion too?" Ginny asked.

"Peeters said *it* was on him, remember? Those were his words. They obviously use some sort of sorcery in the trick they pulled to find the house. I won't let it happen again. It may not be the same thing, but I'm not taking a chance."

Ginny turned from Harry and stared intently at her brother.

"If I'm right," Harry said, "we'll do whatever it takes to get him back. But right now, we mustn't let on that we know. It gives us the upper hand for the moment."

Around the clearing, ghosts were hugging and saying their farewells. In a silvery blur, they began reconstituting, and soon the Grigori reformed.

Everyone except Meriodoc, Boone, and Agnes. They stayed apart, and now they shrank into the deep shadows.

Jones strode up to Harry. He'd been helping Jack and Paula. "They're in rough shape."

"I know," Harry said. "Thanks for helping." He grabbed Jones's arm. "Did you really set them up?"

Jones gave him a sharp look. "Hell no. I believe they were targeted from the beginning. But I had a part to play tonight if I was going to help."

"Looks like you've been playing it for a while. You look pretty good for an old fart."

"Oh, yes, that. A side benefit you might say. I needed a motive. I just couldn't walk over and offer to help. I needed a real inducement to switch sides, something this sorcerer could give me that would make me into a turncoat."

"Will it last?" Harry asked.

Jones shrugged. "Desmin may be the most powerful ever of his kind. He's obviously conquered the problem. I wanted to test it. If it doesn't last, I'm no worse off."

"New life," Harry said, shaking his head.

Jones's eyes sparkled, and he gave Harry a wicked smile. "Have that plane ticket to Hawaii right here." He patted his coat pocket.

"So, how long have you been playing the game with Desmin?"

"Couple of months." He hesitated. "Harry, you do know Desmin was wrong about what he said tonight. My family has been with yours for ages."

The three remaining ghosts walked up to Harry and Jones. "I heard that," Agnes said.

Jones smiled. "You just didn't know it."

"So why was it so hard to convince you all those years ago?" Agnes asked. "I don't understand."

"I didn't need convincing. I just let you be you. I played along so you would remain focused on your mission. I was a good project for that." He looked at Boone. "Sorry about what happened, Thomas. You were brave to come here tonight."

Boone nodded.

"Looks like you get to be with Agnes, after all."

The dead sheriff and Agnes Black smiled at each other.

Meriodoc cleared his throat. "We'll be talking soon, Harry."

"Good job tonight," Harry said. He held out his hand, but Meriodoc just shrugged.

"It isn't over yet," Meriodoc said. "But it sure felt

good giving that bastard his comeuppance. We'll be better prepared next time."

"I sure hope so," Harry said. "You know, I read parts of your passage in the diary. The part where you said it had been a mistake to pick you as Protector."

"The ramblings of a doomed man, I'm afraid."

"Not at all," Harry said. "You were the right choice. Your sacrifice wasn't to fix things or win out. It was to help us now, and for that, you needed credentials as a Protector. I couldn't have gotten through this without that help. Providence knew I guess."

"Maybe you missed your calling, young Mr. Black," Meriodoc said.

"Yeah, how so?"

He poked Harry's chest with a ghostly finger. "You should have been a theologian."

"Nope, I'm a finance guy."

"Oh, yes, filthy lucre," Meriodoc said, smiling. "Use it wisely, young Harry."

Harry smiled as the three ghosts began dissolving. He cried out to Agnes, "Grandmother, wait." The others disappeared, but she remained just as the first helicopter swept over the tree line and descended.

"I just wanted to say—" Harry hesitated.

"Have to leave now, my boy. What is it?"

He wanted desperately to give her a hug and kiss her, to show her the physical affection he'd denied her. "I'm sorry the way I treated you back when you were—"

"Dying?" She smiled. "I know you are." She glanced around the clearing. "You've done well, but there's more to be done. Now finish up here and get the house back in order."

"But why didn't I die? That was the plan, wasn't it?"

Agnes shrugged. "Who can say? Chauncey wonders the same thing."

Before he could ask even one of about a hundred questions banging around the inside of his head, Agnes smiled and disappeared. The twin shadows flickered and blinked out. Harry and the others would have to make it back to the mansion through ordinary means.

He held Ginny's hand as they watched the injured and dead being loaded, comforted in her closeness, thankful she was still alive. Bill Rankin shook Harry's hand and kissed his sister. Neither said a word. Harry got nothing from the physical contact as he had before. That was curious.

Jack and Paula limped to the open bay of a helicopter helped by the state troopers. Before piling in, Jack gave Harry a thumbs-up and said in a weak voice, "I'm billing you for the last forty-eight hours. Medical bills plus quadruple overtime at the going rate of a partner, not an associate."

Harry smiled and nodded.

As the first of the birds took off, he looked past the bright landing lights into the night sky. *Stars and moon.* Meriodoc's words from the Black diaries. It was his power base, whatever that meant. He had so much to learn, but now he was finally ready and willing. And more importantly, he had allies to help his education along.

Harry pulled Ginny closer. They were beginning something he couldn't turn his back on. It wasn't the smart thing to do, but this was the twenty-first century.

He would remake the role of Protector, and Ginny would help him just as he had helped her.

Epilogue

Somewhere near Amsterdam, The Netherlands

"The bitch—the fucking bitch!"

Desmin's rage caused the others to cower as he stalked around the expansive room, ripping his robe from his body. They were all just coming out of their disorientation as a result of Black's treachery, barely able to stand after being deposited in the primary residence of their compound. They had a significant problem. This couldn't have happened, but it had. How?

They had been flung back here by some power Desmin had never before felt. It was certainly none of his doing. He doubted he could have accomplished the feat anyway. Perhaps for himself, but getting the entire group out of that clearing and depositing them half a world away? Never.

Desmin tried to think, tried to clear his mind of the haze wrought by this strange working. The others were strewn about the expansive room, struggling like him, half-drunk. But at least his dignity remained intact. He hadn't fallen over like some common inebriant.

He considered the problem as he fought to regain control of his temper. He hadn't lived two hundred years to be defeated by some upstart Protector barely wet behind the ears. But he wasn't an ordinary

Protector, not as Meriodoc Black had been. This one had some major assistance. The testimony of poor dead Arie Peeters had been right after all. Those things were with this new Black Protector, impossible to believe, but true. It was an almost unprecedented occurrence. His own lore indicated there was only one other time in the history of the conflict when they had been used.

Desmin groaned. So unjust, so damn unfair of that insignificant bunch of English tarts. How could Lord Desmin, long-time head of Clan Mage, be defeated by that hick from Mississippi?

It meant that what he'd felt at the destruction of his psychogeist, no mean feat since he'd poured much of his power into that working, must have been *their* doing. The backlash had killed two of his mages and damaged the mind of a third. That was some pretty powerful—

He stopped himself from thinking the words that had almost come. It wasn't magic or sorcery. That didn't fit at all. It was another power working on their behalf, one that had aligned itself to their cursed clan from the beginning.

"Take off those robes, you fools," he snapped at the group. They were too timid to speak, or just too overwhelmed by what had happened. "Does anyone have an explanation?" He looked at Stanislav Smit. "You are outed now. You will not be able to return to your post at the bank, and we have *not* accomplished our mission." He turned in frustration, speaking into an enormous fireplace. "You *cannot* return. You do realize that, don't you?"

"I have diverted the money, Master. He will be hampered. So it shouldn't matter much."

Desmin gave him a scorching look. “Matter much? Black was to be dead by now. That is what matters much. We have failed. I do not care how weak he was proven to be. Clan Black must end. While the weakest of them live—while they have a foothold in this world—we are in jeopardy. None of our glorious plans will come to fruition. Do you hear me? *None*!”

The sorcerer’s scream reverberated off the walls of the room, forcing Smit to bow low. He cringed when Desmin approached him.

“And the lawyer, Jones. How is it we missed his true intent? He has benefited from the working already. He has his reward. I do not give such things freely. He was supposed to be ours. A valuable resource.” He looked down at Smit with disdain. “Are you sure of the money? Are you absolutely sure? Tell me the patient work of the last forty years has not gone for naught. We cannot start over now. We cannot infiltrate again as we did when I was still weak all those decades ago. All the work your father set up. If we miss this opportunity—” He stopped, thinking. “That work cannot be done anew, Smit. Do you hear? Our contingent plan is suddenly of grave importance in the face of his survival. If we cannot kill him, then he must be stripped of his fortune.”

“If I can get to a computer, I will recheck the accounts. I will not have been discovered yet.”

“Go then, Stanislav. Go.”

Smit left the room, and Desmin convened the others. “How could this happen?”

“If I may, Lord.” Johannes stepped forward from among the group. “They surmised the connection Arie established and knew he was the key. We should not have brought him, Lord. They are smarter than we thought."

Desmin nodded but felt more like breaking this man in two for stating the obvious.

"It was those wretched things, Lord. They worked it out. Not Black. He is too simple-minded as Protectors go. But how did you become bonded to him? Was that necessary for the reestablishment of their veil over the manor house?"

"You tell me."

"It is beyond my understanding, Lord."

"Yes, I see that."

Desmin stalked away from them and went to a bar in a far corner of the room, the plush vermillion carpeting springing back to life after each step. He poured a quarter snifter of Cognac and drank it neat in one gulp. The bond. What was its purpose? They had been flung back here to the compound, but how? Black was weak, shot through by one of Desmin's thralls. If there was any fairness in the universe, he would be dead by now. It couldn't have been some talent he possessed, some unknown skill these Protectors were prone toward. The lore craft of Clan Mage had never cataloged anything of the sort. He poured more of the drink. What was its purpose?

As that question came to mind again, his eyes widened. He spun to Johannes, who had followed him.

"What of the prisoners?"

Johannes clapped, and one of the two servants in the room rushed to a nearby phone.

Both men waited, but after a minute, the servant merely put down the still ringing phone.

"Shall I go see why our guards are not on duty?"

Desmin's mood turned more sour. "You can go, but I know the answer already. They are incapacitated or dead, and the prisoners are gone."

As he finished, Smit walked back into the room. "The news is not good, they have—"

Desmin raised his hand, and Smit stopped speaking at once. "No need to say it, my friend. Our failure is complete."

The sorcerer gulped more of his drink and threw the crystal into the stone fireplace. Gathering his composure once again, he turned back to the bearer of this bad news. He knew an example had to be made. Someone must die.

"Does anyone know where that cursed estate now resides?"

"Mississippi," someone from the back said in a weak voice, "I think."

"In which town?"

This seemed to stump them, but Desmin wouldn't admit that even he no longer knew the answer. Then Smit spoke up.

"It's near Jackson. But, Master, we have always known this. I have worked there for nearly forty years."

Desmin nodded. Black's victory had been complete. Desmin didn't doubt that soon none of them, from the least to the greatest, would remember a thing about the location of Black Manor. Not even Smit. They all might remember the insignificant state, but even that fact would begin to slip from them soon. It was that cursed veil working again. If not for it, Clan Black would have been decimated hundreds of years ago.

Desmin stared at Smit. The banker reacted by

slinking away. "You must go back then."

"But—"

"Not to the bank, Stanislav. That part of your life is finished. Your family will come home, back to Amsterdam where they belong, but you must stay there as a small punishment for your failure." Desmin held up his hand when Smit started to say something more. "Consider it leniency. You really deserve something worse, but it seems that I still need your assistance."

Desmin placed his long arms behind him and paced off a few steps. When he stopped, it was with a sad but determined look. "One of you besides poor Arie was actually in the house, and the rest had sighted it from those damn woods, but we can no longer *see* it."

There was low chattering among the group, but Desmin raised his hand again and they quieted. "Who was it that insisted Arie stay after the rescue? Who was it that made that terrible mistake?"

Johannes raised a feeble hand and, before he could even put it down, there was a rush of wind accompanied by the sound of a distant, forlorn cry, as though it had been carried on the blast the sorcerer had just unleashed. Johannes took a sharp breath and crumpled silently to the plush carpet.

"Many losses tonight. Our ranks grow thin."

The group turned shocked eyes from dead Johannes to their master. Only Smit had the courage or stupidity to speak. "But the larger plan is working. We now have the thrall in place, and he has the ear of their president."

Desmin nodded. "True."

"All is not lost then. We can still win."

The sorcerer paused at this. He liked Smit's

forward-thinking. Perhaps he would let him live a bit longer. "Then we must refocus on Washington. Black will try to expose the senator if he has already guessed our intent. When he shows himself, we must be ready. Is the president's man ours yet?"

"The cash deposit in his Swiss account has been confirmed. I checked it myself a moment ago."

"Good, Herr Smit, good. Make plans to collect more thralls close to those in power. We may not have Black yet, but there will be more opportunities. We shall not miss again."

A word about the author…

Nothing fascinates me like writing, creating stories, or sub-creating as JRR Tolkien referred to it. And, of course, to write and write well, one must read widely. It started early in my life and continues to this day. But, long before I began writing stories, I worked long hours as a college professor, squeezing in time whenever I could to work my hobby."

From the small Cajun town of Plaquemine, Louisiana, SP Brown had limited heroes to choose from besides his father, Joseph Harry, a painter, and his mother, Vivian, a homemaker. Others included his big brother, Harry, and, more prominently, those populating the pages of Marvel Comics. Realizing he didn't have the right stuff to be a superhero himself, he concentrated on academics and took his first post as a college professor at The University of Mississippi. After many scientific publications and several textbooks, the call of storytelling grew. He has been answering that call of late.

spbrownbooks.com

Thank you for purchasing
this publication of The Wild Rose Press, Inc.

For questions or more information
contact us at
info@thewildrosepress.com.

The Wild Rose Press, Inc.
www.thewildrosepress.com

www.ingramcontent.com/pod-product-compliance
Lightning Source LLC
Chambersburg PA
CBHW072254020726
47501CB00002B/260

* 9 7 8 1 5 0 9 2 5 3 1 8 0 *